BORDER AMBUSH
A COLTON BROTHERS SAGA

A Novel

MELODY GROVES

LFP

La Frontera Publishing

Cover illustration from the original painting by Frank McCarthy "Along the Route of the Ancients" © Frank McCarthy. Licensed by The Greenwich Workshop, Inc. www.greenwichworkshop.com. All rights reserved, used with permission

Cover design, book design and typesetting by
Yvonne Vermillion and Magic Graphix

Printed and bound in the United States of America
First Edition

First Printing, May 2009

Library of Congress Cataloging-in-Publication Data

Groves, Melody, 1952-
  Border ambush : a Colton Brothers saga : a novel / Melody Groves. -- 1st ed.
      p. cm.
  ISBN 978-0-9785634-6-2 (pbk.)
  I. Title.
  PS3607.R6783B67 2009
  813'.6--dc22
                                    2009016106

Published by La Frontera Publishing
(307) 778-4752 • www.lafronterapublishing.com

Dedication

To Margaret Dean.
Thanks for the love, support, and encouragement.

A HUGE thank you:

To me, writing is nowhere near the loneliest profession, as it's claimed to be. My mind is always filled with characters, many of whom are quite active. Most days I have to rush just to keep up with their antics. While my characters are busy shooting bad guys or running from the law or just trying to figure out their next move, the real characters in my life are just as busy. As much as I'd like to list them all and thank them for taking time to listen to the characters in my head, a short list will have to do.

Myke Groves—a man of many characters.
Haley Crawford—a character who makes me laugh.
Erin Montoya—a character if I've ever seen one.
Mike Harris—a true character in his own right.
Johnny Boggs—now *there's* a character.
Judy Avila, Sue Brown, Phil Jackson and Dianne Boles-Scott—each one a character worthy of unfettered praise.

Special Acknowledgement:

George Hackler, whose talk in Las Cruces, New Mexico, about the Butterfield Overland Stage inspired this book.

FOREWORD

"To many people who think more of their ease than they do of robust physical health, a stage ride of a thousand or two thousand miles may seem a very formidable undertaking. But for those who had a liking for adventure, and a desire to see something of the world, a long ride of two or three weeks, practically in the open air, possesses a wonderful charm, especially in remembrance." –H.D. *Barrows, 1860 Butterfield Overland Stage passenger*

The Butterfield Stage Lines

Up until 1858, mail traveled to or from the California gold fields either by horseback and wagon down to Panama and then across the isthmus by mule, or by ship around Cape Horn—a three-month perilous journey at best. But more and more gold seekers wanted news and letters from "back home." Pressure was applied on Congress.

Their answer: Collect bids to develop a stage line running 2,800 miles, which would take under 25 days to get from St. Louis to San Francisco. The main objective would be to move mail and small packages across that vast expanse. This project, a first of its kind, would link the coasts and provide the new state of California with the news and the communication it so strongly desired.

John Butterfield, a freight line owner and former mayor of Utica, New York, as well as a friend of President John Buchanan, won the proposal and bid in 1857. Within 12 months, Butterfield selected a route and purchased 1,200 horses and 600 mules (each branded with OM—Overland Mail). He also distributed them, hired a thousand men, ordered 250 wagons, surveyed 2,800 miles, graded fording sites, opened new roads or improved old ones, procured several thousand tons of hay and fodder, built 200 way stations every 20 miles, dug 100 wells, and created the run schedule. All for $600,000.

Thus, John Butterfield created the first reliable line of communication by establishing the longest mail route in the world. The coaches held nine people, riding three abreast, squeezed into back and middle rows. These six faced forward, while the three others faced to the rear. The facing passengers had to ride with their knees dovetailed, baggage on their laps (when it didn't fit up top), and mail pouches beneath their feet. They traveled day and night, stopping 10 minutes or less at way stations. They were allowed 40 minutes for a meal twice a day.

Since the coaches ran around the clock, at night the seats folded down and could sleep up to 10 people. Many chose to sit on top in the open air. The stage averaged 120 miles in 24 hours. Initially, the fare ran $100 in gold for those traveling east from San Francisco, but $200 for those heading west. After a few months of grumbling and confusion, the compromised price of $150 in gold was established, regardless of which way one traveled.

Concord and Celerity stagecoaches were made in Concord, New Hampshire, and were painted either red or green with bright yellow running gear. Inscribed with O.M.C. (Overland Mail Company), the Concord weighed 3,000 pounds and had a load capacity of two tons. Celerity (mud wagons) were used on more rugged areas and across the desert, since their wheels were narrower than the Concords. Both coaches, however, were set on leather straps, which caused "motion sickness" for the passengers.

During its two and a half years of service, Butterfield Overland Mail always arrived within the 25-day contract time. Sometimes the trip took 21 days. The service proved so reliable that the British government sent official correspondence to British Columbia by the Butterfield Overland Mail.

In early 1861, the Civil War loomed in the east. As if that weren't enough to worry about, war with Apaches in what are now the states of Arizona and New Mexico heated up. Meanwhile, the spread of the telegraph had already begun to make the stage obsolete for mail delivery. The telegraph would also doom the Pony Express, which had sprung up in response to demand from residents of Colorado, Utah, and Oregon.

But it was the Civil War that rang the final death knell for the Butterfield stagecoach line. Instead of allowing the Overland Mail Company's property to fall into Rebel hands, the U.S. Postmaster General ordered the Overland Mail to discontinue service immediately and move all the coaches, livestock, and equipment north to the Central Overland Trail. To add insult to injury, the Confederates seized all the Butterfield stations in Texas.

John Butterfield, already in failing health, stepped down as president of his company. He would die in 1869.

Santa Rita, New Mexico Territory

The site of the town of Santa Rita del Cobre sits at the base of the Mogollon Mountains in central New Mexico. A copper-mining community today, it was founded in 1803 by Francisco Elguea, a businessman from Chihuahua, Mexico. Elguea named it Santa Rita del Cobre.

Threats from Apaches were a real problem in the early part of the nineteenth century, so the Mexican government declared an all-out war on the Indians. After 400 Indians were slaughtered at one time, the Apaches, led by Mangas Colorado, retaliated. Miners coming from Mexico as well as people already living in Santa Rita were murdered. Eventually starved out, all of the residents of Santa Rita banded together and left wagon train style for the safety of Chihuahua, Mexico. Of the 400 who left, six made it.

Santa Rita sat vacant for 12 years, until some of the California Forty-Niners made their way toward the Mogollon Mountains and moved in. A company of cavalry then occupied the old Santa Rita *torreon*, or fortress, built by the miners a half-century before, while they protected the gold miners against Apache attacks.

By 1872, Cochise had taken over for Mangas Colorado, who was killed in nearby Pinos Altos, and made a treaty with the government. Santa Rita enjoyed a few years of quiet. Geronimo escaped from a reservation and declared war on all Mexicans and Americans. Within time, however, the Apache leaders were either killed or died, and peace reluctantly spread across the Southwest.

Pinos Altos, New Mexico Territory

"Tall Pines" is an appropriate moniker for such a beautiful little town set in a valley surrounded by Ponderosa pines and piñon-covered mountains in south central New Mexico. Though the mining history of the area dates back to the early 1800s with Mexican miners, it was a later gold discovery in 1860 that brought the fame, fortune, and prospectors to the area. Three Forty-Niners from California found gold in Bear Creek, and this led to the establishment of Pinos Altos (originally called "Birchville") as a mining camp.

It was an unusual camp in many respects. Despite the constant danger of Indian attacks (Cochise and Mangas Colorado attacked and killed over 50 miners), the town had a refinement unlike the other towns around it. For example, the citizens vied with each other for the most beautiful flower gardens and orchards in town. Old orchards are still around today. And, village merchants accepted gold dust in trade well into the twentieth century.

In 1874, Indians and Anglos reached the unusual agreement that as long as a cross stood on a nearby mountain, neither would harm the other. The pact worked. The original cross totally deteriorated by 1907, and then a second was erected. A more permanent cross was erected in 1963.

Mesilla, New Mexico Territory

While the United States grew, so did Mesilla in southern New Mexico Territory. In 1850, 650 people called it home. The Gadsden Purchase, which annexed Mesilla to the United States from Mexico and established the current international borders of New Mexico and Arizona, was signed on its plaza in 1854. By 1858, over 3,000 people resided there, making it the largest town between San Diego, California and San Antonio, Texas.

Mesilla flourished as the center of commercial trade and political events. In fact, Mesilla became the capital of the Arizona Territory of the Confederate States of America (1861-62), which extended all the way to California. The CSA flag flew high over where today's Fountain Theater stands. The San Albino Church was built around 1852 on the south end of the plaza, but three years later, it was rebuilt where it stands today, on the north end.

And yes, Billy the Kid, tried and convicted here in a formal court of law, escaped from jail in 1881. Escaped right on the plaza where he then galloped off into history.

PART ONE

CHAPTER ONE

March, 1860
New Mexico Territory

"You wanna die today, boy?" the bandit asked. "'Nother move like that and I'll be obligin' you."

Cold sweat plastered the shirt to James Colton's back, while desert wind snaked down inside his vest, raising little bumps on his skin. James held his arms above his head, hoping, praying this masked man wouldn't shoot. That .44 Walker Colt's barrel, aimed dead center of James' face, looked to be the size of a cannon.

After being ordered down, James had stumbled while climbing from the drivers' seat of the stagecoach, and he'd come within inches of crashing into the bandit. It was his brother's firm grip on his arm, yanking him back, that kept James from knocking the man down. A second move like that, and James knew he'd be a dead man. There was no doubt this outlaw would just as soon pull the trigger as breathe.

James' leg throbbed and burned, thanks to the bullet that moments before had slammed into it. He shifted his weight as he stood.

The cloudless desert sky blazed blue, as blue as the bandit's eyes. Cactus and yucca swayed behind the gunman. The mule team waited, their tails busy swishing at flies. Boots scuffling. Muffled orders. James chanced a look toward the passengers by the end of the stagecoach. Scared. Their hands in the air trembled.

James counted four masked gunmen. One, his black bandana matching his hat, stood guard over the people he'd ordered out of the stage. His black eyes, hard as coal, stared at the only woman passenger, a middle-aged woman in a modest, dark blue dress. The bandit's lust for her radiated, sending out rays as hot as a fire poker. If he followed up on that lust, James

3

would do whatever necessary to protect Mrs. Anderson. After all, that was his duty.

James stood straighter as one of the other bandits swaggered over, his gait long and deliberate. Obviously, he was the leader. He barked orders at the others.

"Shelton, get the strongbox." A glance at the other two bandits. "Rudy, Billy. Keep your eyes on them passengers. Shoot 'em if they move."

Rudy. Shelton. Billy.

James vowed to remember those names. Rudy was the one with black eyes, the man holding a long-barreled .36 Navy Colt on the passengers.

"You." The brown-eyed leader shoved his gun into Trace's face. "Fetch down that strongbox."

Trace climbed up on the stagecoach, untied the metal crate, then tossed it down. All James could do was watch. A failure. He was such a failure for letting this happen. His first week on the job and he was already a failure. He remembered what his employers had told him before he signed on as shotgun guard for Butterfield Overland Stage Lines. Passenger and mail safety first, last, and foremost. Your job, they'd repeated, was to get to the next way station in one piece. His brother's job was to drive the stagecoach. And Trace had already been doing that for over a year, having driven this Celerity stagecoach from Mesilla, New Mexico Territory, to their turn-around point two hundred miles farther west in Tucson.

A gun shot. James jumped. Two of the outlaws knelt at the strongbox and ripped off the shattered lid. They riffled through its contents. The stoutest of the two men pitched official papers, letters, and documents over his shoulder, and then, as if winning a trophy, he held up a fistful of cash.

Butterfield said James should protect the money and passengers. How could he do that without his new shotgun? Or Trace's pistol?

A failure.

Should've known there'd be a holdup.

The rocks that formed Picacho Pass danced on end. They blurred, then pulled themselves together. James looked at his brother. Trace grew fuzzy around the edges. Voices, distant voices buzzed in his ear. His knees buckling, James leaned back against

4

the side of the stagecoach and watched the blood collect around his boot.

A lake. Looks just like a red lake.

The leader rammed the gun barrel into James' chest. "You deaf? Or just plain stupid?"

James frowned at the man and then at Trace. He'd been listening, he thought. His world, his blurry world, turned black and white.

Trace nudged James with his elbow. "You all right?"

Before James could nod, the leader cocked his revolver, and the scar arching over his eye rose a little as his brows lifted.

"Guess you wanna die right now," he said.

"No. Wait." Trace pushed James sideways. "We're going."

"Damn right you are." The leader waggled his gun toward the gathered passengers. "Now git on over there with the rest of 'em."

James wanted to comply. He wanted to stay alive. To stay in one piece. He eased sideways, but his knees threatened to buckle again. He grabbed for the stagecoach, but instead of the wooden side, he felt an arm stronger than his supporting him, leading him away. His brother guided him the few yards to where they stopped.

After pulling in some air, James felt better. His world colored again. The outlaws were gathered around the stage now. Over their masks, their eyes were clear—real clear. One pair was dark blue, reminding James of late twilight back home in Kansas. Those belonged to Billy. Another pair, gleaming black as bear's fur, belonged to Rudy. The other two pairs were shades of brown, and James made out a jagged scar near the leader's right eye.

Those eyes. That scar. James knew he'd remember them forever.

James and Trace stood shoulder to shoulder with the passengers, all lined up behind the stagecoach. All at the mercy of these four outlaws. James hated them. They'd taken his new Belgian shotgun. He'd only had it for a week, bought the day before he started working. And when he'd shot at the robbers just moments before during their attack, he'd enjoyed its smooth-as-butter recoil.

And he hated them for scaring everyone. Why didn't they just take the money and leave? James watched their every move and flinched as Rudy grabbed Mrs. Anderson's arm.

5

Instinctively, James stepped forward. "Leave her alone."

"Told you not to move." Billy shoved James back against the stagecoach. "You just plain stupid?" He waved his revolver at James.

"You have no right to do this, you low-down outlaw!" Mr. Anderson shook his pointed finger at the masked man. "You kill us and there'll be no place you can hide where they won't find you."

Billy chuckled, while the leader stepped within inches of Mr. Anderson's chest, the nearness sending Mr. Anderson back up against the stagecoach.

More chuckles from the outlaws as they looked at each other.

"I'm scared now." One of them nodded to Billy. "Ain't you, Billy?"

Billy shrugged. "Shakin' in my boots."

Rudy, eyes narrowed into black slits, ran his hand up and down Mrs. Anderson's arm, leering into her face. His gaze followed her body from head to toe, returning to her breasts.

"We'll make this quick. You'll like it." He lowered his mask, pulled her hard against him, then licked the base of her neck. She struggled, protests muffled by her attacker's grunts.

The bandit clutched the front of her dress. She screamed.

"Stop it!" Mr. Anderson shouted, stepping forward.

"That's enough!" James moved closer. Billy's gun cocked. James and Mr. Anderson both froze.

"No need for this," Trace said. "Just take the money and go."

"Shut up!" The revolver swung toward Trace.

Fabric ripped as Mrs. Anderson pounded the man's shoulder. She wriggled with the energy of a snared rabbit. More material ripped.

James clenched his fists.

Remember the outlaw's unmasked face. Black eyes, sideburns down to the chin, mustache. Rudy.

Was the sun going down? Already? A glance told him it was still afternoon, but his strength was fading, and fast, too. If he rushed to Mrs. Anderson's rescue again, the gunmen would shoot him. Maybe her, too. This time it wouldn't be in his leg. He fought to stay upright.

Protect the passengers.

"Leave her alone!" Mr. Anderson lurched at Rudy and

6

managed to grab his arm. Rudy released the woman, and in one quick, seamless motion whipped his gun out of his holster. He swung at Mr. Anderson.

A stomach-churning *whump*. Mr. Anderson reeled back, blood dripping from the wound on the side of his head. He slumped to the ground, then lay still.

The leader snapped at Rudy. "What the hell're you doin', Rudy? Ain't got time for her. Get the money."

"Ain't done yet, Fallon." Rudy stepped toward Mrs. Anderson.

Fallon. The leader.

James memorized the name and scar that went with it.

Rudy, black eyes—matches his heart.

James repeated it over and over. Trace was mouthing something, too.

Fallon turned his .44 Walker Colt on Rudy. "I'm boss and I'm telling you, you're done. Now, get the rest of the money."

Rudy stared at the woman clutching her chest, then shoved her against the side of the stagecoach. After a steel-cold glare at Fallon, Rudy aimed a finger at Mrs. Anderson's chest.

"Next time, Missy," he said. One last leering look, then he walked away.

James leaned over to her. "You all right, Missus Anderson?"

Managing a nod, she peered down at the material hanging around her dark blue skirt like an apron. She pulled it up to cover her bodice. Her eyes darted from James to Trace to her husband.

While James fought to stay conscious, the other two thieves finished collecting money, jewelry, and other valuables from the passengers. Finished, they turned their attention to James and Trace.

"Empty your pockets, driver." Billy nodded at Trace.

Trace hesitated.

"You wanna die, too?" Billy asked. He aimed his gun at Trace's chest.

One arm held out at his side, Trace dug into his vest pocket and handed over all the money he had, not quite three dollars. Billy snorted at the pittance.

James' turn. He looked into a pair of brown eyes glaring over a dirty red bandana. Must be the bandit called Shelton. Something hard bore into James' chest. Shelton's revolver.

"You, tough man. And you call yourself a guard. Hell, can't even shoot straight." The outlaw rammed a finger through the hole in his shirt. "Oughta kill you for this." Shelton extended his hand, palm up. "Give it up."

James' grandfather's watch burned against his chest. Memories of his grandpa and him—the day his grandpa gave it to him. And why. That watch meant everything to him. No one would take it.

James jammed his hand in his left vest pocket, brought out two dollars and change. He offered it to the bandit.

Shelton stuffed the money into his own pocket. "Other one, boy."

"I got nothing else."

"You're lyin.'"

The hammer cocked in his ears. Loud. James fought to breathe. He shook his head.

Hands upraised, Trace peered over at James. "Give it to him. Ain't worth losing your life over."

"I said I got nothing else."

"And I say you're lyin', boy." Shelton patted James' vest. "What's this?"

"Nothing."

James backed away, and Shelton slammed the revolver barrel against James' temple. James slid along the side of the stagecoach, then crumpled to the ground. Shelton rolled him over, fished into his pocket, and brought out James' golden treasure. Watch in hand, Shelton stood and grinned at the victory.

"No!" James reached out a hand, but grasped only air. Fuzzy images grayed.

Shelton held the watch to his ear. "Very nice."

"Let me see," Billy said. He reached for it, but Shelton kept it at arm's length.

"You'll see it when I say. It's mine." Shelton shot a look at Billy, who backed off. Then Shelton knelt by James and aimed the revolver at his forehead.

James' world spun. Was that a gun in his face? He fought to roll away, but his hands wouldn't cooperate. Instead, they flailed like a broken marionette.

"Wait!" Trace wedged himself between Shelton and James. "You got everything. Don't shoot him."

Shelton shoved Trace aside, sending him crashing into a passenger. Before James could take any kind of cover, Fallon marched over. James saw the boot heading toward his chest, but he couldn't move out of the way in time. The blow reeled him under the stagecoach. He felt ribs crack.

"Leave my brother alone!" Trace shouted. He rushed at the leader, knocking him to the ground. Trace threw himself on top and planted a fist in Fallon's face. Someone grabbed the back of Trace's shirt. Arms now pinned behind him, Trace struggled while he was jerked to his feet.

Rising to his knees and then his feet, Fallon glared at Trace and the other passengers. He swiped his hand across his nose, inspected the blood, and touched the growing lump on his cheek. He stepped in close to Trace.

"You're just askin' to die," Fallon said. He pointed his revolver at Trace's face. "I'm gonna help."

"No!" James grabbed at legs. The one he caught kicked back. Although he was on the ground, James could see Trace, that gun pointing right at him. Years dragged while James crawled out from under the coach.

Can't let Trace die. Gotta protect him.

The outlaw leader chuckled, lowering the weapon. He spoke to no one in particular.

"Hell, that's more fun'n shootin' 'im! Did ya see the look on his face? Bet this little coward wet hisself."

"Yeah. He was real scared." Rudy let out a hissing chuckle.

"Come on, Fallon. Let's just get outta here." Billy pulled his stained brown hat down low, pointed over his shoulder. "Law's gonna be on our tail. We got the money. Don't have time for games."

Fallon wagged his head. "Damn, Billy. S'ppose you're right."

Silence stretched across the rag-tag party. Fallon scratched his nose through the bandana.

"Hell," he said, "don't see much sense on wastin' good bullets. Rudy, keep your gun on 'em. Billy, Shelton...unhook the team."

Fallon holstered his gun.

Billy released Trace's arm, shoving him back hard against the stagecoach's side. James was now close enough to reach out and touch his brother's leg. As he extended his arm, another pistol barrel stared him in the face. Rudy's black eyes sparked, that cloth mask now hanging around his neck.

9

"Try anything funny, driver," Rudy said, "and your shotgun guard dies first."

Rudy squatted down, then gripped James' vest. He yanked him off the ground. "Got it?"

James nodded. But he just couldn't let them ride away with his grandpa's watch. The watch he'd do anything to keep. Even die for.

A plan. He needed a plan.

Instead, what he heard was his brother, his voice calm. "No need to hurt him. Nobody's gonna do anything stupid."

James peered around the pistol and up at Rudy's scowl. He memorized every detail of the man's face. Thick mustache. Thin lips. Was he sun-tanned or Mexican? Hard to tell, but his dark skin had that leathery look to it, more like tanned cowhide. If this outlaw's ugly face was on a wanted poster, James knew it'd be easy identifying him. He'd tell the sheriff back in Mesilla as soon as he could.

From this vantage point, he had a clear view of all three passengers and his brother. James searched his memory for the passenger list. Mister...Sandoval? Santos? San something. Something Spanish. Whatever his name was, he glared at Trace and then the bandits. Despite his tanned skin, his face flushed red as his brown eyes narrowed. He glared again at Trace and jerked his pointed finger toward the team. "Wha...what?"

The mules brayed. One danced sideways, bumping into another, while Fallon and Shelton undid the harnesses. Then Fallon slapped the lead mule on its rump, shouted, and waved his arms. All six animals thundered into the desert at a dead run.

Mr. San Something screamed at Trace. "Do something, driver! They're takin' our mules!" He scowled. "*Dios, hombre*, do something!"

"Shut up!" Rudy held up his arm as if to backhand him.

The passenger muttered what James thought were threats, in English and Spanish. More glares at Trace. Mrs. Anderson turned wide eyes on him and moved closer to her husband.

Trace dropped his voice low. "Just let them go, Mister Sanchez. We'll find another team."

Sanchez.

James nodded. Common enough name in this part of the country.

"No other team anywhere around here," Sanchez said. "Going to have to walk. Imagine me, Isaac Sanchez—walking." He swung his narrowed eyes on James and pointed. "And it's all *your* fault. Damn shotgun guard. Damn *kid*. I'd like to shoot you myself."

"I said shut up!" Rudy jammed the gun barrel into Sanchez's stomach. "You. *Pendejo*. You talk too much. Just shut the hell up."

Fallon waved at Rudy. "Looks like we're done here. Let's ride." He sauntered toward his horse as if the sheriff would never catch up. Just like a game.

A plan. James fought for ideas. Something to get these bandits to stop. Return his watch.

"You can't leave me out here to die." Sanchez spread his arms and glanced around at the sagebrush and prickly pear cactus.

"Can and will," Fallon said. "More fun that way." He waved a final farewell. "Enjoy your walk."

The four outlaws rode west, into the sun.

CHAPTER TWO

Even before the dirt clouds settled, James was sitting up, thanks to his brother's strong grip. And Mr. Anderson was on his feet, his wife steadying him.

Desert sand, pushed by a cold spring wind, swirled around James. Behind him was Picacho Pass, those gray boulders signaling the westward turn from Mesilla. But now they signaled a place of ambush, a place of failure.

A finger brushed the side of James' head, pressing gently on the burning knot that came courtesy of Shelton's powerful swing. The gun barrel had left an imprint on his skin. He flinched at Trace's touch, then pushed his brother's hand away. He could take the pain, but damn, that touch hurt. Still, he hoped he hadn't injured Trace's feelings. His brother was all he had out here, so far from home. His brother. His best friend.

Trace pointed to the tin container hanging on the side of the high drivers' seat. "Mister Sanchez," he said, "hand me that canteen, please."

Sanchez took a long swig before he handed it over.

While James leaned back against the coach, Trace untied James' neckerchief, soaked it, then held it against James' throbbing cheek. This time, James let his brother help.

"We were real lucky, Mister Sanchez," Trace continued. "But, if we're gonna get out of this alive, I'll need your help. Think you can do it?"

Sanchez clucked his tongue and glared down at James. "You ain't gonna be much help right now. Not with that head wound." He pointed at the dried blood. "*That* you deserved. You and your pathetic shooting. Some shotgun guard."

"It was the sun, Mister Sanchez." James wondered if his words were pathetic, too.

"Couldn't see 'em coming or I would've shot sooner. I'm sorry."

"Sun in my eyes." Sanchez's sing-song voice mocked James. "Heard that worthless excuse before." He pointed his chin at James' blood-soaked pant leg. "What happened there?"

"Took a bullet during the ambush," Trace said.

James stifled a groan. That leg hurt like hell. How was he going to get the passengers and what was left of the mail to safety? Trace ripped the pant leg, then wiped the wound with his wet bandana.

James jerked away. "Damn, Trace. That hurts."

"Sorry. Awful lot of blood." Trace held his cool palm against James' forehead. "How you feeling?"

James wasn't sure. Head pounding, leg throbbing, cactus, sky and people swirling in shades of gray and blue. He wanted to throw up. The wagon wheel against his back. The ground hard under his rear. His stomach lurched.

Conversations floated around him. Sanchez's voice.

"Looks to me like he'll live, if he don't bleed to death first. Bullet went right into the calf." A pause. "You a friend of his, driver?"

"My younger brother. It's his first week on the job."

Probably my last, too.

James winced. Someone tied cloth around his leg. Tied it tight.

Breathing was hard. The memory of Fallon's boot heading for his ribs exploded in his head. Each rise and fall of his chest brought spear-like jabs. James opened his eyes and sucked in as little air as possible.

Trace offered him the canteen. "You got kicked pretty hard. Hurt?"

James shrugged. He didn't want Sanchez or any of the other passengers to think he was hurt. At least not too badly. He could still do his job. Couldn't he?

But to hell with his job. They'd taken his watch.

James lowered his voice. "They stole my watch, Trace."

A pat of his empty pocket made it real.

Trace wagged his head. "I couldn't stop 'em. I'm sorry."

James' gaze swept across his brother to the passengers, pausing just long enough on each face to note the various expressions. He scowled. "Dammit!"

"To hell with your damn watch," Sanchez said. "If it wasn't for your rotten aim, we wouldn't be in this mess. You're supposed to be protecting me!"

13

Trace raised his fist shoulder high. "My brother put his life on the line for you, Sanchez!"

"No time for argument, gentlemen," Mr. Anderson said. Shorter than both, nevertheless, he stepped in between the two men. "We've gotta work together if we're gonna survive."

Trace dropped his fist. "You're right. I'm sorry." He turned his attention to James. "That leg's pretty bad. Let's get you up."

James found himself upright on his feet before he could say anything. He clutched his ribs tighter. "Can't breathe too good."

Trace wrapped a strong arm around James and guided him to the stagecoach. "Get you out of this sun and put your leg up, you'll feel better."

The first step sent shock waves down into James' foot. Agony knitted his eyebrows. He knew he'd pass out any minute. Instead of screaming, he concentrated on breathing—slow and shallow with each step.

He stumbled through the narrow stagecoach door, then thudded to the wooden bench seat facing forward. While there wasn't much room inside the coach, still it drew around him like a warm blanket. He felt more than saw his brother sit on the seat across from him.

"Can't believe they took my watch," James said. He gazed out the window and saw nothing but the coming darkness.

"There wasn't anything we could do." Mrs. Anderson's voice from the doorway was soft, like his ma's would've been. "They'd have killed you and probably the rest of us. It's just a watch. You can get another one."

"Ain't another one like it!" James shouted. He was sorry for his angry words, but his grief wouldn't let him apologize. "It was my grandpa's. He gave it to me...gave it when..." James wanted to cry, but knew he wouldn't. Not here. Not in front of these people. And he couldn't explain without crying. Instead, he tried to shut out the world.

The tin canteen banged against his shoulder, bringing him back. He heard worry in his brother's voice. "Take a sip, you'll feel better."

Wet coolness soothed his throat. James closed his eyes. Funny silver jagged lines raced across the inside of his lids, and his body sagged. He struggled to stay alert.

Trace leaned out of the coach's door. "Mister Sanchez? You and I are gonna walk back to a ranch I know of a few miles from here. Get horses and a wagon."

"Isn't that *your* job, driver? It's too far for me to walk." Sanchez's arm pointed from coach to desert to Trace's face. "Hell, isn't that what I paid you for? To ride, not walk?"

"Mister Sanchez, you said you'd help and that's what I expect you to do."

Sanchez scowled at Trace's glare.

A groan from James, louder than he'd thought, turned four faces to him.

"I'll go," James said.

"No." Trace patted James' shoulder. The touch was reassuring. "Mister Anderson?"

"I'm fine, driver. What can I do?"

More zigzag streaks. James' stomach boiled, and he pushed down rising bile. Just having his brother close by helped him relax.

"Stay here, Mister Anderson," Trace said. "Watch after James and your wife. I don't think those robbers will be back. Wish they hadn't taken our guns."

"I do, too." Mr. Anderson's words rang cold.

"I can go with you," James said. He pushed himself up straighter.

Trace placed his hand on James' knee. "No. You stay here. I need you to guard the stagecoach. All right?"

James nodded. "Sure. I can do that."

"Right. Mister Sanchez and I will be back soon as we can." Trace tossed a lopsided grin at James. "Don't talk their ears off while we're gone."

James nodded then rocked with the coach as his brother stepped out.

* * *

A cold rag on his cheek. James jerked back and opened his eyes. Mrs. Anderson was sitting next to him. She reminded him again of ma. He grasped her hand, then pushed it away.

"Thanks, ma'am. I'm fine, really."

"I don't think so. You've been out quite a while. Your brother just returned with a wagon and horses."

"Ma'am?" Several blinks, questions not spoken, forehead furrowed. "I only just closed my eyes."

Trace stuck his head into the coach. "Hey, little brother. Thought you'd sleep all afternoon." Trace's grin faded. "You all right?"

"Fine." James studied his brother's twenty-three-year-old face. So much worry there.

Trace stepped into the coach, sat across from James, and examined James' leg.

"Been bleeding pretty bad," Trace said, "but looks like it finally stopped." He held James' chin in his hand. "Got a helluva bruise starting." He poked at the crimson mark on James' cheek.

"Ow!" James recoiled. "Said I'm fine. Don't baby me." After a quick glance at Mrs. Anderson, he swatted at his brother's hand. "Stop poking me."

"Time to get you to a doctor." Trace backed out of the coach and spoke to the three passengers. "We'll take this wagon, then I'll come back tomorrow for the stage. The trip back'll take a couple of hours. We'll get in after dark. I'll drive fast as I can."

16

Surrounded by luggage and mail remnants, James rocked in the wagon bed and fought to stay awake.

"Not too much farther," James said. Someone's body bumped into his. James held his throbbing cheek. "Rough road."

"What? You're mumbling, James. Just rest now."

Whose words were those? Sounded like his brother's. As much as he struggled to keep his eyes open and figure out who was talking, sleep won.

The rattle of a wagon's wheels snapped James' eyes open. He was still in the wagon bed, but his head now lay cradled in Mrs. Anderson's lap. He elbowed his way to sit up. As he did, the clouds lit by the setting sun danced on his horizon. His stomach lurched. James leaned back on the soft lap.

I'll sit up when we get there.

Someone touched his shoulder, and then there was a face inches from his. Trace.

"Gotta get you inside right now." Trace's voice sounded tense, close to panic.

Mr. and Mrs. Anderson were no longer in the wagon, and it was no longer moving. James let his brother help him down to the ground while Mr. Sanchez grabbed his left arm, steadying him. Wincing, James held his ribs. His hands shook.

Trace nodded to Sanchez as he clutched his brother's shoulder. "Thanks, I'll take it from here."

"I just bet you will." Sanchez released James, then ripped his suitcase out of Mr. Anderson's hand. "I'm going down right now to that stage office. They'll get an earful from me!" He sneered at James. "You best start looking for another job, Sonny. I'll see to it you're fired."

Sanchez spun and marched down the boardwalk.

Mr. Anderson stepped in closer. "You'd think he'd be grateful just to be alive."

His knees turning rubbery, James stumbled and reached for the side of the wagon. Anything to stay upright.

"That's a fact." Trace slipped an arm around James' waist. "I'll go down to Butterfield after you're settled and explain things."

Even with his brother's strong grip around his waist, James struggled to put one foot in front of the other.

"The mules," James said. "I lost the mules. Am I gonna have to pay for them?" Were his words really as muddled as they sounded?

A chuckle. Trace's low voice rang close. "No." Another nudge. "Couple more steps. Door's right over here."

James focused on the sign over the door: Ezra Logan, Doctor of Medicine.

He took dead aim for the blue-trimmed door, but before he could take another step, his knees buckled. Adobe buildings spun. His brother picked him up.

Now he was truly embarrassed. Carried in like a baby. But he knew he couldn't make it on his own. Nevertheless, he had to protest.

"I can walk, Trace."

"Uh huh."

Mr. Anderson held the door open as Trace stepped through with James. A man with a concerned but confident look, gray eyebrows pulled together, met them.

James noted two straight-backed chairs against the adobe wall, a small desk on the opposite side. A large painting of what could have been ships at sea, or coyotes in a blue desert, took up half of the wall above the desk. Muffled words floated around his head.

The man, probably the doctor, pointed to a room down a short hall.

The lumpy cotton mattress closed in around James like hands, and he groaned too loudly. He hadn't meant to be dramatic, but *damn* he hurt. Mrs. Anderson patted his arm and produced a motherly smile.

"You'll be fine," she said. "A big strapping boy like you'll be up in no time."

Mr. Anderson winked at him. "Limp as long as you can, son. Gets the girls to take pity on you." He chuckled. "Works every time."

Despite the pain, James had to smile. There was truth in that, he was sure. But right now, a grin was all he could manage.

Mr. Anderson took his wife's arm and led her toward the door. "We'll be over at the Corn Exchange Hotel if you need us, Mister Colton. Hope your brother's up and around soon."

James listened to the outer door close, his brother's labored breathing, the doctor rattling a few metal instruments. Something tugged on his pant leg. Scissors.

Then something wet scrubbed his leg. His bit his lower lip. The pain intensified. He swallowed tears.

Doc poked.

James gripped the edge of the bed and fought the need to scream.

* * *

A bell tinkled. James recognized the sound. He'd heard it all day. People coming in and out of the doctor's office. If that bell was any indication, Doctor Logan was a busy man. James could make out some of the words that had sailed down the hall and into his room. Others were muffled. Maybe it was the laudanum that kept the voices muffled. Most of them didn't make sense.

This voice, the most recent one, James recognized. He couldn't exactly put a name with it, but it was familiar. He strained to hear the words. Mush. Mushy words. Then a couple of words he identified stopped his breath. Stagecoach. Robbers.

Please don't let that be Butterfield's manager. I'm gonna get fired.

Heavy footsteps marched down the hall toward him. James hoped, prayed those were Trace's, but he knew better. Trace wouldn't be back with the stagecoach for several more hours. Probably after dark. And it wasn't Trace's footsteps anyway.

If it isn't Trace, please don't let it be Mister Walters.

A light rap on his doorjamb and Mr. Walters appeared, his shaggy eyebrows pulled together. He extended a meaty hand.

"I understand the surgery went well." Bill Walters nodded at James' bandaged leg draped over a pillow. "Bullet came out slick as you please. Doc says you'll be up in no time."

James pushed himself up farther on two pillows. The mattress under him was hard, just what he expected from a doctor's office.

Walters' gaze traveled from James' leg up to his cheek. Then Walters leaned in closer and frowned at the bruise. "Got a real beaut' there. Hurt?"

"No, sir." James would never admit that its throbbing had kept him up last night almost as much as his leg.

"Need anything?" Walters tilted his head, his wavy hair brushing his shoulders.

"Water, if you don't mind." James licked his bottom lip, his mouth desert dry. "Trace tell you what happened yesterday?"

A nod. "I would've been over sooner to see you, but I had to confirm Trace's accounting of the holdup." Walters handed a water glass to James. "Mister Sanchez came in spouting off accusations left and right. He's one unhappy customer."

James sipped, the cool liquid soothing his raw throat. The glass shook so hard, he used both hands to grip it.

"Mister Walters, I can go back to work today. I'm fit."

Walters took the glass and set it on a nearby table. "You're looking like the losing end of a barnyard scuffle, James. That black eye's the only thing putting color in your face."

"But I can still work."

Or could he? James knew he had enough strength to close his eyes and that was about all.

A couple deep breaths from Walters. His eyes roamed the room, its adobe walls smoothed with mud plaster, the single diploma decorating the wall. The gaze stopped at a spot above James' head, then slid down to meet his eyes. His shoulders sagged a little.

"James, I talked to Isaac Sanchez a long time last night, and he's demanding I fire you."

"Yes, sir, I know." James looked away.

Walters shrugged. "Mister Sanchez is a bigshot in this community. One of Mesilla's councilmen, no less."

A councilman? Hell, why not the President? Might as well get fired from the best.

"Don't want to do it, James." Walters spoke to the wall.

James tried to suck in a lungful of air, but instead pulled in jabs of pain.

"But..." Walters shrugged. "I spoke with the Andersons and they told me how you tried to help her. That was a brave thing you did. They both were impressed and appreciative."

"Thank you, sir."

"Nevertheless, I'm gonna have to put you on one month's suspension." Walters's lips pursed. "I'll pay you for this week, but in a month we'll see how you're doing. If I can, I'll re-hire you then." He patted James' shoulder. "That's the best I can do, son. I'm sorry."

"Yes, sir. I understand."

Another pat, then Walters released James' shoulder and moved toward the door.

"Get some rest, heal up, then come see me. I'll speak with your brother when he gets back with the stagecoach."

The back of Mr. Walters disappeared out the door. James reached for the water glass.

At least I'm not fired—exactly.

Two sips and his eyes closed. What was he gonna tell ma? One week on the job and already robbed, shot, and almost fired.

Helluva way to start a new life.

* * *

James sat propped up in bed and used the last of his tortilla to scoop up the remains of beans and eggs on his breakfast plate. Usually he was hungry in the mornings, but today he felt like he'd never eaten before. His appetite had never been keener, and those eggs were sure tasty. Almost as good as ma's.

Yesterday was all but a blur. There were images of Trace sitting by his bed, much like he was now, and the doc leaning over him...then dark. Then dreams.

During the few minutes he had slept last night, his gold watch danced in his dreams, always just out of reach. He saw his hand grab at it, then miss. Time and time again. Strange chattering, like someone laughing, floated in and out. But what woke him most often were visions of grandpa—his face grimacing yet trying to smile, his brown eyes closing yet trying to stay open, his callused yet soft hand reaching out—giving James his watch. Giving it to him just before—

"You're looking better there, little brother," Trace said. He sat perched in a chair next to the bed and waved a rolled-up tortilla at James' face. "Finally got some color back, but that bruise is right ugly." Trace grimaced. "Lots of purple, black and blue."

"And each color hurts." James sipped his coffee, wincing before he set the cup down. "Soon as I can, I'll talk to the sheriff, see if there's posters on those men."

"Already done that." Trace spoke over a mouthful of tortilla.

"Find out anything?"

"Said he wouldn't come bother you because we found posters on all four." Trace leaned in closer. "They're all wanted for robbery, and that mean one, Rudy, is wanted for murder, too."

"Damn." A cold clot fisted in James' chest. "He could've killed us without thinking twice."

"Uh huh."

Doctor Logan walked in, a fresh roll of bandages in hand.

Somehow, even though he wasn't very tall, Logan exuded authority, a presence that was undeniable. And James suspected that despite the short stature, he was a man who wouldn't back down from anything. He liked the doctor.

Logan peered into James' face and jabbed at the tender bruise. "How you feeling son? See you're eating well. Lot better than yesterday."

He poked harder. James winced and fought down his breakfast threatening to rise. Another poke, then Logan stood back nodding.

"Cheekbone's not broken. Couldn't tell for sure yesterday. Sure was swollen. Looks like those cold compresses helped." Logan's gray-blue eyes smiled. "Yep, coming along nicely."

Today, James felt good. Maybe good was too strong a word. *Better. Yeah, definitely better.*

The doctor straightened up and spoke over his shoulder at Trace. "That leg gave him trouble again last night. He didn't sleep much. Woke up every time the medicine wore off. Gonna need pain powder, at least some laudanum for a few more days so he can rest, build up strength."

"Sure appreciate all you're doing, doc." Trace eased to his feet and stood next to Logan. "Hate to tell you both this, but I gotta be leaving today. Another driver took sick, so the company said I'm taking his place, heading on out to Tucson. Won't be back for about a month."

James let his fork hit the plate. "Today?"

"I gotta do this, James." Trace shrugged. "I'm sorry."

James extended his hand, ready to shake Trace's. "I'll be fine. Don't worry about me." He shook with his brother. "Just be safe and watch out for those outlaws."

A soft chuckle brought Trace's mouth up to a smile. "They

just better watch out for *me*. Walters loaned me two shotguns and another Colt." He nodded. "I'm ready."

"Be sure to hit 'em this time." James felt a twist in his stomach.

"You get well, baby brother," Trace said. "Get on your feet again. No more sleeping on the job. I'll be back before you know it and you'll be riding shotgun for me." Trace paused and grinned. "Oh, and...do some target practicing while you heal up."

James gave Trace a manufactured frown. "Even with the sun in my eyes, I can still outshoot you any day."

Trace ruffled James' dark brown hair. "For a nineteen-year-old pup, you sure got spunk." He looked over at the doctor. "Can he stay here a few more days? Then he can move over to our room at the boarding house."

"Of course. I need to watch him a while longer, make sure that leg doesn't get infected."

Trace squeezed James' shoulder. "I'll come by before I take off this afternoon. Got some business I gotta see about right now."

Doctor Logan gathered the old bandages. "I'll walk out with you. Need you to sign some papers."

A nod, a stiff turn, then Trace with Doctor Logan in front, walked out the door.

A month, James thought. Enough time to heal up, buy another gun, and go after those outlaws. But, would he want to go back there, through that pass—alone? James stared at a spot on the wall.

Yeah, I'll go. Alone or with an army. I'm getting my watch back.

CHAPTER FOUR

The stitches had been out of his leg for ten minutes when James mounted his pinto and headed north out of Mesilla. He passed fields of grapevines about ready to leaf out, and green fields of onions, and adobe farmhouses, all following the curves of the mighty Rio Grande. But what he saw were the eyes. The scar. The faces of those four outlaws. He'd spent a long ten days plotting his moves, how to retrieve his watch, and make those men pay for his pain. Kicking his horse into a hard gallop, he took direct aim at Picacho Peak.

Once there, he galloped around the peak, and then he headed west, straight into the pass—Ambush Pass, as he now thought of it. He slowed his horse to a walk and glanced up at the gray rocks towering over him. Though the spring heat wasn't yet evident, sweat dripped down his forehead and stung his eyes. He pried off his wide brimmed hat, then used his forearm to mop his face.

The noonday sun threw no shadows as he glanced from rock to rock. Heart pounding harder than he knew it should, he swiped his face once more, replaced his hat, then unplugged the canteen hanging around his saddle horn. He took a sip of water.

Gonna be harder than I thought to track those outlaws.

After another sip, he plugged the canteen and hung it on the leather knob.

My grandpa's watch. I'll get it back.

He threw back his shoulders despite the tug of sore ribs, and he nudged his horse into a trot. He followed the stagecoach tracks, and with some effort, he could make out their passing. Spring winds had erased many of the footprints and wagon tracks. He slowed his pinto, and leaned over in the saddle, studying the ground for further signs.

And then, there they were—unmistakable marks of people standing, walking around. James stared at the ground and trembled.

Sonuvabitch.

He swallowed hard and forced air into his lungs. Then he eased out of the saddle and knelt by the marks. His fingers caressed the dirt, running through the prints, tracing the outline of a scuffle.

"Damn, no-good outlaws." He gripped a handful of sand. "Damn them!"

He released the sand and watched it fall back onto the ground.

"Run like the cowards you are. Ain't no place you can run where I won't find you."

Another handful of dirt, then he threw it into the wind.

"Just a matter of time."

As he pushed up to his feet, memories flooded in. James closed his eyes, reliving the holdup. His leg once again burned, and his cheek throbbed. His watch. James massaged his bruised face. A deep breath.

"All right. I begin here."

He knew talking out loud was silly, but somehow it seemed right. More certain. He felt more confident—of himself and his quest. He surveyed the jagged rocks and the crystal blue sky dotted with white clouds while the wind whistled through the pass. A covey of Gambel's quail darted across the road.

Why was he so nervous, so...uneasy? A long scan of the pass revealed nothing but what he'd seen before. No robbers hid behind the rocks, no masked men ready to leap out and shoot him. Nothing. Still, he couldn't shake the feeling of overwhelming alarm.

Just my imagination. Get a grip, James.

James swung up into his saddle, took one more sip of water, and then urged the horse through the pass.

After following the tracks around the boulders, he again dismounted. Those markings were easy enough to spot. According to the hoofprints, it looked like the four robbers were headed toward the tiny mining town of Santa Rita, forty miles away. West. He pulled on his memory. Trace had made him learn the terrain of the New Mexico Territory from the most recent map that'd been made. If he remembered right, between him and them lay plenty of desert, one mountain range, a wide river, and hundreds of places to hide.

I'll find you, you sonsuvbitches. I'll get my watch back. You can't hide forever.

25

He swung up once more into the saddle and spurred his horse. Due west.

* * *

Hours of riding brought him to what looked like an old campsite between rocks—nestled under piñon trees. Stripped lower branches of the trees where the horses had nibbled, fresh but dry dung, a charred stick, and remnants of a campfire dotted the area. He dismounted, then kicked at the ashes. Cold. Dry. Several days, maybe even a week since someone had camped here.

All right, at least I'm heading in the right direction.

A glance left then right. There had been four people, no doubt, four places on the ground where bedrolls were laid out. He spit on the dead campfire. Spitting would have to do until he came face to face with them.

Daylight faded into dark while James spread out his bedroll, started a fire, then heated water for coffee. The flames, orange and yellow spires, licked the bottom of the metal pot and shot up around the sides. Something sizzled and popped under them. While watching the fire dance, he gnawed on a piece of jerky.

Am I doing the right thing? Maybe Trace was right. Maybe my life is more important than my watch.

What if he was no match for those outlaws? What if they hurt him again all the way down to dead? Trace would wonder what had happened to him, wonder where he went, probably spending days, months searching. Endless searching could destroy his brother's life.

Should have left word at the boarding house. Or with the doctor.

James shook off the chill. His plan had seemed simple at the time—find the men, retrieve his watch, get back to Mesilla before Trace. Too late now to turn back. He still needed to retrieve his watch. The coffee and bile burned his throat.

James fell asleep wondering if Trace hated those outlaws as much as he did.

By the time the sun warmed the top of the rocks, James had finished feeding himself and his horse, packed his bedroll, cleaned his gun, and then made sure every chamber in the cylinder was loaded. James put the hammer in the safe position and holstered it. He was one step closer to his watch and maybe even a little revenge.

26

The tracks were easy enough to follow. Those four bandits hadn't bothered trying to cover them, and the wind hadn't erased them. By early afternoon, James stood beside hoofprints intersecting a narrow, dirt road. A road that may have led to a ranch miles away.

The tracks told the story—unmistakable scraping marks, several feet moving around. Someone had been robbed here. He studied the broken bushes where a body had crashed through, the wide marks where someone had been dragged, the swirled dirt where a victim had spent some time on the ground.

The tracks showed four horses still heading west. The horse and buggy tracks revealed that the other group, the victims, had pushed south. James couldn't tell how long ago this happened. He wasn't as good at reading signs as he knew he should be. But, it was plain to him he was getting closer, and the outlaws were still doing what they did best—relieving people of their valuables.

* * *

By late afternoon, James figured those men never took breaks, never got down from their horses, never stopped. As sore and tired as he was, however, he knew he couldn't quit. Wouldn't quit. He'd follow those men until he made them wish they'd chosen a different line of work.

A cold early spring wind whipped around him. He pulled his jacket tighter against his aching chest. His shivering only made his ribs hurt more, but he fought down the pain. Hopefully, this breeze wouldn't bring what he'd heard was a typical spring windstorm. Trace and another driver had swapped stories about these famous winds and how ferocious they could be. Nothing was safe from the sanding such storms brought. They etched windowpanes and stripped the few painted buildings of their color on the wind-side. They were definitely strong enough to wipe out hoofprints. If he lost the tracks, he'd have to go back to Mesilla empty-handed.

He clenched his jaw.

Not going back without my watch.

Just at the top of a low rise, James spotted a small adobe house with a windmill spinning in the side yard, a wooden barn out back, chickens pecking around it, and an old, mangy dog lounging in the shade against the front of the house. As James rode closer,

27

his heart caught in his throat. The tracks led right up to the front door. The robbers had stopped here.

Or they lived here.

James eased his newly purchased Navy Colt .36 out of his old holster and rotated the cylinder. Nervousness. He stuck it back in the holster and continued his survey of the area. No one was working, no kids playing in the yard, no sound of any kind. No horses were tied in front, or even around back as far as he could tell.

More silence.

James rode into the yard, tied his horse at the rail on the side of the house, and then eased back toward the barn, its aging wood creaking in the wind. The barn door was open a few inches, and he peeked inside, but finding no one except an old horse looking back, he opened it wider.

The barn was empty.

Gun drawn, he tiptoed around to the front of the house, careful not to make a sound. As he drew near, the door opened a few inches, a shotgun barrel stuck through.

"Hold it, *Señor*. One move and your head blows off!"

He froze. The voice—female with a heavy Spanish accent. The tone—she would definitely shoot, shoot to kill. His hands inched upward.

"Your gun. Throw it. *Vayase.*"

The shotgun cocked. The metallic grating sped right to his ear. Loud. James' grasp of Spanish was weak, but she meant for him to leave. That much was clear. He hated to relinquish his gun, but he tossed it to the ground anyway. He stepped back. Maybe if he explained…

"I'm not here to cause any trouble, ma'am." Was his voice as high as he thought? "Just wanted water for me and my horse." He pointed to his mouth and remembered the only Spanish word he knew. *"Agua."*

The barrel stuck out farther. *"Vayase!"*

If he left now he'd never find out if she knew about the robbers. On the other hand, if he stayed, he might get shot. Again.

One more chance. He pointed to his chest and produced what he hoped was the famous Colton family smile. Many women said it was disarming. He hoped it disarmed her. At least maybe she wouldn't shoot him before he got an answer.

"Name's James Francis Michael Colton, ma'am. I work for Butterfield Stage Lines."

At least I think I still do.

"Nothing here. Away. Go." The woman's voice softened. "A stream—south." The shotgun poked out another few inches. "Drink there."

In the doorway was the silhouette of a woman holding an older-style double barrel shotgun. What if she really fired it? The recoil would knock her down for sure. Problem was, as close as they were to each other, she couldn't miss. He'd end up with a Texas-size hole in his chest.

James hesitated. The yard revealed that the heavy work hadn't been done for a few days. No man about. And now the wind held a definite chill to it, and it was picking up. Dust swirled at his boots.

"Ma'am, truth is, I'm tracking some fellas I think came by this way. Robbers." He paused. "Can I put my hands down?"

"No." More of her appeared in the doorway. "These men. Why?"

"Well ma'am, like I said, I ride shotgun for Butterfield. They held up my stage couple weeks back, shot me, and took something of mine. I'm aiming to get it back."

His arms losing feeling, they sagged downward.

"Manos. Arriba!"

The shotgun bobbed up and down. James' hands again flew skyward.

The woman eased open the door, then stepped onto the rickety porch. She kept the shotgun aimed at the center of James' chest. Sprigs of black hair stuck out from the bun at the back of her head and her pale face reflected days and nights of sleep lost.

While she didn't shoot him, she didn't lower her shotgun, either. The two stood, gaze locked on each other.

He shivered from a chill that set in. Or was it his nerves?

Gonna get cold tonight. Maybe she'll let me sleep in the barn, at least.

Still they stood. Looking at each other. Little by little the woman lowered the weapon and eased the hammers down. Her eyes scanned James' entire body, starting at his boots and ending at his hat.

"These men. How many days before they rob you?"

29

A quick interpretation of her meaning. "Not quite two weeks, ma'am. About ten, eleven days."

Unable to keep his arms above his head any longer, James lowered them. Inch by inch.

"Stole everything from the three passengers," he continued, "then my brother and me."

The woman's eyes were as black as her hair. She had been pretty once, but hard work had made her rough and aged before her time. She was not very tall, maybe five-foot two, but she appeared to be quite strong. Probably as explosive as a powder keg—ready to blow at any minute. He didn't want to be the spark to ignite her.

The woman lowered the weapon a couple of inches more.

"How I know you are true?" she asked.

"I got a bullet wound that's just now healing." He pointed to his leg. "And my ribs almost got broke and," he pointed to his face, "this black eye and bruises from the butt of one of the men's guns when I wouldn't give him something."

A long pause, then she lowered the weapon to her side. "Come closer, slow. So I can see."

James limped toward the woman, letting her peer at his bruise. The bruise he'd examined this morning using his Bowie knife as a mirror when he shaved. The sun's reflection had allowed him a good, long look at what those outlaws had done. Fading black streaks ringed his right eye, and ugly purple and green marks glowed on his cheek, still tender to the touch.

She hesitated, then sighed. "For now, I believe you. Come."

The inside of the house was warm, and the afternoon light streamed through a single window. Two rocking chairs, their wooden arms dulled with use, and a nicked dining table occupied most of the room. A vase of wilted, dying wild flowers sat on the table. There was nothing in the kitchen but a counter and a wood stove. Behind the woodpile was nothing but kindling.

She stepped inside and shut the door, then pointed to the rocking chair nearest to the fireplace. James eased his sore body to the seat, and he removed his hat while she took the rocking chair across from him. The shotgun rested on her lap.

"Ma'am," James said. "Have you seen those men I'm lookin' for? There were four of 'em, one pretty big, scar over the right eye, one tall, blue eyes."

"*Sí*, they were here." She said it so softly James edged closer to make out the words.

"Three days now, they were here."

"Three days ago?"

He was close.

"*Sí*, they stay *dos dias*, then leave."

She glanced toward a closed door off to the side of the main room. Puzzled, James followed her gaze.

"Did they say where they were heading to?"

"No. *Mi esposo.* They hurt him. I do not listen to their talk. I am glad they leave."

"Isabel? Isabel?" A weak, masculine voice called from the other room. "*¿Quién es?*"

The woman stood, looked again at the door. "*Mi esposo.*"

"You're Isabel?" James asked.

She nodded and motioned to him. James followed her into a small, dark bedroom where a man lay on his side. James waited just inside the door.

Isabel sat on the edge of the bed. "Juan, this is Señor...Señor?" Those dark eyes looked up at James.

"Colton, sir. James Colton. I'm with Butterfield Stage Lines."

The man's fever-red eyes glowed against his pale, drawn face. He glared at James, while his shaking hands tugged at the blankets under his chin. "*No. No. Por favor.*"

James had to lean in closer to hear and understand the words.

"But, I'm not...I won't," James said.

"*Por favor*, don't shoot."

Isabel patted her husband's shoulder, cooed to him. "*Calma. Calma. No bandito.* He helps." She looked up at James. "You will help us, *si?*"

The worry on her face crinkled the corners of her eyes. James held his breath. He couldn't just ride away without helping. He wanted to help, but he sure didn't want to be delayed. He needed... no *had*...to be back in Mesilla before Trace got there. At this rate, he calculated, Trace could make two runs to Tucson before James returned.

"Yes, ma'am, I can help for a day or two, but I gotta go find those men. Soon."

The wind howled now, rattling the windowpane. The tracks would be gone by morning.

"*Gracias, Señor.*" Isabel smiled at him.

"First, we need to get him to a doctor." James scanned Juan's blanketed body. "Where exactly is he shot at?"

"In his back."

Had to have been that pendejo Rudy. Already has one murder on his head.

James prayed Juan wouldn't be number two. Besides, shooting a man is one thing, but you never shoot in the back. It's not the right way to do things.

Bunch of cowards. Not only are they thieves, but they're back-shootin' thieves.

He hated them with renewed passion.

"The bullet out—I take out," Isabel said. "But very much fever. *Muy calor.*"

James wasn't real sure what she'd said, but it was plain Juan needed a doctor. And quick.

"Ma'am, I don't know nothing about doctoring. But I can ride into town and fetch one back. Where's the closest doc at?"

"*Dos días.* Two." Isabel looked at her husband, and her voice dropped to a whisper. "Too far."

James recalled that map again. Another town sprang to mind.

"How about Santa Rita? Don't they have a doctor?"

"*Sí.* But he leave." Isabel sighed. "No doctor."

"Isabel?" Juan whispered. "Who takes care of you?"

"*Shhh, mi novio. Yo te amo.*"

James again guessed at her meaning. The wind gusted outside, and something banged against the side of the tiny house.

"I'll go tend to my horse, ma'am," James said, "and get my gun. Then I'll see what needs doing. But I can only stay two days."

Four days later, they buried Juan.

CHAPTER FIVE

James spurred his horse into a gallop as he waved farewell to Mrs. Villanueva. His heart broke for this kind woman, but he was set on finding those men. It wouldn't be easy. Not now. Not with all the lead-time and the windstorm days before. No, this quest was getting harder all the time.

Trace was due back in Mesilla in about two weeks. Sure wasn't much time to get the job done. Squaring his shoulders, James vowed he'd see those men go to jail.

As he rode due west, James thought about the bandits, about his watch, about killing people. Why did people do that to others? Ma had taught him to treat people kindly, not to take things, certainly not to kill. Would he have to? Could he?

James spent another day and a half of looking...hoping. A track here and there brought renewed determination. They had to be around here somewhere. After reviewing his mental map, he headed for Santa Rita, the bustling mining camp so named nearly sixty years previously by Mexican settlers. He'd heard that in the last year or so, Anglos had come flooding in, building a town where a rough settlement used to be.

On a hill overlooking the town, he rested and took in the few wooden buildings lining the main road. Hundreds of white tents were scattered around the hillsides. Looked like a mushroom epidemic. James chuckled at the image.

The turquoise sky, the sweet, crisp mountain air, the stately Ponderosa pines marching up the hillside. People called to each other. James couldn't make out the words exactly, but he guessed they had to do with mining or striking the world's largest silver vein. Or was it copper? The energy of the town swept him up. He'd never been to a mining camp before. Sure wasn't what he'd expected. It was much better.

Riding down Main Street, he soaked in the hustle and bustle of the miners. A few people, the more levelheaded ones he thought, were making money off of those who needed supplies and beer. On his right was the general mercantile store, smelling of freshly cut wood. It appeared to be the largest building in town. Next to it sat the Tin Pan Saloon where two women, dressed in shades of red and purple, lingered around the swinging doors. If noise was any indication, this was the most popular place in town.

James couldn't help but grin. This burg was jumping. On his left, across from the mercantile, sat another saloon. A man was painting the finishing touches on the storefront: Lazy Dog Saloon. Strange but intriguing name, James thought. Down two more buildings were two more bars, each one noisier than the other. James' grin broke into a wide smile.

This mining camp was going to be fun for a few days. Too bad Trace wasn't here to share in the excitement. Maybe, if the town had an express service, he could contact the doctor in Mesilla and tell Trace to meet him here.

Then it hit him—the reason why he'd come all this way. It wasn't for fun and excitement. It was to locate those men. Something constricted in his chest at the memory of Juan and his widow. James sighed. Was there any real hope of finding those killers?

He reined up in front of a building, its freshly painted sign sporting bright blue letters: Restaurant, Meals $1.

James frowned. Meals in Mesilla usually ran twenty-five cents, or fifty cents with a beer. He felt the twenty-six dollars in his pocket—all that was left of the thirty Trace had given him before taking off for Tucson. Instructions were clear—he was to spend it only on the boarding house and food until they were together again. James shrugged. He could spend it here just as well as in Mesilla. Same expenses, different town.

Farther down Main Street, the sheriff's office was located on the left. This narrow, wooden building, the bars on the window setting it off from the rest of the town, would be one of his first stops. As soon as he could, he'd have a chat with the sheriff about the robbers. Maybe this lawman had heard of them, or at least knew who they were. At this point, any information would be helpful.

A couple miles out of town, he found a perfect campsite nestled under piñon trees. After spreading out his bedroll, he built a small fire, then heated water for coffee. Behind him, a stream gurgled its sweet melody. James breathed in the boiling coffee's aroma.

Nothing better than the smell of coffee by a stream.

Not much had gone right in the last few weeks, and he relished this tranquility. Above him the fading blue sky melted into strands of pink and orange. He poured himself some coffee and thought of heaven.

By full dark, he rode back into town, hoping to be a part of the gaiety of this Santa Rita. He had never felt lonely these last two weeks, but it hit him squarely now. Maybe he would feel less alone sitting in a bar, passing time with strangers and maybe a woman. He chose the Lazy Dog Saloon, the name and noise inviting. As he pushed the new, wooden doors half open, a blast of smoke and laugher hit him in the face. He coughed, his eyes watered, but he stepped inside anyway. The coal oil lamps cast golden glows over the room full of men and the few women. Elbow to elbow, people jostled each other.

After threading his way up to the bar, he ordered a beer. He wasn't a drinker. Never liked the stuff. He and Trace had tried whiskey a few times, but neither one could get the taste for it like others did. Beer was bad enough, but he certainly didn't want any whiskey.

His experience a few years ago with too much of the "amber nectar" only served to remind him he shouldn't drink. Two days surviving a foggy, pounding headache while his pa made him chop wood and set fence posts had taught him a valuable lesson. Even now, the memory couldn't bring a grin.

James took his beer and headed for a corner table, the only one not occupied by at least five other people. Before his rear landed, a plump barmaid sidled up and eased into a chair next to him. Was that the wood creaking under her weight? James peered into a rouged, pockmarked face, too young to be in this business.

"Buy me a drink, mister?"

James' cheeks burned, and he hoped it was too dark for her to notice.

"I guess so."

Did he always have to stammer around girls?

Laughter, glasses clinking, a piano player attempting a tinny version of *Old Joe Clark*—all the sounds mingled together and filled the saloon. Every time the saloon girl scooted closer to chat with James, he found himself scooting away. Not only was he almost deaf from the racket, but he wasn't comfortable around this kind of girl. Not that he'd ever been around saloon girls. But he'd seen a few on the streets of his Kansas hometown.

James tried to feign interest at her small talk, tried to smile, tried to ask insightful questions. He couldn't think of any, his nerves muddling his thoughts. Her pudgy hand caressed the back of his neck, then moved to his arm. When it rubbed down his thigh, his face grew hot. And it wasn't all the beer's fault. Sweat soaked his back.

After what seemed a lifetime, he finished his beer and excused himself, pleading a hard day of digging was causing his eyes to close.

He walked the two blocks down to another saloon. This one was quieter and smaller than the Lazy Dog. He pushed the door inward and was greeted by a green hat complete with feather. His gaze roamed under the hat to a face.

A female face. She wasn't just pretty. She was beautiful. Stunningly beautiful. What struck him most were her bright blue eyes looking up at him and that blond hair hanging under the hat, unusual for this part of the country. Most people were dark, either because of their Mexican ancestry or the sun, which tanned and burned skin until it resembled old boot leather.

He stood frozen, staring, until a voice growled behind him.

"Hey, you're blockin' the door!"

James shook his head and muttered an apology. He sidestepped the grinning woman and eased over to the bar. With one eye still on the woman, he waited for the barkeep to pour him a beer. After a sip, he wandered through the subdued saloon, found a table, and sat. No out-of-tune piano played, and no shouts from drunken miners vied for attention. Although this saloon, The Silver Dollar, was quieter than the other, it felt more comfortable. As he sipped his second beer of the evening, the effects took hold. Warm and relaxed, he didn't feel too bad. In fact, his leg had quit throbbing and his ribs weren't screaming. And if he didn't touch his face, that bruised cheek didn't hurt either.

About halfway through his beer, he looked up. The green-hatted barmaid stood beside him. He couldn't breathe.

"May I sit?" Her southern drawl wafted around James' head.

A nod and grin. Then, remembering his manners, he stood and pulled out a chair. She sat while he plunked into own seat, and then he smiled, still feeling like a fool.

James stared at the most enchanting woman he'd ever seen. She stared back. Two starts and stops, then James sputtered a question.

"May I buy you a drink, ma'am?"

"Thank you. I would love one."

The way she spoke...those words...like music. Her accent reminded him of people who'd visited his family's ranch the year before. Friends of his parents from some place in the South. New Orleans as he remembered it.

"You new in town?" she asked. Her head cocked a bit to the right.

"Aren't we all?" James was surprised he could speak.

"Guess so. Where y'all from?" Her blue eyes lit up, reflecting the lamp's warm glow.

James sat back and thought. He wasn't really from anywhere now. He and his brothers grew up in a small town close to the Missouri River in what was now the Territory of Kansas. He thought back to the talk he'd heard about Kansas someday gaining statehood. His two younger brothers who still lived at home were excited about the possibilities. However, his parents remained uneasy when the question of states rights and slavery arose. In their letters, they had mentioned some shootings and hangings and general mischief by a group of men, but said they still felt safe enough.

Every time his stage brought news from Kansas, he and Trace sat and hashed over the situation. They both promised to rush back home if things got out of control.

But Kansas wasn't home now. Since he'd started working for Butterfield, the stagecoach was more home than anywhere. He hadn't thought of it before, but he didn't really have a home. He frowned.

"I didn't mean to ask such a personal question, sir. I was just making small talk." The saloon girl put her hand on James' forearm and produced a heart-melting smile.

"It's all right, ma'am. It's just...I'm not sure how to answer it." He took in her eyes, the turned up nose, the perfect lips. He forced his brain to form words. "How about you?"

Her face lit up, then a cloud covered it. "Originally, I'm from South Carolina. My mama and me come this way when we heard some talk of the South wanting to be another country, and we've been moving west ever since."

A tear perched on the corner of her eye. "Mama died a few months ago." She took a deep breath, straightened her shoulders and smiled. "But I'm here now, with you." She hoisted her beer glass. "To us!"

Glasses clinked.

"To us!" James smiled. "By the way, my name's James Colton."

"Lila Belle Simmons." She flashed a dazzling smile. "Pleased to meet you."

Maybe he wasn't alone any more.

* * *

The ride back to camp was slow and peaceful, the moonlight throwing a silvery cast on the trees and rocks. He was glad he'd decided to go to Santa Rita. James hummed a tune he remembered. *Camptown Races*—a favorite of his.

Lila Belle Simmons, sing that song...doo-dah, doo-dah. Lila Belle Simmons all night long...oh, doo-dah day.

James considered. Lila Belle all night? Not a bad idea, but he had no girl experience, and besides, she was too nice to think of her like that. He shook his head. Stars spun.

Campsite now in view, trees blurred, his eyes grew heavy. How much had he drunk? At least five. And one shot of whiskey.

He rolled off his horse, and his queasy stomach rolled too, until it rejected both his supper and the alcohol. Kneeling on the ground, he wiped his mouth and his world spun again, this time his stomach brought up nothing.

Glad she can't see me now.

CHAPTER SIX

James clamped one hand over his eyes, the other over one ear. As loud as it was, that stream had to be a full-out torrent, and the sun glowed a hundred times brighter than usual. Rays seeped through every crevice in his fingers to attack his eyes. A groan. Was that his?

A slow roll onto his side. The earth moved. Was it a quake? He waited. No. One eye opened. His horse blinked back, inches away. Another groan. Head thundering, stomach still roiling, he ran his tongue around his lips. Must've been a cotton mattress he'd eaten. Or at least a feather pillow. His horse nudged him. James allowed his gaze to travel upward. The pinto was still saddled.

By mid-afternoon, he'd recovered enough to ride back into town, determined to visit the sheriff. He reined up in front of the office. Maybe this adventure was almost over. Maybe the sheriff knew who those men were. Better yet, maybe they were locked up. James wagged his still-thumping head. No, that was too much to ask for. Information would have to be enough.

James opened the door and stepped in. The lawman, intent on reading some official-looking document, glanced up. He gave a second look, then stood to shake hands.

"Sheriff Lonn Keats," the man said. "Coffee?" He pointed to a pot in the corner, a couple tin cups resting nearby.

One hand held up, James shook his head. "James Colton. Thanks, no."

Strong, black coffee was the last thing James wanted on his stomach right now. Just the smell turned it over and over. James did, however, take the offered chair in front of the desk.

Santa Rita's sheriff was an older man, tall and muscular, perhaps a rancher in a former life. Keats leaned back in his chair with the ease and confidence of a proven man.

"What can I do for you, son?"

James explained his situation, then described the bandits as best he could. He told of the killing of Juan Villanueva, how it left his widow with nothing. Images of digging Juan's grave, Isabel shedding silent tears, and his own grief at the loss of that innocent man brought a knot to his throat. Tightness in his chest kept his breathing short.

"You say they've got posters on 'em already?" Keats asked.

"In Mesilla. Yes, sir."

Sheriff Keats leaned forward, shuffled through a few papers on his desk, and then handed James a thin stack of wanted posters. "Any of these match your men?"

James studied the posters while the knot in his throat dropped and spun in his stomach.

"None are the men I want," James said. "You haven't seen anybody like them around here?"

"Son, there're so many new people come into town every day, I can't keep track of 'em all."

James knew his disappointment showed.

"Tell you what, though." The sheriff pointed a long finger at the calendar tacked on the wall. "Today's Saturday, which means there'll be big doin's tonight. Everybody comes into town Saturday night. If these robbers of yours are near by, they'll be in town probably at one of them saloons."

James flipped through the wanted posters a second time, then laid them on the desk. "One of the saloons, you say? Got any idea which one? There's so many."

"Hell, try 'em all. And if they ain't in the saloons, try one of them red light houses. Guarantee they'll be there."

James' cheeks warmed when he realized what the sheriff was saying. He knew what those houses were. His pa had told him about them and had warned him to stay away. Nothing but trouble, he'd said. His whole body now on fire, James stood.

"Thanks anyway, sheriff. I'll just wait for them at a saloon." He headed toward the door, desperate for the cool outside air, but then he remembered one last question.

"Sheriff Keats, does Santa Rita have an express office? I'm needing to send a message real fast down to my brother in Mesilla."

The sheriff's hands flew out to his sides with his laugh. "Son, we don't got nothin' around here. Hell, we barely got us a town."

James' shoulders slumped and with it, his ribs ached. He rubbed them.

"Tell you what." The lawman pushed his chair back and stood. "We do have a freight company that runs down to Mesilla every once in a while. You might talk to them 'bout deliverin' a message. They're not real fast, but they probably won't charge you too much for it, neither."

James smiled at this piece of good news. "Thanks, sheriff. Where's their office at?"

As James walked the three blocks down to the freight station, which turned out to be a large, white tent, he mentally wrote Trace a note. Luck was really with him. The people at the freight office said they were leaving first thing Monday for a trip to Mesilla. Of course they'd stop at a couple of towns along the way, but they were due into Mesilla in about ten days. And for a small fee, they'd be happy to deliver a message to Trace.

James carefully worded his letter, addressed it to Trace in care of the doctor, handed over his change and smiled. He calculated the letter would arrive one or two days ahead of Trace. The man promised he'd deliver it as soon as he could. He said he knew it was important.

James spent the rest of the afternoon roaming around town, looking into the mercantile, talking to people. He found them usually friendly, but not too willing to talk about strangers. A rumbling stomach signaled time to eat. He guessed he was on the mend from last night's beer binge. He made his way over to the restaurant, still outraged at the prices they were asking.

He took a seat near the kitchen where the smell of steaks cooking and biscuits baking made his mouth water. Aromas wafted around his head and under his nose until he knew if his food didn't appear soon, he'd have to follow his nose into the kitchen. The aroma reminded him of Sunday meals back home. Ma cooked special fixings on Sundays, and lots of it. Her fried chicken was his favorite, but he admitted he was partial to everything she cooked.

Before he attacked the kitchen, a plate of steak and potatoes appeared in front of him. The waitress, a girl younger than him, smiled wider than necessary. While she was a good-looker, she didn't compare to Lila Belle. After she brought the coffee, he couldn't eat fast enough. His plate was quickly clean and his cup empty. He ordered more coffee and blueberry pie, his favorite dessert.

41

The same waitress set a huge piece in front of him.

"Hope you like it," she said, and a giggle erupted before she turned and rushed off.

Fork full of blueberries at his mouth, he glanced up at two men standing at his table. Their hand-sewn clothes and rough canvas pants indicated they were miners, prospectors of some kind.

"Mind if we sit a spell, friend?"

Their beards made it hard to tell how old they were, but they were definitely older than James. And they seemed nice enough. He nodded and motioned to the empty chairs.

"Me and my partner been out minin' for a month of Sundays," one of the men said. The man, his black beard sticking out like a frightened porcupine, pulled out a chair and sat. "Come in for some supper, saw you over here by yourself, thought we'd join you."

"I'm 'bout ready to leave, gentlemen." James wiped his mouth on a napkin. "I'm afraid I ain't gonna be much company."

"We understand. Always lookin' to make new friends, Hal and me are." The other man smiled and extended his hand. He landed in the chair next to his friend. "I'm Abel and this here's Hal."

"James Colton."

They shook. James' stomach turned at these two men after a closer look. They weren't mean, didn't seem to be heeled, but still James was uneasy. Guns or no guns, he didn't want them as friends.

"I'm just passing through," James said. "Leaving at first light."

Hal nodded. "Us, too. Got gold needs to get plucked."

While James finished his pie, the men spoke of their mining claim, how much color showed but how surprised and disappointed they were when all of a sudden it played out. Both seemed determined to make it pay again.

"Tell you what, friend." Abel sipped at his coffee. "Me and Hal here are headin' down to what we're hoping might be an all-night poker game. Wanna come?"

"Thanks, no. I'm not a gambler."

"I beg to differ with you, sir." Hal leaned in closer. "It was a gamble you took just steppin' in this here restaurant. A gamble for you to ride into this here town. A gamble for you to let us—"

"You *do* know how to play poker, don't you Mister Colton?" Abel raised one shaggy eyebrow while his callused fingers combed his beard.

Of course he did. Pa and Trace had spent hours teaching him the finer points of poker. When to raise, when to fold. When to bluff.

"Yes, sir, I do. Just don't feel like playing tonight. That's all."

Who'd these men think he was? Some rube off the farm? Was he?

Hal smacked his partner on the arm, then started to get up from his chair. "Come on, Abel. Let's you and me find some people who do feel like playin' tonight. Somebody old enough to go in a saloon. Leave this plowboy alone."

"Where'd you say that game was at?" James rose also.

"Lazy Dog."

"I'll be there."

* * *

As much as James wanted to visit the blue-eyed beauty at the Silver Dollar, he went to the Lazy Dog instead. He figured he'd go to the Lazy Dog first, beat the miners, then head over to see Lila Belle. Easy. Couldn't lose.

After making sure his horse had oats and water down at the livery stable, he walked into the Lazy Dog well after dark. Hal and Abel were there, just like they said. A couple other men had joined them at their table. And there was an empty chair. James marched over and sat. He'd order one beer. Just one.

After the usual pleasantries, Hal pointed at James' leg.

"That's a damn fine limp you got goin'. What happened?"

James eyed Hal closely. Seemed like an innocent enough question, and his leg had been hurting—more than usual. He'd probably been limping more than usual.

"Nothing much," James said. "Just got shot in a stagecoach holdup a couple weeks ago. Wasn't too bad. They let me have some time off, even though I could've gone back to work right away."

He hoped his poker face was in place.

Spurred by his holdup story, table talk centered on bank holdups, other stage robberies, payroll wagons and the like. James played with the carefulness he'd learned from his pa and the determination he'd learned from his brother. At one point, he realized he was winning a lot—his pile of money was far greater than anyone else's pile. But he was more interested to know about the men he was searching for. Would anyone here know anything?

He spent half an hour describing and asking, but no one had seen those bandits.

Back aching, James twisted in his seat, then stood. There lay that pile of money, mostly bills, a few coins. His gaze swept over the table. Their money was about gone. James picked up the bills and counted. Good Lord! Over three hundred dollars.

One man, Ben he'd said, pushed back from the table and eased to his feet. "I'm about done in, fellas. Besides, I'm tired of losin' all my money to this young jehu." He thumped James' shoulder. "For an honest stage driver, you sure took all my money. Hope I can win it back some time."

James shook the extended hand. "Any time, sir."

A couple hours after midnight, the barkeep declared his establishment closed. A final hand was played, and then the men stood, shook hands, and headed out the door. James, relieved to find his poker partners taking their loss in stride, waved to the bartender before leaving. He'd done a good job keeping the beer flowing and the women hanging onto their shoulders.

The crisp night air of Santa Rita beckoned to James like a seductive woman. Stars winked while a passing cloud darkened the quarter moon, turning the air cold. Shadows were deep. It was hard to see without that full moon sending down light and spreading it over this little town. James, his breath spurting out in clouds, quickened his step. His boots thudded on the wooden boardwalk, the tread echoing against the night's stillness.

He wasn't any closer to those four bandits and his watch, but now there was some money in his pockets. Some real money. Even if he went back to Mesilla tomorrow, he'd be wiser and richer. He decided to send some back home to help feed his other brothers. His folks didn't need any money, but they'd been so good to him, sending them something was the only way he knew to repay. A smile crawled up one side of his face.

Another block down Main, then a turn, and the livery stable was less than five minutes away. He'd get on his pinto, trot back to camp for a good night's sleep, then bright and early tomorrow, he'd locate a bank and get this money to his folks. After that, he wasn't sure, but things were certainly looking up.

Whistling, he passed an alley. Two hands grabbed his shirt and yanked him into solid darkness. A vicious fist in his stomach doubled him over. He fought for air. His sore ribs screaming, he straightened and swung at nothing. Slammed against a wall, he brought his hands up to protect his face, but a powerful fist pounded his cheek, the same place that was still healing. Blood poured into his mouth. He choked, then spit.

His knees plowed into the ground.

Faces. Identify them.

James peered up through blood at his attackers. Blurry, fuzzy. No one he recognized, but he could make out only hands and the top of boots. A roundhouse to his head sent him cartwheeling across the dirt.

He rolled into more legs. But it was hands that yanked him to his feet—by his hair. His arms now pinned behind him, someone's chest pressed against his back. The breathing was labored, but the man's strength was undeniable. James twisted against the hold, but with each move, the grip tightened. More fists in his stomach. He vomited.

An uppercut to his jaw. Globs of warm, sticky blood in his mouth. His arms were released, but then someone shoved him forward—hard. He stumbled and spiraled to the ground.

Dirt crunched in his mouth. Desperate, he tried to curl into a ball, tried to block the blows, tried to scream, but his body refused to help. Instead, he lay gasping as the boots slammed again and again into his ribs.

Then...it stopped. Nightmare over, the attackers slipped into darkness. Not a word said, not a name mentioned. James lay crumpled on the ground, struggling for just one more breath.

CHAPTER SEVEN

The towering Organ Mountains popped into view long before Trace Colton spotted the beautiful valley town of Mesilla. As he drove his stagecoach across the wide-sweeping mesa extending behind him to the west, he realized he'd loved this bustling, yet easy-going town from the first moments his boots had touched the ground. Mountains, valleys, mesas, and a river. What more could he want? Granted, the Rio Grande was unpredictable as it ran along the east side of town. Some years it stayed put, other years, he'd been told, it meandered west and flooded fields. This year, it looked like it might behave itself. From this vantage point on the mesa, the river's path reflected the sun like a silver ribbon.

James sure will be surprised. A whole week early!

What would his brother say? First, it would be surprise and a demanded explanation. Then, it would be hundreds of plans for the next week off for the two of them.

He could see James' face now. The face, barely old enough to be shaving, that wasn't swollen and black and blue from the stage holdup. The face of his younger brother, brown-eyed, with a wide, contagious grin.

When his brother was born, James was the tiniest baby he'd ever seen. Actually, Trace hadn't seen any before. At almost four himself on that cool September day, Trace felt nothing but brotherly love at first sight. And it had been that way ever since. As they grew, the age difference had never been important. They'd played together, done chores together, even gotten into trouble together—more times than he'd like to count. Two other brothers had been born later on, but James was his favorite, his best friend.

The four-mule team slowed to a stop in front of the Butterfield Stage office just off of the plaza. Trace climbed down from the seat bench and stretched. He rubbed his lower back. While the new, temporary shotgun guard tossed the luggage down, Trace helped the passengers out of the stagecoach.

After checking in with the company, he counted his pay and nodded. Not only was he back in Mesilla, but he had money in his pocket. Life was pretty darn good right now.

Trace half-expected James to come bounding down the boardwalk, and he searched the faces as he marched the three blocks to the doctor's office. The arrival of the stage was big doings for the town. Everyone turned out.

Except James.

By the time he opened the door, Trace struggled to hide his disappointment. But he smiled at the doctor who had been so good to his brother and him.

"Mister Colton." The doctor shook his hand. "Glad to see you again. Back early?"

"Yes, sir. Managed to trade with another driver. Wanted to thank you for what you did for my little brother. Seeing him shot and beat like that truly scared me."

"He was shook up, too. But, he's fine now."

Trace couldn't help but grin again. "That's really good news. I'm kind of embarrassed to admit, but I've been worried about him. Real worried." He paused and glanced down the hall, expecting his little brother to be hiding around the corner. "Know where he's at? Thought I'd take him to supper."

Doc's eyes shifted downward, and his lips set a tight line.

"Doc?"

"Mister Colton, I don't know where your brother is. Right after he got the stitches out, he took off. Haven't seen him since."

"What?" Trace ran one hand through his shoulder-length hair, gripped his hat in the other hand. "Took off? He's still in town, isn't he?"

"Haven't seen him."

"He was supposed to stay here."

"I know."

"Well, did he say exactly where he was heading to? What'd he tell you? When's he coming back?"

"Son, I don't know. He didn't say much of anything. But I do know he was mighty upset about his watch." Doctor Logan pointed out the window. "Tell you what. Why don't you check over at the boarding house? I'll bet he told Missus Rosen what he

47

was up to. She's mothered and fussed over him like he was her own boy."

Trace stared out the window at the two-story building across the street, its whitewashed planking reflecting the sun. "Thanks, doc. Guess I'll go ask her. But if you see him, let him know I'm looking for him."

He fitted his hat, then headed for the boarding house.

Mrs. Rosen said the same thing. James hadn't said where he was going, just that he didn't need his room anymore. She reported he was a polite, very nice young man. She'd enjoyed their long talks while he helped her in the kitchen, in between all his target practicing. He shot for hours at a time, she'd said. And, his bruised face was healing and he wasn't limping as badly as earlier. She assured Trace that if she saw James, then she'd tell him Trace was searching for him.

Trace stepped off the wide porch, disappointed and angry. He'd told James to wait, to get well before doing anything. What right did that little brother have to go off without telling anybody? Soon as he found him, he'd tell him loud and clear how much trouble he'd caused.

Irresponsible kid.

* * *

A night's sleep gave Trace time to clear his head, to really think about the situation. Over eggs and ham the next morning, he chewed and figured out his next move. If he knew anybody in this world, he knew James. And James would be following those outlaws' trail. Alone. Trace downed the last bitter swallow of coffee.

Got to find him before he finds those bandits.

First piece of business—a quick chat with Doctor Logan. Trace paid the bill, then headed over to the doctor's office.

Logan met Trace at the door. "You find him?"

"No, sir, I didn't." Something hard pressed inside Trace's chest. "You've been real good to us, sir." His fingers inched along the brim of his clutched hat. "Wanted to thank you again."

"You're welcome again."

"Also wanted to know how much more I owe you. For James' surgery and such." Trace reached into his pocket and pulled out a wad of folded bills.

48

Doc waved his hand. "Bill Walters paid it all off. You're clear."

"That's mighty kind of him." Trace pocketed the money. "I'm wondering if I write James a note, could you give it to him if you see him?"

"Of course. Be glad to."

The doctor rummaged through his desk, brought out a sheet of paper, a pen, and an ink jar. Trace bent over the desk and took his time wording the note just right. He finished, then handed it to Logan.

"I'm heading up to Picacho Peak," Trace said, "then riding west. I'm figuring it's the direction the robbers took. If I don't catch up with my crazy brother in a week, I'll be back here. Butterfield gave me the seven days I had coming, so guess I'll have to use them chasing James."

Trace sighed and stared at the door.

The doctor lay a firm hand on Trace's shoulder. "It's not really my business, but I am curious. Why's that brother of yours all fired up to get his watch back? Never seen a youngster as determined as he is."

The floor held Trace's interest. How could he put aside his own guilt and explain? But the doctor was owed an explanation.

"After grandma died, grandpa came to live with us. He and James were just so alike. Grandpa taught him how to hunt and shoot." Trace lowered his voice. "James is a better shot than grandpa, and grandpa won a trophy for it back in Ireland."

Doctor Logan smiled. "Trophy, huh?"

Trace nodded. "James loved grandpa with all his heart and soul. They were inseparable. So, on James' eighteenth birthday, grandpa had gone outside to chop wood for the stove. Ma was baking James' cake. When he didn't come back in, James went outside and found grandpa on the ground, clutching his chest.

"James held him in his arms until..." Trace swallowed. "Until grandpa died. But just before he did, grandpa gave James that watch. He'd already inscribed it."

Doctor Logan sat down. "That's terrible."

"James was eaten up with guilt, blaming himself for grandpa's heart giving out like that," Trace said. "He still is."

"Not his fault. He couldn't have known."

"You tell James that." Trace studied his hands. "Truth is, I

49

feel guilty because I wasn't there. Should've been me chopping that wood, instead of here driving the stage."

"But, you—"

"I know, doc," Trace said. "I know."

* * *

Trace spurred his horse north toward Picacho Peak. He'd always liked the formation, jagged on one side, smooth on the other, the rock layers an odd gray color. But now it held only bad memories. The ruggedness of the rocks caused him to cringe, complete with a shiver or two. Imaginary bandits hid behind each boulder.

He reined up where the robbery occurred. A walk around the area gave him no new clues. Only thing he could tell for sure was that many people had passed this way in the last few weeks. Some of those old prints were his and James', he knew, but nothing else was evident. He tossed a stick at the rocks, looked into the blue sky, and hoped for a sign.

No sign, just a passing cloud.

Twilight found him making camp beside a small stream. He started a fire, put the coffee on to boil, unsaddled his horse, and then with his coffee cup in hand, he sat back to rest.

Despite his best effort to keep his eyes open, the combination of the gurgling stream and the fresh coffee enticed his eyes to drift closed. He no longer fought the urge to sleep. It took him under.

Somewhere in the distance a bell tinkled. He swatted at the sound. Carriage wheels creaked. His horse whinnied.

Eyes springing open, he reached for his gun. A jingle. A carriage? The weapon in his hand grew warm. Who would be out here making that much racket? Probably not the robbers. The sound closer now, Trace identified the source and relaxed. It was definitely a carriage or wagon. But the bell's tinkle was unusual. He stood and waited.

He didn't wait long. A horse-drawn carriage came into view, and tied at the back of the carriage were two unwilling goats. A woman gripped the reins. No other riders escorted her.

Trace waved at the woman, trying to flag her down.

The woman spotted him about the same time he saw her. She yanked back on the reins, grabbed her shotgun, and then pointed it at Trace's chest.

"What you want?" she asked.

Trace raised his arms, gun still gripped. Would she shoot? Probably.

"Nothing," Trace said. "I'm just camping here."

The woman cocked the weapon, then waved it to her right. "Your gun. There, *señor.*"

Trace tossed his gun toward a mesquite bush.

"This your property, ma'am?" Trace asked. "I'll be glad to get off, if it is. But I'm leaving at first light."

She studied him, starting at the boots and ending at his hat. He cringed. He didn't like feeling like he was being taken apart—analyzed. But, she was more than likely nervous, probably scared out here all alone. He'd excuse her scrutiny.

"Can I put my hands down? I truly don't mean you harm." His arms ached.

"*Sí. Pero,* keep them open." The shotgun lowered.

He wasn't sure exactly what she meant, her Spanish accent heavy. But he lowered his arms, anyway.

"Care for some coffee, ma'am? It's nice and hot. Just made it." Trace jerked his thumb over his shoulder.

"*Gracias, no.* I need knowing."

"Knowing?"

"Mesilla…how far?" She pointed ahead of her, due east.

Trace detected grief in her voice. "Ma'am, it's a good day's ride. Just came from there myself." Armed with courage, Trace moved closer to the carriage. "Don't mean to pry, but you alone?"

The shotgun leveled at his stomach. "I am not afraid."

"No disrespect intended ma'am, but this ain't no land for a lady. Especially alone."

"I do what needs. *Mi esposo está muerto. Mi familia*—in Mexico. I go now."

Glad to know some Spanish, Trace understood.

"Sorry to hear about your loss. But, ma'am, I'd feel better if you'd camp here tonight. Sure be glad to have the company. Then tomorrow I could ride with you back to Mesilla."

Besides, maybe she'd know something about James. Maybe she'd seen a lone rider. A rider with a black eye.

She lowered the shotgun and placed it on the seat beside her. "*Gracias, señor. No.* The sun still shines." A flick of the reins and she started forward. "*Adios.*"

51

"Wait, ma'am." Trace held up a hand. "You seen a man—"

The carriage lurched into a trot.

"—who looks like me? About nineteen?" Trace waved to stop her. "Black eye? Limps?"

He ran after her, but he was no match for the horses. Trace stopped and caught his breath. "Guess not."

CHAPTER EIGHT

Trace's trek the next day brought nothing but confusion and frustration. Plenty of rabbits, cactus, hawks, even mountains in the distance, but no brother. Not even good tracks.

He explored a recently deserted farm—a place belonging to Mr. Juan Villanueva, if the grave marker out back was any indication. The farm probably belonged to the carriage lady from yesterday. Signs of heavy work appeared here and there. Chords of stacked wood, a cleaned-out barn, and the grave. She couldn't have done it all herself. No, more than likely she'd hired some men to dig and help out a bit. Could one of them have been James? Trace knew his brother's conscience would require him to help like that. Goosebumps covered one arm.

Ridiculous. I'm just letting my imagination run. James was never here.

He rode on.

* * *

Santa Rita. Mining town famed for pockets of copper, but most people never glimpsed the elusive metal. Trace recalled what someone had told him about this burg. Starting around 1803, Mexicans from Chihuahua discovered copper in these mountains, the Mogollon Mountains if he remembered the map correctly. They'd named their town Santa Rita del Cobre, but now it was just Santa Rita. Trace glanced down the valley. Yep. Nice little town.

As he sat on the hill's rise, the wind kicked up and Trace pulled his jacket tighter around his shivering body. Late spring in the mountains could get pretty cold. Maybe, if they had a hotel, he'd spend fifty cents or so on a room. Out of the cold. In a soft bed. A bed would feel good after a couple nights on the ground. Trace shrugged.

Must be getting soft.

According to his plan, he'd spend one day asking around town, then two heading back to Mesilla. He hated to leave without knowing his brother's fate, but as much as he missed his brother, Trace understood why James would go after his watch. And at nineteen, he was a grown man and made his own decisions. Trace didn't always agree with those decisions, but he respected them.

Just wish I knew where he was.

* * *

After a good night's sleep at the only hotel and then breakfast, Trace nodded at his renewed energy. Maybe today he'd find James. Maybe.

Trace headed for Santa Rita's sheriff's office. Maybe James had checked in there about those four bandits. At least maybe the sheriff knew James' whereabouts. Maybe, just maybe, his brother was waiting there for him. In a cell. Trace fought dread as he stepped through the door.

The lawman looked up from his paperwork, stood, then shook hands with Trace. He pointed to a chair in front of his desk.

"Lonn Keats. What can I do for you, son?"

Trace sat. The sheriff seemed pleasant enough.

"Trace Colton, sir. Drive stage for Butterfield out of Mesilla. Looking for my little brother."

"Coffee?" The sheriff poured two cups without waiting for Trace to nod. He handed Trace the cup, then shrugged as he perched on the edge of his desk. "Lots of new people around here. Brother you say? What's he look like?"

"Well, he just turned nineteen last fall, 'bout my height. Actually, he's an inch taller 'n me and I'm six foot. Brown eyes, brown hair hits the collar." Trace leaned forward. "Actually, James looks a lot like me."

The sheriff peered at Trace's face, then nodded. "Huh. Think I might've seen him. Black eye?"

"Afraid so."

The officer tapped a long finger on his desk. "Yeah, come to think on it, he *was* in here—lookin' for four men who'd robbed him."

Trace felt his grin stretch his cheeks. "That's him, sheriff. Those men held up the stage I was driving and took James' watch. He was mighty distressed over it."

54

A chuckle from the sheriff bounced off the wooden walls. "Sure was. Determined to find them, too." He grew serious. "Couldn't help him, though."

The last drop of coffee slid down Trace's throat. He stared into the cup then up at the sheriff.

"Do you know where he's at?" Trace asked. "I gotta head back to Mesilla tomorrow and I truly need to find him before then."

"Mesilla, huh? I don't know about now. But he was wanting to send you an express message. We don't got that kinda service, you know. He was headed down to the freight company last I saw him."

"When was that?" Trace knew he was close.

The lawman paused. "Week. Maybe two." He frowned. "You know, thinking on it, I ain't seen him around since. May have took off some place. You know them kids, never do what you want them to."

"That's a fact." Trace sighed louder than he'd intended.

"If it'll help, I'll check with my deputy. He's out chasin' a couple renegade Indians. Might just be he knows something."

"I'd appreciate it, sir."

Despite the frustrating news, Trace now had some hope. At least he was on the right track.

"One last thing," Trace said. "How'd he look? Was he limping? Was he all right?"

"Yeah, just fine. That was a dandy black eye, but fading pretty quick. And he walked like he'd just twisted his ankle or something. Not a bad limp." The sheriff leaned forward. "That from the holdup?"

Trace plunked the cup on the desk and stood. "Sure was. He was damn lucky." Another handshake. "Thanks again, sheriff."

For the first time in days Trace felt like smiling. Wouldn't it be funny if James was sitting in Mesilla right now waiting for him?

Maybe this morning he'd find James. Maybe.

The people at the freight company were little help. They confirmed James had sent a letter to Mesilla, which left with the freight wagon over a week ago. They weren't sure what it'd said, since James sealed it before showing it to them, and no, no one had seen him after that. Trace thanked them and headed for the saloons. If anybody knew anything, he'd hear it there.

Even though the sun beamed, Trace shivered in the wind. He walked the length of Main Street, stopping to look into the mercantile. Sure was a wide range of goods in these stores. Plenty of mining equipment, axes, tin pans, lanterns, but also plenty of calico, button down shoes, and foodstuff.

Freight wagons must be running day and night.

Trace spent the rest of the afternoon visiting each saloon. He soon discovered that the bartenders weren't about to give out any information unless a drink was purchased. Just like James, Trace wasn't a drinker, and he wasted most of it. But he'd do what was necessary to find out about his brother.

He got the same story in each of the six bars. There were too many new people in town, many of them young men who matched James' description. Even the black eye and limp didn't make a difference. With the hundreds of men coming from the California gold mines, many of them scarred and maimed from mining accidents or fights, James just didn't stand out.

Trace's stomach rumbled as he left the last saloon. Supper time. He ambled a couple blocks down Main Street until he found the restaurant he'd spotted earlier. A dollar for a meal? Outrageous. But, if a man wanted to eat, that was the price.

His dollar bought him a steak, biscuits, and corn. The waitress was friendly, but efficient, smiling and then whisking away his dishes. He wasn't allowed to dally long over his coffee. She hovered over him.

"Want dessert?" She flashed a quick grin.

"You have blueberry pie? It's my favorite." Trace could already taste the tart small fruit swimming in a sea of filling.

"We ain't had blueberry pie for over a week." She studied Trace's face. "Actually, sold the last piece to a fella who looked a lot like you. Said blueberry's his favorite, too." Her hands fisted on her hips. "Now ain't that a coincidence?"

She had Trace's full attention now.

"Did he have a fading black eye?" Trace asked. "A limp?"

A coy smile blossomed. "Yeah. Even with that terrible bruise I thought he was awful handsome. And," she lowered her voice, "I'll admit I watched him walk out of here. He did limp some, but I thought it just made him look grand."

"Has he come back in since then?" Trace's heart raced.

She shook her head. "No. I've been watchin' and hopin' every day, but you're the closest what's come in." She grinned. "He some kin of yours?"

"My kid brother. You know where he's at? I've been looking

for him for a week."

"Brother, huh? So that's why you look like him. No. Like I said, haven't seen him. But when you do find him," she ducked her head, "tell him Sally says howdy." She giggled as she walked away.

Again frustrated, Trace stepped into the street. Before he covered ten yards the same waitress grabbed him by the arm.

"Hate to bother you," she said, "but I remembered something which might help."

"Ma'am?"

"Well, I don't know if this'll help, but there were two fellas that sat down with him later. Miners or prospectors I think. They looked friendly enough."

Trace opened his mouth, but she took a breath and continued. "And no, I ain't seen them around here either. And no, I don't know their names. Sorry. Hope it helps."

Maybe those men had something to do with James' disappearance. Could they? Trace reconsidered. If they were miners, they probably just swapped stories then went their separate ways.

As she walked off, Trace couldn't help but sense his brother close by.

Ridiculous. You just want it to be so.

He shook off the sensation, then headed down the street toward his horse.

He searched the face of each person he passed along the way. Why didn't they know where his brother was? His frustration, worry, anger collided in his stomach, the knot tightening with each step. Why did James have to do this?

Irresponsible kid. When I find him, I'm gonna let him know exactly how I feel.

He paused.

If I find him.

His thoughts full of *what ifs*, Trace failed to navigate the corner. Instead of giving a woman room to pass, he knocked into her and she stumbled into the street.

"Ma'am, I'm so very sorry!" Trace said. "Just wasn't watching where I was going." He grabbed her arm steadying her. "Are you all right?"

She tucked a few errant strands of blond hair up under her

hat, the rest dangled in curls to her shoulders. "Just fine, sir. No harm done." She straightened her green dress.

Hat in hand, Trace smiled. "Ma'am, again I do apologize."

She flashed a dazzling grin. "Thanks for your concern." Her slender fingers pointed up at the sign. "I work right here at the Silver Dollar. Maybe when you stop by, you can buy me a drink."

"That would be the least I could do. After you."

As he pushed open the wooden doors of the Silver Dollar, he vowed he'd have one drink, a small chat with this enchanting woman, and then leave. Female companionship would be nice. It had been a while since he'd been around women, and now he realized how lonely he really felt.

It proved impossible to keep her to himself, though. She certainly was popular. Men bought her drinks, told her stories, made her laugh. Made the whole place laugh. Trace stood at the bar until his legs ached, then found a seat with a couple of cowboys. It wasn't until much later that she broke free and sat in the empty chair at his table.

"Oh my feet." She rubbed an ankle hidden by her skirt. "Too long on them."

Trace ordered two drinks.

As they sat and talked, her eyes traveled over him. In the past, he'd been called "sturdy," "muscled," "mildly-handsome," but nothing worthy of such scrutiny. Oddly reminiscent of Mrs. Villanueva's roving eye. Were women that starved for men? A glance around. Hardly.

That southern accent. So foreign, so intriguing. He had to ask.

"Where in the South were you raised, Ma'am?"

"It shows?" Her laughter lit up her blue eyes. "South Carolina, sir. Charleston to be exact." The tilt of her head brought more bounce to the curls perched on her shoulders. "And you, sir? Where y'all from? Or should I guess?"

"I don't have an accent like you, ma'am. So it's not obvious. But go ahead, guess."

She leaned back, those eyes again on the move. "Well, you're mighty tan." That smile appeared once more. "I'd say someplace with lots of sun. Tucson maybe?"

Was it really warm in here?

Trace sipped his beer. "Close enough. Guess I'm calling

Mesilla my home nowadays. See, I'm a stagecoach driver for Butterfield, and I do go to Tucson, but I don't stay in one place very long."

Trace leaned into her, a hint of lilac wafting across his nose.

"Mesilla." She nodded. "Heard of that place."

"Everyone has since it's growing so fast." A second glance around the saloon, this time a bit slower. "Looks to me like there's lots of people from lots of places."

It was getting really warm now.

"Everybody's from some place else." She sipped the last few drops in her glass, then pushed back. "Time for Jim to close up and me to go home." Her slender hand glided toward Trace.

He held it. Warm, soft, sensual. And her eyes. Clear blue, a hint of strength in them. Trace liked her. Liked her a lot.

"Ma'am, I've gotta head back to Mesilla first thing tomorrow, but I truly enjoyed your company. Sure wish I didn't have to go."

"Me, too. Maybe you'll come back some time."

"I'd like that. At least let me walk you home."

When was the last time he'd had a woman on his arm? Too long.

They strolled down the creaky boardwalk, then past a few of the white tents and lean-tos. Two corners, a couple of blocks. She halted in front of a ten-by-ten cotton tent.

"Home. Thanks for walking me, sir. You're a true gentleman." She smiled, then reached up and pecked his cheek.

Thank goodness it was dark. He felt the heat of a blush on his face. Words came out over his pounding heart.

"You know, I've just spent an evening with you, and I don't even know your name."

"Nor I yours, sir." Her soft hand melted in his. "I'm Lila Belle."

"That's the prettiest name I've ever heard, ma'am. I'm Trace. Thanks for a great evening."

Another nod of that beautiful head and she was gone. Disappeared into that tent. Trace stood waiting, hoping she'd come back out. If she did, he'd take her in his arms and hold her, press her against his chest, breathing in lilac and Lila Belle. A long minute dragged by.

Trace's shoulders slumped.

Fool. What in the hell am I standing out here for? What am I?

59

Some lovesick schoolboy? She was just doing her job. Getting men to buy drinks. Fool.

A shake of his head. He turned. What was he thinking?

A voice, words from her tent. Male. Not sweet and soft like Lila's. Definitely male. Sounded sleepy. Trace fisted both hands.

I'm a bigger fool than I thought. What was I thinking? She has a husband, or at least a steady man. One who shares her tent.

Trace frowned at the thought, and bolted into the night.

CHAPTER NINE

There she was. Come back at last. Lila Belle. James squinted. Or was that some other woman? There had been so many, all hazy and blurry...fuzzy. Like a parade of fuzzy angels.

"Lila?"

He prayed his voice sounded clear, but more than likely it was just a gargle.

No response.

Maybe she hadn't heard him. He cleared his throat to speak louder. He thought he'd made a noise. Maybe not. Hazy. Things were so hazy. There she still stood, staring at the tent opening. What could be so interesting? A cough rattled his chest. He grabbed for broken ribs, but his arms lay by his side, all his strength gone.

"Lila?"

His eyes closed. A cool hand on his sweaty forehead.

"Shhh. It's all right. I'm here, Honey."

His eyes fluttered open and his gaze landed on her.

"Who?" The word forced itself over his swollen jaw.

"Just some drifter. Never you mind about him."

Cold. Hot. Really cold. James shivered until he knew he'd fall apart. He gripped the wool blanket and tugged. It didn't move. Lila tucked it around his body. Now really hot.

"I'll get you some water."

Something wet touched his lips. James opened his mouth like a baby bird frantic for sustenance. The water soothed his raw throat, but did little to cool his body. He clawed at the blankets.

That southern drawl came from out of the darkness.

"Sure wish I knew what to do for you." Lila Belle lowered the top blanket. "When you get cold, just pull right here. It'll snuggle in right under your chin." She stroked his head, then planted a kiss on it. "Get some sleep. You'll feel better in the morning."

It was nighttime? Day. Night. It didn't matter. Fuzzy night, fuzzy day. Nothing mattered right now but struggling to breathe, to stay alive. Flashes of a card game, of Lila Belle in a saloon, of a stagecoach. None of it he understood. Nothing he could figure out right now.

James closed his eyes and prayed he'd open them tomorrow.

* * *

Muted sunlight warmed the tent. The glow did nothing for James, however. The more he shook, the more his teeth chattered. Three wool blankets couldn't keep the heat in, but beads of sweat poured down his sore face. A groan escaped his chest. A cool hand on his forehead. He knew this hand. Lila's. He forced his eyes to focus on her face. The mouth curved upward. She was smiling.

"You're doing better, honey. But you sure need a doctor." A wag of her head followed a sigh. She glared at a spot over James' head. "Damn Doctor Williams. Why'd he have to go prospecting? Didn't he know he was needed here?" She reached across James for the folded damp rag. "I need him here."

This must be hard on her.

James wanted to smile. This was the first time he'd thought about her like that since he'd gotten hurt. He must be improving.

"I'm sorry," he said. This time he recognized his own words.

"For what?" Lila Belle dipped the cloth in a bowl of water. "Don't apologize for what happened to you. Wasn't your fault. Glad I can help." She wiped his face. "Without a doctor, I've had to rely on some of the older women around here. They've all helped out one way or another."

"Angels."

Lila Belle chuckled. "I guess they are." She leaned over and straightened the blanket. "You sleep for a while and I'll do more washing. You're keeping broth down better now. Not as much to wash."

Some victory. James didn't move much. Or say much. Lila had told him that besides several ribs, his jaw was just dislocated, not broken. Broken or not, every time he threw up, he'd almost pass out from the pain. So, he stayed still. It just hurt too much to move. Breathing was tough enough. He'd tackle moving later.

* * *

Days melted into one big gray cloud. James couldn't count the passing of time, just knew that the pain wasn't as intense as earlier. Cold stream water helped cool his fiery body. It also helped reduce the swelling on his face. That huge welt over his eye was shrinking, one of the other women told him. She'd also reported that now his face was red, purple and black, with yellows and greens showing through. A sure sign he was healing. Sign or no sign, it still hurt.

James knew he was healing. Every minute he was awake, he worked at getting stronger. He lifted coffee cups, pulled his blanket up or pushed it down, even rolled onto his side. The ground was once again hard despite the layers of blankets under him. Grit and determination in place, he positioned both elbows under him and pushed up. While it was painful, damn it felt good to be sitting up.

A woman, not Lila, knelt by him, bracing his shaking body. She shoved pillows behind him until James was close to upright. She beamed at him, then spoke over her shoulder. "Well look here, Sarah, I do think this young man's gonna make it after all."

Her smile was contagious and James found himself smiling back. It hurt, but *damn*, he was sitting up.

"He's gonna do just fine." Sarah nodded.

His angel. James knew that she and Lila Belle and the other women were his angels. The cold cloth in her hand pressed against his cheek. His entire face tingled.

"You'll be just fine, Mister Colton," Sarah said. "Your fever's down. That's another good sign."

"Thanks." James frowned at the sound. It was more like a growl than words, so he worked his jaw back and forth. Pain. He swallowed, then ran his tongue around his dry lips. "Water?"

The other woman appeared with a bowl of steamy chicken broth, its aroma wafting under his nose. "You're trying to talk, Mister Colton. Good for you. Just a few spoonfuls, you'll feel so much better."

For the first time that he could remember, he was hungry. She held the spoon to his sore mouth. The broth dribbled down his chin, but some managed to find its way into his mouth. James swallowed as best as he could.

"Couple more." She wedged the spoon over his swollen lips. "Lila Belle's gonna be back any second. She'll be so proud of you for eating all this."

A couple blinks and a slow nod. He rubbed his jaw and hoped it would work. "Thanks," he said.

"I have a son, just 'bout your age." The woman's voice turned soft while waiting for James to swallow. "He's off in California somewhere, I think." The spoon rested in mid-air. Her gaze plunged down at James again. Her eyes grew hard. "Does your mama know where you are?"

Ma, pa, his brothers, Trace.

My family.

Hazy memories cleared. He hadn't thought of them in a while, hadn't thought of much for the last several days. A shudder hit him. Nobody knew where he was. Not even Trace.

Images of ma in the kitchen baking his favorite cornbread raced through his mind. Pa and Trace chopping wood while he took as much as his arms could carry into the house. He relived the birth of both of his younger brothers. Grandpa. Tears pressed behind his eyes as he realized he loved them all so much. Trace must be frantic. More thoughts about his family, how much he needed them, how bad hurt he was...his heart shredded. He'd never been so alone in his whole life.

He didn't care if these two women saw him cry. He didn't care what they thought. His hands covered his face as tears rolled down his bruised cheeks. Gulps of air wracked his ribs. He couldn't hold his face and his ribs at the same time. Everything hurt. A new wave of tears. "James, what's wrong?" Lila Belle's voice cut into his misery.

Everything.

Lila Belle brushed the matted hair from his forehead. Her arms slid around his shoulders. Together they rocked back and forth. Now safe in her embrace, powerless to stop the anguish, a new torrent of tears cascaded down his face. He wasn't ashamed. His whole life hurt too much for him to be embarrassed.

* * *

Days melted into each other, eight days now since the beating Lila had said, and with each new day came tiny bits of strength. James sat on the cot and regarded his life. It was time. Time to move forward. Lila Belle had even kidded him that other colors, more normal colors, were creeping back into his face. She liked the pink in his cheeks.

Each day he had sat up longer, stayed awake longer. Even food had stayed down longer. And thanks to the bottles of whiskey Lila Belle brought, the pain was now manageable most times. Other times, he fought to think of pleasant things until the whiskey numbed him. Thanks to the whiskey's magic, he now slept two or more hours at a time. And he no longer woke up in agony.

"It's time." James looked up at Lila Belle and pushed off from the cot. Muscles complaining, he eased to his feet, wobbled, then straightened up. A nod.

Lila Belle gripped his upper arm, steadying him. "Good for you. You're doin' it, James."

A step. Another one. Damn it felt good! Upright, on his feet again.

"Outside. Air," James said.

A third shuffle, this time toward the tent opening. Instead of smiling like he wanted to, James concentrated. He pushed each foot toward his goal.

One hand on James, the other on the canvas, Lila Belle held the tent flaps wide open. A halting step and James blinked at the bright world, then emerged from his canvas cocoon.

"I knew you could do it!" Lila Belle swiped at a tear.

In all his life, there had never been a moment as glorious as this. Here he stood, on his own feet again, upright in the sun. And best part—alive. He was still alive.

First it was those stage robbers, then the money robbers. But you all couldn't kill me. I'm tough. I survived.

Despite his inner strength, James felt his outer strength failing. Just a few more steps. Determined to walk alone, he released the soft shoulders. One step. Another. He looked up at his angel, no longer fuzzy.

"All right," he said.

"Don't over do it. You should rest now."

He waved her away. Another step. "I'm fine."

The next step proved much harder than the last. Were his bare feet in quick sand? He looked down. Just dirt. He picked up a leg, but they both turned to rubber. Lila Belle's arms round him again kept him on his feet.

"I'm so proud of you." Lila Belle strengthened her grip. "But you've had enough for today. Tomorrow you'll be stronger."

Without warning, he turned in close and kissed her. It was

everything he'd imagined and more. Her soft lips tasted vaguely of chicken soup. Delicious. He figured his mouth was still swollen, his lips split but healing. Still, that kiss meant everything. He kissed her again. This time, she kissed back.

They stood...embraced. He wanted to stay like this forever. But his muscles cheated him. Despite Lila Belle's efforts, his knees buckled. He sagged against her.

"Damn. Double damn." Fists clenched, he fought the urge for more tears. Cursing or crying wouldn't help right now. His arms around her shoulders kept his knees off the ground.

"It's just gonna take time." She kissed the top of his head and pulled up him to his feet. "I'll be right here to help you."

"Tomorrow." James held his ribs and forced words over his sore jaw. "I'm walking...to the sheriff's. See if he knows...those men."

Lila Belle shook her head. "*Please* forget about that watch. You're not up to tracking those men—much less fighting. If you *do* find them, this time they'll kill you for sure."

Lila's face again grew hazy. James rushed his explanation.

"I got to. Don't you understand?" The white tent behind her spun. "It's grandpa's watch."

He wanted to explain, but he couldn't get the words, the explanation, out over his swollen face, his jaw that barely worked. Were those tears blurring the world? Even though he was standing upright, he swayed. "I loved him."

"I understand. I do." Lila strengthened her hold and nudged him toward the tent. "But I'm afraid you still won't be strong enough to walk five blocks."

"I will. With your help."

He searched her face for the strength he knew he'd need. He found it.

A slow nod. "All right," she said. "Let's get you inside, then you rest."

Two steps. Halting. Unsteady. Painful.

Lila's words in his ear. "You need new clothes. I'll go buy some while you sleep."

"What's wrong with these?"

"I tried as best as I could to get them clean." Lila wagged her head. "Couldn't get all the blood out. There was too much." She pushed aside the tent flap.

James looked at his clothes for the first time. Now he spotted lines of stitching, repairs to all the rips and tears from the fight. A closer look revealed the faded brownish red blotches covering his shirt, splattered over his pants. It was hard to find a place not bloodstained. A long, deep breath. His words fell from swollen lips.

"Pick out good ones. I'll pay you back."

* * *

Sweat plastering his shirt to his chest, James leaned against the sheriff's door and turned the handle. The door slammed back against the wall. He grabbed both sides of the frame and held on while his world tilted. Someone from behind a desk jumped up. Both man and desk swirled and danced on the wall. Now the ceiling.

Another tilt and James' world turned dark.

One eye forced itself open. The other refused to cooperate. He massaged his eyes. At least they didn't hurt. He coaxed both open. Iron bars pressed against his shoulder, a cot under him kept him off the wooden floor, and a scratchy wool blanket covered him. He tried to sit up, but a hand on his chest pushed him down, while a familiar voice floated around his ears.

"I knew it was too much for you, honey." That familiar hand brushed hair from his forehead. Soft lips kissed him. "Rest now. I'm right here."

"Where?"

Is that all he could say? His strength was gone. Wherever he was, he knew everything was all right. Lila Belle was at his side.

After a long rest, James' strength returned. He propped himself up with the pillows Lila Belle shoved behind him. A better study of the cell revealed nothing but iron bars and cold wooden walls. He'd had nightmares as a child about being locked up and sometimes even now as a grown man. It was a terror he'd always had.

"I've never been in jail before," James said.

"Let's make sure this is the only time." Lila Belle patted his leg as she sat at the end of the cot.

Sheriff Lonn Keats brought in a chair, planted it next to James, then gazed at his face.

"You made quite an entrance, young man," Keats said.

James shook hands with the sheriff. "Sorry about that."

The lawman cocked his head toward Lila. "She tells me you're the kid who got beat up a while back."

James nodded.

Stupid me to get taken like that. Should've known better.

Keats shrugged. "Never did find those fellas or your money." He frowned into James' face. "Ain't you also the one who come in before and wanted to know about an express message to Mesilla?"

"Yes sir." James nodded again. "My brother." Dormant memories flooded back in. "Freighters took a letter." He looked over at Lila Belle. "Did they?"

"We'll talk to them tomorrow." Lila Belle patted his arm. "Take this one step at a time."

Santa Rita's sheriff scratched the stubble on his chin. It was obvious he hadn't shaved yet today. His brown eyes lit up, and a grin lifted one corner of his mouth.

"You know what, son? I think your brother was here."

"Trace?" James pushed up farther.

"Yeah, I think that's what he said his name was." The sheriff pointed a finger at James. "He looked a lot like you, only 'bout an inch shorter. Couple years older."

"That's him. Drives for Butterfield Stage." James looked at Lila Belle and then back at the sheriff. "He was here? Looking for me?"

"Sure was. Right after you got hurt." Keats shrugged. "I didn't know it was you. I mean, my deputy was the one who carried you over to Lila's tent after she found you, and he'd never seen you before. Besides, it was dark. And you sure couldn't give us a name. Just didn't make a connection."

"What'd Trace say?" James threw off the blanket and held his ribs while he sat up. "He still here? Where'd he go to?"

"Calm down, you'll pass out again. Let me think." The sheriff frowned into space. "Let's see. He was headin' back to Mesilla, had to go to work, he said."

James groaned. "I missed him."

"But," Keats leaned forward, "he told me that if I ever saw you, you're to meet him in Mesilla. He'd be waitin'."

James knew what had to be done. What he had to do. He eased up to his feet and extended a hand. Keats and James shook.

"Thank you, sheriff. For all you've done." He turned to Lila

Belle. "Gotta heal up some. Got some business needs tending, then I'll ride back to Mesilla and meet Trace."

James struggled to keep the cell from spinning. His eyes locked onto Lila Belle's crystal blue ones. "Will you go with me? To Mesilla?"

A smile bloomed on her face. "Yes, James, I will."

CHAPTER TEN

James ran the cloth back and forth along the gun's barrel. Clean. He rotated the cylinder again. Something about the gun's weight in his hand and the motion of the cylinder kept him mesmerized. He pointed the gun, sighted a tree branch, then pretended to shoot. No need to pull the trigger—it was unloaded and there was no need for a dry firing. Just might hurt the gun that some day might save his life. He chided himself for not being able to shoot when those men jumped him in the dark alley. Cowards that they were.

When Lila Belle woke up, he planned for them to go down to the general store and he'd buy powder and bullets for this .36 Navy Colt. Correction. *She'd* buy the powder and lead bullets. Lila had the money. He had…well, he still had his life.

He sighted the gun toward a tent several yards away and aimed for a rope hanging from the corner. His chair creaked with the movement, but that sound was barely audible over the noise from the street. Horses, wagons, men, women…all buzzing with the excitement of a new town. James squinted despite the shade his new hat afforded. The sun warmed his face, his whole body. Damn that sun felt good.

"What ya got there?"

James jumped at the male voice in his ear. He fumbled the gun, then peered over his shoulder at a man silhouetted against the sun.

"Sheriff Keats?" James shaded his eyes.

"Mind if I sit?" Santa Rita's sheriff pulled over a chair jammed against the canvas. He eased into the seat and nodded at the gun. "That new?"

"Yes, sir, sure is." James gave it one last swipe with the rag and handed it butt-first to the sheriff. "Lila bought it off a man just coming from the East." His sore jaw was healing. Words formed easily now.

"Bought, huh?" Keats caressed the gun as if it were a delicate woman. His fingers ran up and down the barrel. After touching every inch, he hefted it in one hand. "Nice balance."

"I think so." James held out a hand. Keats had had James' new toy way too long. "Lila paid a good penny for it, but I'll pay her back soon's I can."

"What *did* she pay?" Keats crossed one leg over the other.

"What'd you mean?" Nobody talked about Lila Belle that way. "She paid *money* for it."

"No disrespect intended, son. I'm just curious. These revolvers are hard to come by, being that we're so far west."

James eyed this sheriff, this lawman. While he seemed nice enough, what exactly was he implying about Lila? Did he know something that she wasn't telling? A shrug was all James gave.

"Anyway, son, I didn't come by to talk about your gun," Keats said. "Heard something you might find interesting. Thought you'd want to know right away."

It was James' turn to lean forward. "Something about Trace? Is he back here? You found him?"

The sheriff shook his head.

"Then what kinda news?" James couldn't wait for the sheriff's thinking. "You found the men who took my money? Who beat me?"

The sheriff's eyes trailed up and down James. "Those men are long gone. High-tailed it out of here right after. *With* your money. You're gonna have to accept the facts. Those men won. Your money's gone."

James was afraid that's what Keats would say. And he knew he was damned lucky to still be alive. He turned his attention elsewhere.

"Then what, sheriff?"

"Well, a deputy from Pinos Altos came to town this morning. Told me 'bout a killin' there a few days ago. Seems four men held up a freight wagon, took some supplies, too, but mostly money and such from the drivers."

"Four of 'em?"

Keats nodded. "An outlaw with eyes like coal, he said, was 'specially interested in one driver's watch. Said they'd stole another one like it and was gonna make a collection of pocket watches. The driver objected to handing it over."

71

James clenched his healing jaw.

Santa Rita's sheriff paused and wagged his head. "Shot him right in the heart. Poor fella never had a chance." He raised one hand. "Least the other driver got away."

"Sounds like 'em all right. Guess me and my brother are right lucky. They held a gun at Trace's head. And mine." A shudder jarred his ribs. He winced.

"Son, as you found out, these are bad hombres. They'd just as soon kill you as piss on you." Keats placed a strong hand on James' shoulder. "Why don't you cut your losses, go back to Mesilla with Lila, start fresh? A watch ain't worth losin' your life."

James picked up his gun. "Dammit, sheriff. You sound just like Trace. That's what he said. I can't...won't give up."

"But—"

"Don't forget they also killed a man. A man I had to bury. Can't let them get away with murder. I gotta find those men. And my watch." He sighted down the barrel.

Keats pushed to his feet. "Son, you can't. Even if you were healthy again, completely well, which you ain't, you're no match for them. One against four?"

"I know." James tried to hide his wincing as he stood. "I'll get me some help. Don't you worry. I'm pretty good at shooting. That's why Butterfield hired me to ride shotgun."

"Son, ridin' shotgun's real different from huntin' outlaws. Wish you'd reconsider."

A shake of his head brought zigzag streaks. James' energy waned before he was ready to sit back down. He sat anyway.

A long look at James. Both of Keats's eyebrows rose to meet his hat's brim. He snorted.

"You ain't got enough strength to stand. How the hell you think you're gonna capture those men?"

"I—"

"Just don't go gettin' all shot up. Ain't worth it." Sheriff Keats held up a hand. His gaze roamed up and down James. "Kind of remind me of myself at your age. Bein' headstrong can be a good thing, but it can also get you killed." He turned to go.

"I'll let you know what happens, sheriff." James gripped his new gun. "And don't worry. I'll be fine."

A wave from the departing lawman.

Grit and determination in tow, James tiptoed into the tent,

tugged on his boots, pulled his hat down over his straight brown hair.

Money. Need money.

A glance around the tent revealed no pocket book, nothing that looked like a purse. A flash. Lila pulling a wooden box out from under her cot. Holding his breath, James knelt down and peered under the sagging canvas. Just under Lila's hips was a small box. He slid it out, then using all the finesse he could muster, opened the lid.

Several dollar bills and coins lay amid two sepia toned pictures. A stern man, a smiling woman, and a little girl in a frock dress stared back. The other photo showed several people, all frowning into the camera.

Must be other family members.

James scooped up the bills and counted nine. Enough for ammunition and food. Casting a look at Lila Belle, he folded two and put them back in the box.

An IOU. Need to leave a note.

A diary's empty page and a pencil stub in the box would have to do. Careful to tear out a page, he jotted a note, then replaced the pencil and closed the lid.

He gazed at her. But where to leave the note so she'd find it? On her hat. She always wore this green feathered hat. He felt like a common thief, but he folded the page and stuck it in the hat's front anyway. Then he leaned over and kissed Lila's cheek. A soft moan, she turned her back to him.

Good. Still asleep. Don't want to be frettin' about a woman while I'm gone up to Pinos Altos. No distractions to keep me from finding those outlaws.

Before heading out of town, James stopped by the Silver Dollar. He knew the bartender would tell Lila where he'd gone.

The bartender nodded, agreeing he'd tell her, but changed to shaking his head when he heard where and why.

"Just cut your losses," he said. "Don't go gettin' shot up over a damn watch."

"You sound like everybody else, Nate."

"Hell, James, let the sheriff go after those men. Why're you doin' his job in the first place? Ain't that what he's gettin' paid for?" Nate tossed a towel on the clean bar.

"Guess he don't have time or enough posse to track them."

James produced what he hoped was a confident smile. "Don't worry, I know what I'm doin'."

"Sure hope you do." Nate dried his hand on the towel and extended it. *"Buenos suerte."*

"Thanks. I'll need all the luck I can get." James nodded at the bartender. "Be seein' you."

With that, James turned his back on the barkeep, then stepped into the bright, warm afternoon sun. He limped to his horse.

Swinging up onto his mount was harder than he'd remembered. His ribs reminded him they weren't healed, but he ignored them, as he did anything that got in his way. If he pretended hard enough that the injury didn't exist, maybe his ribs wouldn't bother him. He settled his right boot into the stirrup.

Another beating like that and I'll die. No doubt. Next time, I'll use my gun instead of my fists.

PART
TWO

CHAPTER ELEVEN

A parade of white tents lined both sides of the narrow trail, welcoming James to Pinos Altos. The little mining camp nestled among towering timber was only twenty miles northeast of Santa Rita, but it seemed a world away. There was not much hustle and bustle here as James rode down the main street. Just people doing what they needed to survive. It was so much smaller than Santa Rita that he knew it'd be easy to find those outlaws.

The wind picked up and whistled through the trees, while a sharp chill brought goosebumps and a shiver to his body. Again, those ribs ached. He pulled his coat tighter and jammed one hand under his armpit.

Three buildings made of rock and wood stood among the Ponderosa pines. One building was obviously the jail, its barred windows a dead giveaway. The second building—brand new if the fresh paint on the sign was any indication—was the Buckhorn Saloon. Definitely a place he'd have the pleasure of looking into. He ran a hand across his dry mouth. Beer would taste good about now. He listed what had to be done. Talk to the sheriff, maybe the deputy. Find a place to camp. Eat. Then a drink. Tomorrow he'd find those thieving, murdering outlaws, bring them into town, then head on back to Santa Rita. Back to Lila Belle. Back to a life he'd dreamed of.

The third building was the sheriff's office, and it stood right next to the prison. James reined up in front, tied his horse to the hitching rail, and then brought his shoulders back. He stretched. The buildings, his horse, the people looking at him—they all grew fuzzy, then gray. In fact, the entire world faded.

He leaned against the hitching rail and sucked in air until the dizziness and nausea passed. His hands tingled and shook a bit, and James clenched his jaw until his teeth hurt. He pulled off his hat, ran his one hand through his hair, then reset the hat. Little by little the sky brightened into blue again, and the two women standing near him nodded. "You all right?"

"Yes, ma'am." James touched the brim of his hat with a trembling finger. "I'm fine. Thanks for the concern. Excuse me."

The sheriff's office was a neat and tidy room, well organized. Wanted posters tacked on the wall aligned with the coffeepot in the corner. The desk surface was clear except for a pencil and a piece of paper, partially written on.

"Hello?" James called. "Anyone here?"

He stepped behind the desk, then swung open the door that led, he guessed, to the cells. He leaned farther in. "Hello?"

Both cells empty.

The outer door creaked, and heavy footsteps pounded on the floor. James spun a bit too fast and careened into the door jam. He bounced off, then steadied himself with one hand on the frame.

"Can I help you?" A man with a badge pinned to his vest pushed the door shut with his foot, since both his hands were occupied with a plate and cup.

"Sheriff?" James stood up straight and forced his eyes to focus.

"That's me. Malcolm Dunn." Dunn set the plate on his desk and extended a hand. His grip was strong, despite his slender fingers.

"James Colton, sir."

Sheriff Dunn motioned to an empty chair while he eased down to the one behind his desk. He pointed to his plate full of meat and potatoes.

"Supper time. Want some?" He reached into his vest pocket and pulled out a fork. "Always come prepared." His smile sparked his dark eyes.

"No, thanks, sheriff."

James shifted on his wooden chair until his bruised body wasn't aching too much.

"What can I do for you?" Dunn scooped potatoes into his mouth.

While the sheriff ate, James related everything he knew about the four robbers, including the murder of Juan Villanueva. He also described in detail what he knew of his recent beating, hoping someone had bragged about it.

"Sounds to me like you're on the right track," Dunn said. "More'n likely those freight robbers from the other day are the same men as the ones who robbed your stage." Dunn wiped his mouth on a napkin that he pulled out of his other pocket. He wagged his head. "Poor Mister Tillman never got a chance to defend himself."

James was close now. Damn close. He leaned forward on the edge of his chair.

"Any idea where they might be at?"

"These ain't men you want to be chasin' after, Mister Colton." Dunn pointed at the posters on the wall. "They're killers." He shook his head, then put the cup down on his desk. His steady gaze bore into James. "Don't go after 'em. Just leave 'em be. They'll kill you this time, for sure."

James had to ask.

"Well, sheriff. How come you're not out after those outlaws? I mean, since they're so dangerous and all, shouldn't you—"

"Deputy's out with a posse as we speak." Dunn shifted his weight in the chair. "Just don't you go out lookin' for trouble. I'll do my job. Don't you worry none."

A long, slow breath. In and out. James felt his energy drain. Soon he'd have to rest. Much sooner than he'd hoped. He rushed his words.

"But those men got my watch. They could've had anything else, but they took that. Now they've had it long enough. I aim to get it back."

The sheriff pointed a finger at James. "You're lookin' kinda peeked, son. Those bruises on your face are startin' to glow." Dunn frowned. "Must've been one helluva beatin'."

James lowered his head. It throbbed. He rubbed his temples, then refocused on the lawman. "You know what road they took? Where they're headed to next?"

Dunn dabbed his mouth, then folded the napkin and set it on the desk. "Tell you what, Mister Colton. You go get some rest, then come back tomorrow morning and we'll talk. We'll see about getting your watch back." He rose to his feet. "There's a good camping place just north of town. Nice little stream nearby."

Although the sheriff was a few inches shorter and leaner, something about this lawman drew him to James. Something familiar. Then it struck James. Dunn was just like pa. Just how pa always sat and talked, man to man. James shook the sheriff's hand.

Finally a lawman who'll do something.

* * *

79

From the shelter atop a pile of boulders, George Fallon watched James below make camp. After much preparation, James leaned against a rock while sipping his coffee. Fallon pulled in the smell of the smoke intermingled with coffee. Even though the sun threw deep shadows over the forest, he was still close enough to make out James' features. Yep. Same shotgun guard they'd robbed a few weeks back. The same kid scared spitless, but Fallon still remembered the kid's intensity, his passion about protecting the stage and his stupid watch. Yeah, this James Colton had been willing to die to keep his watch. Fallon chortled.

Maybe I'll give him another chance.

Shelton and Billy knelt on either side of Fallon. Shelton squinted against the sun and pointed. "That the kid gunnin' for us?"

"*Pendejo.*" Billy spit into the dirt. "Who's he think he is?"

"Keep it down. Voices carry." Fallon glared at Billy. Why'd he ever let him join the gang in the first place? He'd been nothing but trouble. "That's James Colton, shotgun guard we robbed back near Mesilla."

"That's the sonuvabitch what shot me." Billy rubbed his left arm.

"Hell, you hardly even bled." Shelton chuckled low and long. "More like a grazin' than a shootin'."

Billy scrambled to his feet, balled one hand. "You callin' me a liar? You wanna see what a real shootin' feels like?" His other hand reached down for his gun.

Shelton jumped up, his hand brushing his revolver. Fallon stood. "Shut up, both of you."

A splash in the creek. Fallon's attention focused on the sound. James stood at water's edge, his fishing line in the water.

"Rudy, over here." Fallon waited for Rudy to join them. Then he spoke just above a whisper.

"Dunn says that kid down there can identify us. He's been goin' around to every lawman within a hundred miles givin' clear descriptions."

"Let me kill 'em." Billy flashed a knife. "I'll do it quick like. Besides, I owe him."

"No, I wanna do it." Rudy pulled a gold watch out of his pocket, pried open the lid, and read the filigreed inscription. "Listen to this. To James. Happy 18th Birthday. Love, Grandpa."

Shelton grabbed the watch out of Rudy's hand. "Now ain't that sweet?" He put it up to his ear.

"Brings a tear to my eye." Billy sheathed his knife, then wrestled the watch away from Shelton.

"Makes me wanna puke." Fallon said. "Give it back to 'im, Billy." He waited until the watch was back in Rudy's hand. "Now Dunn and me talked this out. We can't kill this kid right here, right now."

"Why not?" Billy's mouth curved into a pout. "I got a clear shot of him right over there." He pointed over his shoulder.

"'Cause there's plenty of miners crawlin' all over these hills, and if somebody sees us, it'll be a murder on our heads." Fallon glanced at Rudy. "Two on yours. And nobody knows we killed that Mexican and the freight driver." He leaned in closer. "And because Dunn's got a plan. Dunn says there's another freight wagon headin' this way tomorrow. And he said he's gonna talk that Colton kid into helping guard it. Dunn's thinking if we can get the freight drivers to be eyewitnesses to the kid's death, then nobody's gonna wonder. Dunn'll kill the kid when all the shooting starts, and it'll look like an accident. He was just in the way of a bullet."

Shelton cocked his head and squatted down. "Dunn. Can we trust that sheriff? I mean, hell, he's a lawman, ain't he?"

"Lawman or no, he's still a man," Rudy said. "He's bought and paid for just like the rest of 'em."

"And he'll get his share of the loot like always." Fallon stared down at James, who held up a fish now dangling from the line. "Only Dunn'll be right there when this kid gets killed. The perfect eyewitness."

Shelton bounced a small pebble up and down in his hand. "I don't know. Sounds too simple. Kinda makes me nervous."

"Only thing makin' me nervous is waitin'." Rudy aimed a pointed finger at James' back. "Kid's makin' it too easy for us. I agree with Billy. Let's do it right now."

"Damn if you're both not dumb as fence posts." Fallon gripped Rudy's arm. "We're gonna make sure he comes gunnin' for us tomorrow. And...we'll do it tonight." His gaze roved over all three men. "But it don't involve killing. Not yet." He motioned for the other two men to gather closer. "Now listen up."

* * *

The aroma of roasting fish wafted under James' nose until he almost drooled. Nothing better than fresh fish—unless it was ma's fried chicken. Ma. Would he ever see her again? Maybe his hard-headedness was getting him in trouble. Again. Was he doing the right thing by going after these outlaws?

Sure don't wanna die, but if I turn tail and run, I'll never get it.

Right now, the fish was at hand and sure was cooking perfectly. He pulled in more smells. Crisp piñon smoke combined with sizzling fish. Mountain air brought scents of pine needles. A deep rose sky, complete with a layer of light purple on top, created a perfect backdrop for the trees. James felt a quick shiver with the soft breeze. It was cold enough to see his breath when he wandered away from the fire, but he figured it wouldn't freeze hard tonight. At least he hoped so. He only had a light blanket and the coat he wore to keep off the chill.

More wood. He'd build up the fire, and then throughout the night he'd put more wood on. He'd be nice and toasty. A final check of the fish showed he'd have about ten minutes to gather wood before both supper and sun were done.

He headed into a section of the unexplored forest. Must be plenty of fallen wood here. Before too many steps, a voice behind him made him jump.

"Lookin' for your watch, Jamie boy?"

James whipped around. Strong arms encircled his chest, crushing his healing ribs. James pulled in air to scream, but instead sucked in nothing.

A fist to his stomach doubled him over. James twisted, thrashing against the powerful hold. Whoever it was, the body was bigger, stronger than his. Shadows played. He twisted to see his attacker. Something hard and round pressed against his temple. It cocked, metal scraping against metal.

"Move one muscle, and this bullet goes right into your brain."

James froze. The voice. Familiar. Hands fished into James' pockets, stealing Lila's money. Other hands gripped his new gun in his waistband and pulled it out. More hands dove into his coat pockets. They pulled out his bandana. Before he could protest, it was wrapped around his mouth and tied tight.

More hands grabbed his arms and yanked them behind him. Someone kicked the back of his knees. He thudded to the ground.

A rope lassoed his wrists until he couldn't feel his hands at all. James twisted around in time to recognize Rudy, with that sneer plastered on his face.

Damn outlaws! What the hell? James struggled to yell out, curse these men, demand his watch, but with eight arms commanding his body, he was powerless to fight them off. Before he could stand, they pushed James backwards against a tree. The impact blew out what little air remained in his lungs. He wheezed in fragments, and he fought to keep his head and vision clear.

Rope wound across his chest, around his neck. Tight. He prayed he wouldn't die here, like this. More rope around his legs. Cinched against that pine tree, James strained and pulled, looking for one weak point in the knots or rope.

Fallon bent down and moved in close—so close that James spotted the healed pockmarks on his face.

"Thanks for the pocket change, Jamie boy," Fallon said. He held up Lila's cash and waggled it over his shoulder as he straightened up, then walked off.

How in the hell'd they know my name?

James' breaths were ragged and short.

Shelton turned back. "And thanks for dinner. Fish's my favorite." A cackle exploded from his face.

Billy squatted down inches away. "I owe you a bullet. Might not be today. Hell, might not even be tomorrow. But just like Hell, it's comin'." He poked his finger into James' chest, hard. "And that, James Colton, you can count on."

Billy's stale breath swirled around James until he thought he'd throw up.

"Tick...tick...tick." Rudy sauntered over and stood beside Billy. Rudy's black eyes glowed like ebony fire. The outlaw held up something, something swinging on a gold chain. "Tick. Tick."

James screamed over the gag, screamed at Rudy, screamed at being tied, screamed at frustration.

Like a hypnotist, Rudy swung the watch back and forth in front of James. "Lose something, little boy?"

James strained against the ropes until all his energy faded. He was no closer to freedom than he was to becoming President.

Watch pocketed, Rudy knelt and grabbed James' hair, snapping his head back. It slammed into the tree so hard he knew his neck would break. A gun barrel pressed in under James' chin. Rudy's words sizzled.

"I promised Fallon I wouldn't kill you today." He blew out tobacco-stained breath. "But I didn't say nothin' about tomorrow."

CHAPTER TWELVE

The birds stopped chirping. Nothing but silence, a heart-stopping silence, filled the forest. James tensed. Footsteps. A low chuckle behind him.

Silence.

More footsteps, a branch bending with someone's push. Another chuckle, louder this time. James cringed.

Low-down sonsuvbitches. Probably come back to do me in. Just like Rudy and Billy threatened to do.

"What the hell you doin' here, Colton? All trussed up like a Thanksgivin' turkey." Sheriff Malcolm Dunn stood over James and shook his head. A soft chuckle grew into a full-fledged guffaw that rocked his shoulders.

Shaking from cold, nerves, fatigue, and pain, James grunted at the sheriff. Shafts of sunlight turned the forest golden, the black patches fading to gray. He didn't care right now how pretty Nature was. He just wanted up. To be on his own feet again. More grunts. He fidgeted as best he could, but his entire body, head to toe, was numb.

Dunn squatted next to James and untied the feet first, then worked his way around the chest. What James wanted most of all was that damn gag out of his mouth, but Dunn got to that last. James spit. That dirty cotton taste stayed in his mouth. He spit again.

"Damn, no-good, worthless, sonsuvbitches." James rubbed his sore arms and bent his knees. Every muscle throbbed. "Dammit!"

He accepted Dunn's arm to steady himself as he pulled up. James had to lean against the sheriff until his world cleared. A quick sweep of the area showed his fire out, fish gone, horse gone.

"Sonsuvbitches." James clenched his fists and his jaw. He arched his back, then raised and lowered his shoulders. Anything to get feeling and warmth back in his body.

Malcolm Dunn followed James' gaze, then turned his attention back to James. "You mind telling me what this was all about?"

James tried to take a step, but his legs shook. No way would they bear his weight. He rubbed one thigh. "Them robbers. The four of 'em. Tied me up. Took my food."

Dunn laughed again, this time softer. "You mean you been sittin' here all night?"

A glare was all this sheriff deserved. A second attempt at walking and again James' legs refused.

"Help me get over there, sheriff," James said. He nodded toward the dead fire.

Still chuckling, Dunn slid an arm around James, and together they wobbled to the campfire.

"Found a horse back over yonder," Dunn said. "Thought he might've thrown his rider. That yours?"

The brown and white pinto munched on buckbrush near the water's edge. He seemed unconcerned of the drama playing out around him.

"Yeah." James eyed the horse, halter intact and tied to the bush. He eased down to a rock near the campfire. It had been nice and warm until the flames had died. James had watched them flicker, shrink, then glow as red sticks. They'd turned black before the world turned gray this morning.

"Sonsuvbitches," James said.

Not only did they still have his watch, now they had all his money and his new gun. If they could sneak up like that, couldn't they just sneak up and kill him like that? And why didn't they just outright kill him last night when it was so damn easy?

"I'll start the fire and put on some coffee. Take the chill out of your disposition," Sheriff Dunn said. Then he rekindled the fire, filled the pot with water, added brown granules, fitted the lid, then set it near the flames to warm.

While James and Sheriff Dunn held their hands out over the flames, they compared notes. Same men who'd held up the stage and freight wagon. Dunn mentioned again how lucky James was that he was alive.

"Still can't figure out how they knew me," James said. "I mean, it isn't like I introduced myself and all." He pointed his cup at the lawman. "Tell you. It's kinda scary thinking they know me. Probably know my brother, too. And why didn't they kill me last night?"

Dunn held the cup to his mouth longer than James thought was necessary. The eyebrows knitted under Dunn's hat brim. A shrug, then he looked at the trees. "Hard to tell. Could've been they didn't want another murder on their heads. Could've been you scared them off. And they could've got your name when they robbed you the first time."

James mulled over the answer, which was no answer at all. Nothing of any help.

Sheriff Dunn pulled a strip of beef jerky out of his coat and handed it to James. "Here. This'll help 'til we get some real food."

James took the jerky. Salty and tough, but somehow it was the best food he'd ever eaten. He spoke over a mouthful of meat. "Don't mean no disrespect, but what the hell you doing out here?"

That familiar chuckle. "Looking for you. Figured you'd camp around here and thought I'd come by and tell you."

"Tell me what?"

"There's a freight wagon comin' from Turnerville later this morning. Supposed to be carryin' money with them. A lot of money." Dunn paused. "Perfect candidates for a robbery. Wouldn't you say?"

James swallowed the jerky and nodded. "We gonna follow them and grab those outlaws?"

"That was kinda my thinking. But we'll have to be careful. Damn careful."

"Hell, sheriff. It'll be three against four, right?"

"Four against four. The driver always has a guard with him. Be like shootin' flies off a pie." Dunn aimed an imaginary gun and fired.

* * *

Careful to stay off the road to Turnerville, a small ranching and mining community located near the convergence of two creeks, James and Sheriff Dunn took their time riding east. James didn't know exactly what to expect when he'd meet the freight wagons. Of course there was no guarantee they'd even get held up. He knew if it didn't happen today, according to Dunn, the freight wagon wouldn't be leaving Pinos Altos for another week.

Questions, then doubts. What if this wagon wasn't the target of a robbery? What if the bandits had planned to hit a stage instead of another freight wagon? James chided himself for his lack of planning. Seemed he wasn't doing much thinking lately.

87

As he rode next to the sheriff, he realized most of the thinking and planning had been done by Trace. He'd not actually made many decisions on his own. James smiled.

Finally, I'm becoming my own man, making my own plans, my own life. Right or wrong, they're mine.

Somehow it felt right. But how could it be right if he'd made the wrong decision? Certainly made the wrong choice about his card-playing buddies. He'd carry those scars for a long time, probably the rest of his life.

"Let's stop here, James." Dunn reined up behind a stand of pines. "Good cover in case those outlaws come by first."

James nodded and drew up next to the sheriff. The horse under him blew out air the same time he did. He shifted his weight in the saddle, and the creaking leather broke the stillness.

He didn't wait long. Just as the sun reached its zenith, the rattles of a freight wagon and the commands of the driver clattered through the trees. The narrow road itself was rutted, muddy from recent rains. Two deep grooves in the ground led past pine trees, scrub oak, and a few juniper bushes lining both sides.

Towering mountain peaks a few miles away and boulders scattered up and down each side of the road made ambushing easy. For them and the bandits. James ran his hand up and down the long metal barrel of the Belgian shotgun that Dunn loaned him, then cradled it across his lap. But it was his also-borrowed .36 Navy Colt he'd rely on.

Soon the wagon entered the small clearing, and Sheriff Dunn waved to it.

"Let's ride on up to them, James," Dunn said. "They're expecting us, but I wanna be sure they know it's us." A sideways glance. "I'd hate to get all shot up accidental like."

James gigged his horse alongside Dunn. The wagon master reined the heavy wagon and mule team to a stop. Both the driver and his partner nodded when they recognized the lawman.

"Howdy, sheriff." The driver pried off his hat and wiped the light sweat from his balding head.

"Hi ya, Jake. Just thought we'd ride along, keep you company." Dunn squinted at the driver, then nodded at the other man. He jerked a thumb over his shoulder. "By the way, this here's my friend, James Colton."

"Howdy. I'm Jake and this here's Trent, my partner. Good to know ya."

James shook hands with Jake first, then leaned over and shook Trent's hand as well. Trent's handshake surprised James, bull strong but gentle. The man was big, probably six-three, two hundred forty pounds. What robber in his right mind would challenge Trent?

"I don't mean to be rude, Dunn," Trent said. "But I know you didn't come all the way out here just to ride with us." Trent shielded his eyes from the midday sun. "What's going on?"

Dunn's grin turned downward. "Never did have much of a poker face, did I? Tell you the truth, got word there's some bandits out this way, holding up freighters. Didn't want you to be one of the victims."

The two men looked at each other. "'Preciate your concern." Jake pulled out a well-worn shotgun from under the seat, patted it as one would a child. "But like I told you before, we can take care of ourselves."

"Yeah, I know." The sheriff lowered his voice. "Unfortunately, the last driver who said that's dead."

Jake's chest rose with a deep breath. A slow wag of his head. "Then we're real glad you're here. Wanna ride along?"

"Thought you'd never ask." Dunn reset his wide-brimmed black hat and leaned in closer. "James and me have a plan. James here is gonna ride behind you to the left, hiding in the trees up the hill. He'll be back a ways. You'll probably never know he's there."

Jake and Trent nodded, glancing at James who nodded in return.

Dunn pointed to his right. "I'm gonna be on the other side, watchin' for those bandits. If they do stop you, James and me'll sweep down and arrest 'em, quick as lightnin'. Shouldn't be no trouble."

Dunn's eyes flicked from the freighters to the cover of the trees. He turned in his saddle, a long look behind him.

Why, James wondered, were butterflies scampering in his stomach? Was he nervous about the hold up? The retrieval of his watch? He couldn't decide which as he watched the wagon roll on ahead and Dunn disappear into the forest on the right side of the road.

James followed the wagon well into the afternoon. A few times he lost sight of it as his route wound through stands of trees and around boulders. He squeezed the reins until they sawed into his hand. James focused on sounds—nothing out of the usual. The clattering of the wagon, the metal clanking of the harness, his own quick breathing. If the freighters had been attacked, he would have heard it. He smiled at his foolishness. If he wasn't right there when it happened, Dunn would be. James sat a little easier in his saddle.

Then he heard the distant gunshot.

James spurred his horse down through the brush and onto the road, racing toward the noise. He galloped around a bend where the wagon sat parked in the middle of the road.

James reined up in a stand of trees. Shotgun in hand, he stepped off his horse and tied it to a sycamore. He crouched behind a thick-leafed bush.

There they were.

All four men, all on horseback, bandanas over their faces and weapons aimed straight at Jake and Trent. Just as it was when James was robbed. The four masked men held guns on the drivers, who were handing over the cash box. His gun gripped in his hand, James searched for Dunn. Where was he? Surely he'd heard the gunshot. And from the looks on both drivers' faces, they were asking the same question.

He couldn't—wouldn't—let those outlaws just rob these hard-working men. He thought of dead Mr. Villanueva and the dead freight driver from the last robbery. With or without Dunn, James vowed to stop these bandits.

"Hold it!" James raised his Navy Colt, then with his shotgun in his other hand, stepped into plain sight. He pointed the pistol at black-eyed Shelton. All four robbers spun toward his voice, two aiming their guns at him, the other two covering the freight drivers.

James fired at the man holding the cash box. Shelton flew off his horse, hitting the ground. James then fired at Billy. Blood covered Billy's left pant leg.

Fallon's cold dark eyes turned on James. He pointed his Colt and fired. Dust spurted up around James' foot. He ran for a clump of bushes.

Shelton, still on the ground, clutched his left shoulder while struggling to find his feet, the cash box forgotten in the dirt.

Rudy waved his gun at the freighters. "Keep those hands up!"

James snapped his aim to Fallon and Rudy, both still on their horses. "Don't move."

"Or what?" Rudy glanced at James, then back at the freighters.

"I'll shoot you, too," James shouted.

"I'm scared now," Fallon said. A chuckle followed it.

Where the hell is Dunn?

James wanted to check over his shoulder, but he knew if he took his eyes off these men, they'd shoot and escape. "Hands up!"

"Get him!" Fallon unloaded his weapon at James. Rudy aimed and fired.

James loped away from the brush, hoping to draw fire elsewhere. He headed for a stand of junipers. Twice, bullets whizzed past his ear. Bark flew from a nearby pine. James sprinted from bush to tree.

Where the hell is Dunn?

James holstered his Colt and then cradled the shotgun against his shoulder. He heard the .44's retort but couldn't move out of the way in time. Searing fire streaked across his head, yet his body felt as if it was buried in snow. Waves of burning heat then frigid cold attacked his body, his senses. Something dripped into his eye.

Blurry Trent. Men on horses. Fuzzy red trees. Dazzling white sky. James shivered. Dirt in his mouth.

Must be on the ground.

He gripped his head.

No Dunn. Gotta get up.

James rolled onto his back. Meaningless words peppered the air. Gun shots. He felt for his shotgun but grabbed only dirt.

Dunn's voice cut through the haze. "Drop your guns! Get those hands up where I can see 'em!" The words became clearer. More shots. Horse hooves pounded toward him.

James pushed up on his elbows, then sat all the way up. He squinted at the men and wiped blood from his face. True to form, Fallon and Rudy hadn't done what the sheriff had commanded. Instead, one gun was trained on Dunn, the other on Trent. Shelton still lay on the ground, but Billy struggled to his feet, scooped up the cash box, and loped toward his horse.

91

Trent threw himself off the wagon seat and ran after the man, missing him by inches. As Billy mounted his horse, he kicked out, catching Trent in the chest. James cringed at the whack. The freighter, losing his breath and footing at the same time, crashed to the ground. Puffs of dust danced around Trent's body.

Jake, arms above his head, slid one hand down to his side, reached under the wagon bench, and in one quick motion, pulled out his shotgun. He aimed at Shelton, now on his feet stumbling toward his horse. Jake fired. Bark flew from a tree nearby. Shelton ran faster. James spotted his shotgun lying a few feet away in the dirt. Gripping it, he rose to one knee, pulled back the hammers and pulled the trigger. Nothing. He pulled again. Jammed.

Dunn loaned me a bad gun?

Outlaw curses, threats, and sharp commands faded into the forest along with the four robbers. The trees swallowed them like demons in the shadows.

James sagged back down to the dirt. After a couple of breaths, he focused on Jake, who jumped down from the wagon's high seat and extended a hand to Trent. He pulled the big man to his feet.

"This close." Jake's fingers spread an inch apart. "You almost had 'em."

Trent rubbed his chest and glanced in the robber's direction. "Son of a bitch kicks hard."

"'Specially when he's takin' our money." Jake glared into the forest.

Dusty, scuffed boots stopped inches from his face. James held his throbbing head, then winced at the feel of sticky blood running down his temple and across his cheek.

Not again.

Dunn knelt by James, popped the cork of a canteen, and then tapped James shoulder with it.

James spit and swigged until the taste of dirt left his mouth. He spit again.

Jake untied his neckerchief, poured water on it, then knelt by James and held the compress to his head. James hated to admit it, but that cool against his hot skin felt good. Even though his head was still throbbing, his vision was clear enough to see Dunn's face full of anger, possibly outrage. Who was he mad at? Himself or the robbers?

Sure as hell can't be me. At least I winged two of them.

Jake wadded the wet neckerchief into James' hand, poured a bit more water on the material. "You all right?"

"Good enough, I guess," James said. Blood trickled down his neck before he could sop it up. He turned to Dunn, his anger building. "Where the hell were you?" He dabbed at more blood, then wiped his eye.

Dunn pushed aside James' hand and examined the bullet wound. He whistled between his teeth. "Damn close."

"Yeah. But you almost got us all killed." James found it hard to be mad at a man who seemed so concerned about his welfare. Trent and Jake stood behind Dunn, obvious concern clouding their eyes. James swiped his sleeve across his mouth, studied the bloody cloth he held in his hand, then looked at Dunn.

"Help me up," he said.

On his feet again, James leaned into Jake's strong shoulder as he staggered over to the wagon. As much as he wanted to stand straight, his knees had grown weak, and the trees were tilting at odd angles again. He sagged against the wheel.

"Aren't you goin' after them, Dunn?" Trent said, and he furrowed his eyebrows as he wiped his forehead.

"Yeah. Wanted to be sure James here was all right."

"I'm fine." James rubbed his eyes, while the pounding in his head churned his stomach. "Can't believe I couldn't stop 'em."

"You slowed 'em down, friend," Jake said. "For that we're grateful. They won't get too far. You plugged one of 'em pretty damn good."

James jerked his pointed finger toward the borrowed shotgun. "No thanks to your jammed Belgian, Dunn. You could've got me killed."

"Jammed, huh?" Dunn raised one eyebrow.

"They ain't got much of a lead." Trent retrieved the shotgun from the wagon. "Want me to come along?"

"No." Dunn's words were rushed. "With two of 'em injured they should be easy enough to find. Head on back to town, I'll round up those thieves and meet you there."

"I'll go with you." James pulled in just enough air to fill his lungs, his ribs reminding him again of his recent beating.

Dunn nodded. "All right. Be glad for the company. Those men play for keeps, though." He untied his horse's reins. "Ready?"

93

"Yeah." James swayed with the first two steps. He gritted his teeth, determined to ride with the sheriff, to get those men, to get his watch.

Trent grabbed James' arm. "You crazy? Dunn, he ain't in no condition to go ridin' after bandits."

"I can do it." James turned blurry eyes on Trent. "I can do it."

"I'm takin' you back to town." Trent turned to Jake and Dunn. "I don't care how much he argues, I'm taking him over to Missus Stinson's."

"But—"

Stomach roiling, James turned away and leaned over, afraid he'd throw up on Trent. A hand on his shoulder. A deep breath, then he felt better, the nausea passing without embarrassing himself.

Trent's grip tightened as he led James toward the wagon. "Your eyes are still spinnin' in different directions, son. Missus Stinson's the closest thing we got to a doctor. And since we don't have no hotel, you can stay at the jail 'til Dunn gets back. If that's all right with him."

Dunn patted James on the shoulder as he helped him onto the wagon seat. "Can't argue with Trent when he sets his mind to something. And, he's sure too big to ignore." Dunn mounted his horse, then waved. "See you in town."

He spurred his horse toward the dust trail.

CHAPTER THIRTEEN

Reflecting on the holdup as he rode, Sheriff Dunn thought about the headstrong teenager. James had turned out to be a better shot than he'd thought. Far better than Fallon. In fact, that kid had come close to killing Shelton and Billy. However, someone had come mighty close to killing *him*. An inch more to the right would have made a difference. A big difference.

Dunn's thoughts turned to money. He hated the idea of having to share. Split five ways, the booty was never big enough. And trying to live on a sheriff's salary...hell, that was just a joke. But if he could make a couple big, really big hauls, then he'd head off down to Mexico with the boys. Just like they were planning to do soon.

More money. If he turned in Fallon and the gang, he'd get no extra reward money—just a pat on the back, more accolades from the town's citizens. Accolades wouldn't buy booze and women. He slowed his horse to a walk. An idea came into his head.

However, if I get James Colton to "capture" them, we could split the money two ways. Hell, Rudy alone is worth at least six months in Mexico. Then I'll get rid of my "partner" and keep all the reward money myself.

A smile slid up one side of Dunn's face. He whistled as he rode. Fallon and the gang behind bars or preferably dead. James Colton dead. Hell, by this time next week, he could be in Mexico drinking himself a time with all the tequila his money could buy and loving all the señoritas he could hold. The whistling stopped. He'd have to be careful around Fallon. That man wasn't stupid. So, he would just have to wait and make his move when the time was right.

A mile down the road, in a thick stand of pine trees, Dunn reined his horse into the agreed-upon meeting place. The four men were waiting. Billy, a wad of cash clutched in hand, grimaced in contrast to his gleaming blue eyes. He and Shelton sat propped against a tree.

Fallon ambled over to meet Dunn. "Just like you said, Dunn. Lots of money." Fallon thumbed through the bills.

"Just give me my share, George. Then I'll get out of here." Dunn dismounted and ambled toward the gathered men.

Fallon cocked his head. "What's the matter? In a hurry?" He glanced around at the others. "Maybe he don't trust us?"

Chuckling rippled through the robbers.

"'Course I trust you. Otherwise, I wouldn't let you shoot at me." Dunn lowered his voice. "You missed the kid."

"Yeah. Billy needs more target practice." Fallon knelt by Billy, then peeled up the soggy pant material pasted against his lower leg. "You're gonna live. Just a grazin'."

"Hurts like hell, Fallon," Billy said. "Get me a doc." He elbowed Shelton. "Me and him."

Fallon pried Shelton's bloody fingers from his shoulder. He ripped part of the material and poked. Shelton jerked. Fallon frowned.

"Hold still now," Fallon said. A few more jabs, then Fallon examined Shelton's back. "Damn. Went clear on through. Guess you're gonna live, too."

Quiet until now, Rudy pulled a blade of grass clenched between his teeth and pointed it at his fellow robbers on the ground.

"They gonna be all right to ride down to Mexico with us next week?" he asked. "I sure ain't gonna sit around waitin' for them to heal up while all that Mexican silver's just begging us to come steal it." He lobbed the grass at the ground. "Hell, I'll ride without 'em."

"Thought you were gonna hit that Butterfield stage to Tucson again," Dunn said. "Thought we agreed nobody'll be expecting it to get robbed twice so soon."

Dunn frowned at Rudy, then swung his gaze over to Fallon. Were they changing plans without telling him?

"Mister Quick Gun here wants to rob everything, Dunn." Fallon cocked his head toward Rudy. "Hard to keep the boy from running off and holding up everyone who crosses his sights."

"You need to be careful." Sheriff Dunn thumbed over his shoulder. "Especially with that James Colton. I'll bet he'll be there waitin' for you. Where ever you are." One eyebrow rose. "Pretty determined to get that watch of his back."

Fallon pushed himself up to his feet. "He's becoming a real irritating bee, always buzzing around. Next time he gets in the way, I'll squash 'im—grind 'im into a soggy blob just like the damn pest he is."

"Like that last driver." Billy chuckled. "Huh, Fallon?"

"Yeah." Fallon spit. "And that's a promise."

"I got an idea." Dunn looked into the forest, then up at the sky. Clouds in the west threatened rain. "With him beat up and all, and now his head grazed, he ain't feeling too good. I bet if I gave him his watch, he'd be happy as hell just to have it back in his pocket. I'd make him promise to drop his search and he'd leave. If need be, we'd go kill him later."

Maybe Fallon would be in a hurry to get down to Mexico. Maybe he'd take the bait. Then Dunn and James could get an easy drop on them.

Fallon shook his head, patted his pocket. "He ain't that dumb. Besides, I've grown attached to this time piece. It's right pretty. I'm makin' a collection and don't feel like givin' it back."

Without warning, he grabbed Dunn's coat front and pulled him within inches of his chest, spitting on Dunn as he spoke. "Startin' to like that kid?"

"No."

"You gettin' soft?"

"No."

"Lost your stomach for killin'? Want out?"

"No."

The scar over Fallon's eye pulsated. After a heavy breath, he pushed Dunn away. Sheriff Dunn adjusted his jacket.

"Hell," he said, "four men couldn't kill that kid. Your plan didn't work is all. Maybe mine will."

Fallon swiped his hand across his mouth. One of his eyes narrowed. "Just take your money and ride outta here. Me and the boys'll come up with something else. Something that'll end that Colton kid once and for all."

"Then give me my money." Dunn stuck out a hand.

Fallon counted the bills wadded in his fist, then extracted a few. A glare at Dunn as he slapped the bills into his hand.

"Watch that *kid* yourself," Fallon said. "He's liable to end up shootin' *you*."

Dunn counted, conscious of his roiling stomach, then jammed the cash into his shirt pocket. With nothing left to say, he mounted his horse and spurred it toward town.

* * *

97

A few miles down the road, Dunn caught up with the freighters. Jake reined in the team and braked the wagon, slowing it to a halt. "Find 'em?"

Dunn shook his head.

Jammed between the two drivers, James' face was flushed, yet pale around the edges. His head leaned against Trent's shoulder.

Something tightened in Dunn's stomach. Desperate for a smoke, he fished in his coat pocket for tobacco and paper.

"Lost their trail in some rocks," he said.

"Dammit, Dunn!" Jake yelled. "Now what? Hell, I got another freight run day after tomorrow."

"Calm down, I know you're sore. But I'm plannin' on gettin' a posse together. I'll come back, recover your money." Dunn sprinkled tobacco on the paper and rolled it. "By the way, how much you lose, you figure?"

"Over eight hundred dollars." Jake gritted his teeth.

Sheriff Dunn's hand brushed against his shirt pocket as he whistled. His tongue flicked down the paper. Then he fished a match out of his coat. His gaze returned to the kid and waited for James to focus on him.

"Sure lost some color in that face, son. Don't look too good." Dunn held the flame of his match to one end, puffed, then blew out a gray cloud. He offered James the cigarette.

James massaged his temple and shook his head.

Jake glanced toward James. "Must've lost a lot of blood. Almost passed out on us."

Dunn's eyebrows inched toward his hat while he leaned over on his horse. Despite the handkerchief clutched in James' hand, blood still trickled down his left temple.

"You're lucky," Dunn said. "An inch would've taken your head clean off. Rest now. We'll be in town pretty soon. I'll catch those robbers with the posse, and then everything will be all right."

Smoke curled from Dunn's mouth.

* * *

James watched the back of Dunn as he rode ahead. Where in the hell had he been? He never did answer that question, and James found himself more and more irritated as they rode closer to town. Damn sheriff. If he had been where he said he'd be, then—

"I don't know, but something ain't right, Trent." Jake's words brought James back to the wagon. "Sheriff's got somethin' else on his mind. Don't seem to honestly care about James or the robbery."

"Ahh, just your imagination," Trent said. "That holdup's got you spooked."

Jake expelled a long stream of air. "Maybe you're right." He shifted his gaze to James. "At least Dunn's right about one thing. You're not looking too good."

James hoped he looked better than he felt.

Gotta hold on a while longer. I'll stay in town tonight, then talk to Dunn tomorrow about getting his deputy to help.

Throbbing, pounding in his head brought tears to his eyes. He massaged his forehead, closing his eyes against the pain.

Something shook his shoulder. A firm grip. James' eyes shot open. He stared up into three pairs of eyes staring down at him. A turn of his head brought searing streaks of gray. He grabbed his head with both hands.

"I'll go get her." Three pairs of eyes became two.

"Hey, he's back with us." James put a name to a pair of eyes. Trent. "You've been out for a while. How ya' feeling?"

Head hurts, but I seem to be alive.

James knew words hadn't come out. His mouth opened and closed, but nothing had come out.

"Want some water?" Jake's eyes frowned.

James nodded. Impressions flooded in. Four bandits. Shooting. Dirt in his mouth. The wagon. Before more images appeared, a tin cup pressed against his lower lip. He drank as if he'd never had water. Drank like a cactus dying in the heat. He drank until the cup was empty.

"Missus Stinson's on her way over, James." Trent's meaty hand pushed against James' shoulder. "You need to stay right here until she fixes you up."

"Where...?" James swung his gaze around the room. Blurry rock wall at his feet. Iron bars pressed against his shoulder.

Good God, not again.

The cot under him proved lumpy at best. He squirmed to dislodge what he hoped was just a cotton lump from under his right hip. The wool blanket over him warmed his shivering body.

99

The door squeaked open. A woman was pushing her way into the small cell. Behind her stood Sheriff Dunn. Trent and Jake filled the remainder of the cell.

James glared at the sheriff. "Where were you?"

"Fetching the closest thing we got to a town doctor." Dunn nodded toward the woman, her coffee brown hair pulled back in a bun. "This here's Missus Stinson."

"The robbers. Where were you when they shot me?" James strained to sit up. Strong but feminine hands shoved him back to the cot.

"Lie quiet now, Mister Colton. There'll be talking time later." Mrs. Stinson spoke over her shoulder. "Warm water, towel, strip of gauze." She glared at Trent. "Now."

"Yes ma'am." Trent pushed his way out of the cell.

"You let 'em get away." James locked his gaze on Dunn's face. He detected something else besides worry. What, he couldn't be sure.

Dunn shook his head. "I was more worried about you. Don't fret. I've got a good idea where they're gonna be. And I'll be gettin' a posse together soon and we'll bring 'em in. Them and your timepiece."

James pushed up, propping himself on his elbows. "I'm going, too."

"Move again like that, young man, and I'll tie you to this cot." Mrs. Stinson forced James back down. "You'll get up when *I* say. And not before."

Too tired to fight, too hurt to argue, James squeezed his eyes shut and gripped his head.

Trace'll never believe this.

CHAPTER FOURTEEN

James heard the riders mount up, several men—if squeaking leather saddles were any indication. Last-minute instructions were tossed from Sheriff Dunn to his deputy. The hooves beat out the staccato rhythm of men in pursuit. The sound died as quickly as it had begun.

Lying on the cot, James eased his hands under his head, interlaced the fingers, and then let his head rest in that cradle. Still throbbing. Not throbbing as hard as last night, but that bullet's path along his head let him know he was lucky—damn lucky—to have survived.

The awakening sun spread a golden glow over the rock wall. Stomach rumbling, James knew it was time for breakfast. He pushed upright, despite Mrs. Stinson's warnings, swung his legs over the side, then stood. So far, so good. The walls and bars stayed upright, the floor remained under his feet. He smiled.

After a visit to the privy out back—then a slow walk to the sheriff's office—he returned to jail. As much as he'd wanted to get going, to ride out of town and find those robbers, James spent most of the day lying on his cot in the jail cell. When he wasn't sleeping, or sitting up trying hard to keep his throbbing head from exploding, he was planning and plotting—how to get his watch.

Supper filled his stomach, and the cotton mattress under him supported his still-bruised body. He lay behind those iron bars, thinking how glad he was he could get up, walk away anytime he wanted. He wasn't a prisoner, just a visitor. James cringed at the thought of being arrested and jailed—a nightmare he'd had more than once. To him, the ultimate form of torture would include sitting behind bars and waiting to be hanged. Not much else could be worse.

Horse hooves. The sound brought James' attention to the street. It was dark outside—too dark to see anything. Instead, he lay on his cot and listened to men's voices, the frustration in each word. Words of endless riding, fruitless searching, deep fatigue.

If that posse couldn't find them, then I'll just have to do it myself. First thing tomorrow.

Closing his eyes didn't bring sleep. Nagging thoughts kept him awake long after the deputy had made his final rounds. Lila Belle Simmons. Would she be worried about him?

At least she knew he'd be back. And he knew he'd be back in her arms in a couple of days. With his watch. But what about Trace? His brother would still be wondering...and worrying as he drove that Tucson run. But when he returned to Mesilla, James' message would be waiting at the doc's. Then Trace would relax, not worry so much.

Knowing he'd done what he could with the people in his life, thoughts returned to the task at hand. How could he succeed where the posse failed? He thought long and hard.

A plan. A plan would be a good idea.

James tossed and turned on the hard cot.

Voices. Under his window. James rubbed his eyes and glanced up into the gray pouring through his cell window. It wasn't even morning, yet someone close by was talking. James eased to the window and hunched down under it. He held his breath.

"You're crazy for comin' here, George. What'd you want?"

"Me and the boys made new plans, Dunn. Need a meetin'."

George? James thought he recognized the voice. Fallon? Could it be George Fallon? James envisioned the hard brown eyes above the mask. Cold ran down his back.

"Where?"

"Same place. Usual time."

"You've got to get out of here. What if somebody sees you?"

"So what? Nobody knows me."

Cigarette smoke wafted through the window. James pinched his nose and prayed he wouldn't sneeze.

"You just be there, *lawman*." Another puff of smoke. "You wanna get outta this hellhole, don't ya?"

"Shut up." A curse too low for James to make out. "I'll be there."

Footsteps crunched in the dirt, then died away. Courage gathered, James raised on tiptoes and peeked out the window. He caught a glimpse of a man he recognized, one of the hold-up men. The silhouette confirmed it was the outlaw leader.

James crept back to the cot, then sat, head cupped in his hands. Dunn's actions made perfect sense now. He was a partner, someone who could let the robbers get away with actual murder. James shivered. He'd been resting in Dunn's jail. He thought again how close he'd come to dying. And Dunn was right there in the middle of it.

All right. We can all play this game.

Dunn's deputy. Was he in on it, too? The relationship between Dunn and the deputy was a piece of the puzzle James would have to put together. And soon. Pulling his borrowed black powder revolver from its holster, he slipped the weapon under his pillow.

* * *

Mrs. Stinson woke him at half past ten. After removing the bandage, she cleaned the bullet wound with what James could only guess was whiskey. Cheap whiskey. The stench took his breath. He blinked several times and tried not to cough.

Before he could thank her and leave, she pried the top off a small tin can she'd brought.

"You wanna die from a head infection?" she asked.

"Ma'am?"

"Didn't think so. You just grit your teeth, young man, and keep your rear end on that cot." Mrs. Stinson plunged a spoon into the can of goo.

His eyes watered at the odor—blackjack tar and turpentine. James jerked back, but Mrs. Stinson's vice-like pinch on his shoulder kept him seated. "Might sting for a spell, but..." She dug out an oozing spoonful. "Better 'n bein' dead, I say. After you heal up, more 'n likely there'll be a tiny scar." She waved the utensil in front of his face. "You're lucky that's all you're gonna have."

"Yes, ma'am."

She slathered the concoction over the gash. "Lucky Sheriff Dunn saved you when he did."

"Ma'am?" He struggled to breathe instead of scream.

Mrs. Stinson wrapped a clean bandage around James' head. "If he hadn't been there to ride in when he did, no telling what those outlaws would've done."

103

"No, ma'am." James pushed up a corner of the bandage wrapped over one eye. He swiped at moisture trickling down his cheek.

"No telling at all." Mrs. Stinson tied the ends, then sat in the chair in front of James.

"Thank you again, ma'am, for all you've done. Tell me, how well you know Sheriff Dunn?"

She leaned back in the chair. A tight grin crinkled the skin on one side of her face.

"Sheriff Dunn? He's the greatest lawman around! Everyone respects him." Mrs. Stinson dropped her voice and glanced around the cell, as if the whole world was listening. "Some of the younger women, well, they fancy him, you know. He can't walk down the street without heads turning. A few of them bring him pies and such. If I wasn't a married woman myself and a year or two... why..." A soft giggle erupted as her cheeks pinked.

That answer was unexpected. Were they were talking about the same man?

"He ever do anything...that didn't seem right? Or outside the law?"

This question produced a scowl. "James Colton, what are you getting at? If you're thinking Sheriff Dunn is anything other than wonderful, you've got another thing coming. Why, he's turned this town around and brought peace and prosperity. There isn't anything people wouldn't do for him."

By now James realized he'd asked the wrong question. Or the wrong person.

"And if you've got a notion that Sheriff Dunn's not a gentleman and not the best lawman this side of the Missouri, just ask anyone out there." She waved the spoon toward the street. "Anyone at all and they'll tell you what a fine man he is. He brought this place from being nothing but an old rusty mining camp to the tony village it is today. All by himself. Single-handed. Why just last month, he—"

"Thanks, Missus Stinson. I get the picture." James touched his forehead and swayed side to side. "Think I just need to lie back here and rest for a spell, ma'am. Things are kinda swimmy. Thanks again for everything." He stretched out on the cot and closed his eyes. Maybe she'd quit talking and go away.

Humphs and nose whistles. Mutterings. The tin can slammed down. Silence.

He pried one eye open. She was still there, folding the wet cloth with a vengeance. He draped an arm over his eyes and lay still.

* * *

James ate dinner at the only eatery in town. The largest canvas tent he'd ever seen, probably thirty men would easily fit inside, he figured. The smells of canvas, coffee, stew, tobacco, biscuits, and sweaty men blended together and attacked his nostrils. Scanning the room, he found only a handful of men sitting around shoveling food into their mouths. Most men at this hour, James knew, were out working their claims.

As he ate, final plans took shape. He'd follow Dunn to the meeting place, find out what he could, then ride back to Santa Rita and relay everything to Sheriff Keats. But could he trust Keats?

He'd have to.

Hurrying to finish his meal, he wolfed down the hot coffee and sopped up the remaining stew with his biscuit. One of the men sitting near him had seemed friendly enough. And, he'd glanced at his pocket watch a time or two. The silver casing, with a curlicue etched on top, caught James' interest. He pointed to the watch.

"Nice looking time piece you got. I have...*had* one kinda like it."

"She's a beaut', ain't she?" The man nodded. "Won 'er in a poker game." He held it up. "Keeps right good time, too."

Dunn could leave any minute, and James wanted to be right behind him. He nodded at the watch.

"And it's time for me to go," James said. He brought his gaze up to the man's face. "Keep that in your pocket. I hear tell there's bandits around just itching for watches."

James walked the few blocks down Main to Dunn's office. He stopped just outside the door, straightened his shoulders, and pulled in a lungful of air. While his head's pounding was reduced to an ache, he fought to clear his thoughts. He'd have to be on his toes around Dunn.

Hand on the doorknob, he froze. What if the sheriff had figured out James knew what he was up to? Would he kill him right here or ambush him later?

James pushed the door open, then spied Deputy Ben Wickens sitting behind the desk, feet planted on the wide, wooden top, papers under foot shuffled in no particular order. The deputy jerked his feet off the desk, smacking them on the floor, then leaned over the desk to shake hands with James.

"How's the head?" Wickens asked.

"Mending just fine, thanks to you and Missus Stinson." James glanced toward the closed door leading to the cells. "Sheriff back there?"

"Nope."

"Where'd he go to?"

A frown creased every corner of the deputy's face. The eyes narrowed.

"You're in an all-fire hurry to find him." Wickens leaned closer, shoving the papers with his elbows. "Can I help you with something?"

"No..." Why did he have to stammer at a time like this? Did his nerves show? He shook his head. "Just wanted to tell him I appreciate his hospitality and that I gotta be going."

The deputy stood. "Goin' where?"

"Back...to Mesilla. Meet up with my brother. We're stage drivers you know." James took a step back.

The deputy's eyes softened. Even the mustache over his thin lips seemed to droop a bit. He rounded the desk and stood eye to eye with James. He clamped his hand on James' shoulder.

"I'll tell him where you're heading. And that you said thanks."

The deputy's hand released its tension, then patted James' upper arm, still sore from the beating. "Dunn left 'bout fifteen minutes ago. Rode out headin' east." The lawman pointed his chin toward the door. "That man's gone a lot. Always out chasing bandits. I get to stay back and watch the store." He sighed. "Hope he catches this bunch. They're bad ones."

James swallowed hard. Should he stay now and find out more, or should he rush after Dunn? James stretched out a hand. He'd go after Dunn.

"Thanks, Deputy Wickens. I'll keep my eyes open."

They shook hands.

James shielded his eyes from the afternoon light as he shut the door. He let out a sigh louder than he'd intended. If he rode hard, there was still a chance he'd find Dunn. As he limped toward the livery stable, he paused and turned around. What

106

would he do when he found Dunn? What if those outlaws spotted him? Should he tell the deputy what he suspected? More than that...what he *knew*.

A couple breaths, then he continued toward the livery. No, he wouldn't go back and tell the deputy. The fewer people who knew, the better. He'd just find Dunn, listen in, then hightail it to Santa Rita.

Simple.

CHAPTER FIFTEEN

Dunn hadn't bothered hiding his tracks. Or so it seemed. James followed the sheriff from Pinos Altos south along the same rough trail they'd taken from Turnerville two days before. Tracks meandered through weeds and around rocks. Dunn's tracks were easy to spot—his horse's back left shoe was loose, creating a squiggle where the other prints were half moon. Simple.

The other myriad of tracks had to be from yesterday's posse. They all were headed in the same direction. James trotted his horse alongside Dunn's trail until it disappeared. He reined up, then backtracked.

There. In between two bushes, hoof prints leading away from the main trail, away from the posse's tracks, away into forest. Forest? That same uneasy feeling sent shivers along James' spine.

I've come this far. No turning back now.

He urged his pinto into the clot of brush and pine trees. Several hundred feet later, he dismounted, pushing through mountain mahogany trees and up a small rise. Eerie shadows played with his imagination. Jays squawked at his intrusion. Chipmunks darted out of his way. Old leaves crunched under his feet. He jumped at every sound.

Get a grip, James.

He crept down the other side of the rise. Voices? He froze. More sounds. Definitely voices. After looping the reins around a tree, he crouched low, then fought his way through the woods, through heavy undergrowth. He prayed whoever belonged to the voices wouldn't hear him sneaking up. The words grew louder, clearer as he moved closer.

Anger. Sharp words. Good. It increased his chances of success. On his belly now and using brush as cover, he slithered up a low rise. A couple more yards. He crawled closer. Five men came into view.

He'd half expected someone else. He'd hoped it would be someone else. But there stood Sheriff Dunn and those sonuvabitch robbers. Just as he'd thought—in cahoots.

Tensing every muscle, he pulled in air and straightened up. His head brushed against a branch. A couple pinecones thundered down like bombs. The noise halted the voices. He cringed.

What the hell'm I doing? Standing here like a big dumb target with the words Shoot Me written across my chest.

He sank back down to the ground.

A plan. He needed a plan. If he showed himself, those killers wouldn't let him walk away with his watch. But was he ready to kill five men? Could he?

Another breath and he shook his head. Couldn't kill just for a watch. He wasn't like those men who had no problem murdering people. No, he had a conscience.

His gun was drawn, but he didn't remember whipping it out of its holster. He hunkered down listening in. The voices continued, still heated. His gun slipped back into the leather.

"...not enough money around here, Dunn. We've hit every damn stage and freighter we thought had money."

"Besides, I got a hankerin' to visit Tucson. Know a gal there." A pause and chuckle. "Cute young thing."

Was that Rudy?

James squinted through the brush. Yep. Rudy all right.

"Ain't much in Tucson." Dunn shrugged. "Wagons're busy going through, though."

"We heard they made a big silver strike down around Tubac. Gotta be stages and such that don't need all that money." Fallon blew out smoke, his cigar dangling between two fingers.

The men nodded their agreement.

"Look, George." Dunn said. "I don't have jurisdiction that far. Can't protect you there." His hands spread out at his sides. "You'd be on your own."

"Yeah, we figured that. Guess we'll just have to take our chances. Guess that makes us...well, we ain't partners no more." He turned his back on the sheriff. "Let's go, boys."

Dunn grabbed Fallon's coat and spun him around. "Dammit, I ain't livin' on a sheriff's salary! Why'd you think I took up with you in the first place?" His pointed finger jabbed Fallon's chest. "We made a deal. We'll see this through until I say we're done."

"Not *we*." Fallon grabbed the sheriff's finger and twisted it. "*You*. It's you that's done." He planted a fist in Dunn's stomach.

Dunn doubled over and clutched his stomach. Then he straightened up and swung at Fallon. James heard the impact.

Billy moved in close, despite his game leg, while Rudy pulled out his gun. Shelton, one arm in a neckerchief sling, swung at Dunn. The men hollered and whooped, then moved in close.

Fallon staggered back, swiping blood from his lips.

"Stand back! He's mine," he said, with a wild-eyed glare at his men. Eyes locked on Dunn, he rammed forward like an insane bull. He head-butted Dunn in the stomach, driving the sheriff into the ground. A grunt, then a groan. James winced.

Dunn rolled just in time to avoid the boot careening toward his face. He grabbed Fallon's leg and yanked. Fallon crashed like a sack of rocks. Rolling up onto his knees, Dunn's fist plowed into Fallon's nose. Blood poured down Fallon's chin.

Fallon threw himself on top of the sheriff, landing two punches in his face. Dunn grabbed Fallon's shoulders and somehow—James wasn't quite sure how—managed to throw Fallon off. Fallon plowed into the ground, then somersaulted into a bush.

Dunn, on his feet now, rushed Fallon and picked him up by the front of his shirt. Dunn drew his fist back, but Rudy stepped in behind Dunn, grabbed his arm, then twisted it back and up.

Wrenching free, Dunn spun around. Before the sheriff could strike again, Fallon grabbed the sheriff's gun. A smart whack across the side of the head and Dunn crumpled to the ground. A groan and he lay still.

James swallowed hard. Was he still alive? Rudy pulled out his revolver, then shoved it against Dunn's head. Good God! Just plain execution.

Do I show myself or stand by and watch Dunn's murder?

The answer was obvious. James stood.

"For Chrissake, Rudy, no need to kill 'im. Not yet anyway." Fallon flicked his hand toward his partner. "Put it away."

James froze. Maybe he wouldn't have to rush down and rescue Dunn after all. He sank back down behind a tree.

"Ah hell, Fallon. He'll just make trouble for us. Let me kill 'im and get it over with. He won't be able to tell nobody 'bout us." Rudy cocked the hammer.

James forced himself to breathe.

110

"He ain't gonna be tellin' nobody." Fallon pushed Rudy's hand away. "Hell, as guilty as he is, he'd go to jail." Fallon wiped the blood from his mouth, held his shoulder, and looked around. "And I don't think he wants that. No. He'll be nice and quiet."

Like a rope uncoiling, Rudy eased to his feet and stepped in close to Fallon. The sneer climbed up one side of his face. "When he comes gunnin', and he will, it ain't gonna be me who'll take that bullet for you. I say we kill 'im now."

Fallon leaned in so close that James thought for sure he'd bite Rudy. "I'm boss and when I say kill 'im, we kill 'im. But not 'til then." He stepped chest to chest with Rudy. "Do I make myself clear?"

James knew Rudy would hit Fallon. He waited for the crunch of breaking bones. But Rudy's shoulders sagged and he stepped back. "Yeah. Real clear."

Billy held up a rope. His blue eyes sparked under his wide-brimmed hat. "Can I tie him up, Fallon? I'll do it tight. He won't never get away."

Without waiting for permission, he knelt by Dunn.

Shelton spit a brown stream onto Dunn's leg, then wiped his mouth with his sleeve. "Never thought I'd see the day we'd let a lawman live." He wagged his head. "Just don't seem natural."

Handkerchief in hand, Fallon dabbed at his bloody face. A wince or two. James grinned.

Dunn sure packed a punch.

They tied Dunn to a tall pine, arms behind him around the tree, ankles bound. Same way those outlaws had tied James. After wiping most of the blood off his face, Fallon stepped over to Dunn and kicked him in the leg. Chuckles and guffaws.

Even though Dunn had proved to be no good, he still didn't deserve to be treated like that. A good long time in jail should be enough. Then memories of his holdup hit him. He ran fingers over the knot on his face and knew the scar was still visible.

One of those men over there put a bullet in my leg, put this mark on my cheek. Left Missus Villanueva a widow.

Those men right there had changed more lives than he could count. What was he thinking? They didn't deserve jail time. Not for what they'd done. But still, he wouldn't kill them if he could help it.

James hoped it wouldn't come to that. He had the element of surprise on his side and maybe he could take these men without anyone getting hurt. Maybe.

Or maybe he should go back to town for the deputy. And a posse.

Unconscious, Dunn sagged against the tree while the outlaws stood talking. Just talking like they weren't in a hurry. Like they were planning a Sunday picnic. James considered shooting them from where he was hiding. With his aim, he could hit one for sure, possibly two. They were within easy range.

A grin snaked up one side of his face as he pulled his gun. He wouldn't shoot to kill, just to stop them. The smile dropped to a frown.

I might get two, but there's two more. Not good odds.

He'd have to ride back to town and get help. Might be too late. The outlaws would be long gone, but at least he could get help for Dunn. He inched toward his horse, but he stopped at Fallon's words.

"By this time next Tuesday, boys, we'll all be rich. Richer than we ever imagined." One foot in the stirrup, Fallon swung up into the saddle.

Billy settled in his saddle. "An' drinkin' ourselves a time down in May-he-co."

"Aiyyeee!" Shelton, one arm in a sling, waved his hat with the other hand. "Tequila and señoritas. Here we come!"

Rudy leaned over his horse and gazed down at Dunn. "Sure I can't kill 'im, Fallon? I'll be quick about it." He fingered the gun on his hip, then pulled it part way out of the leather holster.

"You heard me the first time. Besides, we might need him again. Come in useful." Fallon's shoulders bounced with the chuckle. He spit toward Dunn. "Adios, *partner.*" He gigged his horse south.

After James had waited long enough to be sure they wouldn't return, he pushed through brush and around trees to Dunn, then poured canteen water over the unconscious man's head. The lawman sputtered and moaned, struggling against the bindings.

James waited until Dunn opened his eyes, waited for him to be aware of his surroundings before cutting the ropes. He wanted to make sure Dunn would appreciate the rescue.

Ropes cut, James pulled the sheriff to his feet, then handed him the canteen. "How're you feeling?"

Dunn glared at James. "You. What're *you* doin' here?"

"Is that all the thanks I get for saving your life?" James asked.

112

"I followed you. And I know all about you and those robbers, how you've been protecting them and helping yourself to some of the money." James couldn't hide his contempt as he spit the words. "How much you get?"

"Don't know what you're talking about."

"Save it, Dunn. I could turn you over to your own deputy. He'll be glad to see you behind bars. Behind bars for a long time... or even hang. Hell, I should cart you all the way back to Mesilla, to the territory sheriff."

"You ain't got the—"

"I should, but no, I'm not gonna do that." James cocked his head. Was he sure this was the right thing to do? Other than going back to town, it was the only plan he had. "You and me...we're gonna be partners." He chuckled at the shocked, confused look on Dunn's face.

"Partners? I don't have a partner in this."

"You did. But they left you. Right here to die. So, I'm picking up what they left behind. You. Only, instead of robbing freight wagons, we're gonna rob those outlaws."

"What?" Dunn ran a hand across his mouth and fingered his swelling lip.

"Way I got it figured," James said, "I want my watch back, they need to be arrested for murder, and you're gonna help me do it. And this time, *Sheriff*, we're gonna do it right—my way."

Dunn glanced around the wooded hillside, as if expecting Fallon and the boys to appear. "I ain't gonna help you."

"Yeah, you are. Your deputy knows I'm here. I even told those freighters. They're all expecting me to come riding back—right about now—safe and sound. Now, where *exactly* are those robbers going?"

Dunn picked up his hat, brushed the dirt and leaves off, and fitted it onto his head. "I ain't gonna be your partner, but I'll tell you where they're planning to go. Canoa, maybe Tubac. Big silver strike not too long ago down farther south. Fallon and the others plan to hit the stages and freighters in that area."

"They said something about Mexico." James stepped nose to nose with Dunn. "What'd you know about that?"

"Good place to hole up for a while. They'll more'n likely lay low for a couple months down there. Especially with a big silver haul."

James considered. Sunlight filtered through the tops of the towering pines. Mountain jays squabbled over something high in one of those trees. James nodded at Dunn. "Hmm. Canoa, Tubac. I know the area from a map."

"Let's say I do help you." Dunn rubbed a lump puffing up over one eye. "What then?"

"We're gonna let them hit that stage, but then we're gonna rob the robbers. I'll get my watch and you'll arrest those bandits. All nice and legal like. Hell, might even make a name for yourself. At least be a hero."

"Wouldn't it be easier and quicker just to jump them near here? Save us a trip."

James shook his head. "There's just two of us, four of them. I don't like the odds. The way I figure it, the passengers and drivers will help. They usually do. Make it a little more even. Most of those passengers carry guns anyway." He stepped closer to his horse. "And who's gonna be expecting robbers to get robbed?"

Dunn whipped his gun out of its holster and shoved it in James' chest. "That ain't the way it's goin' down. I won't partner with you and I don't owe you nothin'. You ain't goin' nowhere."

"Can't kill me, Dunn." James' heart pounded, his mouth desert dry. "You shoot me, your deputy'll know you did it."

The pressure of the barrel against his chest kept his breathing shallow.

"Know what I think?" Dunn licked his lips. "I think you didn't tell nobody where you went. 'Cause nobody cares 'bout a nothin' kid cryin' over his stolen watch."

Arms out at his side, James itched for his gun. If he moved he'd be a dead man. No doubt. If he didn't go for his gun, he'd be a dead man. Either way, he was in trouble.

"Reach for it, boy," Dunn said. "What's wrong? Miss your big brother who ain't here to protect you? Do your fightin' for you? Or are you waitin' for your mama to come do it?" He drew the hammer back.

Sky, clouds, and trees swirled around James. Hands tingling, his entire body caught fire. In one quick motion, he knocked the gun out of Dunn's hand. It landed three feet away.

A blow to his left cheek staggered James back. He crashed against a tree and slid to the ground. White dots dancing in front

114

of him clouded his vision. What was clear, however, was Dunn scrambling for his gun.

Dunn knelt, grabbed his weapon, and pointed it at James' heart. James rolled to his right, slipped his gun from its holster, thumbed back the hammer and fired.

Twice.

Dunn clutched his chest, then slumped to the ground. Shaking, breath rattling, blood spurting between quivering fingers, he stared at James. He gasped a final breath before his face slammed into the ground.

CHAPTER SIXTEEN

Trace pulled the stagecoach to a smooth stop in front of the Corn Exchange Hotel on the southeast side of Mesilla's plaza. Men, women, and children crowded around waving to the arriving passengers. Smiling faces, some with tears, looked up at him and then into the coach. Warm handshakes, rib-crunching bear hugs, and tearful reunions swarmed around him as the passengers dislodged themselves and fell into loving arms.

Trace looked at all the faces, but James wasn't there waiting at the hotel door. Maybe he'd be on the next block over, at the Butterfield headquarters. Maybe talking to Bill Walters who'd be giving James his old job back. Maybe. Hopefully.

Trace's replacement shotgun guard, who was busy untying luggage and tossing it down to the people, was not much of a talker, certainly not as interesting as James. But, Trace had to admit he didn't cause problems, either. Guess he'd do until James was back. As Trace busied himself with luggage and tickets, uneasiness nagged at him. He pushed it aside while he smiled at children running their hands across the bright red side of the stagecoach. A closer inspection of the crowd—still no sign of his brother.

Trace's shoulders slumped. Everyone else was here, it seemed. Why wasn't James? He couldn't think of a good reason. Unless he wasn't back yet. Maybe James never returned. No, he couldn't bring himself to think any more of those thoughts. Got to be a logical explanation.

Once all the passengers and luggage were deposited, Trace guided the team over to the office two blocks away. He reined to a stop and scanned the street. Again, no James.

Once he'd checked in with Butterfield, he walked the three blocks to the doctor's office. A deep breath, shoulders straight, Trace stepped inside.

"Welcome back," Doctor Logan said. His grin faded to concern when Trace pumped his hand before taking a seat.

"Thanks, doc. Been a long, dusty trip." Trace removed his hat, ran his fingers through his dark brown hair.

"How's your brother? Didn't get in any more trouble, did he?"

Trace leaned forward. "I was hoping you'd tell me. Haven't seen him since, well, since he was here with you."

"You mean he wasn't with you?"

Trace shook his head.

Doctor Logan cocked his head. "No, haven't seen him since he left here. Been 'bout six weeks now, I'd say."

Trace studied his clenched hands. He envisioned his little brother on the ground by the stage, again heard the crack of those ribs as the holdup man kicked him—like he was kicking a flea-bitten cur. He saw James' bruised face smiling as they said a quick goodbye right here in the doctor's office. That might be his last image he'd ever have of his brother. He couldn't breathe.

The doctor fished around in the middle desk drawer while Trace hung his head, trying to decide his next step. The doctor brought out a crumpled piece of paper.

"Ah ha, I was right." He waved the paper at Trace, then smoothed it on top of his desk. "Thought I still had it."

"What is it?"

"A note from your brother."

Trace gripped the paper. He read the scrawling handwriting and then took note of the date. A second reading, then he looked up at the doctor.

"When'd you get this?"

"Let's see." Doctor Logan scratched his head and studied the ceiling. "Freighters brought it in 'bout three days after you left here last time."

"And you haven't seen James since I first brought him in?"

"Nope. Just like I told you." The doctor turned the note around and read it again. "You goin' up to Santa Rita to get him?"

"Looks like I'm gonna have to." Trace let out a long sigh. "I was up there just about when he wrote this. He should've been back by now. Said he'd meet me here."

"You going today?" Doctor Logan asked. "It's gettin' dark."

Trace hadn't thought that far ahead. He hadn't planned on having to go get his brother.

"I'll wait 'til tomorrow. Fortunately, I got close to a week off." More plans shattered. "Guess I need to get some supplies before heading out."

The doctor stood and walked around his desk to Trace. "He'll turn up shortly, son. You know little brothers. Got a mind all their own. Probably bump into him along the road." He patted Trace's shoulder. "He's fine. Don't worry."

Trace eased to his feet, numb all over. "Yeah. Sure."

He offered a limp hand, then walked through the door. A blast of late winter air did nothing to warm him. Something was wrong. He just knew it.

As he stood on the boardwalk, he pulled his coat around his shivering body and looked at the men and women stopping to visit or hurrying about their errands. He stepped into the plaza.

I'm alone. Very alone. All these people around me and I'm the loneliest person in New Mexico Territory.

* * *

Trace had a good sturdy meal, a bath, a shave and a haircut. He was always amazed how much dirt he picked up on the road. There surely couldn't be any more dirt left between Tucson and Mesilla. It had clung to his body like bees on molasses. Any other time, he would've grinned at his new image in the mirror when the barber brushed talc as the finishing touches on the restoration. Trace looked tired, but good. A solid night's sleep should take care of the dark circles under his eyes. Then he'd be rested and ready to go get James.

Trace made his way over to the closest saloon, always the best place to hear the latest news and town gossip. Maybe he'd hear something about James. He pushed the swinging doors wide open, and he stepped into the lantern-lit barroom. Smoke hung from the ceiling like gray icicles. Trace coughed. His eyes watered.

The bartender greeted him like a long, lost friend. Trace grinned back at the man's friendliness and hoped it was a good sign. Maybe his luck was about to change. He stood at the scratched, wooden bar and ordered a beer.

Glass in hand, he leaned against the bar and surveyed the boisterous people in the tiny saloon. Like so many other establishments in the West, coal oil lanterns lighted this one. Their flames cast golden hues over the dozen-plus men. The bar itself was a couple of whiskey barrels with a plank across it. Sturdy enough.

Conversations ran in two languages, Spanish being more prevalent than English. Trace strained to understand. He'd have to learn more Spanish after he found his brother. He took a chair near the front of the saloon, hoping to strike up a conversation with anyone who'd sit with him. Preferably, the conversation would be in English.

The evening wore down as Trace drank his second beer. He'd spoken with a few men who'd come in, but no one seemed to know anything about James. Word was many people were heading over toward Tubac, a couple hundred miles west and fifty or so south of Tucson. Someone struck it rich over there, they'd said, and now the area was crawling with miners hoping to find that elusive silver.

Trace wagged his head at the inane idea of scratching in the dirt, spending hours of back-breaking work. Most people showed nothing for all their hard efforts. So few men made any money, he found it difficult to imagine people leaving their families, friends, and sanity to go dig dirt. Craziness. Men do almost anything for money. Even kill.

Trace frowned at a new thought. Maybe his headstrong little brother would be heading over toward Tubac, trying to scratch out some raw silver. Hardly likely. James was smarter than that. Their folks had taught them that good, honest, hard work was the only true way to make a living. Besides, James still wanted to ride shotgun with him for Butterfield—unless things had changed.

A conversation near Trace piqued his interest. He leaned toward the table next to him.

"Yeah, Clarence, I know. Hard to believe, too. That sheriff. Well, he was a righteous man."

"Got shot, you say?" The second man held his beer mid-air.

Trace turned his chair around and scooted in closer.

"Plugged four times, I heard." The first man looked at each face, then shook his head. "Yep. Once through the heart and the other three through the head. A professional gunman they say huntin' him." He dropped his voice a notch. "The shooter was that good."

Whispers raced around the table, blood and curiosity now throbbing. The rest of the table spoke to each other, lending support and offering other "facts" of the killing.

119

He couldn't help himself. Trace had to know.

"Where'd this happen?" he asked.

"Where you been, friend?" Beer sloshed over the side as the man swung the glass toward Trace's chest.

"Just got into town. I drive the stage." Trace's smile was rewarded with a handshake.

He pulled his chair closer, introduced himself, although it wasn't necessary. No one cared who he was. They were much more interested in this sheriff and the man who'd shot him.

"Happened up around Pinos Altos, I heard. Guess it's that sheriff up there."

"Best sheriff this territory's ever seen," another man said. "Why, he captured outlaws that the U.S. Marshals only dreamed of gettin'."

"Hell, he's a downright legend."

"*Was* a legend."

"Real shame."

The general muttering of agreement drowned out any other noise in the room. More and more people gathered around his table, more people interested in this killing. Accusations, speculations, tales ran rampant.

Trace raised his voice over the din. "Who did it?"

Like plugging up a dam, all talking stopped, the silence—a vacuum. Trace glanced from face to face.

Someone spit next to Trace's boot. Another man leaned over the table, his chest scraping against the wood.

"Already told you, stranger. A professional from the East." The man's answer was edged with sarcasm.

"Then it wasn't anybody local?" Trace asked.

Why did he feel relief?

"Couldn't have been." The man brought himself up straight, glanced around the other faces. "Nobody'd ever think of killing such a great lawman."

"Tell you what, though." Another man hoisted his beer mug. "They'll string up whoever killed him. Never get a trial."

A range cowboy, a three-day stubble shadowing his face, clinked glasses with the first man. "Hell, won't last a day once he's found." He sipped, then spoke over a foamy mustache. "Hell, I'll see to it myself."

Cheers and threats filled the saloon. Trace finished his beer. He was tired. No, not tired. Exhausted. James had him more worried than he cared to admit. And now with some sheriff being killed, it all added up to frayed nerves. He hoped nothing else would come up tonight. A night's sleep should help. *If* he could sleep.

Trace nodded to the men at his table, but none took notice of his standing. As he threaded his way toward the door, another conversation caught his interest. A man, looked to be a merchant of some kind, shook his head. He met Trace's gaze.

"Yeah. What a shame," he said. "A pure tragedy. I knew him."

"Who?" Trace just couldn't let it rest.

"Sheriff Malcolm Dunn. The lawman what done got murdered. Senselessly murdered."

The bartender leaned across the bar, rag in hand. "Don't know what the territory's gonna do without Sheriff Dunn." He wiped a tiny spot of liquid on the bar. "As honest as they come."

"Well, if he was such a terrific fella," Trace said, "then why would a gunman from the East come all this way to kill him? What'd he do that he deserved to die for?"

The bartender jumped in before anyone else could explain. "Word is that more'n likely he was protecting a citizen, doing his duty when he was gunned down in the prime of life. He was always tryin' to protect the weak."

The conversation continued for a few more minutes, expounding on the qualities of the fallen sheriff. By the time Trace elbowed his way into the street, Dunn had been anointed a saint and the killer had been declared Lucifer himself. Trace knew if and when the accused man was found, a lynch mob would have trouble finding enough pieces of him to hang. People were so worked up over this killing that the assassin had better be in another country by now.

Since James had let the room at the boarding house go, Trace treated himself to a room at the Corn Exchange Hotel. Sometimes he slept at Butterfield's stage house where a room was set aside for the drivers, but it was tiny, cramped, and uncomfortable. Tonight he needed room to stretch out, relax and think this through.

While he yanked off his boots and rubbed his feet, he thought about the conversations in the saloon. Most interesting. He lay back. The cotton mattress had a couple of lumps, but with a certain amount of squirming he found parts that were comfortable. He closed his eyes.

121

I gotta find you. I don't care how long it takes.

He wasn't ashamed to admit he honestly missed his brother. Trace shuddered at a sudden burst of cold wind. He got up and latched the window.

Something in the air bothered him, but still he scolded himself for being on edge. Why would he think James was in trouble? True, he wasn't where he said he'd be, but James didn't always have the same sense of time that Trace did.

As Trace climbed back into bed and pulled up the quilt, he remembered all the times when James had been distracted, especially on new adventures. One time his little brother, six at the time, wandered away from home to follow quail tracks for hours, hoping to catch the birds to keep as pets. Such a look of relief then anger on pa's face when they found James. His kid brother had the same narrow focus now when it came to retrieving his watch.

That damned watch. Must be why he'd been in Santa Rita and why he wasn't back yet. Guilt punched Trace in the stomach as he thought of the holdup, the robbers. He knew James loved his watch, even cherished it, but he hadn't realized what he'd do to get it back.

Trace decided that at first light he'd stop by Mesilla's sheriff and have a talk. Maybe he'd know something.

CHAPTER SEVENTEEN

After a hearty breakfast of *huevos rancheros* and *papitas*, Trace stepped into the sheriff's office on the southeast corner of the plaza. The deputy greeted him at the door.

"Sheriff's out guzzlin' down a pot of coffee. Probably polishin' off pork chops and flapjacks, too." The lawman pointed to a chair. "Oughta be back momentarily. Big day today."

Trace sat in the offered seat. "How's that?"

"Maybe you ain't heard. Big killin' up in Pinos Altos. We're gonna go haul back that Wicked Willie." The deputy poured a cup of black coffee and handed it to Trace. "I'm Thomas Littleton." A sip from his own cup brought a light cough.

"Trace Colton. Thanks." He blew on his cup.

The deputy's shirt stretched tight across his belly. Judging by the tufts of gray hair jutting out from his temples, Trace figured Littleton at least fifteen, twenty years older.

"So, they found him?" Trace asked.

"'Course they did. Otherwise we'd be goin' up chasin' nothin' but our tails!" Littleton's eyes lit up, a hint of mischief behind them. "Story goes, that dumb-headed killer brought the dead sheriff in himself." The deputy shook his head. "Hard to figure people."

"Why's that?" Trace blew on the steaming coffee.

"Well, from what I understand, the man who brought Dunn in says it was self-defense."

The deputy perched on the corner of his desk, then leaned over to Trace and spoke slowly, as if explaining to a child. "Now we all know it wasn't like that."

"Why?"

"'Cause Sheriff Dunn was the fastest gun around. He'd never let anyone get the drop on him." The deputy leaned back and shook his head. "Not no way, no how."

Trace used his cup to point north. "*Somebody* did."

The deputy scowled. "Struck from behind. Shot in the back, I heard."

Just as Trace was about to relate the gossip from the saloon, a man sporting a shiny sheriff's badge stepped in. Another man followed on his heels. He shut the door.

The deputy slid off the desk, pointed at Trace. "This fella's waitin' for you, sheriff."

"Trace Colton, sir." Trace stood and stuck out his empty hand. "Good to see you again, Sheriff Fuente."

Alberto Fuente's dark eyebrows merged as he eyed Trace. A nod and the brows parted. "I remember you. Stage driver that got held up couple months ago."

"Yes, sir."

"This's the mayor, Gordon Ignacio." Fuente pointed to the chair Trace had been sitting in. "Sit down, son." He turned to the mayor. "Never did find those outlaws." Back to Trace. "What can I do for you?"

The four men repositioned chairs and placed them around the sheriff's desk. Fuente sat behind it. Trace looked into his coffee cup as if the grounds would organize his thoughts.

"My brother's missing." The words choked him. He'd never thought of James in those terms, but now he had to admit it was true.

Trace told the story, leaving out nothing. When he finished, Sheriff Fuente eyed his deputy. "You hear anything, Littleton? See any posters?"

A shake of his head.

"Mayor? You heard anything?"

A shake of his head.

Fuente sat back and fiddled with his empty tin cup. His dark eyes fell on Trace's face. "You say your brother's the same shotgun guard what got shot in that hold up?"

"Yes, sir." Trace wondered where the sheriff was going with this. Hadn't he already told him?

"Too bad me or the deputy never got over to visit with him. If we had, one of us would've known what he looks like." Fuente shrugged. "Sorry, Mister Colton. Looks like we can't be of much help. Nothing's come through about anybody that sounds like your brother. But we'll keep our ears and eyes open."

Trace slumped back against the wooden chair, the coffee now

unappealing. He set the tin cup on the desk and pushed to his feet. He'd have to ride out within minutes if he expected to get anywhere.

The mayor shifted his coffee cup to his other hand and cleared his throat. "You say you're a stagecoach driver?"

Trace nodded. "Yes, sir. For Butterfield. Over a year now. I was one of the first on the line."

Mayor Ignacio turned to the sheriff. "How about him?" He pointed his coffee cup toward Trace.

Sheriff Fuente's eyes roamed up and down Trace's body. His eyebrows dipped with a frown, then raised when the frown changed to a smile. He leaned back in his chair and pressed his fingers together into a steeple, and then he gazed over the pyramid at Trace.

Unsure about the silence, Trace nevertheless decided to leave. He headed for the door.

"Just a minute, Mister Colton." The sheriff rose to his feet. "We've got a problem maybe you can help us with."

Trace glanced from face to face, the problem hidden on each one. Although he was in a hurry, his curiosity sparked. "Sir?"

"Well, we gotta go up to Pinos Altos today, retrieve the prisoner. You know, the desperado who killed Sheriff Dunn? Gotta bring him back here for trial." Fuente pointed north, then back behind him, toward an open door which revealed an iron cell door standing open.

Mayor Ignacio stood also.

"We need a driver for the jail wagon, Mister Colton. Our regular driver's too sick to go and no one else's willing to drive."

"Sorry." Trace edged toward the door. He had to find James. "Can't your deputy here do it?"

All three men shook their heads—the deputy's faster than the other two.

Ignacio wedged himself between Trace and the door. "Seeing how it's such short notice, we're willing to pay you a month's salary if you'll do it."

Trace looked from the mayor to the sheriff to the deputy and then back again. Was this for real? Or some sort of joke? A month's pay? To drive a wagon?

Sheriff Fuente lay a hand on Trace's shoulder. "We really need someone today. You won't have to do anything but drive. That's it.

We'll take care of guarding the prisoner. Won't be any danger to your person, Mister Colton." His coffee-laced breath hit Trace's face. "Up there and back. Simple."

"And who knows?" The mayor smiled a practiced politician's smile. "You might even run into your brother along the way. Wouldn't that be something?"

Trace knew he needed to spend time finding James, but that much money for six days' work was hard to resist. "I'm not sure. I gotta—"

"Two months' salary." Ignacio's smile reached ear to ear. "And not a penny more." He held out a hand. "You drive a hard bargain."

Must be some prisoner.

Trace returned the mayor's smile. James' note had been sent from that area. If he had enough time, Trace might even get a chance to ask around. Hell, since he was doing the mayor and sheriff such a favor, he'd *make* time to ask around. Somebody up there had to know something.

"All right, sheriff," Trace said. "I'll drive for you. But, I gotta be back by Tuesday when my next run to Tucson begins."

Sheriff Fuente pumped Trace's hand. "You won't regret this, Mister Colton."

"Call me Trace, since we're going to be working together." A glance at each face showed huge relief.

Maybe there's something they're not telling me.

"Good to have you on board, Trace." Sheriff Fuente opened the door. "Be back here in an hour and we'll take off. If all goes well, and I know it will, we'll be home by Monday."

Trace checked out of the Corn Exchange Hotel, and he informed the hotel clerk where he was going, just in case James came by. On his way over to the sheriff's, he stopped by the doctor's office.

"Just wanted to let you know I'm heading up to Pinos Altos, doc."

"You think that's where he's at?" Doctor Logan coiled a stethoscope into a black circle and shoved it into a leather bag.

"Not sure. But remember hearing about the sheriff up there getting killed?"

The doctor nodded.

"Well, the killer turned himself in."

"You don't say."

"Yeah." Trace found himself more excited about this adventure than he'd thought. "And our sheriff wants me to drive the jail wagon up to Pinos Altos. Go collect that outlaw, bring him here for trial."

Logan turned to Trace. "You just be damn careful. I'd hate to have to sew you up, too. One Colton's enough."

"I plan to be extra careful. You can bet on that." Trace grinned at the doctor. "We're supposed to be back some time Monday." He extended a hand.

"And I'll tell your brother to wait for you. If I see him." Doctor Logan gripped Trace's hand and shook it. "I'll tie him to a chair if I have to."

Trace nodded, then headed for the door. A hand on his shoulder stopped him. Doc's intense eyes met his gaze. "God speed, son."

Another nod, then Trace stepped into the cool air. He marched across the plaza and into the sheriff's office, where he shook hands with two other men sporting badges. They introduced themselves as Roberto Reyes and Sam Kidd. Both said they were temporary deputies, hired on just for this little outing. Three deputies and a sheriff was a bit of overkill, Trace mused, but all he had to do was drive.

Deputy Littleton shoved powder flasks and pouches of lead bullets into a black bag. He looked over at the sheriff. "Think it'll really go smooth?"

"Don't know why not. I hear the prisoner's pretty tame. But anybody who'd back shoot a man can't be trusted." Fuente spun the cylinder in his black powder revolver. "We'll take extra chains and cuffs, just in case."

Now that's overkill.

Trace lent a hand where he could—holding bags open, folding a blanket, filling canteens. Last-minute preparations now centered outside, around the jail wagon. Trace surveyed this portable prison as he circled it. Barred windows, maybe twelve by twelve inches on both sides. Even smaller window in the back door. Barred. On tip-toes, he managed a peek inside. Nothing unusual. He knocked on the side. Hard wood, probably oak, painted black. His eyes riveted on the lock on the back door. The clasp it pierced had to be inch-thick iron. The lock—big, imposing. Just like the jail wagon. Correction. The black jail *box*. That's how he now thought of it. The jail box.

Trace checked the team's harnesses again. Good leather, no cracks or wear. He packed a couple of bedrolls behind him in the wagon's boot along with food supplies and extra water.

Mayor Ignacio inspected each activity with the pomp of a true politician. Trace chuckled at the look of this self-important man. His chest thrust out as he strutted from one end of the wagon to the other. His words of encouragement were edged with civic duty as he directed each and every man—with great enthusiasm.

Trace watched the show.

Hell, this mayor will declare himself king if he brings the killer to trial.

Sheriff Fuente shook hands with Ignacio. "All set, mayor."

"Got enough deputies?" The mayor's face revealed true concern.

"Yeah. I'm taking two more men besides Deputy Littleton here. We'll be fine." The sheriff turned to his second-in-command. "Reminds me, Tom. Make sure the other two deputies have extra powder, shot and caps, just in case. Don't want to leave nothing to chance."

"Already done, sheriff."

* * *

As Trace guided the mule team north out of Mesilla then west around Picacho Peak, his chest tightened when he spied the pass. What he really wanted to do was close his eyes until this area was well behind them. But, open they stayed. He watched those outlaws hold up his stage again—the memory playing over and over. With teeth gritted, he urged the animals forward, as fast as he dare let them.

After a full day of traveling, they made camp along the wide Mimbres River. This late in winter, the river was full with runoff from the snows. And it had been a good year for wet weather. Plenty of rain and snow, especially this far north of Mesilla.

Trace studied the map in the fire's glow. Looked like the road crossed the river three times. The fordings would be tough. Because of such high water, the crossings could prove difficult, if not impossible. Trace eyed the mules. If the team didn't spook and things went right, they'd all have a good chance of getting through. He'd done it many times on his Tucson run, but still, he didn't cherish the idea of swift water sweeping the wagon side to side, rocking like it would topple over. No, he'd been in swift water before and wanted no part of it.

Trace squatted by the sheriff and the other men lounging around the campfire. "Just thought I'd let you know, sheriff. Stock's strong and healthy, but tomorrow we ford the river in a couple of tough spots. May need you three to help guide the team."

"No problem." Fuente handed a cup of coffee to Trace. "We're ready for whatever comes our way."

CHAPTER EIGHTEEN

Trace's concerns were overrated the next day. The strong mule team plowed through the Mimbres River as if crossing a trickle. Even though the water hit the top of the wagon wheels, the mules pulled through without so much as a grunt. Trace relaxed after the third fording. From here on, it would be an easy ride.

The clouds were thickening over the Black Range, though. If the rains came, as Trace figured they would, tomorrow the river would spill over its banks. He pushed that thought to one side. Nothing he could do about it now. He'd worry about it tomorrow.

They rode into Pinos Altos mid-afternoon. It was one of the prettiest little villages he'd ever seen—trees surrounded the bright white tents dotting the hills. The wind whistling through sixty-foot pines captured a pre-spring freshness.

The sweet scent calmed nerves he didn't realize were tense. A pair of women who were chatting on the boardwalk stopped to stare at the procession. Trace touched his hat brim at the ladies and mumbled a greeting. One of them blushed while the other smiled and nodded.

The jail proved easy to find. Trace spotted the rock building with barred windows before Fuente pointed. With the finesse of an artist, Trace pulled the team to a stop in front of the jail, and then set the brake.

"And now, sheriff?" Trace pulled off both leather gloves.

"We go get him." Sheriff Fuente jumped down, then opened the back of the wagon to release the three deputies inside. They scrambled out and glanced around, making a show of cocking their shotguns.

Trace wagged his head.

Big-city, tough-man bravado.

Who did they think they were impressing? More than likely each other. He climbed down from the wagon. His curiosity, he hated to admit, was piqued and he wanted to see what this killer looked like. He also looked forward to hearing this deputy's account of this whole affair. He wanted the truth.

While Fuente and the deputies busied themselves loading weapons and unlocking handcuffs, Trace stepped to the jail door. He grasped the handle. It grew warm in his hand. Before he could turn it, the door swung open. The deputy of Pinos Altos, that badge glinting in the sun, stepped out. Red hair streaked with gray stuck out from under his hat and brushed his shoulders.

"Howdy. Ben Wickens. Deputy." He extended a hand. "Been waiting for you."

"Trace. Driver. Nice to meet you." They shook hands. "Finally here."

Wickens cocked his head toward the jail. A shotgun rested on his shoulder. "Got that prisoner ready for you."

"Thanks. I'll just go take a look."

Fuente grabbed Trace's arm. "We'll take care of this. You're hired to drive." He nodded to Roberto and Sam. "See to the prisoner."

Although he was a bit disappointed, Trace shrugged it off. He'd have plenty of time to see this killer. Might even get his side of the story. He turned to Fuente.

"I just remembered, sheriff. I need to go down to the livery, get some extra tack in case one of those harnesses breaks in high water." Trace stepped around the sheriff and Deputy Wickens. "Be back soon as I can."

"Make it quick," Fuente said. "That prisoner's a bad one, and the sooner we get going, the sooner he'll stand trial."

Trace studied the sheriff's face. Fuente wanted this prisoner and he wanted him bad. Anything to bring him in. Was it for the glory? The fame? Maybe a promotion. Whatever it was, Trace would watch. He wouldn't let anyone hurt the prisoner until he was found guilty in a court of law. His pa had taught him that, and it was a rule he believed in.

Trace nodded once, and then he headed down toward the livery stable at the end of town. This little trek to Pinos Altos was proceeding just as planned. Far easier than he'd expected. What he hadn't expected, however, was how he felt about this little mining camp. He liked it. A lot. Somehow it felt like home. Almost seemed as if James was right around the corner. Trace reminded himself that his little brother was probably a hundred miles from here, heading back to Mesilla right now.

The livery stable had everything Trace needed. However, the owner, while fast at talking, was slow at working. He took his time locating harnesses and a few extra rawhide lacings. While he dug through piles of straps, bits, headstalls, and harnesses, the owner related his version of the killing. Trace only half-listened, having heard most of it before in various translations. Nothing new. When the man took a breath, Trace changed the subject.

"Since you've been around here for a spell," Trace said, "I was wondering if you've seen a man, a stranger, who looks a lot like me. Younger, an inch taller, might be limping. Probably came through a couple weeks ago."

The man turned his dark blue eyes on Trace. His gaze trailed up and down his body. "Hum." He straightened up, leather strap in his callused hand. "Young fella, you say?"

"Yes, sir. Nineteen."

"What kind of horse he ride?"

"I don't know." Something lumped in Trace's throat.

The owner used his free hand to scratch his chest. "Let's see. I heard of a fella needed tending by Missus Stinson. Kind of young they said."

"You get a name?"

"Nah. And he's gone now. Just up and disappeared." The man held out the straps. "That'll be three dollars."

Half an hour had passed by the time Trace headed back to his wagon. The extra tack and gear he lugged were not particularly heavy, just bulky and awkward. Maybe if Fuente wasn't quite ready to go, Trace would have time to find this Mrs. Stinson and see what she knew. It was a long shot at best. The several blocks to the jail seemed to stretch for miles.

Trace turned the corner onto Main Street, then froze. More than forty people crowded around his wagon. Some peered through the small barred windows, while others shouted insults. A few raised their guns overhead, yelling. Trace picked up his pace.

As he slung the tack over the hitching rail, Trace caught Deputy Wickens's eye. He shoved his way through the throng.

"What's going on?" Trace shouted to be heard.

"Killer's in the wagon! People just want to take one last look before he's strung up!"

"Any problems getting him in?" Trace focused on the jail wagon and wondered how it felt to be confined in there.

"No. But he sure didn't want to go." Deputy Wickens kept his eyes on the crowd. "Strong fella. Said he hated being locked up, but we had to pry his fingers loose from the cell bars. Kept screaming he was innocent. Self-defense. The usual. Got so bad, one of those other deputies cold cocked him. That ol' boy went down slow—melting like a snowman in springtime. Hell, he's still out. Made it a lot easier getting him in your wagon, though."

Trace stepped closer to the lawman. "Tell me honestly. Is he dangerous?"

Wickens took a deep breath, removed his hat, then mopped his forehead with a bandana. He thumped Trace's chest with his hat brim.

"Just between you and me, he's about as dangerous as a jack rabbit." Wickens leaned into Trace's ear. "Just between you and me, I think he's a real nice fella. Just in the wrong place at the wrong time."

Wrong place. Wrong time. Trace knew all about that. Now was as good a time as any to ask about James. "Deputy, you seen—"

"Better get going, Trace." Sheriff Fuente fought his way through the people. He nodded to Deputy Wickens. "Crowd's gettin' riled up. Best we go now. Right now."

Trace knew he only had seconds to ask about his brother. But with this crowd turning blood-thirsty, Wickens had to concentrate on crowd control. Trace moved in as close to the deputy as he could.

"My little brother's supposed to be up around this way. You seen a fella kinda looks like me, might be limping? Young."

Wickens cocked his head, his eyebrows knitting. "Hum..."

Before Wickens could explain, four men crashed into him, knocking him sideways into Trace. Deputy Wickens pulled out his gun. "All right, you men! Move back! This ain't no lynching party!"

"Gotta go *now*." Fuente said. He shoved Trace away from the deputy.

Trace found himself tugged through the ever-increasing throng. With the sheriff's help, he hoisted the harness and tack to the wagon top, then secured it with rope. Trace clambered onto the wagon seat and picked up the reins. He tried to shout at Deputy Wickens above the din.

133

"My little brother! You seen him?"

The deputy pointed to his ear. "What?"

Jeers, shouts, threats enveloped Trace. Angry men rocked the wagon side to side. The crowd was turning into an out-of-control horde. He'd just have to come back.

One man whipped out a gun. He fired into the sky. "Killer! Hanging's too good for 'im!"

Deputy Wickens rushed the man and wrestled the gun out of his hand. He waved at Trace and Sheriff Fuente.

"Go now!" Wickens yelled. "I can't hold 'em much longer! Go!"

Another man picked up a rock and heaved it at the wagon. It slammed against the side, splintering the wood. Someone hurled a larger rock, which sailed through the wagon window.

Trace snapped the reins over the mule team. "Step up, mules!"

Men and boys ran with the wagon as it picked up speed.

"String 'im up now!"

A rock whizzed past Trace's shoulder.

"Killer!"

"You'll never see the rope! We'll take you apart piece by piece first!"

"Murderer!"

Gunshots cracked the air. A bullet dug into the wagon. Trace whipped the mules into a gallop.

The crowd rushed through the streets of Pinos Altos, hurling insults and threats until Trace's ears rang. Little by little, the people fell back, until the wagon was alone. Quiet once more.

* * *

His nerves still a bit on edge, Trace kept the mules at a steady gallop. He wanted more distance between them and that town. Within minutes, the sun would touch the horizon. The earth would turn pink, gray, then dark. Usually, Trace enjoyed the evening, but not today. The end of daylight meant a long night of sleeping on the ground and hoping that prisoner didn't escape. Or worse.

The wagon approached the first Mimbres River crossing. The water lapped higher on the banks than it had the day before. And the current raged much faster than yesterday. It must've rained somewhere. A knot tightened Trace's stomach at the thought of trying to make it across this late in the day.

He pulled the team to a stop at river's edge. Fuente glared at the water, then at Trace.

"Can I help?" Fuente asked.

"Water's running awful fast and deep." Trace pointed northeast. "That rain up in the Black Range isn't helping things." He shrugged and studied the river. Way too swift.

"I'll go check it out." Fuente jumped down from the high seat, walked to the water, then marched back to the wagon. He peered inside. "How's the prisoner, Sam?"

"Awake. Says he's got a bad headache, though." Sam snorted. "Oughta be grateful just to be living."

"Make sure he stays that way." Fuente stood back.

Trace stretched around on the hard wagon seat and looked down. No chance to see inside.

"Sheriff? They need water back there?" Trace asked.

Fuente fingered the gun in his holster. "You give him some water, Sam?"

"Won't need water where he's going," Sam said.

Sheriff Fuente exploded. "Get that man water right now! He may be a killer, but he's not gonna die in my wagon. I'll let the judge and jury decide how and when he dies."

"Yes, sir."

Fuente's chest rose and fell until he calmed enough to speak without yelling. "Tom, check the cuffs and shackles. Make sure they're nice and tight." Fuente looked around at the darkening sky while waiting for confirmation.

"Tight like a Scotsman with a nickel, sheriff."

"Good. Got a rough ride ahead of us, then we'll make camp in about an hour. Tom Littleton, you and Sam come on out and help with this crossing." The sheriff walked around to Trace, and then he threw his shoulders back. "Let's go."

Trace frowned at the sheriff. "I think we'd be wise to wait until tomorrow. Water's awful fast."

Deputies Tom and Sam took their places on either side of the team. Fuente waited by Trace. "Let's go," Fuente said. "It's fine. Water won't get lower the longer we stand here."

"But—"

"I said now. Let's go."

135

Trace shrugged, then cracked the reins over his team's backs. The wagon lurched forward as the mules stepped into the current.

Water lapped against the bottom of the wagon, then pushed against floorboards as the team fought the current. At one point, the wagon started to float with the high water. Just when Trace doubted their chances of making it across without incident, the wagon charged up the bank's other side.

* * *

The sun hugged the horizon when Sheriff Fuente decided to stop for the night. Trace found a sheltered campsite where a few trees perched along the river. Trace followed Fuente around to the back of the wagon. Maybe now, with just enough light, he could see who he was hauling.

Sheriff Fuente pulled his gun before unlocking the door. "Everything all right, Roberto?"

"Fine. Prisoner kept griping about his ribs." Roberto backed out of the wagon as Trace moved around. The deputy blocked Trace's view. "Damn killer keeps talking. My ears're still ringing."

Tom climbed out. "You clamped his mouth shut tight, Roberto. Buffaloed him awful hard. He's out."

"What?" Fuente frowned at Tom, then at Roberto.

Roberto shrugged. "Wouldn't shut up. I asked him nice. Didn't I, Tom?" He played with his handlebar mustache. "Had to use the butt end of my gun for some peace and quiet."

Fuente's hands fisted. "There's no need for—"

"Hell, he ain't dead, sheriff. Just quiet." A glare. "For once."

Fuente holstered his weapon and leaned inside. "How's he doing, Sam?"

"Trying to come around. He's gonna be as grumpy as a hungry bear when he's full awake."

"You're probably right. Just watch him. We'll get grub for you and him directly. Make sure those cuffs are secure."

Before Trace could peer inside, Fuente straightened up and shut the door.

Dark gray dimmed the campsite. Trace unhitched the team, then led them to the river to let them drink all they wanted. While he waited, he remembered how James was kicked during the stage holdup. It had hurt his little brother—bad. Did James' ribs still hurt, or were they healed by now? A pang of guilt slapped him in the face.

Should've been me. Should've kept him safe.

Trace squatted by the river. Was it too much to ask to see his brother again? His chest tightened. He sniffed. Too much to know if he was all right? Alive? He sniffed again. Something stung his eye. Despite what he'd thought earlier, he had to admit it'd been a long, hard three days and it wouldn't get easier soon.

Trace led the team back to camp. The orange glow of the campfire, with its sizzling and popping, quieted Trace's doubts. After tying the mules to a nearby tree, Trace ambled over to the three lawmen, all perched near the fire. He spooned stew into an offered plate, then found a log to sit on. He ate like a starved man. Second helping proved as tasty as the first.

Appetite now sated, he pushed up off the log and ambled over to the wagon. Roberto leaned against the side, cigar in hand, smoke looping from his mouth.

What would Trace find when he saw this prisoner? A devil? Lucifer himself? Trace hated to acknowledge his morbid fascination.

"Mind if I take a peek?" Trace asked. "Kinda like to see what I'm hauling."

"Ain't nothing but a low-down, back-shooting *pendejo*. Don't see why we're wasting our time." Roberto pointed his cigar at Fuente. "That man right over there oughta let us hang this bastard right here, right now, and be done with it." Another drag on the tobacco. "Hell, we'd all be heroes. Save the taxpayers trial money."

"Ain't the way it's done, Roberto." The sheriff called out over a mouthful of food. "I better not see you with a rope in your hand. I'll shoot you myself."

Tom pointed his tin cup at Roberto. "We're takin' him in all legal like." He glanced at the sheriff. "Maybe we oughta put that deputy in cuffs, too." A chuckle grew from his chest.

While this banter and posturing among the lawmen did nothing to make Trace feel better, he still wanted a look at the prisoner. He aimed his question at Fuente. "You mind if I take a peek? Won't open the door or anything."

Fuente nodded. "Be careful. Don't put your hand in there. He's liable to bite it off."

Trace peered in between the high bars.

A man. Huddled on the floor, back to the door, pressed into the corner of the wagon. Just a dark, cuffed, gagged, defeated blob of a person hunkered back there. Trace stepped back and shook his head.

Some tough killer.

Trace sighed, then turned to find a place for his bedroll.

CHAPTER NINETEEN

A quick, cold breakfast eaten before sunrise would have to satisfy Trace until they stopped for their mid-day dinner. By then, he figured, they'd be close to Mesilla and the end of his journey tomorrow. He counted the hours. He'd get his money, walk away, and enjoy his freedom. Unlike that man behind him in the jail box.

Images of the prisoner haunted him—all night, all day. Unable to shake that woeful, lonely picture, Trace felt genuine sorrow for the man. Whether the man was a killer or not, he seemed so pathetic.

With each mile closer to the river, Trace kept one eye on the thunderheads building over the mountains and the other eye on his team. He chewed on the inside of his cheek. They would have a hard time trying to get through the water, and he prayed they could find sure footing for the animals and wagon.

He pulled the wagon to a stop in front of the swirling, muddy Mimbres River. Just like yesterday, water topped the banks, covering the road for several yards in both directions. Trace swiped at a bead of sweat threatening to trickle down his temple. He turned to the sheriff sitting next to him.

"Gonna be rough," Trace said. "Never seen it this high or this fast." He pointed north. "Only other crossing is about twenty miles up that way."

"Too far. It'd take too long." Sheriff Fuente said. "Better get going or the water's gonna be even higher."

Trace nodded. "All right. Get the prisoner out and everybody can help guide the wagon and team." He shifted his weight on the seat.

The sheriff held up a hand. "No. Don't want to risk losing him. I'll keep the prisoner and one deputy inside. The rest can help."

Before Trace could object, Fuente leaped off the seat, shotgun in hand, then headed around back. Within a minute, Deputies Roberto and Sam squinted up at Trace. Fuente joined them.

"I told Tom we'd stop on the other side," Fuente said. "Take a quick break."

Roberto whipped his gun out of its holster. "Maybe that *pendejo*'ll try to escape."

"Wouldn't get far with those shackles." Sam thrust out his chest. "I made sure they're nice 'n tight. Walking's damn near impossible."

"Just hope it don't come to that, men." Fuente swung his gaze up river then down. He shook his head. "Let's go, Trace."

"Sheriff, I think—"

"I said go. Now."

Trace straightened his shoulders and pulled in air.

Let's get this over with.

He snapped the reins over the mules' backs. Men and mules lurched into muddy water.

He fought the current as the water lapped at the mules' legs. Before he could get the team a third of the way across, the current pulled at the wagon. And just like yesterday, water rose halfway up the sides. The deputy and prisoner would be fine unless the water came in through the windows. In that case, they'd be trapped. And drown.

Trace couldn't spend much time thinking about drowning. The mules fought the currents and the driftwood that was rushing through the water. They stumbled over boulders hidden by debris and churning water. Trace feared one of them would break a leg on this crossing. If he lost one mule, the other would have a tough time pulling this much weight. Most of the men would have to walk back to Mesilla. Maybe even the prisoner.

The two deputies in the water held onto the wagon as it swayed and jolted forward inch by inch. Roberto grabbed at any part of the rigging he could keep a grip on as he struggled through the torrent. Sam clung to the other side, frantic to stay upright.

Halfway across the river, the wagon drifted downstream, then jackknifed against a pile of large rocks. The front wheel jammed between two boulders. Trace called out to the team, snapping the reins. The mules strained forward, then panicked. Pulling and tugging against each other, they rammed into the wagon, then bounced off a boulder.

"Sheriff!" Trace hollered over the rushing water and thrashing mules. "Grab the lead lines and pull!"

Fuente raised his hand in answer and turned to guide the animals, but before he could grab the lead, a surge of roiling water hit him, sucking him under. After a few seconds, he surfaced, arms waving like a mad man. He fought against the raging water and tried to get his balance, but another current pushed him under one of the mules struggling to stay upright. Jammed against the animal's rear leg and unable to pry himself off, Fuente thrashed. The current was relentless.

Sam, gripping the right side of the wagon, stepped into a hole. Water swept over the top of his head as he went under. He came up gasping, but another wave hit him, taking him under. He somersaulted downstream.

Trace yelled at the mules, at Fuente, at Sam, at Roberto. He stood. A jolt tossed him back to his seat. From where he sat, Trace's view of Sam rolling over and over in the water was clear. So was the gut-wrenching impact of a tree limb smashing into the back of Sam's head. Sam's arm reached for the sky, then was caught up in the raging torrent. His body tumbled downstream.

Fuente slid around the mule, grabbed hold of the harness, and yanked. The mule reared.

Both animals and man crashed into the river. Water swirled over their heads as they fought their way to the surface. By some miracle and with Trace's encouragement, the team righted itself. They strained against the harness, frantic to escape, but the stuck wagon kept them in place. Fuente clung to a wheel and fought off sticks and tumbling rocks.

Trace snapped the reins again and again. No success. That wagon was jammed and not even the mules on a good day would have the strength to get it loose. He'd need men to help. Trace spotted Roberto near the far side of the river, water at his knees. He'd made it out alive.

"Roberto!" Trace shouted. "Grab a wheel and push!"

The deputy nodded and headed back into the water. The mules, ears laid flat against their heads, eyes bulging with panic, lunged side to side. Roberto clung to a mule as he fought his way to the wheel.

Fuente was useless. It was obvious he had just enough strength to hang on, but none extra to help push the wagon forward. Trace

141

considered releasing the other deputy and prisoner. They could help. A glance at the swirling water told him he couldn't get the door open right now. No, it would have to be just him and the two lawmen.

Trace scrambled down from the seat, landing in chest deep water. He gripped the side of the wagon, praying he was strong enough to save their lives. He neared Fuente first. Fuente's tanned face had paled, and his entire body shook.

Trace shouted over the water's roar. "Hold on! Gotta get this wheel unstuck."

A nod, but Fuente's strength failed. He released the wheel and slid under the water. Trace grabbed a foot and pulled. Fuente surfaced, sputtering, water washing over him again. Flapping his arms, he managed to keep his head above water. Trace grasped the sheriff's vest.

Another boiling rush of water crashed into the sheriff, knocking him into the side of the wagon. *Smack.* Like a watermelon against a rock. His body sagged.

Trace pulled Fuente toward him, draping the sheriff over his shoulder. Then he plowed his way through the rapid water to the closer bank several yards away, and once they reached the shore, he released the sheriff. Like a wet sack of grain, Fuente's body crumpled to the ground. He lay motionless.

Trace headed back into the river, but before he could reach the wagon, another tree limb tumbled toward the team. It struck one mule in the shoulder. Panicked, the animal reared, then fell sideways on top of the other. Both animals thrashed, pulling and tugging in different directions. Caught between the animals, Roberto was tangled up in the web of harness, reins, and headgear.

One of the mules kicked Roberto, then fell on him. Both went down and under. Roberto screamed as he surfaced, rawhide in hand. Another crushing wave and he careened downstream. Gone.

In complete panic now, the mules broke the rigging and harness, then tore loose from the rocking wagon. They bolted toward Trace, but the heavy current took them downstream, missing him by inches.

As the mules thrashed onto the bank only a few feet from where Fuente lay, Trace headed toward the teetering wagon that was rocking in the river. Water lapped at the windows. Before he reached the pitching jail, a surge of water hit the wagon and rolled it over twice before it ground to a jarring stop—lodged upside down against a boulder.

Trace fought to stay upright as he swam against the current. Reaching the wagon, he ducked under the water, yanking the door. He shook the handle. Stuck. Surfacing for a quick breath, he fought his way to the side window. He dove under and kicked. Once. Twice. Tight. No amount of force budged it.

He pushed his head into the fresh air again, while water pulsed around his body. As he struggled to stand, he listed his options. A rock. He could use a sharp rock to smash the side of the wagon, and squeeze the men out through the opening.

Seconds raced by. The men were running out of air. Dying. Might already be too late.

Trace held his breath, ducked under the water again, and grasped at a rock near his foot. Then he hit the wagon side with as much force as he could. The surging waves ate away the sand underneath him, and he fell backwards, sucking in a mouthful of water. He stood up gasping, spitting out sandy melted snow.

Maybe a thick, hard branch might work. As if in answer to a prayer, a driftwood branch slammed against the wagon. He grabbed the limb. If that jail box slid just a little bit farther around the boulder, it would be lost forever downstream. Another deep breath, and Trace plunged under the water where he had tried smashing the wagon side. He felt the dent and knew if anything would work, it would be right there.

Frantic now, he rammed the branch into the wooden side. Nothing. Again. Nothing. Again and again and again. One last heave.

Wood cracked. He was through. Trace surfaced for a quick breath, then kicked in the broken planking. He stuck his head inside. The deputy was wedged in a corner just out of arm's reach. Water lapped around Tom's face, his nose covered, the air pocket gone.

Trace grabbed at his legs, then pulled him through the narrow opening. Both surfaced, Trace gasping for air. He stood, throwing the unconscious man over his shoulder as best as he could, then fought his way to the nearest bank. He dropped him in the dirt.

Panting, wiping water and mud from his mouth, Trace knelt by Tom. A hand on the chest and Trace knew Tom was breathing.

After a couple more breaths, Trace stood, pushed his hair back, and felt the afternoon sun. Warm. His attention shifted to the water. Swirling, rapid, cold, deadly. Could that prisoner still be alive? If so, did he really need rescuing just to be hanged next week?

Trace knew the answer. If he didn't at least try to rescue that man, it'd eat at him for his entire life. He walked toward the water. Then stopped.

What if I end up dying and this fella lives? Do I really want to risk my neck for some low-life killer? But...what if the prisoner's innocent?

Again, he knew.

Dammit! Why's it got to be so cold?

Trace plunged into the swirling river.

Once again he peered into the wagon. Through the muddy water, he spotted the prisoner, face stuck in a corner way in the back, struggling for breath in a tiny air pocket. The prisoner clawed at the gag tied over his mouth, but his feeble attempts couldn't loosen it. Little opportunity to suck in air. Trace cursed Roberto.

Muscling himself in, Trace reached the shackled man, then grabbed him around the chest. The prisoner thrashed against the wagon sides while Trace tugged him out into freedom.

Trace's arms wrapped around the trembling man, keeping him upright against the current. He couldn't see the man's face, since the prisoner's back was against his chest, but he knew that even if this fella had killed a sheriff, he didn't deserve to drown. No one deserved to die like that.

The racing water pressed both men against the upturned wagon. Unwilling to let go of the prisoner, Trace held on to him with one arm and used the other to pull down the gag. Before he succeeded, the prisoner's knees buckled. Trace yanked up, and with that, the wagon dislodged.

Trace fell back. Both men plunged under water again. Trace lost his grip, but despite scraping his face on the river bottom, he managed to pull himself upright. He stood waist deep. The prisoner's head bobbed not ten feet away. Trace lunged and grabbed him again.

Wood crunching. Trace turned to see the wagon swirl around the boulder and shatter into hundreds of splintery pieces against the jagged rocks. Like matchsticks, they cascaded downriver in the torrent.

Thankful to be alive, Trace pulled the prisoner to his feet. The man's manacled hands tore at the gag. Trace coughed while the man spit water. Chest heaving, the prisoner pulled in air then turned around. Water spurted from his nose. He blinked at Trace.

Trace froze. James? Couldn't be.

James stared back.

Without warning, a surge of water washed over both men. Rocks plowed into Trace's leg.

He stepped back, sinking into a hole. James flew forward, knocking into Trace's shoulder. They had to get out of that river, or they'd both be swept under and drown.

Words refusing to form, Trace chose action. He tugged James to the bank, then shoved his brother into the safety of the trees.

CHAPTER TWENTY

When the river was behind them, the brothers collapsed onto the forest floor. Trace rolled then sat up, his chest still pumping for air.

"All right?" he asked.

Leaves and twigs stuck in his hair, James flopped back and forth on the ground before rolling up onto his knees. "Couldn't breathe." He said, turning his terrified eyes on his brother. "God, I couldn't breathe."

Questions, images, worry swirled inside Trace's head. He focused on the questions. They spurted between gasps. "You. In there. How? Why?"

James' long strands of wet brown hair were plastered over one eye. He draped his hair behind his ear, and he sat up straighter. "Me?" Water dribbled down his chin as he spit. "You were driving. I recognized your voice."

"Why were you in there?" Trace swiped his face with his wet sleeve. "How?"

"Don't tell me you didn't know."

"I didn't." Trace held out one hand palm up. "You all right now?"

"No." James shook harder. "You're...supposed to be in Tucson, not driving the jail... How could you *not* know?" He blinked around water drops. "And why the hell didn't you?"

His shock receding, Trace pointed toward the rock where the wagon had been. "I'll ask again. Why the hell were you *in* there?"

James looked everywhere but at his brother. Words started, stopped. Shoulders sagged. James took a deep breath and tugged at the handcuffs. Trace's anger faded.

"All right. No arguing," Trace said. He ran his hands through his wet hair, his hat now more than likely cascading downstream. "Whatever trouble you're in, I'll help. Better hide you."

146

James rolled up onto all fours, struggling to stand.

"This way." Trace clutched his brother's shirt and hoisted. James wobbled to his feet. Loping like a drunken marionette, his shackled ankles kept his running slow and awkward. He stumbled twice, each time plowing face first into fallen leaves and pine needles.

The brothers ran five full minutes before Trace stopped. James collapsed to his knees, rasping, wheezing, the roar of the river now just a memory.

Trace knelt by his little brother, then slid a protective arm around James' shoulders. God, it felt good having him here. Trace squeezed, then released him.

"Gotta get those bracelets off," Trace said.

"How?" James' breathing slowed. Both hands shook.

What could he use? Trace held one wrist and examined the thick iron wrapped around it, the rusty spring, the lock. His brother's wrist was swollen from the pressure. Trace ran his hand across his face, over his eyes. He rubbed them. Suddenly tired. No. Exhausted. A scan of the forest revealed a rock, solid and sharp. He draped James' wrist chains over another larger rock, then struck. Again and again. Nothing. The iron dented, but remained secure.

"It's no use." James slumped back against a tree, his head cradled in his hands. "Just leave me here."

Trace turned a frustrated eye on his brother, then sank down next to him. Silence wedged itself between them. How to ask the question? Trace chose the direct route.

"Did you kill him?"

James' brown eyes met his, misted, then looked away.

More silence.

"Did you?"

James mumbled something. Trace leaned in close. "What?"

"I don't want to talk about it."

"What!" Trace grabbed James' shoulders, twisting him around. Then he clutched the front of James' shirt, the material bunching in his grasp. "Won't talk about it! I'm out here risking my life, and you won't talk about it?" He shook his brother harder. "I've spent weeks looking for you! Been worried sick about you! Answer me! Did you kill him?"

Nose to nose, James searched Trace's eyes. "Yeah." He looked away.

There. It was said. Out in the open. His own brother, his little brother, a killer. Trace shook his head. How in the hell could James be a back-shooting killer?

Trace shoved him back, releasing the trembling shoulders. He'd have to think about this for a while. Could it be that the gossip in Mesilla was true?

"It was self-defense, Trace. I swear on grandpa's grave it was. You gotta believe me." James buried his face in his chained hands. "Hell, it don't matter if you do. I'm gonna hang."

Trace closed his eyes and squeezed the bridge of his nose. Something he'd seen his pa do when he was worried. Real worried. His eyes flicked over to James. Instead of an innocent teenager, there sat a terrified old man.

"All right. I believe you," Trace said. "But there's just one thing you gotta know."

"What?"

Trace grabbed James in a bear hug. "Glad to see you again. Love you, little brother."

"Love you, too, Trace."

Instantly awkward, the two men pushed away from each other, then grinned. Trace pointed at the handcuffs. "That iron's tough. Gotta get something else. Wait here. Maybe I can find the key." He pointed a muddy finger at James, then at the ground. "You. Stay here."

A nod. "Trace?"

Trace raised his eyebrows.

"I'm sorry." James wagged his head. "Sorry for everything."

"I know." Trace squeezed his brother's shoulder. "I'll be back directly."

Five minutes later and emerging from the forest, Trace spied the sheriff across the river on the far bank. Fuente was thrashing like a dying fish, flopping side to side. Mumbling.

At least Fuente's alive.

Trace didn't want to think about the two men already lost. Maybe Tom would die, too. He pushed those thoughts away. Another glance at Fuente. Still now. Was he dead?

Tom was closer. Trace rushed to the deputy sprawled a few yards down the bank. He checked for the rhythmic pulse of the unconscious man. Alive. So far so good. Trace hated himself for digging through a man's pockets, but he searched Tom for the keys nevertheless. He found nothing but change, which he replaced. Standing, he ran his hand across his mouth. He'd have to wade.

Fuente better have that key.

Frigid, roiling, life-taking water. Between him and the key. There was no other way. Trace steeled himself for the freezing rapids, then stepped in.

This was the strongest current he'd ever tried to cross, even worse than back home during the spring flooding. As he struggled to ford, he remembered playing with his brothers in the rising water back home and his mother screaming at them all to stay away, to get out right then and there. Now he understood her panic. It was easy to die in this.

What felt like hours passed before Trace managed to haul his body onto the bank. Collapsing next to the sheriff, he sucked in air and blew out steam.

When he had recovered enough to sit up, he ran his fingers through his hair, pushing most of it out of his eyes. Trace shook Fuente's shoulder. "You all right, sheriff?"

Fuente moaned and brought a hand up to his head. "Tom?" It flopped back to the ground.

Trace knew this might be his only opportunity for the keys. "Sheriff?" He patted his shoulder. "Sheriff?"

More moans.

Trace fished in Fuente's pockets until he found a hard, metal object that was the right shape for a leg iron key. He shoved it in his own pocket, amazed the key had survived. Amazed anybody had survived.

After another inspection of Fuente to be sure he wasn't bleeding to death, Trace waded back into the water. His strength had drained by the time he reached the other side. He allowed only a moment to catch his breath, and then he plunged back into the forest.

Trace found his brother where he'd left him, leaning against the trunk of a towering pine, fidgeting with the shackles. A smile from James when the key fit into the leg iron lock. Wide smiles from both when the same key released the handcuffs. James rubbed his ankles and his wrists as the iron restraints clanked to the ground.

"Thanks, Trace. I owe you."

"Damn right."

149

James dug a hole in the soft dirt, and he dropped the manacles, leg irons, and key six inches down into the grave. Trace pushed dirt, leaves, and twigs over the burial site.

With that first piece of business taken care of, Trace turned to his brother. Light purple marks on James' face, a scar, a bump in his nose—all new. Trace frowned, then held James' bruised chin in his hand. He turned it side to side, that red scar on the side of his brother's head standing out like a flare in the night.

"Those stage robbers do all this to you?" Trace asked.

"No, not them. In Santa Rita, I got beat up pretty bad, almost killed." He hung his head and turned away. "Then nearly shot." One side of his mouth curled up. "But, I'm fine. Really. Best part is I met a girl—"

"Don't want to hear about a girl right now." Trace saw the love on James' face. This was going to be a long story. "We don't have time. But, I'd like to hear all about her—later. What about your watch? You get it back?"

James frowned.

"Then why'd you get thrashed, James? What happened?"

James gazed into the sky. "Card game. Robbers took all my winnings. I was sending it all home to ma and pa. They were gonna be so proud of me."

"Guess they'll just have to be proud to have a son who's still alive."

Trace studied his little brother. Six weeks of hard living. What really happened he could only guess. The whole story would come out in time. Trace hoped he'd be ready to hear it then, because he sure wasn't ready now.

James took a deep breath, winced, then massaged his ribs. "Don't know what to do next. If I run, I'll have to run all my life. But, I can't face any more time in jail. Too closed in. Those handcuffs. It terrifies me, Trace, the thought of spending years behind bars. Hate to admit it, but it does. And if I turn myself in, I'll hang for sure."

"We best get more distance between you and the sheriff." Trace extended a hand and pulled James to his feet. They walked in silence until James stopped and turned to Trace.

"So, let me get this straight. You were driving the jail wagon to fetch me down to Mesilla. To stand trial."

Trace knew it'd have to come out sooner or later. He hated

himself more with every step. How in the hell could he have been so blind? Not knowing it was his own brother back there? The memories of that dark, defeated man huddled in the corner of the jail wagon made it hard for Trace to breathe. What else had they done to his brother? Maybe he didn't want to know.

"Trace?" James gripped Trace's arm and shook it. "What're you not telling me?"

It was Trace's turn to peer into the sky. How could he tell James everything he'd heard? He'd soften the words. A deep breath.

"There's talk in town that you backshot the sheriff."

"What?"

"The town's in an ugly mood. They're not gonna let you stand trial. There's talk of lynching. Sheriff Fuente and the deputy're ready to protect you, but they're not in good shape right now."

"Lynching?" James slid down to the ground and sagged against a tree. "I can't hang. It was self-defense." His frantic eyes turned to Trace. "Self-defense."

Trace eased down next to his younger brother. "Tell me about shooting this sheriff. Just that part."

After a long breath, James related the freight wagon attack, Sheriff Dunn's suspicious behavior, and the lawman's capture by the stage robbers. He finished by describing Dunn's last actions.

"I've gone over it a million times in my head," James said. "Been trying to figure out what went so wrong. Can't believe I was stupid enough to walk into that trap. Dunn almost killed me."

And now he would hang.

Trace's shoulder bumped him. "If it had to be either you or him, better it was him."

James tossed a pebble at nothing. "Don't excuse the fact I killed a man. Took a life. I didn't mean to, just trying to save my own skin." He buried his face in shaking hands. His shoulders rose and fell. Sobs escaped.

The tops of the majestic pines glowed with early-spring sun. White clouds skittered against the blue sky. Jays squawked in search of food. Squirrels rustled under leaves. No footsteps, no sounds of people in pursuit. Nothing but the pounding of Trace's heart. He slid his arm around his brother's shoulders and pulled him close.

CHAPTER TWENTY-ONE

Trace stood by Sheriff Fuente's bed in the doctor's office. Alcohol, bandages, and medical instruments—their use Trace could only guess—sat on the table wedged against the wall. Fuente's black eyes roamed the ceiling, the adobe walls, then landed on Trace. Fuente squeezed his eyes tight and rubbed his bandaged head.

Doctor Logan shook the sheriff's shoulder. "Alberto. Alberto? Can you hear me?"

Fuente moaned, his head rocking side to side.

"He gonna be all right?" Trace asked.

The doctor glanced over his shoulder at Trace, then nodded. "He's coming out of it. Good thing you got here when you did."

"Sure is." Trace thought back to his relief when that farmer and his wagon showed up. Thanks to the high water he'd made a detour. And with the promise of a reward for his trouble, the farmer was more than happy to haul Fuente, Tom, and Trace back to Mesilla.

Doctor Logan pulled up a sheet around Fuente's shoulders. "Might be a while longer before we know anything. Took quite a blow to the head. We'll just let him rest."

He started down the hall then stopped and turned to Trace behind him. "You get a chance to ask about James while you were up there? Did you find him?"

Now wasn't the time to tell anybody about James, not even the doctor. No, Trace wouldn't reveal the location of the little cave they'd found not too far from the accident site. And James had promised he wouldn't venture out of the hiding hole until Trace returned.

"Trace? Did you find him?" Doctor Logan frowned. "Is he all right?"

"No, didn't find him." Trace shrugged. "How's Tom?"

Doctor Logan pointed down the hall.

Trace followed the doctor down the hall to the room where Deputy Tom Littleton lay. For some reason, Trace liked this deputy, even though Tom was a bit crusty and spoke his mind. No pretenses with this man.

The doctor peeled up Tom's eyelids and peered in. "Still out cold. Leg's broken in a couple places. Probably never be as good as it was." Logan straightened up. "How long did you say he was under water?"

"Five minutes, maybe. Hard to tell for sure."

Tough decisions had to be made. Trace figured Butterfield wouldn't give him time off to clear his brother, so he'd have to quit. He'd already missed this last run. At least he'd been able to find a substitute driver in time.

Shoulders slumped, heart heavy, Trace left the doctor's office and trudged around the Mesilla Plaza toward the stage office. One of the last things he ever wanted to do was quit. He loved driving the stage, watching the desert landscape change into mountains. He was awed by the sunrises bursting with orange and gold, and he was equally amazed by the sunsets melting into shades of crimson and purple.

The strength of the mules pulling the stage always astounded him. He admired the muscles rippling across their wide shoulders. And their incredible endurance. The idea of animals running for miles while pulling the stage with its passengers humbled him. The stage alone weighed almost a thousand pounds. But nothing would stand in his way of clearing James. Nothing. If he spent the rest of his life proving his brother's innocence, he'd do it. Gladly.

Lost in thought, he rounded the corner to Butterfield's office.

"Señor Colton?" A voice shot above the town's murmur. "Trace Colton?"

Trace scanned the dusty street, shielding his eyes from the noonday sun.

Mayor Ignacio waved from across the plaza. "Señor Colton. Wait a minute."

Trace waited. They shook hands.

"Need to talk to you, son. Can I buy you dinner?" The mayor wiped his forehead with a well-used handkerchief.

"I was just going over to the stage office," Trace said. "Got some business there. What d'you need?"

153

"Some business and town matters. Can I buy you a drink at least?"

"Why?"

A chuckle shook the mayor's shoulders. "Your mind. Whatever's there—mighty consuming." He patted Trace's arm. "Said I'd like to talk—something important."

An hour either way wouldn't make his business with Butterfield any easier. It'd been a while since breakfast, and he sure could use a bite. After the mayor was done, and after his stop at the stage office, he'd go over to the general grocery, pick up some food for James.

Trace unfolded his arms and raised an eyebrow. "Tell you what. If that offer for a meal still stands, I'd be glad to hear what you have to say."

Mayor Ignacio guided him down the street and around the corner to a small, crowded restaurant. They ordered and ate their food before Ignacio got down to business.

"The town of Mesilla wants to officially thank you for saving two lives," Ignacio said. "Sheriff Fuente and Deputy Littleton, well, they're alive today because of you."

"Mister Ignacio, two men also died." Trace stared into his coffee cup.

"Two? What about the prisoner? Doesn't he make three?"

Trace's stomach turned. "I'm sorry. I was just thinking of lawmen." A quick sip of coffee. "You're right. Three lost."

Mayor Ignacio turned his dark eyes on Trace. One lone line zigzagged its way across Ignacio's forehead. Ignacio leaned back. "I have one regret, though, Señor Colton."

"How's that?"

"That damn prisoner."

Trace spoke without breathing. "Sir?"

"By getting himself drowned. Hell, that murderer cheated this town out of a good neck stretching. Most of the people here already were planning a hanging party."

A pretty Mexican waitress appeared at the table and poured fresh coffee for the mayor and Trace. She flashed a shy grin at him.

"Biggest trial and hanging this decade, maybe even century, and he has to go and get himself killed. Damn prisoner." Ignacio stirred his coffee, then met Trace's gaze. "You look tired. This must've been an unsettling experience."

154

If you only knew.

Trace took another sip. What did the mayor want? Something—more than just giving a pat on the back. Trace hadn't done anything extraordinary. Any man would have done the same.

Ignacio's gaze followed the waitress across the room, then turned to Trace. "Señor, Mister Colton...May I call you Trace?"

A nod.

"The town council here in Mesilla had a meeting last night."

Trace's coffee refused to slide down his throat.

"I'll be direct, Trace. As you know, the town has no sheriff or deputy for now."

Another nod.

"We'd like you to be sheriff until Fuente recovers." The mayor rushed his words. "Now, please, keep in mind, it's only temporary. Until he gets on his feet again."

"What?" Trace opened his mouth twice before more words tumbled out. "Why me?"

"You proved you can keep your head in an emergency. And you're strong as an ox, as they say."

Trace realized his cup was held halfway to his mouth. It banged down on the table.

"You were willing to drive the jail wagon on a moment's notice," Ignacio said. "You risked your life crossing that river. And you seem to know right from wrong. We think you are the man for the job."

If he was sheriff, how in the world could he help James clear his name? Trace shook his head.

"I can't. Appreciate the offer, I do. But I've got some important personal matters to take care of."

"We knew that would be your answer. But Trace, the town really needs you now. We will double the salary if you'll do it. And, you will stay for free at the boarding house. Missus Rosen already has a room for you."

Trace was quiet for a few minutes. The idea began to intrigue him. This might give him a chance to help James on the side. Maybe even legally.

"Now, mayor," Trace said, "if I take this job, just what is it you expect me to do?"

"The usual—keeping peace around here." Mayor Ignacio finished his coffee, searched the bottom of the cup for an answer.

His eyes trailed up from the cup to Trace's stare. "We need you to find the three bodies."

Trace choked.

Ignacio patted him on the back and offered him water. "I know it's not pleasant, but we must find them, bring them back for proper burial. Even that prisoner, whoever he was, his family needs to be notified."

Trace managed to catch his breath. "So no one knows who the prisoner was?"

The mayor glanced around the restaurant, then leaned in close. "No, but we're trying to find out. We sent an express message up to the deputy there in Pinos Altos. He knows the name." Ignacio leaned closer. "Don't let it out that Fuente...that, we...he made such a mistake. We want people to think he knew exactly who it was."

That was a promise Trace would be glad to make.

"What if I can't find the bodies?" Trace asked. "What then?"

"You must find them. Especially the prisoner's. Those bodies must be buried. They are out there somewhere."

Trace pictured his brother in the forest, hiding in the safest place they could find. Yeah, his body was out there without a doubt, and Trace knew where it was.

"I guess they are." Trace pursed his lips and played with his fork. "You're gonna have to give me time to think on it, mayor."

"Take your time, Trace, but we need to know by tonight." Ignacio stood, tossed coins on the table, then produced that half-sinister, half-angelic grin. "Food's on us. Thank you again for saving those men."

Trace nodded at the mayor's back disappearing out the door.

CHAPTER TWENTY-TWO

Trace threaded his way across the river, then up between a stand of pines. His two horses carried saddlebags full of supplies, plenty of food to last a week. The storekeeper even threw in a plug of tobacco, although neither brother had acquired the habit or the taste for it. He said it just might come in handy down the road. Trace didn't disagree.

Dismounting at the base of a steep hill, Trace tied the horses to a scrub oak, then removed one bag and slung it over his shoulder. He wagged his head at the crazy turn of events. Would James believe him?

Trace had to scramble up steep yards of shale to the hidden cave where James was waiting. The rock pieces made Trace's footing precarious at best. Twice he slid before reaching the cave's mouth.

"Heard you coming a mile away." James' familial grin spread across his face.

Trace tossed the saddlebag to James and squatted down near the cave's entrance, then leaned against a boulder and watched the distant trail. His chest heaving, Trace wiped the sweat from his forehead. "Not as young as I used to be."

James opened the pouch, fished out two red apples, then held one at arm's length. "Want one?"

"Yeah." Trace stood face to face with his brother.

James, his arm still suspended mid-air, stared at the shiny badge pinned to Trace's shirt. He stepped back, with his chin pointing toward the badge. Then he clutched the saddlebag in front of his chest like a shield.

"What's going on? You the law now?"

"Yeah, but it's not what you think."

"Not what I *think*?" James inched sideways away from Trace. "You know what? I think you're here to take me in. That's what I think."

"You're wrong." Trace held up a hand. "It's not like that."

"Then tell me what it is, *brother*."

A few more steps and he'd be gone. Down the shale hill and into the forest. Disappearing again. Trace slid in behind James. His brother would have to climb over him to get out.

"Calm down and I'll tell you," Trace said.

Silence. James turned around to Trace, then hung his head. His shoulders rose and fell.

"Sorry. It's just that—"

"I know. You gotta trust me." Trace pried an apple of out James' grip, then gestured with it. "Look, I'm your brother. I'd never do anything to hurt you. You know that, don't you?"

A nod. Another breath.

"Sit." Trace waited until James eased down and sat cross-legged against the cave front. Trace slid to the dirt next to him. Then he explained the situation to James.

"If we're careful," Trace finished, "it'll work to our advantage. Anyone recognizes you, I can say you're my prisoner and I'm taking you to jail."

James took a deep breath. "Makes sense."

Trace took a bite of apple. "And since I'm supposed to be recovering the bodies, I'll be gone from town for a while. Nobody even questioned the amount of grub I asked for."

James sunk his teeth into his apple, broke off a piece, then chewed thoughtfully. "Just can't believe the mayor would ask you to be sheriff."

"It is a strange turn of events all right."

"Kinda like hiring the fox to guard the hen house." James laughed, and the sound soared into the forest.

"Keep your voice down. Don't know who's out there."

Trace peered out over the tops of trees, north toward Santa Rita. The branches glittered from the brilliant sun. Was he ready for this next step?

A deep breath, his voice low. "It's time you tell me everything, James. What's happened these last six weeks. I'll need to know every detail if I'm gonna help you."

James' smile plummeted. His shaky hands combed his hair, then swiped across his face. He tugged at the beginnings of a prickly mustache. The last couple of days in the jail wagon hadn't given him the chance to shave.

Ramblings of bandits, beatings, Lila Belle, dishonest lawmen, a widow woman, trusting the wrong people, gunfights, cards games. James explained it all in agonizing detail. Trace stole glances at his brother, but most of the time he kept his eyes trained on the treetops. The last story described the several days he'd sat in the Pinos Alto jail. Not fun, but at least the deputy fed him three times a day and escorted him to the privy out back when needed. They'd even played poker once or twice. James ended the recitation with a sigh.

"I asked Deputy Wickens not to send word to Lila Belle. I wouldn't want her to see me behind bars. No, not like that."

Trace tossed his apple core into the air and watched it land on a rock below.

Silence.

"That's a helluva story." Trace shook his head. "You've lived three lifetimes in six weeks. Wish I'd been there to...to protect you. Don't know what I would've done if you'd died."

James smacked Trace's leg, the moment shattered. "You'd have got the girl." They looked at each other. James smiled. The same smile their pa had. "But because I'm quicker and much better looking, I got her!"

Both men laughed for a half-minute, jabbing each other with soft punches.

Now that he knew the whole story, Trace realized what had to be done. He grew serious again.

"All right. We gotta clear your name, but Fuente and Littleton can't help. And if I bring you into town now...well...it'll get ugly." Trace stared into sky. "It's only a matter of days before Mesilla knows your name. Maybe make the family connection. I don't know."

James rubbed his throat. "You got a plan?"

"Maybe. Gotta get those four robbers back to Mesilla. They gotta admit it was them that started it, tell their story, their involvement with Dunn, so you can go free. To tell the world that you shot in self-defense. Their testimony's crucial."

"Without it?"

Whispered words pushed their way into the cave. "You'll hang."

* * *

159

Next morning, plans were made. Trace knew the bodies were downstream somewhere and he needed to recover them—soon. The town expected to bury its dead within a day or two, and he needed bodies. Trace was willing to find two, but bringing in the third was going to be more difficult. Actually, impossible.

Trace's foot swung into the right stirrup as he settled his weight in the saddle. He waved to his brother squatting at the cave's mouth. Just to be on the safe side, they'd both decided that James would stay behind, out of sight. At least for today. The sun caught the side of James' face, his profile revealing a nervous teenager. Trace snugged his new hat down on his head, and thought about that third body he was waving to. He'd bring it in, but when he did, it would be alive. And, by damn, it would stay that way.

As he traveled downstream, second horse in tow, Trace considered his brother's story. He shook his head at how often he'd missed James, sometimes by hours it seemed, and he thought about Lila Belle. She was pretty even when he knocked her off the boardwalk by the Silver Dollar Saloon in Santa Rita. James chose a beautiful woman. Or did she choose him? And how could Trace ever repay her for saving his brother's life? James must have been badly beaten, surprising he'd even survived. Trace tried to push aside imagined scenarios—the beating, Lila's discovery of him, his brother's struggle to recover. But those images returned, each time bigger and bigger.

The first body Trace found was Deputy Sam Kidd's. Trace discovered it shortly after noon that same day. Lodged against a mountainous pile of brush near the bank, it was easy to spot. Like a flag, Sam's red plaid shirt stuck out between the mishmash of branches and rocks. If things hadn't been so grim, Trace would have laughed at the ease of this assignment.

Trace panted and wheezed as he draped the body over the extra horse. Sam Kidd was not a small man, and his dead, wet weight measured well over two hundred pounds. The horse, frightened to have death hanging over it, whickered and pulled at the tether, but Trace patted her neck and spoke soothing words. After much encouragement, she gentled enough to accept the burden.

Trace rode farther downstream, stopping at every large brush pile and logjam. Several areas along the bank held the promise of Deputy Roberto Reyes's remains, but when twilight arrived, his body was still hidden. Five miles of searching brought an ache to

160

Trace's six-foot frame. As he walked along the east side of the river, he decided to call it a day, go back to his brother, stay overnight, and then at daybreak, head into town with Sam.

* * *

Early evening of the second day, Trace was back at the cave. "Sam's wife appreciated having his body back," Trace told James, "but the mayor's demanding the other two. They were surprised I didn't bring in all three at once." Trace shrugged. "I promised them Roberto's body soon."

James spit. "That *cabron* who kept hitting me?" He rubbed the back of his head. "Still got a knot back there. Just leave him wherever he is. Hope it's in Hell."

"You know I can't do that."

Trace fed a small stick into the fire at the back of the cave. James shoved the remainder of his ham sandwich into his mouth.

"He's gotta be close by," James said. "I mean, devils don't float, do they? And wouldn't his pitchfork get caught in the debris? Maybe his horns got stuck in the mud."

Trace chuckled. "Whichever. Hopefully I'll find him tomorrow." He turned around.

"Town's in an even uglier mood than before. I'm afraid your body wouldn't even make it to the undertaker. And they want it *pronto*." Trace eyed his best friend. "From what you say, that Sheriff Dunn sure had people fooled."

"Guess he did. I didn't know he was so famous." He met Trace's gaze, then hung his head. "I didn't want to kill him. Didn't mean to."

"I know." Trace slid his arm around his brother's tense shoulders. "It'll be all right. We'll work this out."

"I'm gonna hang."

"Never. They'll have to kill me first."

* * *

They'd been searching less than three hours when seven miles downstream James waved and whistled at Trace on the other side of the river.

"I see something. Think it's him." James pointed. A boot stuck up between two large limbs, a boulder hiding most of the crumpled body.

"Good eyes, James." Trace rode across the water, now more a stream than a river, and swung out of his saddle. "Glad I changed my mind and let you ride along. I never would've spotted him by myself."

"At least he got what he deserved." James waded into the water alongside Trace. "Guess what ma always preached is true."

"Yeah? What's that?"

"Do unto others." James pried a large limb off Roberto's leg. "He's been 'done unto,' I reckon."

"I reckon." Trace grunted as he pulled the tangled dead weight from the river. "But he didn't have to pay with his life."

James dropped his load of the body onto the riverbank.

"Hell, Trace. That's the price he wanted *me* to pay. I remember him threatening to hang me every time I moved. He was gonna just out and out shoot me one time. Even put the gun to my head, cocked the hammer. Littleton stopped him. Hell, I couldn't even ask for water without a death threat. Nothing was good about him—nothing."

Images of James, that gag tied around his mouth, shackles and handcuffs too tight, stuffed in the back of that jail wagon. Roberto's snorts at having to keep the prisoner alive. Trace rethought the man at his feet. Still, it wasn't right to speak ill of the dead. Ma had taught them that, too.

But his brother was right. There wasn't much good to be said for Roberto Reyes. Trace pointed to the man's legs and then at the horse. "Help me with him."

After draping the body across the horse and tying it down tight, Trace swiped his hand across his forehead. Beads of sweat and river water dripped to the ground.

"I'll take him back to town," Trace said.

"Then we'll go find those robbers." James glared at Roberto.

"Right. We'll clear your name and get our lives back." He gripped James' shoulder and shook it. "And that, my little brother, I promise."

CHAPTER TWENTY-THREE

After depositing Deputy Roberto Reyes's body in Mesilla, Trace met up with James at the cave.

"Tomorrow," Trace said, "we'll head south, toward Mexican Springs."

"Ain't that down by the border?" James, a biscuit held halfway to his mouth, slid his eyes sideways at his brother. "What are we doing? Running? Crossing the border and running? I thought you said—"

"Silver strike down there's sure to draw all types of outlaws. The smell of money's bound to attract…what'd you say his name was? Fallon?"

A nod.

"Fallon and his boys are gonna be there. If not today, soon." Trace swigged from the canteen.

A grin drew up one side of James' mouth. "Yeah, thinking back on it, I remember them talking about riding south. Bet you're right." He held up a thumb and forefinger, half an inch apart. "We're this close, Trace. This close."

All the next day they kept a steady, mile-eating trot, knowing their time was limited. Trace needed to get back to Mesilla soon; Sheriff Fuente was on the mend and already grumbling about having nothing to do. Trace pushed hard.

Horses tired, backs aching, Trace and James rode into a sea of canvas tents just as the sun made a final plunge toward the horizon. This was no town, not even a village. Just an encampment. It was nothing like Pinos Altos—smaller, dustier, no wooden saloons.

A stream snaked through the white tent settlement. Trace, with James right behind, followed it past all the tents to a stand of trees. Remnants of an old campfire beckoned them. Perfect place to spend the night. A few boulders scattered nearby would give them cover, if needed.

They made camp with just enough time to find firewood, make coffee, and throw a pot of beans on the fire before true dark overtook the brothers. In the distance, men's voices shouted to each other—offers of poker games and calls for food drifted over the camp. The glow of other campfires dotted the landscape.

Trace drained his coffee cup, then stood and stretched. His back popped again. Third time today. At least his stomach was full. He wiped supper crumbs off his face.

"You best stay here, James. I'll ride back into town, have a look around, ask some questions." He pointed to the badge reflecting the campfire's glow. "This'll give me the right to ask questions."

"And make people answer them." James poured more coffee into his half-empty cup. "You just be careful, big brother. They might not like the questions you ask."

A chuckle. Trace swung up into the saddle. "You just keep the coffee hot and I'll be back quick as I can." He reined around, then peered down at his brother, perched on a log by the fire. He had to ask. The six weeks of searching, not knowing, still ate at his heart.

"You'll be here when I get back?"

Brown eyes met his. A nod.

* * *

By the time early-morning sunrays bathed the world in pinks and golds, Trace and James had fed the horses, fed themselves, and washed the dishes. James rearranged supplies in the saddlebag and spoke over his shoulder. "You never did tell me what you found out last night."

Sticks and coals sizzled as Trace poured water over the campfire. "Hard to talk to you over the snoring."

"I was awake when you got back. I was just...resting."

Trace kicked dirt over the sticks. "Uh huh." He headed toward the stream to fill the canteen.

"And?" James tightened his horse's cinch.

"And there's not much going on." Trace waited until the canteen was full, then replaced the cork and returned to camp. "There was some talk about someone getting robbed on the south road over to Georgetown. They thought maybe there were four robbers, but they weren't sure." He shrugged. "Nobody got killed, thank goodness, just lost some change. And no one'd even heard about Dunn."

James turned his back to his horse and stood eyeing his brother. "You know, I'm hoping you're telling the truth, because it's making me feel a whole lot better."

More sizzling from the campfire, then silence. Trace straightened up and studied his brother. Despite an uninterrupted night's sleep, James looked tired. Scared and tired.

"Are you saying I might lie to you?" Trace spread his arms and forced a half-smile onto his face.

"Nah." James shook his head. "I'm just saying you're my protective older brother." He chuckled. "No telling what you'll do."

"That's what I say about *you*." Trace swigged from the canteen as he walked toward his brother and the horses. "No, I'm telling the truth. But if you don't get your rear in that saddle pronto, we ain't never gonna catch 'em."

Trace looped the canteen strap around the saddle horn, untied the reins, and then swung up into his horse. That broad, familiar smile stretched across James' face. He settled his weight in the saddle, then turned bright brown eyes on his brother.

"Maybe, Trace. Maybe those bandits are right around the corner. Maybe by this time next week, our lives'll be back to normal."

Trace wagged his head. "Whatever *that* is."

The brothers trotted around hills, across another stream, up and down arroyos; their eyes scanned the desert for any sign of the men. Those outlaws. Mostly they rode in silence, each lost deep in thought. Minutes melted into hours.

Sweat trickled down Trace's temple, the noon sun unrelenting. He crested a hill and pulled up sharp. A swipe of his sleeve across his cheek, waiting for James to catch up. Trace pointed to a brown line in the distance.

"Stage road to Tucson, James. Look there."

After a long drink from the canteen, James offered it to his brother. "Road to the gallows if we don't find those robbers." He wiped a water drop from his chin.

The breeze cooled Trace's face, sending bumps up and down his arms. Again, his brother was right, but he wouldn't think like that now. He wouldn't let James think like that now. Wouldn't do either any good. Trace concentrated on the positive.

"About three miles from here's a way station, Cowboy Creek, part of the San Diego and San Antonio Stage Line." Trace pointed west and a bit to the south.

"I remember driving past it." A wag of James' head. "Never understood why the stage lines don't use the same way stations. Don't make sense."

"I know. Be easier to have one station, but I just drive the stagecoach." A hawk circled something in the distance. Trace's gaze trailed over the sand, sage, and mesquite. "Station manager doesn't know me there."

"You going alone?" James frowned. "He won't know me, either."

"Sorry. I'm not gonna risk it."

"You think they'll recognize me?" James lowered his voice, as if someone would hear him out in the desert.

"I don't know what to think. Just don't want to take the chance." Trace searched the area.

"Need to find a place for you to wait. Out of this sun."

A rock outcropping held promise. Trace pointed with his chin.

"Let's head up there," Trace said. "Give your horse a chance to rest, too."

Before James could argue, Trace gigged his horse.

* * *

Trace reviewed his mental list of questions as his hand fisted to knock on the way station's door, but before his knuckles touched wood, the door creaked open. A man, empty plate gripped in one hand, appeared. Aroma of something cooking wafted through the door.

"Saw you ride up, sheriff. Hungry?" He nodded at the tin plate.

"Always." Trace choked at the word sheriff. Would he ever get used to that title?

"Nice to have some company over dinner." The man, with sprigs of gray peeking out from his mop of black hair, stepped back to allow Trace room to enter. "Don't have many visitors out here. All I get are grumbling passengers, hot, tired and complainin' about the dollar I charge for grub. Nope, not too many visitors." He pointed to a chair at the nearest table, then headed for the pot hanging over the fire. "Course I won't charge you, sheriff. On the house."

"Appreciate it."

166

The man whirled around. His empty plate stuck out behind his ear. "What? Don't hear too good. Not since a fever I had as a child. Nope, not since then."

Trace fought a grin at the plate used as an extended ear, then sat and wiped his hands on his shirtfront. He spoke slower and louder.

"Said I appreciate it."

The manager dished out large dollops of stew into both plates. After the man sat, Trace reached across the table, shook hands. "Trace Colton."

"Eli Lester. Good to meet ya, sheriff." He broke off a piece of tortilla, popped it into his mouth. "Yep, good to meet ya."

While the men ate, they exchanged pleasant tidbits of information in a loud conversation. Trace learned that Lester had headed east after years of ranching in California and was now quite content managing this particular stage station. He'd been here more than a year.

"Never did tell me what brings ya out this way, sheriff." Lester finished his coffee. "Nope, never did."

"Looking for some men. Four of them. Stage and freight wagon robbers. Two have black eyes, one a scar on his face."

Lester frowned, possibly lost in thought, possibly trying to figure out what Trace had just said.

Trace spoke louder. Was he shouting?

"Four men," Trace said. "Held up wagons over at Picacho, Turnerville, Santa Rita, Pinos Altos. They might be heading this way."

Even if he received no useful information, this stew was sure tasty. Best he'd ever had, and he wasn't real fond of stew.

Lines trailed across the station manager's forehead. His lips pursed as he stared into his empty cup. A shake of his head.

"Nope. Can't say as I've heard." A stronger wag. "Nope, nothing."

"When's the next stage due in?" Trace set his cup on the wooden table.

Lester pulled out a pocket watch and studied it. Gold filigree and curlicues swooped across the top. Sure looked a lot like James'. Trace focused on the inside cover. No engraving.

"Almost three hours now. Where does time go?" Lester shrugged. "Where?"

167

"Three hours? Stage is that late?"

"Not usually three. Sometimes as much as two, but ol' Bill's pretty punctual. Not like him to be this much behind schedule." Lester stood, cup in hand. "Nope. Not usually behi—"

"I'll ride out that way. He might've had a broken wheel or something. More'n likely he's fine, Mister Lester." Trace stood, arching his back. The stretching felt good. "If you hear anything about those robbers, could you send word over to Mesilla? Sure would appreciate it."

"'Course, sheriff. Glad to."

As he headed out the door, Trace stopped. He turned around. "Just remembered."

Lester's hand cupped his ear. He leaned close. "You say something?"

"Said I'm meeting my deputy later today. You got a small bucket of stew I can take him?"

"'Magine I can rustle it up." Lester's eyes flicked from Trace's empty plate to the pot on the stove.

"I'll pay for it, Mister Lester." Trace struggled to hide a grin as he dug into his pocket for change. "And for the bucket."

Lester nodded and returned to the stove while Trace waited. After handing the tin pail to Trace, the station manager followed him outside.

"Thanks for the company, sheriff. Enjoyed it." He extended a hand. "Yep. Sure did."

Trace made sure he spoke loudly. "Me, too. Take care now." He mounted his horse and waved.

* * *

Still there. Trace relaxed as he spotted his brother sitting against a rock in the only patch of shade they could find. Trace chided himself for doubts. He would have to just trust that nothing would happen to James again. Out here in the middle of nowhere.

Now within a few yards of James, Trace reined up. "You asleep?"

Eyes still closed, James grunted. One hand attempted a limp wave. Sweat glistened on his cheek. Trace wiped his own forehead. It was spring, wasn't it?

James fanned his face with his hat. "Find out anything useful?"

"Maybe." Trace stepped around a mesquite bush, then stood in the shade next to his brother. "Stage is about three hours late."

"So?"

"Station manager says the driver's always on time."

Sniffs. A grin. More sniffs. James opened his eyes and smiled toward Trace's horse.

"That stew?" He scrambled to his feet, bolting over to the horse. "You bring me stew?"

"It was supposed to be a surprise. Yeah, dinner." Trace nodded at his brother's back. James untied the bucket from the saddle horn, raised the lid. His eyes closed with another whiff.

James wolfed down the warm stew, polishing it off with water from the canteen while Trace perched in a square of shade. Although for both men another plate of stew would've been welcomed, they knew to push on.

An hour later, they topped a hill and scanned the horizon for any sign of life. Fifty miles away rose Pyramid Mountains, and the rolling hills were dotted with clumps of yellow flowers that shimmered silver in the sun. The brown road under foot wound through mesquite bushes, around alligator junipers, and past purple and gray striped boulders.

"Spooky, ain't it?" James turned in his saddle. "Haven't seen any rabbits, hawks, quail, or nothing else for that matter. Just that old coyote a ways back."

Trace nodded. "Like Old Man Death put a spell over this area." He scanned the rocks and bushes for some shade.

James pointed west along the road. Down about half a mile or so, people, all afoot, trudged toward them. One stumbled, lagging behind.

The brothers rode out to meet the ragtag party. Trace's foot touched ground before his horse stopped. His badge was a welcome sign, he knew. He handed a canteen to the only woman in the footsore group.

"Howdy. I'm Sheriff Trace Colton."

"Sure glad to see you, sheriff." One of the men pumped Trace's hand. "Been a long walk. Lonely, too."

They looked to be in good shape, except for one man who was probably the driver. He wobbled as he stood. The dust smeared across this man's face did not hide the fatigue. Trace offered a canteen.

"Where'd you come from?" Trace asked.

"Stage...back yonder." The driver swayed. James grabbed both arms, eased him to the ground, and held the canteen up to his lips.

The woman passenger related their story. "Four men came outta nowhere." She glanced back over her shoulder. "Took all our things...strong box, too."

A third passenger, his sunburned face glowing red, waved his arms up and down, as if to accentuate his grievances. His terse words shot across the desert.

"Then, if that wasn't enough, they ran off the team. Scattered 'em everywhere. They left us to die out here. Just to die." He grabbed a breath and stuck his chest out farther. "And I want to know what you intend to do about it, *sheriff.*"

Trace leaned back, afraid this man would pummel him with his clenched fists, but before Trace could answer, the driver pushed away the canteen.

"We might've died if you hadn't come along when you did," the driver said.

"You must be Bill." Trace shielded his eyes against the sun.

"How'd you know?"

"Mister Eli Lester over at Cowboy Creek way station thought you might be having some trouble."

The third passenger wedged himself between Trace and the driver. "I'll ask again, sheriff." He stood nose to nose. "What are you doing to do?"

A glance behind him and Trace knew what had to be done. "Looks like I'm riding down to the nearest way station and get you some horses."

The woman fanned herself and clutched the arm of the man next to her. James offered a canteen, then turned to Trace. He cocked his head at a boulder not far from the road.

"They can rest over there. Little bit of shade. Looks cooler," James said.

Trace scanned the nearby hills. "Good idea. While they're resting, I'll go see how many horses I can get." He nodded to James. "You stay here with them."

Before Trace could get to his horse, the third passenger grabbed Trace's arm. "But what about those outlaws coming back?"

"Mister...?" Trace waited for the passenger's name.

170

"Finnegan." He lifted his nose. "John Robert Finnegan. From San Francisco."

"Well, Mister Finnegan." Trace glanced at the passengers. "Soon as you release my arm, I'm going. And it's pretty much a sure bet those outlaws are long gone by now. No need to worry."

Trace turned to the other passengers. "We'll send another wagon for your suitcases. All right?" Trace nodded to James and tossed a raised eyebrow at him. "Be back soon as I can."

James glanced at the passengers, his brother, then back to the people. "They're safe with me...sheriff. Don't worry."

CHAPTER TWENTY-FOUR

Left in charge, officially, James watched his brother ride off, then dug the last two apples out of his saddlebag. After halving the fruit, he offered it to the passengers. They ate like hungry bears starved after long hibernation.

On his left, the woman sat munching around the apple seeds. Dainty. She was looking better, not so frightened. Had she been attacked like poor Mrs. Anderson? Should he ask? No, her clothing wasn't torn or too dusty, and if she'd been attacked, they'd have said something. Instead, he returned his attention to the driver.

"Mister...Bill?" James asked. "You get a good look at those robbers?"

"Too good if you ask me." Bill's shoulders rose with the deep breath. "Come on us all of a sudden like. Fired a few shots. Nobody hit."

"Well, that's good news right there."

Bill spit out apple parts. "First time with no shotgun guard and look what happens."

James rubbed his aching ribs. "You get names?"

"Names? You expect me to get names? This wasn't no social dance, and they didn't introduce themselves. No, I didn't get no gal-darn names." Bill grunted up to his feet.

"I did." The woman reached out for James' arm. "One called another one Rudy."

This close. He was this close again. James' excitement sparked. Maybe by next week—

Finnegan, who up until now had done nothing but lurk in the shadow, stepped forward.

"That's right, deputy," he said. "Now that she mentioned it, Rudy told one of those other robbers to shut up. Called him... " His eyes turned to the driver. "Called him Billy."

Rudy. Billy. The other two were Fallon and Shelton. James knew those names well. Knew those eyes, those faces. They were so damn close, he could smell them. James paced a path around a cluster of prickly pear, tossed rocks at nothing, and failed at small talk with the passengers. He even took a quick hike to the top of a hill. At long last, James spotted a cloud of dust in the eastern distance. Had to be Trace with the horses. He wanted to shout out to Trace that the robbers were close. Maybe by nightfall he'd have his watch back along with his cleared name. Maybe by next week, he'd be a shotgun guard again, and he and Trace would be driving the stage along this same road.

Somehow, James managed to wait until his brother rode up and stopped. "Wait 'til you hear, Trace," James said. "Those robbers...it was them. Fallon and his gang. It was them, Trace. This woman...she remembers names."

Tired brown eyes and a nod greeted James.

"Now, Trace...now we know for sure where they went to. Just a matter of hours now, I'd say."

"And I'd say we need to get these people back on the road."

"They're about as rested as they'll ever be." James nodded to Finnegan, who was scrambling up to his feet. "Here comes one who's pretty angry, though."

Finnegan stormed over, glaring at James until he stood within inches of the brothers. His glare shifted to Trace.

"You brought horses. At least you did one thing right."

"Again, I apologize for—"

"You can bet you sorry salary the company will hear about this," Finnegan said. "Yes, indeed, sheriff. They'll get an earful from me." He spun around and stalked back to the shade.

James leaned into his brother's ear. "Glad he's on the other stage line."

A nod and raised eyebrows from Trace. A deep breath, shoulders pulled back a bit, then he pointed at the horses.

"If it'll make you feel better, Mister Finnegan," Trace said, "I'll be escorting you all to the next way station. Mister Lester over there even has stew waiting. Next stage should be able to get you into Mesilla shortly."

"That's the least you can do in this uncivilized country— *sheriff*." Finnegan spit out the last word as if it were vile, filthy, dirty.

James knew Trace wouldn't argue. It was useless. Trace pointed at the horses. "Best be going now. Way station's just a few miles on east."

The driver extended his hand. "He didn't even thank you for bringin' back these horses. Guess he thought that's part of your job." A quick handshake, then Bill swung up onto a roan. "I want you to know that I appreciate you, sheriff."

"Thanks." A corner of Trace's mouth curved upward.

"Just don't 'member seein' you before." Bill frowned into Trace's face. "You new around these parts?"

"Yessir." Trace patted the horse's rump, then swung up onto his own horse.

James helped the woman into a saddle. Her husband settled his weight on a big gray. With everyone now ready, James untied his horse's reins and walked over to Trace. He'd been trying to decide how to ask his brother just right. Now was the time.

He looked up at Trace and dropped his voice. "You don't want Lester seeing me, right?"

Trace nodded.

"And you said we needed to save time, right?"

Another nod.

James jerked his thumb over his shoulder. "So, I'm thinking I'll ride on to the stagecoach and guard it 'til you get there."

"Guard it?"

"Don't want anybody messing with the luggage 'til they can send a wagon out. Right?"

Was Trace buying this or not? Hard to tell with the way he was squinting into the sun.

Trace's eyes flicked from the road to James' face and back to the road. At long last a third nod.

"Just to the wagon, James. Stay there. If you see any sign of those outlaws, you hightail it back this way."

James nodded.

"Any sign..." Trace leaned in close. "You just watch yourself."

Lines etched Trace's forehead. James felt sorry for him... the worry, the fear, the uncertainty. It was starting to age his brother.

"I'll follow the road and see what happened," James said.

"Right." Trace reset his hat.

James knew he shouldn't joke at a time like this, but he couldn't resist. He swung up into his saddle and gripped Trace's shoulder. "Maybe I'll even find those robbers and get my watch."

"Don't—"

"I know, I know." Grinning, James held up a hand. "Don't worry."

* * *

James gigged his horse into a trot before Trace could get his bedraggled brood headed east. Bill had reported the stage was about three miles back behind them west, but a combination of excitement and uneasiness kept James from enjoying the short ride.

Then there it was. Just as the driver described it. The large, red Celerity stagecoach sat in the middle of the road, naked without its team of horses and load of passengers. It seemed to be intact, except for the empty strong box tossed under the tongue and the scattered suitcases pulled apart. Passengers' strewn garments littered the road and hung on the bushes. The scene looked like the losing end of a tornado.

The robbers' tracks would be easy to follow. They led off southwest, more than likely headed toward Mexican Springs and that supposed silver boom. James pried off his hat and wiped his sweaty forehead. The low hills, mesquite bushes, and frightened jackrabbits offered no hint of the bandits. If they knew, they weren't telling. A long breath, then he planted his hat back on his head and swung up into his saddle.

It would be at least an hour before Trace met up with him. That time could be better spent following the gang's trail. After all, Trace had agreed that they needed to save time. Made perfect sense. He'd just go a little ways. Be back before Trace came along. Easy.

James gigged his horse into a gallop. Soon, very soon, he'd clear his name and retrieve his watch. How he was going to accomplish it, he wasn't exactly sure, but he knew he couldn't, *wouldn't,* spend the rest of his life behind bars. And he sure as hell didn't want to swing.

Living behind bars.

On second thought, he'd rather swing.

Riding along, James' thoughts turned to Lila Belle. It had been days since her image had played with his emotions. He'd never said good-bye. Properly. After all she'd done for him, how in the hell could he treat her like that? What kind of man was he to run off without as much as a thank-you for saving his life? Hell, by now she probably knew he'd shot Dunn. Everybody knew. And, she'd probably already left Santa Rita. Wouldn't blame her, either. Probably moved on to some place where he'd never find her, never explain things, never win her back.

The horizon stretched forever. Endless blue skies melded into brown and green rolling hills. Hawks circled overhead, watching for the unsuspecting rabbit or mouse to make the wrong move.

Life is like that. One wrong move and you've had it. You're done. Take the wrong step and something or someone is waiting to eat you.

The hair on the back of his neck stood at attention, and his skin crawled with small bumps. He jerked his horse to a stop. Those outlaws were probably watching him right now, waiting for him to take the wrong step.

He turned around in his saddle and couldn't see the stagecoach. No amount of stretching or craning his neck would bring it into view. Damn. He'd gone much farther than he'd thought.

Trace is gonna kill me.

He reined his horse around and spurred him back toward the stagecoach.

After a few frantic minutes, he recognized a rock formation coming into view. The stage was now about a mile away, and he hoped he'd make it back in time.

And then like magic, Trace on horseback materialized not ten feet in front of him. James jerked back on the reins. Trace did the same. They froze, face to face.

"Where the hell were you?" Trace yelled. He launched himself off the horse.

"I—"

"What the hell were you thinking?" Trace's hands ripped James from the saddle. He seized James' shirtfront and shook him. Hard.

"I—"

Trace drew back a clenched fist, shoulder high. James squeezed his eyes shut, knowing he deserved it, and that it would hurt. He turned his head, waiting for the agony, the bright lights to dance around his body as he hit the ground. It was all too familiar.

"I oughta beat you senseless!" Trace shook James. "Give me one good reason why I shouldn't." He shook him harder. "One!"

James steeled himself. And waited. Labored breathing. Trace swallowed. Mumbled curses. When the pain didn't come, James opened his eyes. Trace's eyes were riveted on his. Inches apart, neither brother moved.

A deep sigh. Trace unclenched his hand and dropped his arm to his side.

"Dammit, James. You still got bruises from the last fists." His shoulders sagged. "I can't put any more on you."

James touched the sorest place on his cheek. "I'm sorry."

"What got into your brain to go running off like that?" Trace released James' shirt. "When I saw four sets of tracks, then yours... I thought you were...that you.... Don't ever do that to me again."

"I'm sorry. Didn't mean to...just got carried away." James raised both shoulders. "Thought I could save some time by seeing where the tracks went. Didn't mean to alarm you."

Trace ran the back of his hand across his mouth and gazed toward the hoof prints.

"What'd you find?"

"Nothing yet. But they're out there. I know they are." James glanced up at the sky. "Bet we can get 'em by dark if we hurry."

Trace's gaze trailed over James' shoulder to the desert, then back behind him toward the stagecoach. "All right. Don't wanna rush things and get us killed. We got to do this smart. But they've got a good head start on us."

"If we ride fast we'll be able to spot them. What're we waiting for?" He slapped Trace on the back, then stepped into his saddle.

After an hour of tracking, James hoped they were close. "Tracks are still leading right toward Mexican Springs in Mexico, right?" James pointed to the southwest as he slowed his horse to a walk.

Trace nodded.

"Anything between here and there?"

"Cuerva."

"Never heard of it."

"It's more an encampment with a couple of adobes than anything else. Every outlaw and third-rate bandit hides there."

"What's so great about Cuerva? Sounds like just a dusty, nothing town."

"Dusty? Yeah, but it's in Mexico, close to the U.S. border. Thieves and murderers come and go at will. Closest law is sixty miles away."

"But…you're the law."

All James received was a shrug from his brother.

The two men rode in silence for several miles. James surveyed the sky, then pulled in air. A breeze kicked up dirt. To the west, a sheet of clouds blocked the sun. Purple thunderheads loomed in the west.

"Smells like rain or dust," James said. "Looks like we're gonna get wet."

"About time you had a bath anyways." A grin flitted across Trace's face as he scanned the horizon. "Gonna be a downpour. Probably be over in a matter of minutes."

Gusts pushed tumbleweeds against the horses' legs. Off in the distance, a quick streak of lightning and a low rumble announced the storm's arrival. The desert grayed with the clouds.

A sharp crack. Gunshot? No. James relaxed. Lightning.

James spurred his horse. "I don't feel like getting fried. How about hurrying a little?" A half-mile down the trail, James pointed to a mound of boulders on their left. The angle of the rocks formed what could be a cave. At least it would provide some shelter. Trace nodded, urging his horse that way.

The storm struck. Wind howled, and rain hammered sideways. The overhang provided protection from most of the rain, but there was no real dry place. After the brothers had tied and unsaddled their horses, James tucked his body into a crevice and covered his face with his hands. He shivered. Trace pulled his knees in tight and turned away from the entrance. They waited.

By the time the worst of the storm had passed, James knew the robbers' tracks were gone. He could only guess which way they were heading. Probably to Cuerva, but there were no guarantees now.

"Might as well make camp here," Trace said. He swiped the saddle blanket over his horse. "Get an early start in the morning."

"Can't we go now? A couple more miles anyway." James stared out into the desert, then back at Trace. "Look. Maybe they're gonna make camp tonight right where they are. So—"

"While you might be right about a couple things, this is a good place to make camp. We'll head out at first light, aim for Cuerva, and see what happens." Trace spread the saddle blanket over a mesquite bush. He nodded at James. "Best see to your horse now."

Instead, James pulled the coffeepot out of the saddlebag.

Trace held up a hand. "No fire tonight. Wood's too wet, and we don't want those robbers knowing we're following them. Better make a cold camp."

More mumbled curses. James just wasn't ready to stop for the day. Why did Trace always have to make the decisions? Just because he wore the badge, did that make him boss? Here they were, out in the desert, a cold night ahead, and those outlaws were probably already sitting in Cuerva, lifting a beer and laughing at the rain. Why in hell did Trace decide to wait?

James scanned the horizon for signs of life, signs of their quarry, but there was only the retreating storm. He shivered again and reeled in another oath.

After a cold supper, the Colton boys sat in front of the overhanging boulders late into the evening. Stars glowed against a velvet-black sky.

James picked up a stick and drew lines and circles in the dirt.

"Taking a man's life, Trace, I just can't get over it. I know he would've killed me and that I was luckier, maybe quicker with my gun. But I sure didn't want to kill him." He looked at his brother. "Is that what life's about? Being quicker than someone else?"

"Maybe." Trace raised an eyebrow and gazed at James' crude drawings.

"The guilt's eating my heart away." James wiped his nose on his sleeve.

"Wish I could help you figure it out. Guess it's just like being born or dying. You gotta do it all by yourself." A deep breath. "But, just like when you were born, I'll do what I can to help."

"Thanks. But I don't think boiling water will help this time." James attempted a smile, but couldn't manage even a tight grin.

"Think you're up to killing those men if need be?" Trace asked. "Tomorrow or the next day, we're gonna catch up with those outlaws. When we do, I need to know that you'll back me up, be willing to take their lives if necessary." He glanced at James. "If you're not, I need to know now."

Was he? He'd thought about this often. Torn between life and death and who decides, James studied his clenched hands. Trace

179

was right. He had to be able to shoot and shoot to kill.

James brought his eyes to his brother's. Decision made. A nod.

James' gaze shifted to the moonlit openness of the desert. Coyotes sang to each other. Something skittered away. Trace squeezed James' upper arm.

A sudden chill sent shivers over his entire body. James leaned against a boulder, pulling the blanket tight around his shoulders. He searched the stars.

PART
THREE

CHAPTER TWENTY-FIVE

L ila Belle Simmons dealt cards at a table in Santa Rita's Silver Dollar Saloon and thought about her man. James had been gone a while, hadn't even said goodbye. Just up and left. How could she have let herself get so involved with a man who'd just love and leave her? How could her heart pound so hard when it was so broken?

She focused on the game and her job as a smiling bar hostess, and she decided to put that worthless James Colton out of her mind. Then she surprised herself by thinking that her sweetheart wasn't worthless, but gentle and kind. In the next breath, she remembered how disappointed she'd been when she woke up to find him gone. She recalled their last kiss—tender, love-filled, passionate. Genuine. How could she be so wrong about James?

One of the men sitting at the table nudged her. "Hey, Missy, we wanna play cards, not day dream."

"Yeah, deal the deck!" Another player tapped his coin on the table.

Lila Belle mumbled an apology. She was hired to keep the customers happy, not mope.

Close to midnight, Sheriff Keats pushed open the wooden saloon doors and looked around the dimly lit room. Lila Belle took little notice of him. Every night he came in about this time on his rounds. As usual, she was glad to see him just in case any of the men got too rowdy.

The sheriff waved to the bartender, then threaded his way toward Lila's table. He chatted with bar patrons along his route, until he stood next to her. Lila Belle glanced up, flashed a wide smile, then continued dealing. His face next to hers, he whispered in her ear.

"Lila, we need to talk."

Was he serious? He teased her often, but this sounded more business-like. She met his steady gaze.

"Somethin' wrong, sheriff? I'm dealin' proper. Do you need me right now, or can it wait 'til tomorrow?"

"Right now, if you don't mind, and if these gentlemen can figure out how to deal their own cards." He nodded at the four miners.

"It's all right with us so long as you don't keep her more 'n two minutes. Ain't nobody 'round here pretty as she is." The men chuckled and lifted their glasses to her.

Lila Belle's elbow in his firm grip, the sheriff nodded. "I'll return her good as new. I promise."

He led her out into the cool evening air, stopping on the boardwalk down from the saloon. Deep breaths. His hand combing his hair. Another breath. He turned to her.

"You seen or heard from James lately?" he asked.

"James?"

"Yeah. You know, the kid whose life you saved?"

"I know who you're referrin' to, sheriff. I'm just surprised you mentioned him, bein' as that's all I think about it seems."

Lila Belle cocked her head. Just what was he getting at?

"I know he was real special to you, Lila. Only wondering if he's showed up and I just haven't seen him." Keats ran his hand over a face that needed shaving. "Been gone for some time, hasn't he?"

Lila stared off into space, addressing the twinkling stars. "Exactly three weeks. A long three weeks."

"And he hasn't been back?" The sheriff leaned in closer.

A shake of her head, a tear trickled down her cheek. Sheriff Keats' hand reached out and held hers. The touch wasn't comforting. Wasn't what she wanted. She wanted James. The grieved look on Keats' face brought to her a deep fear she hadn't known for years. The same fear when she and her ma faced the fever. People died. Her loved ones died.

He patted her hand. "Lila, I've got to tell you something you're not gonna like. But I feel it's my duty—as a friend—to let you know." Keats shrugged. "You'll find out one way or the other, and I'd just as soon it come from me."

Lila wrenched her hand from his grasp. "James is dead? Did he get killed over in Pinos Altos?" She tried to hold back the tears, but one slid down her cheek anyway. "Is that what you're tryin' to tell me, sheriff?"

He handed her a handkerchief from his pocket.

"I'm afraid it's not that simple, Lila."

"Not that simple?" Lila Belle dabbed at her cheeks. "He's either alive or...not."

Another deep breath. "Remember that sheriff over at Pinos Altos being killed a while back?"

She nodded.

"Well, the deputy from there came by today. Seems James is connected to that killing. Matter of fact, he's been arrested for the murder. That's why he hasn't come back to you."

Lila swayed on the boardwalk, her knees like butter. Sheriff Keats led her to a bench in front of the general store. She melted to the seat, tears now unleashed.

"I'm sorry, Lila." The sheriff gripped her upper arm. "Please don't faint on me."

Lila wadded the handkerchief in her hands. "Poor James. He must be terrified! I've gotta go to him."

Keats shook his head. "Not possible. There's more. Seems James was being taken down to Mesilla to stand trial. Murder cases are always held where the judge—"

"I can be there in three days."

"Stop interrupting and just listen." He looked away, then turned back to her. "Sorry to be so sharp, but this is tough for me to say. You're not making it any easier."

Lila wiped another tear cascading down her cheek. Keats stared at the black sky.

"About thirty miles from Mesilla," he said, "the jail wagon they was taking him in got caught in a bad flood. Two of the deputies drowned, but the sheriff of Mesilla and his deputy survived, as well as the driver." He swung his gaze to Lila. "But...well, they can't find James. Dead or alive."

* * *

Lila made the trip in three days. It wasn't safe for her to drive the buggy alone, she knew, but she had to go. James needed her now—if he was still alive. Her throat closed and tears pushed against her eyes. It just wasn't possible that James would be dead. Gone from life, her life, forever.

Mesilla was the largest town she'd seen in a long time. But she took little notice of the bustling people, the noise of the town. She had to find James. Somehow. Once he was safe in her arms, then she'd take time to enjoy this pretty valley.

After securing a room at the Corn Exchange Hotel, she received directions to the sheriff's office. She stood outside the office door, frowning. What was she going to do if they'd found James by now and he was dead? What if he was alive but in jail? What if she never found him, never knew what happened?

Her hand grasped the doorknob, then released it. How could she face the truth? Could she continue if James was dead?

She opened the door and stepped in.

The office looked like the few law offices she'd been in—wanted posters dotted the walls, the desk hidden by stacks of papers. Normally, the coffeepot resting in the corner on the potbelly stove would be welcoming. But not today.

A man behind the desk groaned up to his feet and extended his hand. "Howdy. I'm Sheriff Fuente, ma'am."

"Lila Belle Simmons, sir. Nice to meet you." Lila looked around for a place to sit. Scattered papers hid every flat surface in the office.

Fuente limped over to the nearest chair, scooped papers off the seat, and held it for her.

"The temporary sheriff is out doing fieldwork while I'm healing up from an accident," Fuente said. "I'm trying to help with the paperwork." He smiled at Lila Belle while he dropped the papers on his desk. "Looks like I'm not doing a very good job."

Lila glanced toward the back. Was James behind those doors?

Fuente waved a hand over the desk. "But you didn't come to hear how messy I am." Another groan escaped as he eased to his chair. "What can I do for you?"

She took a long look at the sheriff. Should she just leave, or would he be someone with answers? With his deep-set brown eyes and crooked grin, he looked to be honest enough. Besides, what other choice did she have?

"I'm lookin' for someone, sir. His name's...James. James Colton."

"James?" Fuente leaned forward, his bushy eyebrows pushing together. "Don't you mean *Trace* Colton?"

186

"No, sir. James. Trace's younger brother. James is the man I understand was arrested in Pinos Altos for killing that sheriff."

Fuente fell back into his chair, gripped a wanted poster until his knuckles turned white. He sat for half a minute glaring into space.

"You're sure James and Trace are related?" Fuente's fast-clipped words spurted like bullets hot out of a gun barrel.

Lila perched on the edge of the chair and nodded. "Of course I'm sure. I spent a lot of time with James, and he told me all about his family. His brothers, his folks. Said Trace drives for Butterfield Stage."

Fuente frowned. "What's your connection to Mister Colton, anyway? If you don't mind my asking."

"He...I...well, I saved his life up in Santa Rita. He was badly beaten, nearly died. I nursed him back to health. Then he went up to Pinos Altos to find the men who stole his watch, and...he never came back. The sheriff told me that James was arrested for murder there."

Sheriff Fuente nodded. "That's right. He was being brought here when the wagon he was in had an accident. Still haven't recovered the body."

Hope erupted. Lila's hand flew to her throat. "So he could still be alive?"

"Not likely, Miss Simmons. Water was too fast, too deadly. Officers are out looking for him now. I'm sorry to say, but we're positive the prisoner's dead."

Lila dabbed her eyes with the handkerchief. "You're sure he killed that sheriff?"

"Ma'am, he brought the body in himself. Told the deputy, Ben Wickens, what'd happened."

Lila dropped her head, twisting the white cotton fabric around her fingers. "He couldn't have done anything like that, sheriff. Couldn't have killed anybody. I know him too well." Her words hovered just above a whisper. "But if he did, I'm sure it was self-defense."

"People do things we never expect. I see it all the time in my business." Sheriff Fuente pushed up to his feet, holding his still-bruised head. "Just what exactly can I do for you?"

"Find James. One way or the other." She rose, stared at the floor, then brought her gaze up into Fuente's eyes. "I love him."

CHAPTER TWENTY-SIX

Alberto Fuente held his head in his hands. How could he have been so stupid? So blind? Well, it wasn't his fault. After all, the mighty town council had pushed him into hiring Trace without thinking it through. And it wasn't his fault the prisoner was Trace's brother. Just a bizarre coincidence. How in hell was he supposed to know? Or make the connection? Wasn't his fault.

Of two things he was certain. One, Trace wanted to be sheriff so he could protect his brother, more than likely hide him out somewhere. Maybe Mexico. And two, the town council wasn't going to be happy when they heard the news.

By the time Mayor Gordon Ignacio and two of the council members had gathered in the sheriff's office, Fuente had convinced himself that James had survived the wagon accident. Now, how would he break the news? His gaze swept the room. Each face revealed impatience and confusion at being called to this hasty meeting.

The men grew silent. Fuente knew it was time. He pulled in a deep breath.

"Men, we've been had. Turns out our new sheriff, Trace Colton, is the brother of that prisoner from Pinos Altos."

"What?" Councilman Emilio Sanchez pushed forward in his chair, piles of paper underfoot. They slid along the rough wooden floor as Sanchez moved his boot.

Mayor Ignacio brought himself upright. "How in the world did you make such a ridiculous connection, Alberto? What you're saying is preposterous! There's no way Trace could be remotely related to that murderer." His arms flew out to his side as his face reddened. "Hell, he even drove the jail wagon."

"I realize that." Fuente's shoulders rose. "Our new Sheriff Colton's been gone from town now for what, five, six days? Plenty of time for him and that murdering brother of his to escape to Mexico. I think there's a strong chance we'll never see him again."

Sanchez leaped to his feet. "You're saying the murderer is the same worthless shotgun guard I had Butterfield fire? The kid who couldn't hit a barn if the whole damn thing fell on him?"

Fuente nodded. "One and the same."

"That's ridiculous! You mean to tell me, he shot...and killed... Sheriff Malcolm Dunn? The fastest gun around? A sheriff with years of experience? A sheriff who—"

"One and the same, Emilio."

Councilman Isaac Montoya spoke for the first time. "How do you know they're brothers?"

"A girlfriend of James Colton's in town looking for answers, too, Isaac," Fuente said. "Came right out and told me that our Sheriff Trace Colton is older brother to our missing prisoner."

"I'll see that boy on the end of a rope!" Sanchez balled his fists and glared at his fellow politicians. "He'll swing for this."

"Too bad those bandits didn't kill him when they had the chance." Isaac Montoya nodded to Sanchez.

Mayor Ignacio held up his hands. "Calm down, both of you. Just calm down. Nobody's gonna swing until a court of law decides. Won't have an illegal hanging in my town while I'm mayor." He turned eyes on Sheriff Fuente. "You'll back me on this?"

Fuente nodded, hoping it wouldn't come to that.

Ignacio shook his head. "Sure had me fooled. First, he was mighty reluctant to hire on. Then, he suddenly decides to accept the job, even found two bodies right away. Thought it peculiar that he couldn't seem to find the prisoner's. No wonder he practically begged me to be sheriff." He looked at Fuente. "Do you suppose that murderer...*James* Colton, you said?"

Fuente nodded again.

"...that he survived the accident and Trace has him hidden somewhere? Could that be the way it actually happened?"

Fuente shrugged.

Mayor Ignacio played with a pencil on Fuente's desk. He used it to point out the window.

"Now suppose," Ignacio said, "just suppose, that the prisoner *did* die in the accident and Sheriff Colton simply can't find the body. That's another possibility. And...did Trace really know that it was his brother he was carting back for trial? Probably to hang?"

"How could he *not* know?" Isaac Montoya pointed an angry finger at Fuente. "Unless he's just plain stupid. In either case, I don't want him to be sheriff any more." He turned to the others. "Temporary or otherwise."

Sanchez continued pacing. "I agree. And of course he knew. Why'd he take the job if he didn't?"

Sheriff Fuente watched Sanchez's marching. It made him dizzy. "Colton hasn't brought the body back yet, because more 'n likely it ain't dead yet."

"We've been had, all right." Mayor Ignacio stood. "Question is, now what?"

One minute stretched into three before anyone spoke. Mayor Ignacio exhaled a long, slow breath. He dropped his voice. "First, gentlemen, and most important, we can't let this piece of news out of this room. Mesilla just doesn't need to know. It'd be political suicide. Agreed?"

Nods around the room.

"Second," the mayor continued, "we've got to find our new *sheriff* and make him pay for the humiliation he's brought on us. Not to mention the advance pay I gave him."

"And the supplies he took." Montoya glared toward the door. "Did wonder why he requested so much food."

"Had us all fooled." The mayor shook his head. "I hate to admit that I've been so wrong about someone. Thought I could trust him. You know, stage driver and all. Seemed like a good man." He sighed. "Next time, I...*we* will be much more careful."

Heads nodded.

Sheriff Fuente fished paper from his drawer, picked up a pencil. "First things first. Gotta find Trace Colton. Might even snag his brother. Two birds with one rock, so to speak."

Councilman Isaac Montoya walked to the window and peered out. "Where're you gonna look first? Have any idea where he went to?"

Sheriff Fuente shrugged. "Guess I'll go back to the accident site, work from there."

Mayor Ignacio pointed his pencil again at Fuente. "Whatever you decide, do it quick. Word'll get out sure as we're sitting here, and we're gonna look pretty silly. Never should have trusted him in the first place."

Montoya spoke over his shoulder as he stared out the window. "I'll go with you, Alberto." He turned around. "Just the two of us should be able to track them down—bring them in."

"Alive?" The mayor cocked his head.

"Maybe."

Ignacio slammed the pencil onto the desk. "This won't be a lynch party. Better take a posse, sheriff."

Fuente held up his hand. "No, no posse. Don't want to attract any attention to us. I think Isaac's right. Trace'll never be suspecting me to take him in. We'll be able to get him by surprise."

Ignacio stood and leaned over the desk. "Alive?"

"We'll do our best, mayor."

"You do that, sheriff." Ignacio narrowed his eyes. "Keep him alive, and you just may keep your job."

CHAPTER TWENTY-SEVEN

Trace unpinned his badge, then cradled it in his hand. The afternoon sun glinted off the nickel-plated emblem.

"Best keep that thing hidden, don't you think?" James swayed with his horse's easy gait. It matched Trace's horse as the two brothers rode side by side. An adobe building came into view. Cuerva lay ahead. James straightened his shoulders.

"Putting it in my pocket now, little brother." Trace shielded his eyes as he glanced at James.

"But what if they find out you're the law?" James squinted despite the shade his hat brim afforded. "I mean...they'd probably—"

"Don't even want to think about it. Just pray it doesn't fall out at the wrong time." Trace reached inside his vest and shoved it into a hidden pocket. He patted it and tossed a raised eyebrow at James. "There."

The town itself was dusty, dirty, and unnervingly quiet as the brothers rode in. A few low adobes stretched down what James thought might be called a main street. Hand painted signs identified two of the buildings: *El Perro Gordo Cantina* and *Mujeres Aqui*. He laughed at the bar's name. A fat dog? Why would someone name a saloon something like that? The blatant advertisement for women surprised him. Must be one of those red light houses the sheriff in Santa Rita talked about. His cheeks burned.

Farther into town, a couple more adobes and one wooden, two-story building appeared down near the end. The rest of the community consisted of tents and open fire pits scattered around. No pattern to the tents—they just seemed to be erected at random, wherever people wanted. No living person was in sight.

"Where's the people at, Trace? Suppose they're all dead or something?"

"*Siestas*. Everyone takes a nap in the heat of the day. We oughta do the same thing." Trace reined up in front of the two-story structure. "Looks like a hotel, or at least a place to get a meal. What say we get out of this sun?"

"Good idea. I could sure go for a big glass of water right about now."

Sweat rolled down James' temple. He swiped his arm across his mouth. His gaze roamed the town as he dismounted. A stretch produced a couple of pops, his vertebrae finding their place again. He massaged the revolver on his hip.

After spotting a sliver of shade on the east side of the wooden building and tying their horses there, James and Trace sauntered into the hotel. It wasn't much cooler than outside, but the shade was a welcome relief. Cowhide chairs in the empty lobby looked about as comfortable as his saddle. At least they offered a place to sit out of the sweltering heat.

Both brothers stood at the hotel's counter waiting for a clerk to assign them a room. James scanned the small lobby. No one. Not even a sleepy boy appeared to take care of customers during siesta.

"Must take nap time seriously." Beads of sweat rolled down the back of James' neck. He pointed to an open door off to his left. "I'm gonna look over in that other room. Be right back."

Three rickety tables each with three broken-down chairs filled the other room. The furniture looked to be held together with twigs and string. James doubted the chairs would hold up under any weight. There was a man in the corner, his dilapidated chair kicked back at a steep angle. Why didn't that chair slip out from under him? Both man and chair crashing to the floor. James envisioned the resulting cursing and bedlam that would follow.

James approached the man. Was he asleep? James placed a hesitant hand on his shoulder.

"Sir? *Señor?*" James said.

A gun appeared at the end of the man's hand. It jammed under James' nose. His eyes still shut, the man cocked his pistol.

"Don't sneak up on me, *señor*. What do you want?"

James' hands shot up, reaching for the ceiling. "Nothing."

James backed away, keeping his eyes riveted on the pudgy man. The thick, black hair, matching mustache, heavy jowls covered with beard stubble—they reminded James of a bear. A bad-tempered bear.

The man's black eyes glowed. "You want nothing, *señor*? Yet you interrupt my *siesta*—for nothing?"

James eased his hands down and considered reaching for his gun. Bad idea. He'd be dead in a second if he tried to outshoot this man. Instead, he stammered.

"Well... not exactly."

Trace was standing in the doorway now. Courage gathered, James continued.

"We're needing a room. My...my brother and me."

The man regarded James, starting at his boots then traveling upward. Then the man eased down the gun's hammer and slid it back into his pant's waistband. A chuckle jiggled his belly.

"You're brave. For a *gringo*!" The laughter grew into a full-blown guffaw.

As the chortling subsided, James drew his shoulders back. "Are you the hotel manager, *señor*?"

"*Sí*. And you?" The belly shook again. "You are nothing but a *niño*. Even a child should know you never approach a man when he is sleeping. Especially here in Cuerva. You can get yourself killed. *¿Comprende?*"

With a shake of his head, he plopped two chair legs on the floor, pushed up his body weight using the table, then stood scratching his ample belly.

"Yes, sir." James knew the man was right and he'd been warned. He'd definitely take it to heart.

Trace moved aside as the man lumbered past him, through the door, and into the lobby. James followed. Trace leaned in close. "What's so funny?"

"Me, I guess." James shrugged. "Anyway, got us a room."

Trace signed the register, handed over a dollar, and waited for the key. The manager pointed up the stairs.

"Room *siete*. That's *seven*, for you gringos." A chortle. "Second door on the right."

"The key, *señor*?" Trace stretched out his hand.

The man laughed again. "We don't lock our doors. Besides, all the keys have been stolen!" He ambled back toward the other room. "Ahh...*gringos*."

He turned the corner and was gone.

James kept his voice low, not wanting that trigger-happy innkeeper to come back.

"Guess this isn't a real fancy hotel. Hope the beds are better than the reception."

James followed Trace up the narrow stairs and located number seven. The room matched the drabness of the lobby. A rickety chair, tilting on three good legs crowded one corner, and a quilt-covered bed pushed into the opposite corner filled the room. James pushed on the edge of the mattress. Firm enough. He sat, then lay back.

"Ahhh." James closed his eyes, cradling his head with interlaced fingers. "Finally, a bed. Last one I slept in was...jail..."

Handcuffs pinched his too-swollen wrists. A gun barrel pressed against his temple. Iron bars closed in, crushing his body. James leaped up, bolted across the room, then plastered his body against the closed door. His shaky hand felt for the doorknob. He pulled, pushed, twisting metal until the door sprung open.

James ran. Ran until he couldn't pull in air. Ran until his world came into focus. Outside. Not in jail. He slowed, then stopped. Wheezing, he bent over with his hands on his knees.

Running footsteps behind him grew louder. James figured it was Trace. Sure enough, within seconds he recognized the boots and out-of-breath voice.

"What's wrong?"

James sucked another lungful of air, then straightened up. Cold sweat pasted his shirt to his back. His knees turned to rubber. James studied his shaking hands.

Wrong? Hell, going to jail is wrong. Hanging for self-defense is wrong. Having to run is wrong.

"I'll ask again. What's wrong?"

Trace's strong grip on his arm was both reassuring and frightening. Would he arrest him now and take him in? Even though he promised not to? Or would Trace keep on helping him find those outlaws?

An even tighter grip on his arm and a shake. "James?"

"Jail." Nausea boiled to the surface. James fought it down. "Can't do it. Can't go to prison. I'd rather hang."

Trace released his grip, then held James' shoulder. "Won't come to that. I've already told you. We'll get these men, persuade them to testify you shot in self-defense." He stepped in front of James. "I'm gonna tell you something straight up."

"What?" Why did his heart beat so hard?

"More than likely you'll spend a few days, maybe a week, behind bars. But I promise, it won't be very long."

"You can't promise *me* anything." James planted a finger in his brother's chest. "But here's what I can promise *you*." He dropped his voice to an iron whisper. "If I go back, I'll hang."

CHAPTER TWENTY-EIGHT

Sheriff Alberto Fuente and Mesilla town councilman Isaac Montoya reined up at the Cowboy Creek way station far west of Mesilla. After dismounting, Fuente twisted his stiff back then rubbed the lower part. When did that saddle get so hard? Montoya reached overhead, stretching side to side.

Fuente led his horse to the water trough, and then removed his hat and squinted at the late afternoon sun.

"Be glad when the sun goes down, Isaac," he said. "Too hot for anybody 'cept lizards. And it ain't even summer yet."

He untied a bandana from around his neck, dipped it in the trough, then swiped it across the back of his neck. Even though the wet bandana was warm, it cooled his skin.

Montoya removed his black hat, then dunked his head into the water trough. The horses didn't even seem to notice—they drank around him.

"Aye!" Montoya straightened up, water dripping down his face. "Too hot for me." His black hair hung straight down over his ears.

Shuffling feet. Fuente's hand flew down for his revolver. He spun toward the noise.

"Welcome, *amigos.*" A man stepped out of the barn and pointed to the water trough. "Help yourself." His quick strides covered the distance in seconds. He extended a hand. "Name's Eli Lester. I run this place."

Fuente relaxed his grip, then shook the manager's hand. He introduced himself and Montoya.

Lester pointed toward the adobe building. "Let's go inside... and sit. Too hot out here. Ain't even summer yet. Nope, not yet."

The adobe breathed out cool air. The smells of cooking stew rumbled Fuente's stomach. He re-knotted his neckerchief as he sat on an offered chair. The room was small, with a table and chairs, a desk with scattered papers, and a bedroom off to one side. Typical

197

way station. He sat while Montoya stood looking at the map on the wall next to the posted stage schedule.

Lester produced two glasses of water from a bucket inside the door. "You look thirsty. Nice to have some visitors." The manager pulled up a chair and sat while Fuente gulped his water. He drained the glass.

"What brings you way out here?" Lester leaned forward.

Fuente used his hat to swat at flies landing on his glass. "I'm the sheriff from over at Mesilla, and we're lookin' for one, possibly two men. Brothers."

"Sheriff from Mesilla you say?" Lester scratched his balding head. "Don't hear too good. Nope, not after the fever. Nope."

Fuente nodded.

"How many sheriffs Mesilla got, anyway?" Lester asked.

Montoya turned from the map. "Why you asking?" He raised his voice. "Why you asking?"

A chuckle from Lester. "No reason, I suppose. Just another Mesilla sheriff came through a few days ago. Nice fella, too." He wagged his head. "Big appetite, though."

Could it have been Trace Colton that came through here? If it was him—why? Fuente caught the look on Isaac's face. It was obvious he was wondering the same thing. Maybe they were on the right track. The time they'd spent searching for Trace, which turned up nothing, had only served to make them angry. And now, on a hunch they'd headed southwest, down toward Mexico. Would it pay off?

Fuente leaned back in the chair, relaxed as if he had no cares. "Mister Lester. This fella who come by last week?"

The station manager nodded over his own glass of water.

"What'd he look like?"

"I remember him good. Yep. Sure do. Six foot, brown hair, brown eyes, maybe twenty-three, twenty-four. A youngster."

Montoya eased down to a chair. "He give you a name?"

"What?" Lester cupped his right ear.

"A name?"

"Oh, *yeah*." Lester nodded at Montoya.

This man was taking way too much time. Fuente's impatience surfaced. "And? What'd he say?"

"Ain't you the one to be in a hurry." Lester's eyes flitted from Montoya to Fuente. He took his time breathing out. "Colton. Trace Colton."

Montoya also leaned back in his chair while he took a final sip of water. "That's him. Was anybody else with him? Maybe somebody couple years younger?"

"Why all the questions?" Again, Lester looked from Montoya to Fuente. "Don't you sheriffs ever talk to each other?" He lowered his voice to a near whisper. "What's he done that you need him for?"

"Nothing...that we know of," Fuente said. "It's just...he's been missin' for a while and the town's worried about him. That's all."

Fuente considered. It looked like Councilman Sanchez was right all along. James was alive, and Trace was taking him to Mexico to hide out. Or maybe the two of them were planning to meet there and run. This way station was nowhere near Mesilla. And if his brother's body had been found, Trace would have taken it back to Mesilla. It all made sense.

"You sure there was no one else with Sheriff Colton?" Fuente asked.

"Sure, I'm sure. Fed one man, just him. Yep, just him." The station manager paused, scratched the stubble of beard shadowing his face. "But you know, he did mention meeting his deputy later. I sent extra stew."

Fuente gripped the empty water glass and stared into it. He spoke more to himself than the other two men in the room. "Of course." He looked up at Lester. "Anything else?"

"Nope. Nothing else. He left after bringing in those people from that robbed stage. In a hurry, if I remember."

"The stage? They came through here? Tell me what they said."

Fuente, of course, had been told about the holdup and had filed the necessary papers, but he hadn't realized that Trace was involved. Another important piece of information he had overlooked—first the prisoner's name and now this. Maybe he *was* getting too old for law enforcement.

Fuente wrestled his focus back to the station manager, who was still droning on about the robbed stage. Isaac Montoya had been paying attention. He could fill in missing details later.

Ten minutes dragged as Lester recounted the excitement. He closed the subject of Trace Colton.

"And I haven't seen him. Now, you want some supper?"

* * *

199

Late evening found the Colton brothers full from *frijoles*, *menudo*, and *tortillas*. They headed for Cuerva's most popular saloon, if noise indicated popularity. A step into *El Perro Gordo,* Trace and James stopped just inside the door, eyes adjusting to the kerosene-lit surroundings. Smoke stung James' eyes and lungs. He coughed.

His gaze flitted from table to table, man to man. Another cough, then sneeze, James turned to his brother.

"Bigger than it looks from outside," James said. "There's what...at least thirty people in here?"

A nod. "Yeah, I'd say. A few empty tables, too." Trace leaned in close. "You see those fellas in here? You remember better than I do what those outlaws look like."

Smokey haze. Drinking men. Laughing women. No one he recognized.

"Not yet. Too damn dark."

"Sure hope they're here." Trace patted James on the back. "Buy me a beer. I'll get us a table." He threaded his way across the saloon toward some empty chairs.

James stepped up to the wooden board set across two barrels, which served as the bar. After ordering, he leaned against the plank and surveyed the crowd. No one resembled the men he was tracking, but the room's lighting sure wasn't the best. Shadowed faces, indistinct forms sat at tables. He'd have to get closer to be sure the outlaws weren't here.

The bartender pushed two glasses toward James, raised his eyes to him, then gripped the glasses in his hands. A grin spread ear to ear.

"Hey, *señor*. I know you." The bartender pointed a beer glass at James. "You're the *gringo* who put on a play in the street this afternoon." A chuckle sloshed beer over the sides. Sarcasm and clear distaste for outsiders punctuated each word. "We liked parts of it—especially when you ran 'round and 'round in the street. Like maybe you were on fire or something."

Good grief. Everyone saw that.

"But, the ending, *señor*." The bartender wagged his head and lowered his voice. "It needs work. Just walking away. Not very entertaining."

A guffaw erupted. Other patrons broke into peals of laughter. Heat flashed across the back of James' neck. He pushed a coin toward the bartender, grabbed the glasses, then headed for Trace.

"Making new friends already?" Trace asked. "Best keep a low profile, brother."

"Trying to." James sank down to his chair. "Appears they weren't taking *siestas*, Trace. They were watching us, instead." He sipped his beer and eyed the men at the next table. "I don't like this. Feel like a sitting duck."

"Just keep those brown eyes of yours open and we'll be fine." Trace fidgeted with his glass. "No one matches your description of those men, James. No scars over the eyes, no nothing. Maybe it was a mistake coming here."

"Maybe." James sipped his beer as he studied each face in the bar.

Every time a new face appeared at the door, James hoped it was their quarry. But it was never familiar eyes, familiar scars. No one he even half-recognized. Trace slumped in his chair while James counted the nicks in the table—again.

"I've had it." Trace drained his second beer. "They're not coming. Let's head back to the hotel. Get a good night's sleep for a change." He plunked the glass on the table and pushed back.

James grabbed his brother's forearm. His eyes riveted on the bar.

"Wait."

Four men stood at the wooden plank, three of them leaning against it, backs to the bartender, surveying the room. The short one pushed coins across the bar. James sat upright.

How could I have missed them coming in?

"That's them. Just standing there." James elbowed his brother. "We found 'em."

"Now all we gotta do is make them surrender. I'm sure they won't mind doing that."

The four men scooped up their glasses, then ambled toward the opposite side of the room. Each pulled out a chair and sat.

James forced his throat to swallow the last of his beer. His gaze steady on the outlaws, he flicked the safety loop off his gun. He knew it was loaded, ready to use if needed.

James sucked in a deep breath, then rose to his feet. Trace's grip pulled him back down.

"You wanna get us both killed?" Trace asked. "What're you doing?"

201

"My watch." His eyes darted from Trace's concerned face to those outlaws. "It's right over there."

"So are half the *banditos* in the Gadsden Purchase. You'd be dead before you stepped out that door. Use your head. We'll watch and wait. You'll get it back."

Again, his brother was right. James nodded. Another deep breath. He spun his empty glass, picked it up, then examined the bottom of it. Something to do with his hands. Anything to keep from pulling out his gun and rushing over.

Trace grabbed the glass out of his grip and stood. "We'll have another beer." He pointed with it. "Watch your friends over there."

While Trace made his way to the bar, James studied the men. Each bandit sported double holsters. Pearl-handled Navy Colts peeked out from the leather. Just like Deputy Wickens had said— those outlaws were a bad bunch.

Refills in hand, Trace clutched the two glasses, then headed back to the table, navigating through the bar patrons. Hopefully, no one would notice him. Trace was half way across the room when gang leader Fallon stood, then walked toward the bar.

James itched for his gun. Trace and the outlaw passed shoulder to shoulder. His brother's eyes grew wider than usual, his brows pulled together. His lips set a tight line. A couple more steps and chances were it'd be all right. Maybe Fallon hadn't recognized Trace.

"Hold it!" Fallon said.

Would James and Trace have to kill? Right now? Maybe Trace could talk his way out. James caught his brother's eye and nodded encouragement.

Trace turned around. "Are you speaking to me?"

"Yeah, you." Fallon, that scar on his face, stood nose to nose with Trace. "I know you. I never forget a face I robbed."

Several patrons stood, backed away.

James listened hard.

He just admitted to robbery. Out in the open. Back in the States you'd never boast about that so openly. This Cuerva must be a true den of thieves, just like Trace said.

Fallon nodded toward his table. "Me and my boys held up that stage you were drivin' a few weeks ago. I remember your shotgun guard pitched a fit when we borrowed his watch." A roar of laughter bounced off the adobe walls. "He didn't take too kindly to that. Kinda fun shootin' him, too."

More laughter.

A plan. Just talking to these men wouldn't work. Their first plan hadn't been well thought out, James realized. Right now he had to get to the door and outside. Somehow. And take Trace with him.

Rudy leaned across the table, his voice rising above the other customers' whispers. "Where's that sonuvabitch guard at, anyway? He ain't around here somewhere, is he?"

Billy jumped to his feet, his pistol appearing in his hand. "I owe him. Where's he at?" He turned in a circle.

James shrunk back into what he hoped was shadow.

Trace shrugged and shook his head. "Out to California, I suspect. Said he wanted to get rich before he got old." Another shrug. "Told him it was a waste of time, but he don't listen to me."

Pretty good story telling. If it hadn't been such a serious moment, James would've smiled. But, instead, his attention stayed on the thieves.

Fallon reached into his pocket and took out a gold watch. He held it up. "Great time piece. Works good, too." He swung it in front of Trace. "There's even some writin' inside. See?"

Trace glanced at the inscription, then nodded.

Fallon clicked the lid shut and slipped it back into his pocket. He thumped Trace on the shoulder. "Come over and sit with us. It's not so often we have a beer with men we rob."

"Sorry." Trace cocked his head away from where James had been seated. "I'm entertaining a lady friend—if you get my drift. And, truth is, she's prettier than you."

Both Fallon's eyebrows shot up. Then he threw his head back and laughed. He nudged Trace with his elbow.

"Mister, an old goat would be prettier than me. Enjoy. Maybe some other time I'll rob you again, then we can have a beer together."

Chuckles died away as he made his way up to the bar.

James licked his dry lips as Trace sauntered with the two beers over to a table where a woman was sitting alone, obviously waiting for someone. James strained to hear the conversation.

"*Señor?*" The woman flashed a seductive smile.

Trace said something that must have garnered sympathy. She ran her hand down his arm. He ducked his head. She giggled. Trace's lips puckered into a pout.

The *señorita* leaned over, amble bosom straining her low-cut blouse. "You're kinda cute for a *gringo*. I'm sure *mi esposo* won't mind my sharing your *cerveza*."

She took a glass from Trace and ran her tongue around the rim. Even from this distance, James could feel his brother blush. His own cheeks grew warm.

Trace nodded at the woman. While his brother and that *señorita* spent time together, James threaded his way up to the front side of the saloon. Just as James reached the door, a man appeared at Trace's table. His voice boomed across the entire saloon, drowning out the drunken voices.

"Carmela! *¿Quién es esto?*"

Trace looked up into the face of an angry husband. The muscles that stood out from the man's neck and shoulders made him look more like an enraged bull than an irate husband. He hoisted Trace up by the front of the shirt.

"Who do you think you are, *gringo?*" The man spit. "And what are you doing with my wife?"

Before Trace could do more than stutter and stammer, the man grabbed him by the shoulders and flung him across the room. Trace somersaulted over two tables and thudded to the floor, sliding to a stop against one of the barrels holding up the bar. He shook his head and leaped to his feet. Swaying, he held onto the wooden platform.

James used this distraction to slip through the wooden batwing doors and move outside. He waited in the dark and peered between cracks in the door.

All eyes turned to Trace who bowed with great flourish.

"*Señora*. Thank you for the company. *Adios*."

He patted his head for the hat that was no longer on his head. As he made his exit, the table of outlaws stood and applauded his efforts. He waved, then stepped into the street. His hat sailed over the top of the saloon doors, landing in the dirt. Shouts of '*Olé!*' erupted from the cantina.

His brother's hat at his feet, James picked it up and tapped Trace's shoulder. Trace jumped.

"Here." James offered the hat. "That was quite a show."

"Let's get out of here." Trace slapped his hat on his head, then marched toward the hotel. "Not quite what I planned, but it worked out all right."

"I'd say." James trotted to keep up. "Almost got a girlfriend, too."

A glare was all James received.

By the time they entered the hotel room, James struggled for a better plan. He turned the well-worn chair around, straddled it, and faced his brother perched on the bed. Folded hands cushioned his chin. Both men studied the floor for a few minutes, deciding their next step.

"I'll tell you what," James said. "I'll stay by that saloon 'til they come out, then follow to see where they're sleeping. Once they're settled, I'll come back and get you. Then we can get the drop on 'em at sun up."

Trace pursed his lips. Something their pa and he did when they were deep in thought.

"You'll arrest them," James continued, "and haul them back to Mesilla. I'll stay here in town. They'll confess and you'll come fetch me." He raised a shoulder. "Simple."

"Too dangerous. How about if we both wait and follow? I'm not crazy about letting you go off alone watching those men." Trace looked into James' eyes. "You know sometimes, little brother, you don't think things through like you should. Could get yourself killed."

James knew his brother was right. He didn't always think. Just reacted. But he sure as hell didn't want to die because of it.

"Here's another plan, James. After we nab them, they'll confess here in Cuerva, then we'll all head back to Mesilla." One corner of Trace's mouth curved upward. "It'll save me a trip back over the border."

James studied his fingernails. Trace meant well. But if he didn't get these outlaws this time, they'd hightail it somewhere else and he'd never find them. He'd never be able to go back...ever. This plan would have to work.

CHAPTER TWENTY-NINE

James and Trace spent a long night crouched down in an alley, waiting for the bandits to emerge from a red-light adobe house. As the sun rose, so did the four men who pulled on britches as they stepped into daylight and headed toward the stable. James and Trace followed, then slunk back against a shadowed alley wall. They watched. Waited.

Tapping his finger against the wood, James bit his lower lip, and turned to Trace.

"I've made a decision," James said.

"Yeah?"

"I'm not going back to Mesilla with you. Not crossing that border again. Even if they do confess here, I can't."

"But I gotta take you back. Uphold the law. I'm sheriff. "

"And I'm your *brother*."

Silence wedged itself between the men. James pushed down fear.

"If I go back, they'll just lie. I'll hang for sure, Trace. Don't care what you promise."

"Don't put me between you and the law."

"Seems like you put yourself there. I had nothing to do with that." James raked his hands through his shoulder-length hair.

"But—"

"Only way you'll get me across that border is headfirst down over a saddle. Only way."

"But—"

"I'll go with you and those outlaws as far as the border. After you clear my name, come and fetch me. Just like I said before."

A long look at Trace, then James reset his hat. Trace let out a stream of air.

"All right," Trace said. "I can understand how you feel, but what if those men don't talk? What if your name's never cleared?

We agreed you weren't running, didn't we?"

"Yeah. I've done a lot of thinking on it. A lot. You can't protect me from a jury. I'm staying here. I'll do anything not to swing." The rope tightened around his neck, squeezing out his last breath. He closed his eyes, listening to his heart pound in his ears.

Trace nodded. "Maybe you're right. Don't know what I'd do if they found you guilty." He gripped James' shoulder. "There's no way I'll let them hang you."

* * *

Following the outlaws was easy. James rode behind Trace, down in the arroyo.

Don't like this. Just don't feel right. Excellent place for an ambush.

But that's where the tracks led.

Unmistakable tracks of four horses. Mile after mile, the sandy arroyo curved east, west, then north, meandering like a drunken snake. Every turn, every creak of his saddle, every burst of wind jostled James' nerves. The arroyo banks towered over his head. Too high. Too hard to see above and in front. Too easy to get trapped. He fidgeted with the revolver strapped to his hip.

The sun perched high overhead before the tracks of the four men made an unexpected detour. As if knowing they were being followed, the hoof prints split, leaping out of the arroyo. James, then Trace reined up. James pried off his dusty hat and fanned his face. The breeze cooled his skin.

"I'm not liking this," Trace said.

James shielded his eyes. Nothing but empty arroyo behind him. Nothing but rocks clinging to the sides. Nothing but a lizard darting under a creosote bush.

"Me neither, Trace. Let's get out of here while we still can." James gigged his horse out of the arroyo, following the hoof prints. Trace did the same.

Two sets of prints headed north, the others south. James turned in his saddle, his gaze trailing over the desert. The sand and sage of the Sonoran Desert stared back.

"I'm *really* not liking this." Trace shielded his eyes against the glaring sun.

"They just vanished, Trace."

A bluff and a slight rise lay behind and to the right, while endless miles of desert stretched out before them into the distant blue mountains.

James cocked his head. "I'll take the south tracks. Try to find out what they're doing."

"No. Stay together. Looks like they're gonna try to outflank us."

"Damn. You're right. They're gonna catch us if we don't get moving."

"Too late, friends." A familiar voice echoed behind James, followed by the distinctive clicks of guns cocking.

Rudy.

James recognized that killer, the black eyes and sneer. Even the horse under that bandit was black, a shiny black like Lucifer himself. Was that a gleam in the horse's eye? Maybe it was that Colt pointed at James' chest. Maybe that sneer. Maybe the memories.

Shelton pulled up alongside Rudy, his .36 trained on Trace. Brush cracking, horses plodding through sand. Fallon and Billy materialized from a stand of piñons.

Can't let them see me scared.

James cut his eyes sideways at his brother. Trace's shoulders were thrown back, his chest out a little farther than usual. He'd do the same. Maybe that defensive posturing would throw these outlaws off balance. Maybe they expected people to quiver and grovel. Well, he and Trace wouldn't.

"Toss your guns over there." Fallon waggled his pistol to his right. Trace and James did as told.

"Now, off your horses."

James froze. Trace's face paled despite the sun, but his shoulders remained straight. He didn't move, either. James knew he'd have to dismount, but his muscles refused to cooperate. His heart pounded.

Bang!

Fire burned James' left upper arm. He grabbed the wound and slumped forward. His skin sizzled.

"He said off your horses. Now!" Rudy rode in closer and gripped James' arm. "Next time I won't just wing you." He yanked.

James sailed out of the saddle and crashed to the ground. He struggled to his feet while silver streaks zigzagged across the desert. His world spun and blood oozed through his fingers.

"You'll never get away with this!" James shouted. He wobbled toward Rudy's horse. "What gives you the right to shoot me again?"

Laughter soared across the desert.

Trace's voice penetrated his darkening world. "Calm down, James."

"The hell I will!" All semblance of reason gone, James yanked Rudy from his horse. His fist rose shoulder high as he drew it back.

But before James could strike, someone leaped on his back, both men tumbling to the ground. They rolled over and over before James found himself on his back, rocks poking him. Someone heavy sat on his stomach. Billy.

"I owe you, *cabron*," Billy said. "I owe you for shootin' me."

James squirmed, but Billy's weight kept him down. James could do nothing but watch that revolver in his assailant's hand come up and smash into the side of his head. His world lit up like white-hot pokers. Stars. Lots of spinning stars. Then pain. James grabbed for his head, but his arms remained pinned under Billy. Words, angry words, flew overhead while he waited for the pain to subside and his world to quit dancing.

Boots hitting the sand. Someone walking behind him. A voice in his ear.

"He's mine," Fallon said. "Billy, get off."

Without speaking, Billy stood. James curled into a tight ball, hoping more fists wouldn't pound his face. A tug on his shirtfront sat him up. The barrel of a Colt filled his world.

"I oughta kill you right here, right now, boy." Fallon pressed his revolver harder against James' forehead.

Trace's voice. Pleading for James' life. The words were mumbled, mushed. James knew his brother was panicked.

James stared up into cold, brown eyes. The scar running above the leader's right eye and into his temple gave the bandit that pirate look James remembered seeing in books. Sneering, deadly, one-eyed killers. Black Beard must've been an angel compared to Fallon.

Somewhere above him, a bird cawed. Fallon pulled in air. More boots scraping across sand. Was this a dream? Was he asleep and when he woke life would be normal? His gaze swept across the faces looking down at him. He located Trace. That panicked look in his eyes again.

Nope, not a dream.

Fallon eased down the gun's hammer.

"This is gettin' to be a habit. Every time I see you, I shoot you." James' shirtfront still firmly in his hand, Fallon yanked James to his feet, then stood within inches of James' face. "You *like* bein' shot?"

James shook his head, the rest of his body trembling, knees threatening to buckle. He couldn't let it happen, wouldn't let it happen.

Remember Mister Villanueva, that woman from the stage. Hell, even Malcolm Dunn.

After a deep breath, James straightened as best he could.

Fallon turned to Trace. "You're that fella from last night at the cantina. Not too good with the ladies I noticed." More laughter.

Boot steps behind James. A hand slapped on his shoulder. The grip had the strength of two men.

"Well, looky here Mister Stage Driver. We done found your shotgun guard." Billy rocked James—hard. "Thought you was out in Californy scratchin' in the dirt."

Only Fallon's grip kept James upright.

Billy's eyes roved up and down James, then turned to Trace, his eyes tracking hat to boots. A cock of his head.

"Well, well, well." Billy glanced at Fallon. "Them two ol' boys look alike. Same brown hair, brown eyes. Same ugly face. Damn, them two could be twins."

Shelton moved closer. "Sure as hellfire do. Gotta be brothers."

Fallon spit on James' boot, then wiped his mouth. "Brothers, huh? There's a surprise." The half smile on his face mocked James. "You're more 'n likely pondering on why I don't just kill you right now. Or let Billy do it."

James hadn't truly thought about it, but now he did. He shrugged.

"Way I figure it," Fallon said, "we owe you."

"What?" The knot in his throat kept James' words soft.

A nod from Fallon. "We heard you killed ol' Sheriff Dunn. You did the job for us. Reckon you remember, we left him tied up in the woods, figuring he'd die there."

"And if Dunn did escape," Shelton said, "he's too stupid to ride after us." He moved in close. "We'd kill him next time he got in our way."

Fallon waved his gun at James. "Hell, didn't know you'd come along and do it for us." He laughed long and hard.

"It was an accident." James ran his fingers over his aching temple.

Harder laughter. Fallon's shoulders shook. "I'm sure it was, boy. I've seen you shoot."

"Dunn was the fastest gun around," Rudy said. "Hell, a pathetic shot like you could never've taken him. Must've shot him in his sleep." Rudy shoved James backward. "Coward. Ain't nobody could've outshot him." Rudy looked at the others for agreement. He hit James again.

Knocked off balance, James stumbled backward, but Fallon grabbed his arm again, the grip so tight James' hand grew numb.

"We knew you were on our trail up there in Pinos Altos," Fallon said.

"Yeah," Billy's top lip tugged upward. "Had a fine time tying you up, eatin' your supper."

"Ever wonder why ol' Sheriff Dunn just happened on you...out there in the woods...all trussed up like a hog at butcherin' time?"

James had to admit he figured it had been luck. Why didn't he see what was going on?

"Dunn wanted you out of the way." Fallon spit again. "He was gonna shoot you during that freight wagon hold up. Had hisself a couple of reliable eyewitnesses. And with all those bullets flyin' here and there, why it was a real shame you got hit with one. Real accidental-like. Dunn figured those drivers would've told the whole town how you got shot while he was busy defendin' that wagon."

"An' if he missed, we'd get to." Rudy leaned within inches of James' face, his voice dropping to a whisper. "Almost had you then. But I'd take pleasure in finishing that job, right now."

There it is. They just confessed.

Trace edged closer.

"I'm sure you would, Rudy." Fallon breathed out, the sigh louder than necessary. "Tell you what, James Colton. Just because you killed Dunn, we ain't gonna kill you today." His smirk melted into a glare. "No, no killin' today. You two ain't worth wastin' good bullets on."

Fallon pried James' bloody fingers from his upper arm, then ripped the sleeve where the bullet had struck. He poked at the wound.

211

"You'll live," Fallon said. "Took off some hide, just grazed you. Like your head. Now *that's* a good shot." He stretched his arm out behind him. "Billy."

Billy opened his mouth in protest, but with an over-the-shoulder glare from Fallon, he shut it, untied his neckerchief, then tossed it to the leader. Billy looked over at Rudy, who shrugged.

James wanted to step back, but Fallon's grip kept him in place. He couldn't move.

"Hey, you." Fallon cocked his head at Trace. "Brother." He tossed the material at Trace. "Get that bleedin' stopped."

Trace wrapped the cloth around James' arm. Before he could tie it tight, red soaked through the fabric.

Fallon's voice dropped low as he watched. "Lots of blood there. Can't have you bleedin' to death." His brown eyes trailed down James' chest and stayed there. "My kid brother died like that. Choppin' wood. Hit his leg. He sorta looked like you."

As if being poked, Fallon recoiled from his reverie. He snorted at James. "Three times now I've run into you. The first was on accident, but the last two, thinkin' on it, I don't think was. You got sand, that's for sure." His eyes roamed up and down James. "You're followin' us. What exactly d'you want? What? Join us? Rob us? What?"

James pulled in air. He had nothing to lose.

"My watch. I want my watch."

His voice was more hollow than he thought it should be. James pointed to Rudy. He shuddered, remembering those black eyes staring over the bandana.

Silence. James knew the next sound would be a click, then a gunshot. A couple maybe. Then lightning would sear inside his chest while his world spun to black.

Instead, Fallon let loose a laugh so loud the horses shied. The rest of the bandits snickered.

Fallon stuck his hand in his vest pocket, then pulled out James' treasure. He held it up, sun glinting off the gold case.

"You mean this?" He taunted James, holding it at arm's length, then raised his eyebrows at Rudy. "Nice, ain't it?"

"Grandaddy's watch." Rudy's growly voice turned soft and sing-songy. "All that pretty writin' inside." He sniffed. "Well, it just rightly brings a tear to my eye."

"Mine, too." Shelton pretended to dab at a tear on his face.

"Not *grandaddy's* watch, you *pendejos*." Billy elbowed Rudy. "Some ol' haggy whore give it to him for his first time."

"Which whore? Who'd wanna touch him?" Shelton raised a shoulder.

"The ones who ain't got no teeth!" Rudy's lips peeled back, revealing his own brown teeth.

"Bet he likes them kind." Billy ran his tongue around his lips.

The four bandits chuckled and snickered.

Laugh all you want, make fun of me. Gonna get my watch.

James focused on it right there, right in front of him. All he had to do was reach out and take it.

Fallon snatched the watch from James' view, then shoved it back into his pocket. "Mine, little boy." His eyes narrowed. "Get your daddy to buy you another one."

James glared back.

"We're wastin' time, Fallon," Shelton said. "Just kill 'em. Shoot 'em both and be done." He wagged his gun and stepped shoulder to shoulder with Fallon. "Besides, he put bullets in two of us. He needs killin'."

"I said we ain't wasting no bullets." Fallon frowned. "No, we ain't gonna shoot 'em, though that does sounds like fun. And I agree, he does need killin'."

Shelton pointed at the desert. "How about we could give 'em a head start and snare 'em like rabbits?"

James eyed his brother. Trace's straightened back and steady gaze reminded him of an oak. Could he be strong like that?

Billy moved in close. "Or we could just wound 'em so bad that by tomorrow they'll be beggin' us to finish 'em off." His right eye twitched.

Snickers all around. Fallon raised one eyebrow. "Good idea. Real good idea."

"Last time was fun." Rudy's gun cleared leather. He used the barrel to push his hat up his forehead.

Fallon nodded at Rudy. "Sure was. But...no. What we're gonna do is take their clothes, tie 'em up, leave 'em here for the sun to bake. It'll be nice and slow—kinda like roastin' pigs." His laugh crackled across the desert sands.

CHAPTER THIRTY

James' left arm and face throbbed, but he couldn't let these outlaws hogtie and kill him and his brother. Fallon and his gang had to be taken down.

But how?

Fallon turned to Trace. "You. Ladies' Man. Take off them clothes." He gripped Trace's vest and yanked. The badge flew out of its hiding place and landed at Billy's feet.

Billy scooped it up and turned it over in his hand, then held it up like a hard-won trophy.

"Well, looky here, Fallon. Look what I found," Billy said. He held out the badge and read from it. "Says here, Sheriff. Mesilla, New Mexico Territory."

Trace turned wide eyes on James.

Fallon plucked the metal out of Billy's hand and waved it in Trace's face. "What d'we have here? A lawman? Sheriff no less." He moved in close.

"Seems to me he kept pretty quiet about it, too." Shelton nudged Fallon.

"Sure did," said Fallon. His eyes narrowed in on Trace. "I don't like bein' lied to. Here I was gonna let you live. Leastways for a while longer, and now you go and do something like this." He ran the side of the badge down Trace's left cheek. "I just can't let you live now."

Trace jerked away and instinctively swatted at Fallon's hand, just missing the badge and the man. Rudy pressed his Colt against Trace's temple.

James squirmed against the hold on his arms. They were going to kill Trace, he was sure, but he couldn't let that happen. He squirmed harder.

Fallon gripped Trace's vest again. "Well, Mister Law Dog

man, looks like you're dead either way you go." He nodded toward James. "Either your brother shoots you, like the last sheriff... or we do."

"I'm taking you in for murder, Fallon," Trace said. "You and the rest of the boys here."

Fallon laughed loud. "You? And what army?" He thumbed toward James. "Him? You and him gonna take us in?" His laughter stopped.

"Can I shoot him now?" Rudy asked.

Fallon stepped back. "Yeah."

Not my brother.

James swung at Rudy, fist plowing into his face. The gun flew out of his grasp while Rudy reeled back. An over-the-shoulder glance at Trace. Still standing. James lunged, fist connecting again.

Rudy fell back on the ground, James on top, and both men somersaulted over and over like men in a prison-yard brawl. Rudy's fist smashed into James' cheek.

Stars exploded. James blinked toward Trace. Splatters of dust. Trace and Shelton were locked in a fistfight.

Despite the searing pain shooting down his arm, James dredged up energy from weeks of pain and anguish. He scrambled to his feet and pulled Rudy up, too. James landed a gut-wrenching blow to his stomach. Rudy doubled over, but came up with an upper cut to James' jaw. Warm, thick blood filled James' mouth. Memories—fists, blood, pain. Death. Renewed rage surfaced. A roundhouse took Rudy in the gut, and his knees hit the ground before he keeled over.

"Get up, Rudy!" Fallon's shouts cut through the groaning. James looked up.

"Move aside, Fallon, so's I can get a clear shot!" Billy's voice rang over the melee.

"He's mine, Billy!" Fallon aimed his gun at James. "Get the sheriff."

Shaking, exhausted, James stared into Billy's .36.

Fallon's voice reverberated against James' ears. "I told you he's mine. *Mine.*"

"My shot's clear, Fallon. Move." Billy crouched for the shot. "I'll take him down."

Before Billy or Fallon could shoot, Trace plunged headfirst

into Billy, taking him to the desert sand. He grabbed Billy's shirt with one hand while pounding Billy's face. Again and again and again. Shouts, grunts, and curses peppered the air.

Someone grabbed the back of James' vest and pulled. Arms still swinging, James found himself on his feet, someone's arms wrapping around his chest. Fallon. James' arms now pinned, he spotted Rudy and Shelton lying on the ground.

Two down, two left.

Fallon released James, shoving him so hard he stumbled several yards forward. Grunts and groans from Trace and Billy. James crashed into a mesquite bush, its thin branches scratching his face. He took part of it down with him as he sank to the sand. As much as he wanted to squeeze his eyes shut and wait for this to be over, he trained his eyes on Trace. Billy was now a rag doll in Trace's grip. Then Fallon's gun slammed into Trace's head. Both Trace and Billy crumpled.

A gun. I need a gun.

James spotted what looked like Rudy's gun not too far away. Could it be within reach? James crawled toward it.

"Watch out, James!" Trace shouted, but the words didn't make any sense to James. He filled his lungs with the dusty desert air and continued his trek to the gun. He pushed down the ham and tortilla breakfast threatening to come up.

The gun within reach now, James stuck out his arm, his hand touching the barrel. Fallon lunged. Both men struggled over the gun. From his knees, James launched himself at Fallon, then grabbed the hand holding the weapon. The gun pointed away from James' face.

Bang! The noise reverberated off the rocks, sailing across the desert.

James' ears rang, but he shook off the roar and plowed into Fallon, fists swinging. An animal growl rumbled, erupting from James' chest. From his soul. His vision narrowed in on Fallon. This outlaw was going down.

James smashed Fallon's face—again and again. At long last, like a coal in a hot fire, Fallon crumbled to the ground.

Then, all the energy, all the pent-up anger, all the frustration drained out of James. He was finished. Done. It was over. Fallon lay still at his feet, face covered in blood. Rudy lay crumpled in the dirt. Billy and Shelton also lay askew—out cold.

And then...silence.

His labored breathing, wind whipping through the creosote bushes, a horse blowing out air. Silence.

His world froze. Trace. Where was Trace?

James turned like a broken wheel in a buggy. Little by little images focused.

Finally, not twenty feet behind him lay Trace, propped on his side, blood blanketing his back.

Trace?

James took what seemed like years to get to his brother. Everything ran in slow motion. Although his hands were now swollen and bruised, James managed to untie the bandana around his arm. He wadded it, then pressed it against Trace's lower left side. A groan rattled Trace's chest.

"Trace? Trace!" James grabbed Trace's shoulder and shook it.

Another groan. This one louder. Trace coughed.

"I'm sorry. So sorry. Don't die!" James' gaze darted from Trace's face to the wound and back.

Did I shoot my brother?

"Don't...you can't..." James' cries quieted into pure anguish. He shook his brother. "Come on, Trace."

Eyes fluttered open, then shut. After a few tries, Trace's eyes remained opened. They met James' gaze.

Maybe his brother would live. Maybe they'd get out of this mess yet. Maybe. James had to believe. Just had to. For his brother's sake if not for his own. He patted Trace's shoulder.

"Stay right here, Trace. I'm gonna get water. You're gonna be all right. Just fine."

James stood, wiping his nose on his sleeve. Then he retrieved a canteen from one of the horses' saddles. Trace sipped the offered water and grimaced.

"It hurts." Trace's words sounded raspy over his shallow breaths. Another quick drink. "God, it hurts."

"I know. Lie still now. I'll see what I can do." James gave the fallen outlaws a second look.

Better get 'em tied up before things get outta hand again.

James headed for the leader first. Using his own bandana for binding, James tied Fallon's hands, then dug into Fallon's vest pocket. James grasped his stolen watch. It slid it out easy, almost like it knew it was going home. James massaged the filigree cover.

217

As much as he wanted to just enjoy this moment, time was precious and his brother needed help. He shoved the watch into his vest pocket.

After trussing up the rest of the bandits, James rechecked Fallon's bindings. Nice and tight. A nod. They weren't going anywhere. James rushed back to Trace and forced him to drink more water.

Getting his watch back didn't hold the excitement James had anticipated. It was tainted, the whole episode turning so ugly, so deadly. The price was way too high.

James patted his pocket.

"Trace, I got it back."

"Hmm." Trace's eyes glazed, then cleared.

James wagged his head. "You're right. It's not worth losing a life over. I'm sorry. Didn't mean to get you shot."

Trace reached out and patted James' leg. "All right."

No matter what Trace said, it wasn't all right. He'd have to make amends somehow, and saving his brother's life didn't come anywhere close. But, first things first.

"I'm gonna have to get that bullet outta your back. Roll over so I can see better." James pushed Trace's shoulder.

"Mesilla. Doc." Trace twitched, wincing with the movement it caused.

"Too far. We'll go back to Cuerva. Gotta be a doctor there."

Trace rolled his head back and forth. "No doc, no sheriff." His red-rimmed eyes rested on James. "You're not...going...Mesilla. Help me on my horse...I'll go alone."

"For being such a smart older brother, you sure can be dumb. I'm not letting you go anywhere by yourself. Hell, Trace, you wouldn't even make it to the border."

James glanced up at the unending afternoon sunshine, wiped his forehead, then studied his scraped knuckles. Deep breaths. Decision made.

"We'll go together."

"No."

"Yeah, we will. I'm boss now." James spoke over the lump in his throat. "Roll over so I can look. I'm good at taking care of people. Been around a lot of doctoring lately."

James pushed his brother onto his stomach, then peeled off the blood-soaked neckerchief.

He pulled up Trace's shirt and probed the small, round hole. Slug was still in there.

James turned around, glaring at the four bound men. Two of them moaned, struggling to free themselves. Rage surfaced again. All James wanted now was to hurt them, kill them for what they had done to Trace and himself. Pay them back for all the torment and pain they'd caused.

James clenched his teeth and fists, tensed his muscles, then stood.

"Leave it be." Trace grabbed for his brother's shirtsleeve, managing to grip the pant's leg instead. "Don't. I need you."

James froze.

What'm I doing? No time for revenge.

Not now. Maybe not ever. If he could save his brother and clear his name, it would be enough. It would have to be. No more killings, no more pain and suffering. There had been more than enough to last a lifetime. It stopped now.

Let it go.

A longer look at the wound. That bleeding was bad. What would help staunch the blood flow? James searched his memory. Tobacco. Trace had a plug of tobacco in his saddlebags. Good thing neither one of them used it. That would soak up the blood well. He knelt and patted Trace's shoulder.

"I'm gonna get something from your saddlebag. Won't be long. I promise."

After smoothing the tobacco over the wound and watching the bleeding ease, James pulled out his pocket watch. As if seeing it for the first time, he opened the cover and read the sentiment his grandfather had inscribed. He rubbed a bloodied finger across the words, reliving the moment it was given to him.

He held it up. The gold case glinted in the sunshine, but it reflected only pain. It was tarnished. James turned it over. Blood covered the watchcase, staining James' hands. Whose blood was it? His blood? His brother's? And the outlaws'?

Too much. Too damn much.

219

It had been a lot easier getting Trace on his horse than James had first thought. Trace had had just enough strength to help hoist himself up and into that saddle. James pushed as best he could, his own arm throbbing, but still, it helped having Trace able to sit upright part way.

The bandits had been another story. All four were awake, but certainly not cooperative. Each one had tried either crawling out of reach, getting to his feet and running, or head-butting James. One by one, however, James had them lashed to their mounts. James mused that their own saddle strings, those rawhide strips hanging down on the saddles, had come in handy strapping each outlaw into the saddle. A few loops around the saddle horn, up between their hands, then a tight knot would keep them in their leather seats. If they tried to escape, they'd have to take the whole saddle with them. James chuckled at the mental image.

Also, thank goodness, Trace was able to guide his own horse. James' hands were full of the outlaws' reins. Given the chance, they'd hightail it back to Mexico or at least across the next rise faster than a rabbit with a coyote on its tail. He wasn't taking any chances on losing them.

Trace hadn't said much since James had removed the lead ball. At one point, James had thought the bullet would be impossible to remove, the bullet lodged too deep and only Trace's Barlow knife available, but he remembered grinning when that bullet gave up and let go.

A cool wind sang down the narrow valley just as the last of the sun's rays sprayed gold over the desert. It'd be dark soon. They'd have to stop for the night. Or would they? Maybe if they kept moving, they'd make it to Mesilla by this time tomorrow. James glanced at his brother. Pale face, shoulders sagging, body slumping forward. Nope. They'd have to stop soon.

Somehow, he'd have to keep Fallon and his gang tied up all night, which meant he wouldn't be able to sleep at all. Deep down exhaustion settled into his bones. He shook it off. He couldn't rest until...until what? Until Trace was in the doctor's care in Mesilla, and...James didn't want to think about it. He pushed aside those thoughts.

Jail and the gallows would come soon enough.

"Hold it!"

A rider materialized from behind a couple of piñon trees.

The shotgun aimed at James' chest resembled a small canon. Another rider pulled up alongside the first, pistol at the ready.

The setting sun glinted off something pinned to the first man's chest. James squinted. A badge. Instant relief washed over him. He eyed his brother, still sagging in his saddle.

"Glad to see you, sheriff," James said, "I—"

"Throw down your gun, nice and easy now." Sheriff Fuente trained his shotgun on James as he rode in closer.

"But, sheriff, my bro—"

"You don't listen too good, boy. I said drop it!"

James opened his mouth, then thought better of an immediate argument. He tossed his Colt to the sand and raised both hands. Fuente wagged his gun.

"Now, off your horse. Easy, easy. One wrong move and I'll shoot you quicker'n you shot Sheriff Dunn."

James froze. Good God! Who was this sheriff, this lawman who recognized him?

Fuente bolted from his horse, reached up, and jerked James out of his saddle. Nose to nose, James smelled stew on Fuente's breath, felt rage in the clutch of his shirt.

"You back-shootin', snivelin', no-good little..." The fabric bunched tighter. "Got ya. Not as smart as you thought you were." Fuente turned his attention on Trace. "Sheriff Colton. You got the look of someone who betrayed the trust of the good people of Mesilla."

Isaac Montoya dismounted, gun pointed at James. He strode up alongside Trace. "Yeah, like a real traitor."

Then it hit James. This was Sheriff Fuente of Mesilla, out to bring both him and Trace in. Like common criminals. "Sheriff," James said, "you gotta get a doctor for Trace. He's shot. May not make it 'til tomorrow."

221

The outlaws behind him snickered. One whistled. Fuente glanced toward Trace. "Isaac, see about him." Fuente's gaze riveted back on James. "You about cost me my job and my life. I aim to see you get what's comin' to you."

"He's shot all right, Alberto," Montoya said. "Not doin' good at all."

James pulled against Fuente's grip. "Sheriff, I can explain—"

"Shut up!" Fuente shook James so hard that his knees buckled and plowed into the sand. Fuente grabbed the back of James' neck and shoved his face into the dirt.

"What'd you do now?" Fuente asked. "Killin' one sheriff wasn't enough? Had to make it two? And your own brother, no less."

Snickers from the outlaws.

"Hey, sheriff!" Rudy called. "After shootin' his brother, that Colton kid tried to kill us."

"Damn right," Billy said. "Better watch yourself. He hates law dogs."

More chuckles.

Even with his face smashed into the sand, James struggled. Somehow, he managed to get his arms under his body. He pushed up to his knees, then glared at Fallon's gang.

"Liar! Liar!" James shouted.

Another shove plunged his face back into the sand. The more he squirmed, the harder Fuente pushed. James sucked in dust.

"Sheriff Fuente," Trace said softly. "Let me ex—"

"I said shut up. All of you!"

Finally, Fuente's grip lessened. Before James could even think, his arms were pinned behind his back, and that distinctive cold metal of handcuffs wrapped around his wrists. A terrifying *click*, and they were locked.

Fuente jerked James to his feet, and his eyes searched James' face. "Looking pretty good for a dead man, James Colton. You and your brother have a nice little reunion?"

Snickers. A low outlaw whistle.

"Yeah, sheriff. It was a right-fine tear-makin' reunion." Rudy's sing-song falsetto rolled down the valley. "Oh, Trace, I missed you so much!"

"Then he just up and shot his brother." Fallon said, leaning forward on his horse. "He's a damn fine shot, sheriff. You oughta hire him."

"You lying sonuvabitch!" Yanking out of Fuente's grip, James rushed Fallon and planted his teeth into the robber's leg, biting with the rage of a wounded puma. The outlaw screamed, jerked, and kicked. James caught a boot square in his chest. He thudded back on his cuffed hands, rolling once before careening into a horse's leg.

"Colton!" Fuente planted a foot on James' chest.

"He...those men, sheriff. *They're* the outlaws. They robbed the stages. They shot Trace!" James screamed at Fuente.

"Did not!" Billy glared down at James. "You did. You picked up that gun and fired. Saw you do it." He turned to Fuente. "I'm a first-class eyewitness, sheriff. Hell, I'll even testify in court."

"Liar. Sonuvabitch liar!" James yelled.

The boot's pressure stomped James farther into the sand, his manacled hands digging into his back. A revolver barrel pointed at his face. Montoya's face behind it. The unmistakable click of a cocking weapon.

"One move, one word...you die," Montoya said.

It was over. Over and done. Trace would die and James would hang. They wouldn't believe him. Hell, they wouldn't even believe Trace. James swallowed his pounding heart.

"Hmm." Fuente moved from bound man to bound man. He pointed at Rudy. "Seen your ugly mug on a wanted poster." He waved the same finger at the others. "Fact is, you've all got posters. Murder, robbery, horse stealing...a long list of bad ideas."

Fallon squirmed in his saddle. "But he bit me, sheriff. You saw it! That *pendejo* bit me!"

"You gonna let him get away with that?" Rudy spit toward James.

"Shut up, all of you!" Fuente stood back, surveying the group. "Yep, all of you got a price on your head. Thanks to Sheriff Colton. He identified each of you back when you held up his stage. I've been on your tails ever since."

Rudy leaned as far over his horse as his bindings allowed. "You." His chin pointed at James. "Soon's your neck's stretched, we're gonna kill your brother."

"Pay him back for pointin' his finger." Shelton nodded.

"You ain't gonna kill nobody, any of you." Fuente wagged his shotgun at the outlaws. "And if you're thinkin' of doin' any bushwhackin', this here shotgun's got two barrels. And neither one misses."

The boot pressure off his chest relieved some of the tension. At least now James could breathe. He sat up as soon as Montoya moved back. Fuente lifted James to his feet.

"But my brother!"

"Shut your mouth, boy! You're in enough trouble as it is!" Fuente shook James by the shirtfront. "I should hang you right here and be done with you. That what you want?"

A headshake was all James could muster.

If Trace dies, they'll blame that on me, too.

"No. Leave him alone," Trace said. He slid off his horse, landing on his knees.

Desperate to go to his brother, James twisted his hands, his wrists chaffing under the biting metal. Still in the lawman's grip, he wasn't going anywhere.

Montoya walked over to Trace. "Don't fret, Colton." He gripped Trace's arm to keep him steady. "You probably won't hang like your brother. Prison time's more like it."

"No." Trace turned red-rimmed eyes on James.

"Fuente, he ain't doin' too good." Montoya unhitched the canteen hanging on Trace's saddle. "He needs a doctor." He allowed Trace a long drink.

"Right." Fuente regarded the four bound men, their faces bruised, bleeding. His gaze returned to James and lines wrinkled the sheriff's forehead. "You and Trace did all this?"

Snickers and chuckles from the outlaws.

"Pure devils they are, sheriff."

"Fought like crazed demons, that's a fact."

"We're lucky to be alive!"

Fuente silenced them with a stare.

James spoke just above a whisper, his words rushed. "I know you don't believe me, sheriff, and I guess if I was you, I wouldn't believe me, either." Tears blurred his world. "But please, help my brother. He don't deserve to die like this."

CHAPTER THIRTY-TWO

Low adobes on the horizon. Plowed fields and ditches glowed pink in the setting sun, and the Organ Mountains turned purple. Even the dust brought up from the horses' hooves mottled the world in shades of rose. Mesilla was close. It was only a matter of minutes now before Trace would be at Doctor Logan's. For that, James was grateful.

Trace sagged in the saddle, barely able to keep his head up. At times, he almost fell off his horse. His cheeks were gray, as gray as a coyote's fur, and dark circles under his eyes reduced him to an old man. His posture resembled a beaten man—exhausted, injured, defeated.

They rode into the outskirts of Mesilla. It had been a long, hot, dusty, slow parade for the eight men. They'd pushed on to town, spending only a few hours for rest. In an odd way, James looked forward to being in jail. At least he could sleep.

He'd be hanging at the end of a rope soon—no doubt. But Trace, his brave, steady brother, shouldn't die. He should live and keep driving for Butterfield, do what he loved to do. Maybe even get the girl. His girl. His Lila Belle. James fought tears.

Tears? What good were tears? Would his pa and ma want him crying right now? No. They'd insist he think this through. Be strong. Be brave. James sat up straighter and brought his shoulders as far back as he could. All right. It looked bad, but maybe he could find someone who could help. Someone besides Trace. In his mind, he ran through a list of possible witnesses. There was nobody who could or would come forward to keep him from swinging.

Nobody.

Fuente, on his left, sat taller in his saddle, pulled his hat lower on his forehead, and waved to a couple men who'd stopped to watch the procession. At this time of day, most women were inside preparing dinner, but the men were coming in from the fields or taking their teams into the barns.

Mumbles, then distinct shouts. James turned around. A crowd followed, men and boys pointing, a few children skipping alongside, each jeering at the tied men and shouting congratulations to Fuente and Montoya. The group reminded James of stories his ma had read to him about the Pied Piper of Hamlin. They'd been lead down the wrong path, and that's exactly what Fuente was doing now.

The procession reined up in front of the sheriff's office and jail. By now, more than one hundred people crowded around the prisoners.

Fuente yelled at Montoya to be heard. "Take Trace over to the doc's. I'll take it from here." Fuente pulled his revolver from the holster and pointed it at James' head. "One wrong move, boy, I'll shoot you before you can even blink."

James wanted to laugh. What was he going to do? His hands were still cuffed behind him, there was a throng of people he'd have to run through, and there was nowhere to go. He was no threat to anyone. The sheriff knew it, too. Fuente was just trying to be a big man, trying to keep his job.

A strong yank on his arm, James flew out of the saddle and hit the dirt street. He looked up just in time to see Fuente point his gun at several red-faced men standing inches away, pointing and jeering, ready to rush James.

"Back off now. Ain't gonna be a lynchin'." Fuente moved closer to James. "Not yet, anyway."

The door to the office creaked open. A man sporting a badge, the deputy James figured, stood in the doorway, gun in hand. He stepped out to Fallon's gang as Fuente led James inside. A strong push on his shoulder, countless steps through the dark office, then James found himself face to face with two empty jail cells, side by side. The sheriff pushed him toward the far end.

The barred door swung open. James' heart pounded hard. He couldn't breathe. The walls, the bars, the cots faded to gray. He couldn't go in. Just couldn't.

Another shove and he stumbled across the wooden floor, crashing into the stone wall.

Once James was inside the jail cell, Fuente released James' hands. That click was more like music. His fingers tingled as he brought his arms in front, then rubbed his wrists. His shoulders screaming, James shrugged a few times, hoping the movement would release the tension. It didn't.

Clang. Click.

Here he was. In jail. He focused on Fuente smirking at him on the other side of the bars.

"You just shot your last sheriff, boy." Fuente turned, leaving a string of chuckles in his wake.

The only good thing so far, James reckoned, was he had a cell of his own. Those robbers, those ruthless killers, would be crammed into the other cell, all four of them. At least he hoped so.

As he perched on the hard cot, head in his hands, he thought about how he'd ended up in this predicament.

He felt for the gold watch in his pocket.

* * *

Late evening found James finishing his beans, tortillas, and some watery something that could have been stew. He sipped the last drops of coffee, wondering what his final meal would be. Probably more beans and tortillas. The inner jail door squeaked open, and the sound of heavy footsteps followed. James didn't even bother to look up. Instead, he took the last bite of tortilla.

The footsteps stopped at the cell next to his. Mumbled curses, loud questions, sharp answers. James ignored them all. Those outlaws had done nothing but harass him since they'd been forced to cram inside their own cell. They wouldn't let up. He tried to turn deaf ears on them. Think of more pleasant things.

Footsteps stopped in front of his cell.

"I have good news and even better news, James Colton," Fuente said.

James set his cup on the tin tray, eased up to his feet. His sore muscles and ribs made the rise difficult. He eased near Fuente with the wariness of approaching a wounded bull.

Fuente cleared his throat. "Circuit judge's riding in tomorrow morning, which means we can get your trial started tomorrow afternoon."

"What's so good about that?"

"Don't have to sit around and wait." Fuente moved in closer and lowered his voice. "And the doctor says your brother's gonna make it. Fever's down a bit, too. Says you did a good job gettin' the bullet out."

"Thank God! Thanks, sheriff. Great news. Thanks for letting me know." James didn't try to hide the blooming smile stretching his swollen cheeks. He turned around, stopped, then turned back to Fuente. "Did Trace talk to you? Tell you what really happened out there?"

Fuente glanced at the men in the other cell, then turned his gaze to James. He shook his head. "He mumbled about you shootin' Sheriff Dunn. Didn't say nothin' about self-defense."

James shut his eyes. Without Trace's testimony, it was a done deal. Jury wouldn't be out more than two minutes.

"He's still outta his head with fever," Fuente said. "Probably by tomorrow he won't be strong enough to talk, even if the judge *were* to let him speak."

"You mean the judge might not? But those outlaws admitted to Trace that they killed Villanueva and were gonna shoot Dunn. They said they were gonna kill us both!" James gripped the cold iron bars. "The judge's gotta let him talk."

"Not if he has good reason, boy." Fuente stepped back from the cell. "He'll be figuring that Trace, bein' your brother and all, likely won't tell the truth." He jangled the keys and walked toward the inner door. He turned back. "By the way, thought you'd want to know. The judge that's comin' tomorrow is Jacob Falls...The Hangin' Judge."

The scrape of the closing door and click of the lock bounced off the stone walls.

Unable to breathe, James watched his feet carry him to his cot. Numb, he thudded to the bunk. Whistles and insults shot his way. Again, he ignored them.

James lay back on his cot, arms under his head. All right. Time to get life in order, finish everything left undone. First, he'd need to write a letter to his family back home. Tell them how much he loved them and wished things could have turned out different. Second, he'd have to write to Lila Belle, confess his love but tell her to find another man to make her happy. Try to forget him. Third, he'd leave a note for Trace, thanking him for everything and telling him not to feel guilty about how things turned out. He did his best, and he had nothing to blame himself for. James also wanted to make sure Trace was given the watch.

There he lay, head cradled in his hands, staring at the blurred ceiling.

Another squeak of the inner door. More footsteps. He didn't bother to look over. In fact, he didn't have the energy.

Just leave me alone. I can't be strong or brave right now.

Fuente's voice at his cell. "Colton. Got a visitor." The voice softened. "Don't know why such a looker would want to see an ugly killer like you."

James shook his head. The only person James could imagine coming to see him was Trace, and Trace wasn't able to walk over.

Another ploy to berate me, to get my hopes up.

He shut his eyes and rubbed them, vowing to keep them closed until this nightmare passed.

"Colton! Pay attention, boy!"

All right. I'll play your game.

He looked over and frowned. Lila Belle? Was he dreaming or already dead? Either way, questions raced around his head. What was Lila doing here? How did she know where he was? How long had she been here in Mesilla? Had she really been waiting for him all this time?

James rolled up to his feet, sore ribs forgotten, and smoothed his hair. He looked from Lila to Fuente to the outlaws.

"Five minutes, Colton." Fuente backed to the wooden inner door. "Better make 'em count."

James held the bars in front of his face and gazed into Lila's eyes inches from his. He ignored the catcalls and whistles from the other cell.

Tears trickled down Lila's cheeks as she put her hands over his.

James kept his words low. "Lila. Glad you're here, but I didn't want you to see me this way."

"James Colton, I've seen you in much worse condition than this." She flashed that mesmerizing smile, lighting up the dim room. "I've even seen you without your—"

She looked over at the four men in the other cell. Two pressed against the iron bars, inches away. Her smile faded as she turned back to James.

"I've seen you nearly dead," she said.

Catcalls and whistles erupted from the adjoining cell. "You strip bare naked for her, Jamie boy?" Billy pretended to unbutton and remove his pants.

"Ooohhh, Jimmy, I'm *dyin'* in your arms!" Rudy's falsetto

229

rang against the walls, fading under the men's snickers. Sucking, kissing noises punctured the cackles.

"Shut up! Just shut up!" James yelled.

He'd had enough. He couldn't handle the outlaws and Lila Belle at the same time. There was only so much he could take. His knuckles turned white as he gripped the bars.

Sheriff Fuente jerked the inner door open, then stuck his head in. "Quiet down, all of you. Can't even hear myself do that stinkin' paperwork." He pointed at the four bandits. "Another outburst like that and I'll gag you 'til next Tuesday."

Rudy, his high voice bouncing off the stone walls, moved toward the sheriff. "But, sheriff, I'm innocent and I love her sooooo much!"

More whistles with oohs and aahs.

Fuente marched the few steps to the outlaws' cell, then stood with his chest against the bars. Anger brought a flush to his cheeks. "I said shut up." He balled his fist and brought it shoulder high. "Next person makes a sound, eats this."

The outlaws stifled their chuckling. Fuente glared at everyone, then spun on his heels and marched through the door, slamming it behind him.

James turned to Lila. "I was gonna write you a letter tomorrow." He reached through the bars and ran his fingers over her soft cheek. "I don't know how you found me."

"That doesn't matter," she said. "I'm here now and everything's going to be all right."

Be strong.

"Lila. Listen to me." James pushed words over the knot in his throat. "It's not going to be all right. I go to trial tomorrow, and next day they'll hang me."

Lila shook her head, a blond curl dancing around her right temple.

"Here's what you've got to do," James said. "Walk away from here. Say good-bye right now. Forget about me and move on with your life."

How could he speak without breathing? Her hands, so soft, warm, trembling. His gaze trailed from her hands up to her eyes.

"James—"

"You'll never know how much I love you and appreciate what you did for me. But now, if you really, truly love me, you'll leave. Leave Mesilla tomorrow, never look back."

"James, I can't leave you."

"Yes, you can." He pulled her hand through the bars and kissed each finger. That cool, soft skin held against his bruised cheek eased the soreness. His eyes caressed her blue eyes, the creamy pink cheeks, those lips he'd never...

"I love you Lila Belle Simmons," James whispered. "I always will."

Dredging up courage from the bottom of his soul, James released her hand, turned around, and trudged to his cot. He lay with his back to her, glad she couldn't see the tears streaming down his face, pooling on the lumpy mattress.

CHAPTER THIRTY-THREE

"Guilty, your honor. The jury finds James Francis Michael Colton guilty of the murder of Sheriff Dunn." The jury foreman nodded, then eased down to his chair.

James' heart pounded so hard he thought it'd explode right out of his chest. He knew this would happen, but still he'd prayed the truth would come out and he'd go free.

"Do you have anything to say before sentencing, Mister Colton?" Judge Falls picked up his gavel.

James stood. "Yes, sir, I do."

He looked at the judge and the six-man jury, forcing his knees not to buckle, to keep his weight.

Be strong.

"I admit I shot Sheriff Dunn. I've never said otherwise. Hell, I'm the one who brought in his body. But, like I told you, it was in self-defense. Dunn was in cahoots with Fallon and his gang. The ones locked up in Sheriff Fuente's jail. Ask them, they'll tell you that they was gonna kill me and then decided Dunn was gonna do it."

"They're not on trial here, Mister Colton. You are." The judge leaned over the bench. "They'll have their day in court just like you."

James couldn't keep his temper under control. His words boomed.

"I don't deserve to hang, judge! All I wanted was to get my watch back. The one that Fallon stole. I did all the things I was supposed to, like going to the sheriff, trying to help him arrest that gang. Remember I said I rode with him to bring in those four robbers? True, Dunn and I planned to stop them. But *I* ended up shot, almost killed, and Dunn let them get away. And this is how I get paid back?"

He brought his handcuffed fists up to his face. Sheriff Fuente grabbed his hands, lowering them. James faced the people in the crowded room.

"I hope no one in this courtroom ever has to go through what I did," he continued. "I've been beaten, shot, robbed, arrested, and humiliated. There ain't much else that can happen to me."

James' words echoed off the silent courtroom walls. He inhaled stale, smoky air. The people in the room fidgeted, and a couple people raised eyebrows at him. He dropped his voice.

"I don't deserve to die. It was self-defense. Any one of you would've done what I did."

Silence.

A cough. Feet shuffling. Falls clearing his throat.

"James Colton."

James turned to face the judge. There was a pinched look on Falls' face, his eyes having lost their fire. The judge removed his glasses, rubbed the bridge of his nose, then replaced the spectacles.

Falls fixed his stare on James. The words turned cold. "You have been found guilty of the murder of Sheriff Malcolm Dunn. Therefore, James Colton, I sentence you to be hanged by the neck until dead. Tomorrow at sunrise."

The judge's gavel smacked his desk.

Cold metal locked tight around his wrists. Fuente turned him around, so that James faced the crowd. A nudge and his feet moved forward. Before any more steps, men jumped up from the benches and rushed toward James.

"Murderer!"

"String him up now!"

"What're we waitin' for?"

James froze. Maybe he wouldn't get back to jail after all. Would Fuente let these people rip him apart? Judging by the outrage planted on their faces, there wouldn't be enough of him left to hang. He scrambled backwards. The mob grew, their voices reaching a furious crescendo.

Hands grabbed at his shirtfront, one managing to grip a sleeve. Bodies behind him wouldn't move, let him escape. He pressed against someone, while another hand clutched his vest and tugged him forward. A fist brushed his cheek.

"That's enough! Back off now!" Fuente yelled. He wedged himself between James and the crowd. "He ain't goin' nowhere right now except to jail—with me! So, just back off!"

By now the crowd waiting outside had pushed inside. Would Fuente be able to control all these people? James doubted it. And would the sheriff want to? After all, these were relatives, friends, neighbors. When it came right down to it, who would Fuente protect? James pushed down the knot in this throat.

It sure as hell won't be me.

Fuente stepped back, running into James. He half turned and spoke low.

"We'll go out through the alley. I don't think they're gonna let you through that front door."

James turned around and spotted the newly appointed deputy, Toots Magill, standing near the back of the courtroom. Magill waved, then pointed to a door leading to the judge's chamber. It was the only escape. Weaving past Judge Falls, then between a couple jurors, James bolted for the back.

Magill slammed the door just as James' boot cleared the frame. The judge's chamber. Next to a diploma hanging on the wall, a photograph of a man, a woman, and three children. A short stack of papers sat on one side of the desk, while a milk-white glass inkwell sat within arm's reach.

Close enough for the judge to sign my death certificate.

James turned his eyes on this new lawman, the man who'd replaced Thomas Littleton, the only kind deputy during that entire wagon ordeal. Littleton, he'd been told, was still recovering from his near-drowning, but he would never have the physical strength to be a lawman again.

"That t'was a close one, Mister Colton." Magill's hard Massachusetts accent sounded foreign, especially compared to this region's lilting Spanish.

James nodded, desperate to pull in enough air to speak.

"We'll wait for the sheriff, then walk ya down through the alley to jail." Magill's thin mustache twitched as he glanced at a door on his left. His hand rested on the butt of his .36. "Hope nobody tries anything, but if they do, I'll be ready."

Where was Fuente? James wondered what exactly was being said out there. Were there promises, threats, or just what? A glance down at his manacled hands. If that crowd got in here, James couldn't defend himself. Not with cuffed hands.

"You know how to use that Colt, Mister Magill?" James nodded at the lawman's holster.

Magill chuckled, a smile raising both corners of his mouth. "Sure enough do, son. In my younger days, I used to be a shotgun guard for a stage line back east. Shot me a fair number of road agents, I do remember."

James brightened. "I'm a shotgun guard, too. For Butterfield here in Mesilla." His shoulders slumped, and his stomach turned. "*Was* a guard." James closed his eyes. "Was."

A sharp rap on the door, Fuente's voice. "Let us in."

The deputy unlocked the door, then held it just wide enough to allow Judge Falls and Fuente to squeeze by. He slammed it shut the moment after they stepped through.

"I convinced them that waitin' 'til tomorrow for a proper, legal hangin' was the right thing to do." Fuente flicked a bead of sweat off his cheek.

"He sure did." Falls sank into his chair behind the desk. He nodded toward Fuente's holstered gun. "Took that hogleg of his to persuade some of them to go on home to supper. But I think they've all seen the light."

Magill gripped James' arm. "You ready to take him back, sheriff? One of us in front and one in back should be enough protection, don't you think?"

Now would be James' only chance to convince both judge and sheriff he was innocent. He pulled out all the stops.

"Judge, I respectfully request a retrial. That lawyer fella you appointed me slept through about half the trial. And I didn't even get a chance to talk to him all that much, sir."

Both of Magill's eyebrows arched toward his hat brim. Fuente frowned, while Falls picked up a pencil from his desk. James prayed the answer would be yes. Anything to give him time to really think this through and to give Trace a chance to heal up enough to testify. Maybe even some miracle would appear and erase this nightmare.

Falls took a deep breath, then shook his head.

"It's an open and shut case, Mister Colton. I don't think a dozen lawyers all together could get you off."

* * *

James stood in the middle of his cell and held out his arms for Fuente. *Click* and the cuffs opened. How many more times would that happen? Once.

A solemn Sheriff Fuente locked the cell door behind James. He stood on the other side and cocked his head. "Quite a speech in the courtroom, Mister Colton. You really believe all that?"

James stared out the high window above his cot. Clouds skittered across the darkening sky, the wind pushing them along.

"It's the truth," James said.

"Son, your trial was fair. You had your chance. There just wasn't anybody to speak on your behalf. Nobody'd seen you or knew anythin' about it."

"They did, sheriff."

James pointed at the other cell. Shelton and Rudy lay on their bunks. Billy sat on the floor, while Fallon stood grinning, one shoulder against the wall.

"You just can't have other prisoners testify," Fuente said. "It flat ain't done. Besides, who's gonna believe them?"

"I do, sheriff. I believe me." Fallon poked his chest with his thumb. "I would've been glad to testify. Tell 'em everything I know."

"Shut up." Fuente glared at Fallon. "You'll have your day."

A deep breath hurt James' ribs. He held them. "Sheriff, is there any way I can get just a little whiskey? My arm's on fire and these ribs are truly paining me."

Fuente shook his head. "You know the rules, no whiskey for prisoners. And Doc Logan's already been over to see you. Says you're fit. Nothing else I can do."

"Damn right, sheriff." Billy stood up, his hand around his own throat. "No need patching up somebody who's swingin' tomorrow."

Chuckles from the cell. "Waste of good medicine," Rudy said.

"What'd I tell you boys?" Fuente whipped around to the outlaws. His pointed finger shook. "Shut up!"

James moved closer to Fuente. He kept his voice low. "Got a favor to ask of you, sheriff. Kind've a last request, so to speak."

Fuente nodded.

"Ask the doctor to keep Trace on that sleeping powder until after...well...until after it's all over. I don't want him seeing me like that."

Another nod from the sheriff. Fuente looked down and fidgeted with the handcuff key. A frown. His gaze trailed up to James.

"Damn," he said, "you know I almost halfway believe you. Your testimony's got me to thinkin'. You could be tellin' the truth."

236

"Liar! He's lyin', sheriff." Rudy bolted from his cot and rushed over to Fallon. "Don't believe a word he says." Rudy pointed through the bars. "He's a damn liar."

Fuente's .36 materialized in his hand. He aimed it at Rudy. "Get back. One more word, I'll shoot you." Fuente glared. "And that's a promise."

Rudy slunk to his cot, while Billy eased down to the floor.

Fuente holstered his gun, then turned back to James. "If any new evidence or eyewitnesses were to come forward, the judge'd probably open up your case again." He tugged on the cell door. Locked tight. "You might think real hard on it."

CHAPTER THIRTY-FOUR

Had he slept at all? Probably not. The cell had been dark, only a half moon pouring what light it had in through the window. Then the moon had moved on, revealing a sky full of stars. From his cot, James watched those stars until they grayed into mush. His cell took form as pink then gold light filled the space. Snores from the other cell punctured the morning stillness. James pulled in air, and with one hand under his head, he lay on that bunk and thought of his life. He'd only lived nineteen years. There were still so many things he wanted to do. But now—it would be over much too soon.

Memories from his childhood and young teen years played in his mind. Images of his parents, his brothers, his home raced across his memory. He'd been happy. Certainly there were squabbles with his brothers, but nothing serious. His ma and pa had understood when he needed to leave and join Trace. They didn't much like the idea, but they knew he had to go. James blinked against the pressure behind his eyes. Why did it have to end this way?

The inner door squeaked open. James sat up. It was time. His stomach knotted, and he knew he'd throw up.

Sheriff Fuente and Deputy Magill walked in, stopping in front of his cell. James stood, then gazed into the cell next to his. Fallon, the man who should be on his way to the gallows instead of James, lay on his cot, sleeping. Two others were definitely asleep, both snoring. But Rudy sat on the floor grinning. No, not grinning. Smirking.

Fuente placed the key in the cell door. "Move back over to that wall, turn around, put your hands behind you."

The rock wall was cold as James' chest pressed against it. "Fuente? You heard about Trace? Is he—"

"Already talked to Doc Logan this morning. Your brother's better. Fever's down."

Metal clicked around James' wrists again.

Fuente turned James around. "The doc did like you asked. Trace's been sleeping like a baby. Doc gave him enough pain powder so he'll sleep 'til Sunday, most likely."

At least that's going right.

"You won't give me any trouble, will you?" Fuente asked.

Was Fuente's voice just a bit sorrowful? It sounded shaky, almost uncertain. James shook his head and looked deep into Fuente's dark eyes. He and the lawman stood for a moment as if reading each other's thoughts. Fuente couldn't keep the contact long, his gaze melting down to his feet.

A grip on James' arm nudged him toward the cell door, but his feet wouldn't budge. No. It wasn't fair. He wasn't supposed to die. He hadn't done anything wrong. He pulled out of Fuente's hand.

"It ain't right, Fuente! I shot in self-defense. Should be those fellas going to their maker. Not me!" James backed to the other side of the cell.

The snoring in the other cell stopped. Fuente clutched James' arm again, this time much tighter.

"They'll have their turn," Fuente said.

"You keep saying that. They're the ones that should be hanging. Not me! Dunn was gonna kill me! It was self-defense!"

Soft laughter rolled from the adjoining cell.

"I don't deserve to hang!" James stared at Fuente's eyes. "I don't."

Deputy Magill appeared on the other side of James, then gripped his arm with the same force as Fuente's. James found his feet heading for that cell door. He watched each step get closer and closer, then out through the door.

He froze, tugging against both grips. James glared at the four men, now all awake, now all watching.

"You'll go to hell for this, Fallon!" James yelled. "You'll all go to hell!"

"See you there, farmboy." Rudy saluted James, then turned to Fallon and snickered.

"I'm going someplace else, *pendejo!*" James leaned as close to the bars as possible. "I did nothing wrong. I don't deserve to hang. I don't deserve to die!"

A jerk on his arm knocked him off balance. He stumbled away from the cell, through the door, and into the office. James thought he knew where he was, but his vision brought him only a black tunnel. Was he dead yet? Another glance down at his feet, and his boots were hitting a wooden floor. Not yet.

A yank on his arm stopped him. Shouts, threats, murmurs outside. A crowd. Sounded like a big crowd. Someone pounded on the door.

"What's takin' so long? String 'em up!"

James' vision cleared. The sheriff's office. People outside angry and upset. Would they turn into an ugly lynch mob before he could get down to the gallows? Neither were pleasant thoughts. Which would be better?

A hand on his shoulder. He jumped. Magill leaned in close. "You know, if there was anything either one of us could do, we'd do it."

"I did some thinking, sheriff," James said. "I know an eyewitness, somebody who could stand up for me. That deputy up in Pinos Altos. Ben Wickens. He knows me. He can speak for me."

Why had he forgotten this until now? James searched Fuente's and Magill's faces.

A slow headshake. Fuente shrugged. "I sent word up to him two days ago, right after we rode in with you. I never figured on the judge comin' in so soon. Ain't no way my messenger could've got up there and have him come back before you... Well, before four, five more days at the earliest."

James hung his head. The rest of his world had fallen out from under his feet. Why not this one little straw of hope?

Magill's words in James' ear did nothing to make him feel better. "Sheriff Fuente and I've done some thinking and discussing too, and we understand why you shot Dunn." He squeezed James' shoulder hard. "But, we have to uphold the court's decision."

"I know. I ain't blaming you." James looked from Magill to Fuente, then back. "What made you change your mind? Two days ago you thought I was Lucifer himself."

"We listened to your testimony during the trial," Fuente said, "and we thought about what you've been sayin'. You did what you had to."

"So why can't—"

"No hard evidence, son. No use opening up your case again just because me and the deputy believe you." Fuente dropped his voice to a whisper. "I'm sorry."

James looked down. The wooden floor under his feet creaked.

Magill shifted his weight.

Fuente cleared his throat.

Magill stepped in close. James had to keep talking. He had to explain. Had to live.

"Those people out there don't know Dunn would've killed me if I hadn't been lucky enough to shoot. They should know that, both of you. They should know that before I die. They need to know who they'll be hanging next." James dropped his voice to a whisper. "Tell them they hanged the wrong man."

Magill looked away. "Son, there just isn't anything we can do. Our hands are tied."

"No, *my* hands are tied!" James swallowed hard.

Be strong.

"Last few details I need looking after," James continued. "There's a letter on my cot for Trace. Would you see he gets it?"

Sheriff Fuente and Magill nodded.

"Also, the letter I wrote my folks needs to get sent. Could you do that, please?"

"Of course." Magill glanced toward the door. Louder angry shouts, threats. The door handle rattled.

"One last favor, sheriff." James thought his chest would explode. Words were impossible to form. He licked dry lips. "In my right vest pocket is my watch. Would you get it out and put it in my hand? I wanna die with my watch."

Fuente nodded, fished out the precious timepiece, then placed it in James' manacled hands.

The watch—it fit in his palm like it was made for him. Like it was always his. His and grandpa's. Maybe after he died, James thought, he would see grandpa again. Explain things to him. Would grandpa understand? He had to. James closed his fingers around the watch.

"Sheriff, make sure Trace gets this after...after..."

"I will." Fuente gripped James' arm and tugged.

Two steps, then James froze.

"Sheriff?" James asked.

Fuente's steady gaze. James forced sounds over his pounding heart. "How bad does hanging hurt?"

Fists pounded on the door. Faces shoved against the windows.

241

Angry voices yelling outside. A gunshot.

Magill rushed to the door now pulsating with frustrated men. He leaned against it.

Fuente pulled in air, stood up straighter, then nodded at the deputy. "Come take charge of the prisoner. I'll see what I can do outside. Wait here 'til I say it's clear."

Voices, Fuente parting the crowd, threats subsiding. All this James took in but didn't understand. All he knew was he was about to hang. Now would be a good time to pray. Nothing came to mind. Before James could force his memory to kick in, Fuente opened the door and waved at Magill.

"Don't want to lose him now," Fuente said. "Somebody might wanna be famous, take a potshot, so keep your eyes peeled. Let's move."

James, with Fuente on one side and Magill on the other, stepped into the Mesilla morning air. The crowd opened up just enough to allow passage. Sun. Bright sun. James squinted at faces in the crowd as his feet took him down the boardwalk.

The white plaster of the Corn Exchange Hotel reflected the rising sun. James turned his head and winced. More walking. Numb. His world grew fuzzy around the edges. Bright white throbbed gray.

One foot pushed in front of the other. The Butterfield Stage office. He slowed. Out in front, on the boardwalk, stood Bill Walters, the manager. A couple other drivers and one guard he recognized stood in the doorway.

James wanted to yell he was innocent. Unjustly hanged. That all he'd wanted was his watch. Instead, his mouth opened, but nothing came out.

The office's single window. James stopped. A reflection. There stood a man, his brown hair plastered with sweat, the blue and white striped shirt soaked under the arms. Even through blurred vision, James noticed the shaking, the terrified expression of a man about to die.

An innocent man.

A push on his shoulders moved him forward. More steps and he passed Sam Bean's Saloon. The dark brown adobe walls melted into the ground. The green of the trees in the plaza shimmered with budding life.

Buzzing words called out all around him. They sounded like

"murderer," and "string 'em up." Nothing he understood. Nor wanted to.

Then, like a demon rising from a nightmare, a wooden platform grew out of the ground, reaching to the sky. It grew and shrank with each breath. A rope, a noose, hung still in the morning air. Somewhere above, birds shrieked.

A tug pulled him forward. How could he move without walking? A glance to his left and there was Fuente, his paw-like hand clutching James' arm. The lawman growled and barked at some of the bystanders. On his right, Magill did the same, his grip more powerful than Fuente's. Could they be nervous? One corner of James' mouth lifted.

Why should they be nervous? I'm the one about to die.

Now within a few yards, he passed over the *acequia madre*, the main irrigation ditch, the lifeblood of Mesilla. He paused at the base of a towering, gnarly cottonwood growing less than twenty yards away. This hanging tree had always served the town well, but for a crime as well known as his, the people used the formal wooden framework, complete with swinging trap door. The platform sat several feet above the ground so all the spectators would have a good view of the lynching.

Now at the base of the steps, he froze. His gaze trailed up until it stopped on that rope noose. Would grandpa be on the other side to greet him? He prayed he would. Peace. Calm. Someone wrapped him in invisible protective arms. It was going to be all right, after all.

The pain would last but a second or two, then it would be done.

No, I will be done.

"One step at a time, James. I'm right here." Fuente's voice startled him. Who was this man from another place, another world?

A nudge. The steps up to the platform unfolded in front of him like the paintings he'd seen of heaven. Maybe there really was something to this heaven and hell thing. He'd find out, but he'd never be able to come back and tell Trace.

Fuente's grip on his arm—comforting in an odd way. It was reassuring to know someone still cared enough to walk with him, catch him if he tripped.

Then the sheriff's grip loosened, and James looked where the sheriff had stood. No one was by James' side now. He was up there alone, except for the black-clothed hangman. James peered over the crowd, praying he wouldn't see his brother or Lila Belle. He didn't. He let the corners of his mouth turn up. At least something was going right.

Someone stood next to him. James stepped aside, but a hand grabbed him, held tight. The growing throng of people eight feet below spread out into the street and over the boardwalks. A few men leaned against the old cottonwood.

Children laughed and pointed, women pretended to look away, but gawked instead. James shut them out. All of them. They didn't matter any more.

Breathing was all but impossible, and his heart pounded until he thought it would explode. Death looked him in the eye.

James glanced at the man standing next to him, that thick noose in his hand. A dream. Anything this terrifying must be a dream. The man draped the scratchy, heavy rope around his neck. James closed his eyes and clenched the watch in his fist.

The knot tightened.

James' rapid breaths brought tingles to his hands, his feet, his entire body. As if still in a dream, James opened his eyes in time to see the hangman's meaty hands grasp a black hood and shove it toward his face.

James shook his head. "No. Please, God, no. It's too soon to die."

The hangman shrugged and tossed the material to one side.

As the hangman adjusted the noose, James struggled. He strained his neck left then right, trying to take some of the pressure off his throat. He tried to bring his bound hands in front of him, to loosen the rope, to take the tension off. Impossible. The iron bracelets held firm.

The sky and clouds melded into gray swirls, while the tops of buildings blurred. The cottonwood's light green leaves pulsated in rhythm with his heart.

A pinching grip on his arm brought James' world back into focus. He peered at the executioner holding him. The hangman shook his head, and then he grabbed James' other arm until James stopped squirming.

"Take longer to die if you keep movin' like that," the executioner said.

Breaths rasping, spurting like a terrified bull, James' body tingled all over. Electrifying jolts raced from his feet to his scalp then back down. He shook.

The executioner stepped over to the lever at the edge of the platform.

James clutched his watch, caressing it as he squeezed his eyes tight. He mouthed what he thought might be a prayer, and he took one final deep breath. He waited for the rope to squeeze around his throat, waited for the excruciating pain he knew would happen, waited for his world to end. All he could do was stand and wait.

And wait.

Should've been done by now. Should've been swinging from that rope.

Maybe I'm already dead and don't know it.

His breath erupted in sharp bursts.

Do it! If I'm gonna die, do it now!

Shouts. Voices. Footsteps on the wood. People calling out. Nothing made sense. James kept his eyes squeezed shut. More yelling, more words.

When he didn't hear the trap door spring open, didn't feel air under his feet, didn't feel the rope strangle him, he opened his eyes. He looked over at the executioner standing next to him, lever handle in hand, watching people below shouting.

Sheriff Fuente, now standing on the first step of the wooden frame, held his hand up to stop the executioner. James took all of this in, but he wanted the torture to be over. It was time for him to die. It wasn't right that even this was going wrong.

Mayor Sanchez was yelling at James and the sheriff, but James still couldn't understand the words. The executioner loosened the rope, then removed it from around his neck. Numb, James spun around with the sheriff's nudge, and sailed back down the gallows' steps.

He caressed his watch. The only thing in his world that made sense right now. The gift from his grandfather. His father's father. A gift no one could take from him.

"James." Sheriff Fuente grabbed him by the shoulders shaking him. "James. Look at me!"

It was hard, but he focused on the sheriff.

"Gotta get you back to jail."

CHAPTER THIRTY-FIVE

Words would not form enough to make sounds. James could only nod as Magill and Fuente pushed him through the crowd. Roared threats, shouted indignation, and screamed outrage pierced the air, all growling like a hungry tornado.

The deputy shoved the sheriff's office door open. How did they get to the jail so soon? James stepped into the darkened room, then froze. Someone behind him slammed the door. The lock clicked.

Grayed figures filled the office—some sat and some stood. Several men, it appeared. When James' eyes adjusted to the inside light, he recognized Deputy Ben Wickens now rising to his feet. Their eyes met.

A glance around the room revealed more people he recognized.

The two freighters also from Pinos Altos.

Maybe he wouldn't hang after all. Maybe he'd be freed. Maybe he would live.

"Who...wha...?" James took it all in, but nothing made sense.

Strong hands on his shoulders, a nudge, not too gentle. Fuente's words, hard, sheriff-like.

"Gotta lock you up again."

"No." James found his voice. "These men, sheriff." His shoulder pointed toward Deputy Wickens and the freighters. "They can help."

"Uh huh." Fuente pushed harder. "Move. Now."

"Trace?" James resisted the pressure on his shoulders. "Wh—?"

"Not here." Magill gripped the front of James' vest and tugged.

James lurched through the inner door of the cell. Snorts, sneers, curses flew around the room from the second cell.

"What the hell, deputy? What's he doin' back?" Billy asked. "Why ain't he stretched yet?"

Rudy grabbed the bars. "He oughta be stinkin' up the air by now."

All four outlaws crowded against the bars, their taunts and threats growing louder and louder. James ignored them. He had way too much else to think about.

Instead, he turned his back on Magill and waited for that too-familiar click of his wrists being released. There. He whipped around.

"What's going on? Am I free? Do I get a new trial? I saw the judge out there. And those freighters, that deputy from Pinos Altos." James didn't want to stop talking. Too many questions.

"Am I still gonna hang?"

His voice was raw, his throat sore. It had been close. Damn close.

Deputy Magill locked the cell door. "I'll see what's going on, then come back. Don't be getting your hopes up, though. I've heard stories about that judge."

Before James could ask any more questions, Magill turned his back and disappeared into the outer office. The door squeaked closed.

More curses and questions from the outlaws. Didn't they ever just shut the hell up?

James gripped the bars. "Magill! Fuente! Judge Falls! What's going on?"

Cackles and low whistles from the outlaws. If he didn't get his emotions under control, James knew he'd reach through and strangle the next man who even breathed. Then he'd hang for sure—as a guilty man. Instead, he turned his back on the bandits and moved as far away as possible. Then he sat on the edge of the cot and stared at the wall. And waited.

And waited.

And waited.

The door scraped open. James jumped up and rushed to his cell door. Magill stopped in front of the other cell. What the hell was going on?

Magill pointed his drawn gun at the four men. "All of you. Back against that wall." He waited for them to do so.

James couldn't stand the suspense. "Deputy. How about me?

What's happening with me?"

The deputy leaned over toward James. "Need to ask Fallon some questions, is all. But like I said, don't get your hopes up." He holstered his gun, then inserted the key into the lock.

"Nobody do anything stupid, and I won't have to shoot you. Fallon, come with me. The rest of you stay put."

Before James could ask more questions or even demand answers, Magill and Fallon were gone. Disappeared into the outer office.

More curses and threats from the other cell. James turned his back and dragged himself to the cot. Didn't those outlaws ever run out of bad things to say?

More waiting.

Endless waiting.

The inner door scraped open again. Fallon entered first, followed by Magill. The deputy unlocked the cell door, then locked it the moment Fallon stepped through.

James jumped up. "Magill. You gotta tell me. What's goin' on? Am I still gonna hang?" The iron bars turned hot in his grip.

Magill cocked his head at James. "It's not up to me, son."

He moved over to James' cell. Those gray-green eyes of Magill's roved up and down James' trembling body. Magill pointed to the wall.

"Move back over there," he said.

James did as told. He stood with his face to the wall, hands behind him. A firm clamp on his shoulder, Magill's voice in his ear.

"No handcuffs right now. Just behave yourself and I won't use them. All right?"

Could James nod faster or harder? Probably not. James faced the deputy. Was that relief in those eyes? Something he couldn't quite identify. Magill pointed to the open door, and James stepped through his cell door, then through the inner door. He froze. There sat Judge Falls behind the sheriff's desk, pen in hand. In front, sat Ben Wickens. Was that a smile on his face? Off to James' left stood those two freighters from Pinos Altos. What were their names? He pulled at memories. Ah yes. Trent and Jake. He nodded to them. Sheriff Fuente occupied a chair pulled up near his desk. All eyes were on James. He couldn't move.

Judge Falls pointed to an empty chair. "Sit down, Mister

Colton. Got some questions for you."

How James managed to get to the chair and sit was a mystery. Surely this was a dream. Or would it turn into a nightmare? He waited for someone to speak. A light cough and air pulled in. Otherwise, the office echoed silence.

Falls played with the pen, rolling it between two fingers. He looked at it, then James, then over at Wickens.

"Tell James what you told us," Falls said.

Wickens scooted around in his chair until he half-faced James. "Few days ago I was cleaning out the safe there in the office." His shoulders straightened. "Now that I'm *sheriff* of Pinos Altos, thought I should know what all I had in there. Dunn never let me get too close to that safe when I was his deputy."

Was there hope after all? James thought he saw a glimmer in Wickens' eyes.

Wickens took a deep breath. "Anyway, after Dunn was killed, I went through that safe, and came across a pile of cash that wasn't accounted for." Wickens pointed at the paper in the judge's hand. "I went back through our records and came up with nothing."

Freighter Trent stood. "My partner and me just happened to come into the sheriff's office about that time and told him how much we were missing."

"That's right." Jake moved next to Trent. "Turns out it was exactly one-fifth of what was taken from us." He trained his eyes on James. "To the penny."

"But that doesn't mean Sheriff Dunn was working with Fallon and his gang," James said. He prayed the answer to his next question would free him. "How can you prove anything?"

Fuente held up a piece of yellowed paper, crumpled and well worn. "Right here. It's a note from Fallon telling Dunn where to meet him."

James wanted to jump up and shout, but instead he looked from face to face—all the men in the room.

Judge Falls nodded toward the closed cell door. "And Fallon just corroborated the note, Mister Colton."

Sharp knocking, kicking at the door. Until then, James hadn't been aware of the shouts and threats, the crowd noises from outside. A voice rose above the din.

"Let me in! It's me! Trace Colton!" More pounding. "Let me in!"

Trace? Was it really him? James struggled to take all this in. For all of this to make sense.

Judge Falls frowned at Fuente.

"That's the prisoner's brother." Fuente stood. "He's a former sheriff here."

"All right. Let him in." Falls nodded. "No one else."

A quick turn of the lock and the door flew open. Trace leaned into the door jamb, his fever-red eyes scanning the room.

Fuente gripped his arm, then slammed the door. "Surprised to see you, Trace."

"You can't hang him. You gotta listen to me." Trace's words spurted between quick breaths. "My brother shot Dunn in self-defense. Fallon admitted it over in Mexico. I heard him say it." Trace wobbled toward the judge, but stopped in mid-stride. "James?"

Unashamed of his love for his brother, James leaped up and bear-hugged Trace. They stood, each trembling, until James knew his brother had to sit. Otherwise, they'd both end up on the floor.

"Mister Colton?" Judge Falls shuffled papers. "James Colton, please take your seat."

Fuente helped Trace to his chair next to James.

The room soaked in the breathing, the words started and stopped, the pounding hearts.

Falls' gaze riveted on James. He removed his glasses, set them on the desk, then leaned forward as if confiding a secret.

"You're a helluva lucky man, Mister Colton," Falls said. "Seems that Sheriff Wickens and these boys were already on their way when Fuente's messenger found them. Otherwise, all they could've done was put flowers on your grave."

Chills and goosebumps raised the hair on James' arms. He shivered.

Falls cleared his throat. "They didn't get to town until this morning, fortunately for you just before you swung. The final piece to this puzzle just confessed, Mister Colton. Fallon sold out his gang. He'll go to jail but won't hang. Not like the others."

Judge Albert Falls let out a slow breath, rubbed his eyes then fitted his glasses back on his face. "James Francis Michael Colton, please rise."

Using every ounce of energy available, James pushed his body from the chair, somehow managing to keep his knees from buckling. He stood straight, squared his shoulders, and stared at the judge.

Be brave.

Falls scribbled something on a piece of paper, then placed the stylus back on the desk. He looked up at James. "I've officially reopened your case, and now I'm officially closing it. Here's my final, and I do mean *final*, decision."

James' heart thumped so loud he knew everyone could hear it. He held his breath.

A long look at James, then Judge Falls nodded. "Due to the new information presented here today, I'm inclined to agree that you did kill Sheriff Dunn of Pinos Altos...in self-defense."

Heart now in his throat, James swallowed a last bit of moisture and waited for the final decree.

Falls continued. "However, there is no hard, clear evidence to support this, Mister Colton."

Walls blurred. James knew he'd pass out if the judge didn't hurry.

"While Dunn has proven to be a rascal, full of heinous crimes, a villain full of spite, he was also a fast gun." Judge Falls leveled his gaze on James. "As I understand you are."

"No, sir, I'm not." James shook. "I only shot 'cause I had to. And I was lucky." He glanced over at Trace. "I'm just a stagecoach shotgun guard. Nothing else."

"You're more than that, son," Falls said. "You're brave." He pulled his shoulders back, then let out a long breath. "So, with all the new information presented, and in consideration of your testimony, I'm going to grant you the benefit of the doubt. I hereby find you innocent of the murder of Sheriff Malcolm Dunn."

James held his breath.

The judge banged his hand on the desk. "You're free to go."

CHAPTER THIRTY-SIX

Evening shadows stretched into twilight by the time James and Trace sat down in the best restaurant in town, *El Patio*. They ordered the finest steak and the best locally grown wine.

"I wanted to take you to dinner the first night I got back into town, James." Trace held up a glass of wine. "Couldn't find you."

James took in his brother's pale face, the dark circles under Trace's eyes. "I still say you should be in bed, resting. But I'm glad you're feeling up to eating." James sipped his wine, and then he peered over the rim. "Thought the doctor gave you enough sleeping powder to keep you under for days. What happened?"

Trace's eyes sparkled. "I'd heard talk there was going to be a hanging, knew it was you. So, I didn't take all the pain medicine doc gave me. Lucky for me, he got busy with someone else. By the time he got back, I was already out the door."

James held up his glass of wine. "Here's to you, Trace, for putting up with me, always believing in me, and coming to find me." He lowered his voice, clinked glasses. "I owe you my life."

"You don't owe me anything," Trace said. "Besides, aren't you the one who took the bullet out of my back, brought me to the doctor, gave up your freedom when you'd sworn nothing would get you over the border? You knew you'd swing when you crossed over." He paused. "I owe you *my* life."

James smiled. "Guess we're even."

The Colton brothers looked at each other and nodded. Their quiet conversation was interrupted by a waiter who stood beside James. He leaned in close.

"Someone's requesting to see you, sir." The waiter paused and nodded toward the door. "Says it's urgent."

James looked up at the man, over at Trace, then in the direction of the restaurant's entrance. Had the judge changed his mind again?

Had Fallon reversed his testimony? Was James going back to jail?

James stood, tossing a second questioning look at his brother. Who wanted him now? Within five feet of the door, he stopped. A woman in a green dress stepped out from behind a partition.

Lila Belle. James moved in close and slid his arms around her. She smelled of lilacs and lavender. He buried his face in her curly blond hair.

"I thought you'd already left," James said.

"I couldn't leave without knowing what happened, James. You mean too much to me."

After leading her back to the table, James held the chair as she seemed to just melt into that seat. Remembering his manners, James introduced her to his brother.

"I know you." Trace and Lila Belle spoke in unison, then laughed. Once the stories were told and retold, the three wiped tears from their cheeks. Lila Belle held her side.

When the laughter died, Trace turned to James. "Wanted to wait until after dinner, but there's something I need to tell you. Guess I might as well get it out now."

James' smile melted. His brother's face—serious.

"While you were napping this afternoon, the station manager at Butterfield sent for me." Trace played with his cloth napkin.

James banged his glass down on the table. "What'd he want?"

Trace stared at James, Lila Belle, then back. He lowered his voice. "They're looking for you."

James' world spun again. How much more could he handle?

"What? I haven't done anything. Don't they know those charges were dropped?" James pushed his chair back, running his hand through his hair. A glance at Lila Belle revealed pretty much what he was experiencing—surprise and confusion. He frowned. "I can't go back to jail. I just can't."

Trace spun his wineglass then set it on the table. "Said they'd hunt you down if necessary."

Worry lines spread across Trace's forehead.

James took a quick breath. "They gonna send me to jail?"

"They don't want you in jail, James." A grin split Trace's face. "They want you to ride shotgun with me again!"

"What?" James crashed back against his seat. "They what?"

A long, loud laugh, then Trace explained. "They offered both of us our jobs back. The southern New Mexico Territory run is ours if we want it."

"Hell, yeah." A glance at Lila Belle. "I apologize for the language." His eyes met his brother's. "When do we start?"

ABOUT THE AUTHOR

"I don't believe in reincarnation," says author Melody Groves, "but tendrils of the Old West keep me tied to stories yet untold. As long as I can remember, I've lived in the Old West, walked the plank streets, listened to the clip clop of horses trotting out of town, the occasional gunfire of cowboys whoopin' it up, or a sheriff going toe to toe with an outlaw."

For years, she denied this connection, but the people, the stories, the tendrils kept pulling. She lives, she says, not only in the real West, but also in the Old West. Groves is a member of New Mexico Gunfighters, a group of Old West re-enactors who perform skits and shoot outs in Albuquerque's Old Town every Sunday. Therefore, she knows what it's like to face down a sheriff or to stand with her "gang" and harass the "law." Her .22 Ruger single-action six has been busy—shooting hundreds of times—almost as often as she's "robbed" the bank! A performance highlight came in the form of performing as Morgan Earp at the famous shoot-out in Tombstone's OK Corral. As a writer, she uses those experiences to enhance her western fiction stories.

Groves grew up in Las Cruces, New Mexico, in the far southern part of the state, and rode horses and explored the desert. Heading for a jaunt in rodeo as a barrel racer, her life sidetracked when she moved to Subic Bay Naval Base, Philippines. As a teenager during the Viet Nam War, and only 800 miles from there, her life experiences were drastically different from her friends' back in the States, her barrel racing career extinguished.

She returned to attend college at New Mexico State University, earning a bachelor's in education. After moving to Albuquerque, she worked for the public schools and earned a master's degree in education. While sitting with students in front of her, Groves says, her mind raced with shootouts, dastardly outlaws, and women and men who wanted to tame the West. "Finally," she says, "I allowed the tendrils to take hold, the stories to unfold, and my pen to take flight." She quit teaching and now writes full time, magazines, screen plays as well as books.

A contributor to *True West, New Mexico Magazine*, and *albuquerqueARTS*, Melody Groves is the publicity chairman for Western Writers of America, the public relations chairman of SouthWest Writers, a member of New Mexico Gunfighters Association, and a member of the New Mexico Rodeo Association. Groves' first non-fiction book, *Ropes, Reins and Rawhide: All About Rodeo*, explains the ins and outs of rodeo. It is designed as a "how to watch rodeo" book, complete with 93 photos.

Border Ambush is one of the stories in her Colton Brothers Saga, published by La Frontera Publishing. Other books in the Colton Brothers Saga include *Sonoran Rage* and *Arizona War*. Melody received a 2008 New Mexico Book Award for her novel, *Arizona War*, winning in the Best Historical/Fiction category.

Ordering Information

For information on how to purchase copies of Melody Groves' *Border Ambush, A Colton Brothers Saga,* or for our bulk-purchase discount schedule, call (307) 778-4752 or send an email to: company@lafronterapublishing.com

About La Frontera Publishing

La frontera is Spanish for "the frontier." Here at La Frontera Publishing, our mission is to be a frontier for new stories and new ideas about the American West.

La Frontera Publishing believes:
- There are more histories to discover
- There are more tales to tell
- There are more stories to write

Visit our Web site for news about upcoming historic fiction or nonfiction books about the American West. We hope you'll join us here — on *la frontera.*

La Frontera Publishing
Bringing You The West In Books ®
2710 Thomes Ave, Suite 181
Cheyenne, WY 82001
(307) 778-4752
www.lafronterapublishing.com

OldWestNewWest.Com
Travel & History Magazine

It's the monthly Internet magazine for people who want to explore the heritage of the Old West in today's New West.

With each issue, **OldWestNewWest.Com Travel & History Magazine** brings you new adventures and historical places:

- Western Festivals
- Rodeos
- American Indian Celebrations
- Western Museums
- National and State Parks
- Dude Ranches
- Cowboy Poetry Gatherings
- Western Personalities
- News and Updates About the West

Visit **OldWestNewWest.Com Travel & History Magazine** to find the fun places to go, and the Wild West things to see. Uncover the West that's waiting for you!

www.oldwestnewwest.com

La Frontera Publishing's eZine about
the Old West and the New West